The room _____ *ntified a*
nanoscope, a _____ *els, and a*
surgical table h.......... appeared to be the corpse of a call-
oraptor. Cormac slapped a contact charge against the window
and stepped away. The charge blew, and its metal disc went
clattering across the floor. The glass remained intact until the
decoder molecule began unravelling the tough chain molecules
of the glass. After a minute the entire window collapsed into
powder, and Cormac leapt through.

"Skellor!"

Cormac hesitated before moving beyond the corpse, as now he
saw that he had been mistaken in thinking it a calloraptor. He
had never seen anything quite like it: greyish veins seemed raised
up from the inside, and had a slightly metallic hue; the face was
also distorted—much more flattened than a calloraptor's and of
a simian appearance—and the forearms were bigger, the claws
more like hands. It had also, obviously, been able to walk more
upright, and in its ocular hollows gleamed a line of pinhead
eyes. He recognized that there was much of calloraptor in this
corpse and also something of human being, and surmised that
this creature must be the result of some experiment of Skellor's.
He moved on and scanned his surroundings further.

There.

Skellor stepped out from behind the insectile chrome night-
mare of the surgical robot. The hologram Cormac had studied
earlier had not shown a particularly distinguished-looking
individual: he was short, muscular, with brown hair and
brown eyes. Fanatical as Skellor was about his work, he had
apparently never bothered with cosmetic alteration, nor any
form of augmentation. The latter situation, Cormac now saw,
had changed: a crystalline aug curved from the man's right
temple, down behind his right ear, and terminated in three
crystalline rods that entered the base of his neck. Recognizing
just what this device was, Cormac felt inclined to put numerous
holes in him right there and then. He restrained himself.

"Cormac, Earth Central Security. I've come to get you out."

THE
LINE
OF
POLITY

THE
LINE
OF
POLITY

THE SECOND AGENT CORMAC NOVEL

NEAL ASHER

NIGHT SHADE BOOKS
NEW YORK

First Night Shade Books edition published 2014
First Night Shade Books mass market edition published 2018

Published in the United Kingdom by Tor, an imprint of Pan Macmillan, a division of Macmillan Publishers Limited.

Night Shade books may be purchased in bulk at special discounts for sales promotion, corporate gifts, fund-raising, or educational purposes. Special editions can also be created to specifications. For details, contact the Special Sales Department, Night Shade Books, 307 West 36th Street, 11th Floor, New York, NY 10018 or info@skyhorsepublishing.com.

Night Shade Books® is a registered trademark of Skyhorse Publishing, Inc. ®, a Delaware corporation.

Visit our website at www.nightshadebooks.com.

10 9 8 7 6 5 4 3 2

Library of Congress Cataloging-in-Publication Data is available on file.

ISBN: 978-1-59780-979-5

Cover artwork by Steve Stone
Cover design by Neil Lang/Pan Macmillan

Printed in Canada

For Dawn, Samantha and Rebecca, Lorna and Jack, and all ensuing generations of readers.

ACKNOWLEDGEMENTS

My thanks as always to Caroline for encouragement and support even when subjected to my readings, or tirades, about obdurate plotlines; Peter Lavery for his judicious pencil and lavish patronage; Stefanie Bierwerth for all her efficient help; Steve Rawlings, Richard Ogle and James Hollywell for those stunning covers; Jason Cooper and Chantal Noel for infiltrating my books into Germany and America; and to all the other staff at Pan Macmillan for their hard work.

Further thanks to all those people grafting in research establishments and laboratories across the world: people who will in years to come be putting wheelchair manufacturers out of business, restoring sight and creating artificial limbs—when not finding ways to grow new ones—finding cures for cancers and other ills, and generally bringing closer a future only small aspects of which the likes of myself attempt to imagine.

PROLOGUE

Eldene felt weak and light-headed for the second time that morning and wondered if her scole was preparing to drop a litter of leaves. Running her thumb down the stick-seam of her shirt, she opened the garment to inspect this constant companion of hers that oxygenated her blood in exchange for a share of it. The scole clung to her chest, between and below her breasts, like a great flat aphid coloured in shades of dark brown and purple; however, it was a relatively small creature, as she was still a young woman. Observing a reddish flushing in the crevices between its many segments, as it rippled against her body, confirmed for her that it was drawing blood, and such frequent feeding in the course of one day indeed meant it was preparing to litter. She closed her shirt and gazed across the square-banked ponds to where shift foreman Ulat was speaking to Proctor Volus—the latter easily identifiable by his white uniform—and decided now was not the time to ask for a lighter work assignment. Gritting her teeth, she hoisted up her cone basket and moved on.

The squerms remained somnolent under the aubergine predawn skies, but that would change as soon as she started casting in the dried pig-meat flakes that were their favoured food. As she walked, Eldene observed her fellow workers scattered between the ponds that chequered the land to a horizon above which the gas giant Calypse ascended ahead of the sun. These ponds reflected the red, gold and opalescent green of the giant, and her fellows were sooty silhouettes against this reflection, weighed down by their huge cone baskets as they tramped along the banked-up paths for the morning feeding. Every now and again one of those ponds lost its reflectivity as squerms fed voraciously, disturbing the turgid and slimy water. Eldene supposed the scene might be considered a beautiful one, but well understood that beauty was something you required energy to appreciate.

After propping her pole-grab and net against a nearby flood-post, Eldene lowered her basket to the ground, took up the scoop from the dried flakes it contained, and gazed down into the water. The squerms in this pond were each over a metre long and the thickness of her arm. Their brassy segmented shells gave the impression of something manu-factured—perhaps items of jewellery for some giant—rather than of living creatures. The tail of each squerm tapered into a long ovipositor that Eldene knew, from experience, was capable of penetrating both flesh and bone. The head of each creature was a slightly thicker hand's-length segment that extruded a bouquet of glassy hooks to pull in food to be ground up by whirling discs deep in the creature's throat. Those hooks were not so lethal as the ovipositors, but they could still strip the skin off a worker's hand for a moment's inattention.

She tossed some meat-flakes upon the pond, and the water foamed as the squerms writhed and fed, their bodies gleaming in the lurid morning, feeding hooks flashing in and out of their mouths. A second scoop caused further frenetic activity, till some of the squerms were surging half their body-length out of the water. The third and final scoop quietened this activity a little.

Only one deader in this particular pond, Eldene was glad to see, and that one a fresh, so therefore unbroken, squerm. Stepping back, she retrieved her pole-grab to see if she could reach it from the bank, but it was too far out. She sighed, pulled on her armoured gauntlets, and waded in, treading down the mat of silkweed and algae rumpled up at the pond's edge, while the hooks and ovipositors of the squerms grated against her armoured waders. With the deader positioned in the jaws of the grab, she almost dropped the pole when a live squerm rose out of the water beside her, flashing out its glassy hooks only a metre from her face. She backhanded the creature, slapping it down into the water, before pressing the trigger of her pole to close its jaws round the deader, then she turned and trudged out of the pond, hauling it behind her. Once back on the bank, amongst the wild rhubarb and clumped flute grass, she paused to swallow bile—feeling sick with fear and the weakness caused by the constant drain on her by her scole. After dropping the dead squerm on a mossy patch next to the path, she took up her feed basket again and moved on to the next pond. She'd collect the deader on her way back, along with any others, once she'd emptied this load of meat-flakes into the twenty ponds that made up her round.

As Eldene trudged towards the next pond, she gazed up at the satellites glittering in the sky, and tried to believe that beyond them lay wonders, and those seemingly magical worlds that had been described to her—but it was difficult to see anything beyond this orbiting metal that might just as well have formed the bars of a prison.

The Outlink stations were poised on the surface of the sometimes expanding and sometimes contracting sphere of the Human Polity. They marked the line beyond which AI governance and Polity law no longer applied. Most of this sphere's border lay in intergalactic space, but on the edge of it facing towards the centre of the galaxy, the density of stars increased and the Line was still shifting as worlds were subsumed by or seceded from the Polity. Here was a buffer zone of human occupation, beyond which lay numberless unexplored systems where people had ventured, but where hard fact blurred into strange tales and myth.

Each station had its own character, its own shape, and its own distinctive society. Over the centuries better materials and methods of manufacture had become available—also fashions had changed. Some stations were spherical, others were ovoid, and others still were like steadily growing arrows. Station *Miranda* had the shape of a corn-stalk with accretions like fungus down its eight-kilometre length—additions made during its long history—and those who dwelt within it were strange to the transitory runcible culture.

Apis Coolant was one of the more exotic examples of his kind. He was so thin and lacking in muscle that gravity above one quarter of a gee would have collapsed him as if he were made of sugar sticks and tissue paper. He avoided the runcible travellers, who mostly kept to the one-gee areas—death to him—as even a friendly pat on the back from an Earth normal or near equivalent would break his spine. He did not mind this isolation: he preferred the warm electric atmosphere of the station near the scoop-field generators, just as he preferred the company of his own hairless multi-hued kind. However, the station was not small, and back near the fusion engines Apis had relatives—but he never went there to see them. They were strange.

The Coolant clan was mainly concerned with maintenance, and the only contact necessary for them was with Miranda, the AI that ran the station and its runcible. To this AI they put their requests for equipment, chemicals for their floating gardens and crop cylinders, and for information, gossip, news . . . It was a fallacy, which Apis and his kind allowed to go unchallenged, that they were stupid or socially crippled. They were just perfectly happy where they were: looking at the galaxy voyeuristically and taking what they wanted from it with eclectic reserve.

Apis's tasks were educative rather than necessary, as he was too inexperienced to have qualifications to put him in a position to challenge the station drones. Yet, at fourteen solstan years old, he was a fast learner and knew he would soon be graduating from stress data collation to direct testing and recrystallization. But today this was not his greatest concern and, as he hauled himself between the D-section struts of Skin Heights, he contemplated his technical future with a lack of excitement that was uncharacteristic.

Apis had just discovered sex.

In the Coolant clan, polyandry was the rule; most of the women took three or more husbands, and there was not a great deal of civility in the taking. The women were bigger and stronger, and the selection process they used was one of attrition. First husbands were normally those with the greatest stamina, and therefore the ability to take punishment. Second and third husbands were usually the casualties of this selection process. Apis, only just into puberty, was completely new to it all and had countless bruises. He was feeling a little shell-shocked, hence his confusion and long-delayed reaction to what he now saw beyond one of the flickering shimmer-shields.

At least a couple of minutes passed before Apis realized that what he was seeing should not be there. There was something unusual on one of the obsolete communication pylons. He pushed himself away from a strut and floated across the face of the shield to catch at another strut on the further side. He still could not quite fathom what was out there. The pylon itself contained a chaotic collection of tubes and dishes, but he was familiar with its every angle and curve—it was his business to know them. He saw that there was something caught in it that had no right to be there. Something amorphous? A product of life?

Silently damning the fact that he was too young yet to be allowed an aug, he spoke into his wristcom. "Apis Coolant M-tech number forty-seven. Anomaly on com pylon three six eight six bee. Respond."

"This array is disconnected and not available to ship systems," Miranda told him. "Ah yes, I have it on visual now. A sampling drone is on its way."

"Not necessary. I will investigate," Apis told the AI, feeling an excitement he had not felt since . . . his last intended sleep period. He plunged his arm into the shimmer-shield and stepped through into vacuum.

Not only did Apis look very different from the rest of humanity, he *was* very different. Four centuries in the past, his ancestors on the Sol-system bases had been eager users of adaptogenic drugs, and recombinant and the later nanochanger technology. Apis did not have pores; his bright yellow skin was impermeable and, if stretched enough from its filament ties to his bones, it became rigid. He had sphincters to shut his nostrils and ears, and on his eyes nictitating membranes like glass cusps. He could live without breathing for fifty minutes. He could survive vacuum.

Once on the other side of the shimmer-shield, the air jetted from Apis's lungs, and when it was mostly gone, the saliva on his lips turned to resin, sealing them. His body bloated and stabilized, and, using an old handrail attached to the hull, he moved ponderously towards the pylon. Five minutes later he was below it. A few seconds after that he was studying the anomaly at close quarters.

Between the metal struts it clung like a slime-mould, only it had the colour of green metal, and the texture—as Apis discovered when he touched it—of wood. Apis was first intrigued, then worried, when he noticed the fibres etched into some of the nearby struts. With trained precision, he took a sample of the substance with a small field-shear, then went on to press his M-tester against the strut itself. The strut snapped off. Apis returned the tester to his belt and pushed against another strut. This one also broke and a piece of it floated away. A third strut shattered—frangible as burned bone—and a receiving dish made a slow departure from the pylon. Apis pulled himself down from the pylon, some struts breaking in his hands, others holding. As he hurried back to the shimmer-shield, he felt panic—another new experience for the precocious fourteen-year-old.

1

With the small blond child balanced on her knee the woman managed the awkward task of one-handedly turning a page of the picture book, and ran her finger down the border between text and picture, to set the superb illustration moving—the long legs striding through the reeds, and the sharp beak snapping in silhouette against a bruised sky.

She continued, "For the brother who had built his house out of flute grass there came misfortune indeed; that very night a heroyne came to stand over his house . . . and what did it do?"

The child reached and stabbed down with one stubby finger, leaving a jammy imprint on something that bore only a passing resemblance to a wading bird. "Heroyne," he said, blue eyes wide at his own cleverness.

"Yes, but what did it do?"

"It huffed and it puffed, and it puffed and it huffed," said the boy.

"And it blew his house down," the woman completed. Then, "Now, do you remember what the brother said when his house was gone?"

The boy frowned in concentration, but after a moment grinned with delight, knowing the best bit was coming. "Don't eat me!" he said.

"And what did the heroyne do?"

"It gobbled him up! It gobbled him up!" the boy replied, bouncing up and down with the excitement of it all.

*

"Once more: tell me of your death."

Gazing at the weird view of pink striated sky and twisted shapes, and seeing more with his new eyes than ever before, he clearly recalled the words. Because memory to him could be only as fallible as he wished it, he knew every intonation, every nuance—just as he remembered every vivid second of his own demise:

"I was leading the way down, when it came up the shaft and hit me . . ."

And thus it had gone: words spoken while his senses came online, sounds impinging, light illuminating the map of artificial veins in his eyelids, gravity holding him down on a warm but hard slab. He never heard the beat of his heart, never would again. His speech finished; he'd paused before saying, "Value judgements."

"You are no longer in virtual mode. The reality you will now experience is really real."

Oh, he was a joker that one. Gant remembered the feel of human bones breaking in his hands, the screams, the blood—the sheer terror of movement, past now.

"There's a difference then," he'd asked with some sarcasm.

"Virtual mode is fine for physical training—in it you have been made aware of your capabilities, but too long in it can affect value judgements. In virtual mode you have learnt that you can kill a human being in an eye-blink, and you have learnt how to control your new body. You learnt nothing of consequences though."

"You think I don't already know?" he'd asked, then thinking: *human being*. The AI had been way ahead of him though.

"Yes, in VR you have killed twenty people, many of them by accident, and there have been no consequences. All the time you have been aware that these people are not real. It would have been possible to quell this awareness, but the disorientation can sometimes drive a mind into paranoid schizophrenia."

"My mind is made of silicon," he pointed out.

"Your brain is made of silicon. Your mind is made of memories and patterns of thought little different from how

they were in your organic brain."

"I can't hear my heart beat."

"You chose to have the memplant, trooper Gant. Would you prefer termination?"

"No . . . I guess not."

Gant remembered opening his eyes and staring at the tiled ceiling. He'd sat upright and, out of old habit, moved his head from side to side. There was no stiffness, though, no aches or pains of any kind—not a trace of humanizing weakness. He could feel, oh yes he could feel, and it was with a clarity that was as hard and sharp as broken flint. Scanning the room, he'd flicked his vision to infrared, ultraviolet, wound his hearing to each limit of its scale, before abruptly leaping from the slab and standing beside it. He'd been naked, his body free of scars. Touching his genitals he'd found them no less sensitive than he remembered.

"I'm not really Gant any more," he said.

"No, you are a recording of Gant."

"I mean, all that was Gant: the glands, the aches and pains, the body. I'm not human, so I won't act the same."

"Does that matter?"

"I wanted immortality."

"You have it."

"Gant does not."

"There is no such thing as immortality: death is change. A human being is dying every day that it lives. The material of its body is exchanged for other materials, its thoughts change. All that lives is the DNA, and what does that matter to you? In the end it is your mind that is important. The mind you have now is closer to the mind you had when you died on Samarkand—than the mind you would have now, had you not died. The memplant crystal does not get everything, but the margin for error is smaller than the alterations to an organic brain in—"

"Oh yeah," Gant interrupted, chuckling inside.

A taste he could replay was the one in his mouth when he had taken his first ever breath with this artificial body. The air tasted sweet, though he did not require it then, nor did he now. And he'd thought somewhat on what lay ahead—a future that death had not denied him. Now, still gazing at the horizon, he breathed air that would have killed the man he had once been.

Cormac clicked his intensifier into place on the goggles of his hotsuit and then, from the tracer clipped on his utility belt, uploaded the signal code to the image intensifier's CPU. As he increased the magnification by several orders of magnitude, chameleon lenses whirred and shifted as they compensated for the involuntary movements of his head, and in his visual field a frame was thrown up, centred on the shimmering horizon. Nothing came into view other than tilted slabs of rock that were harsh white in the scalding sunlight, plasoderms rooted like giant metallic birds' claws in the arid soil between, and the occasional flickering movement from the abundant lethal fauna. It was, Cormac felt, the calloraptors that made this place such a hell, not the temperature that remained constantly above fifty degrees Celsius, not the desiccating air laden with cyanide compounds, nor the gravity of two gees. The calloraptors were what could tear your suit and expose you to the killing conditions; they were the creatures that would chew you down to the bone even while your flesh poisoned them. All things considered, he was glad of the pair that accompanied him, though he wondered what Earth Central had thought was the benefit in partnering these two.

"Nothing yet," said the first of those individuals.

Cormac unclipped the intensifier and returned it to his belt. Of course, Gant had no need of an intensifier, as he had one built-in. Cormac glanced at this Golem with its human mind uploaded from the dead soldier: Gant did not wear the mask or the hood of his suit, and it was this that revealed his unhumanity as he casually surveyed their surroundings, his multigun resting across his shoulder. Had he himself done the same, Cormac wondered what would kill him first: asphyxiation or desiccation. He studied the individual with whom Gant had been partnered. This one's unhumanity was mostly concealed by his hotsuit, until he moved legs that were hinged the wrong way—birdlike. But then the dracoman was, by a convoluted route, descended from the same ancient species as birds.

"No sign," Cormac agreed. "I thought they'd have towers up. You'd think they'd have autoguns for our friends here." He gestured to their right where a raptor had leapt onto a rock slab and was inspecting them with its bright orange eye-pits. He inspected it in turn. The creature could, with a stretch of the imagination, have been a relative of Gant's partner. Its name was an amalgam of the name of this planet, "Callorum," and of the dinosauroid raptors that had once roamed ancient Earth. It stood a metre and a half high, on two legs, but closer study revealed forelimbs branched at the elbow into two forearms, which each in turn terminated in three bladed fingers. Its mouth, below the disconcerting eye-pits, opened into three independent jaws lined with back-curved slicing teeth, and its utterly smooth skin was a dark purplish red.

"Mine," said Scar, the dracoman.

Gant, who had lowered his multigun, gave a deprecatory smile and waved him on. With his strange reverse-kneed gait the dracoman advanced on the creature, his own multigun held at his hip. Cormac wondered why Scar found it necessary to be so confrontational. The raptor made an easy enough target where it was, so there was no real need to provoke it.

As Scar reached the edge of the slab they were presently upon, the calloraptor opened its mouth and no doubt emitted the subsonic groan that was the challenge of its kind. When it attacked, it came in with a kangaroo-bouncing from slab to slab. The triple thud of Scar's multigun came as the creature was in midair between two slabs. It shuddered at the terminus of a broken blue line, then hit the next slab on its back, its head missing and its internal fluids streaming into the thirsty air. Then it rolled down to come to rest at the base of a plasoderm.

"Are we all having fun?" Cormac asked.

Gant, grinning, glanced round at him, then wiped away the grin and shouldered his multigun. Scar swung his toadlike head from side to side, searching for something else to shoot, before giving a grunt and returning to join them.

"We'll get on now, shall we?" said Cormac, and led the way onto the next slab.

Even though his clothing effectively kept out the searing heat, Cormac felt hot and tired. Despite the exoskeletal help he was getting from his hotsuit—it was set to multiply his strength sufficiently to compensate for the doubled gravity—he was really feeling his weight. The other two, of course, made this particular mission seem like a jaunt in holiday sunshine.

"You never explained why Central paired you with chummy here," Cormac said, before leaping a gap from which a somnolent raptor observed him for a moment, before returning to sleep. Its bulbous stomach attested the fact that it had recently eaten one of the root-suckers. It would now, if the survey probe's information was correct, be digesting its meal for a solstan month.

Gant followed him across the gap, then said, "Even though Scar is now considered a free citizen of the Polity, he's not entirely trusted. We work together, and I watch him."

They both glanced back as Scar hesitated at the same gap, his muzzle directed towards the sleeping raptor. When this provoked no action, the dracoman followed on.

"Should we trust you, Scar?" Cormac asked.

Scar growled but offered no other reply—as talkative as ever.

Cormac felt that whether or not to trust the dracoman was a tough call, as he was the creation of a transgalactic being calling itself "Dragon"—a being as untrustworthy as it was immense. Dragon had first proclaimed itself as an emissary of an alien race, but had then caused wholesale destruction and slaughter on a world called Samarkand, in its anxiousness to kill one of the aliens searching for it. It was during a mission to that world, led by Cormac, that Gant had died, so perhaps

Earth Central's choosing him to keep an eye on Scar was not such a bad idea after all.

It took the rest of the Callorum afternoon for them to cross the slab-field and come at last to an easily traversable saltpan. Here plasoderms had spread like a marching army of avant-garde sculptures and amongst them could be seen the occasional timorous root-sucker. These were utterly strange creatures: three-legged—a truncated tail forming the rear one of the three—and almost lacking in anything that could be called a body at the juncture of these three legs, merely having an eyeless oval head from which extended a long curved snout terminating in a ring of black tentacles. The creatures were harmless, subsisting as they did on sap tapped from the roots of the plasoderms.

Cormac again studied the dracoman as they moved on across the weird and arid landscape. Scar now purportedly had self-determination, and was no longer controlled by Dragon, for Cormac's mission had resulted in that entity's destruction . . .

Partial destruction, Cormac reminded himself. When the human race had first found Dragon on the planet Aster Colora, it had consisted of four conjoined and living spheres, each a kilometre in diameter, with pseudopods like giant snakes rooted in the two-kilometre perimeter all around it. There it had apparently destroyed itself, at the termination of its supposed mission to deliver a warning to the human race. And that had seemed the end of it until one of those spheres turned up at Samarkand. During that same encounter they had learnt that out there somewhere were the three remaining spheres. That they had indeed been parts of an emissary had turned out to be true. But now they were rogue biological constructs—like three round dots below three huge question marks. And a similar question mark hung over Scar himself.

The sun, which was so bright that one glance at it left the reactive glass in a hotsuit's goggles black for some time afterwards, ate into a chain of globular mountains eviscerated from the white crust of the planet, then blinked out. The blue twilight was an immediate thing: there was no gradual change. In this light, the grazers headed for the shadows, and the raptors followed after them to play the nightly lethal game of hide-and-seek.

"I see a tower," said Gant.

Cormac clipped his intensifier into place, and at the centre of the signal frame he spotted the squat tripod with its swing-ring-mounted autolaser. Even as he watched, the two rings shifted to bring the gun to bear on something near to it, and there was a brief ruby flash.

"Okay," said Cormac, lowering the intensifier, "nothing fancy. We'll find out what their perimeter is, and spot that tower for the *Occam*. Once it's down we go in. You two find their 'ware generator and take it out. I'll go after Skellor."

"If he's still alive," said Gant.

"Will Occam *see*?" asked Scar, his muzzle pushed forward as he peered into the twilight. Cormac wondered if the dracoman could even see the tower. It was possible: the dracomen had certainly been made with combat in mind.

"That we won't know until we try it," Cormac said.

"Never expected them to become this sophisticated. Even our chameleonware isn't that good," said Gant.

"That'll be Skellor, and he *is* still alive. His implant signal would have changed, otherwise."

Gant nodded, then said, "I still don't understand what all the anxiety is about this guy. I'd have thought if he'd been that dangerous, Earth Central would have had him whacked long ago."

"Skellor's a top-flight biophysicist, highly rated even by an AI like Earth Central, but his methods have always been dubious to say the least. It was rumoured he was using human subjects in some of his experiments, but insufficient evidence was found for any kind of prosecution . . . or whacking as you so charmingly put it. I think EC was reluctant to act against him because of the possible huge benefits deriving from his research. Now the Separatists have him it's a different matter. He was screwing around with nanotechnology and biological systems—and it doesn't take much imagination to work out what our home-grown terrorists might do with such tech."

"Well, best we resolve the issue," said Gant, unshouldering his multigun and swiftly tapping a new program into its side console.

"*Whacking* Skellor is not an option yet," Cormac told him. "We still don't know if he was kidnapped or went willingly."

"Gotcha," said Gant, clicking the three barrels of his multigun round by one turn, before swapping magazines. He glanced at Scar. "Night work," he explained. The dracoman likewise adjusted his weapon.

"What setting?" Cormac asked.

"Rail," said Gant.

Cormac nodded before moving on. Rather than firing bright pulses of ionized aluminium dust, their guns would now be firing tipped iron slugs; whether those tips were ceramal, hollow, or mercury was a matter of choice. He of course had his own preferred armament. He initiated the shuriken holster strapped on his wrist, and the weapon gave a buzz of anticipation—something he suspected was not in the user's manual. He then drew his thin-gun and wondered just how many Separatists he would kill tonight.

It seemed that his work for Earth Central Security consisted mainly of such killing. Expanding into space the human race brought with it all the traditional troubles of old Earth, and it seemed that all who had once been labelled "terrorist" now called themselves "Separatists" as if that would provide their nefarious activities with some cachet. In Cormac's experience they only really wanted wealth and power—as always. This swiftly became evident on any world that seceded from the AI governance of the Polity when, usually, the inhabitants started screaming for the Polity AIs to be brought back in.

"Gant, I want you to spot the tower for me," Cormac said, glancing at the Golem.

Gant grimaced, peered at his own weapon, then shrugged. "Never really aligned it," he said.

With Golem eyes, he had no need of a laser sight.

Cormac turned to Scar. "I take it the sight on your weapon is aligned?"

"It is," Scar grated.

"Well, *you* can spot the tower for us."

Scar gave a sharp nod in reply. Cormac felt that the mask of his suit probably disguised the dracoman's characteristic gnathic grin.

Hot darkness swamped the blue twilight, however through his intensifier it seemed almost daylight to Cormac, but with an odd lack of shadows. In this weird gloaming, the perimeter of the autolaser tower soon became evident. Thinking of other perimeters he had known, Cormac involuntarily glanced over at the dracoman. Scar was obviously fascinated by a curving line of hollowed-by-fire corpses of calloraptors. It was fast becoming apparent to Cormac where the dracoman's interests lay.

Beyond the tower, three geodesic domes had been erected amongst a scattering of low barrack-like buildings, and beyond these the other perimeter towers were just visible. At the centre of this encampment stood a complicated scaffold. It held something canted above the ground so it was possible to see it was a huge flattened spiral of reddish metal, wavering behind distortions like heat haze. The frame cast up by the intensifier had narrowed and centred on one of the domes. Cormac signalled a halt and pointed to the centre of the encampment.

"That thing in the scaffold has to be your target. Skellor is in the dome on the far left," he explained, before squatting down and turning on his suit's comlink. "Tomalon, do you still have a position on us?" he asked.

"I do," came the reply. "You're about two hundred metres in from the edge of the 'ware effect. By my scanning, all that lies beyond you is empty saltpan."

"Scar," said Cormac, nodding to the dracoman, "is going to send his multigun code to you, then range-spot an autolaser tower. On my signal I want you to take it out."

"Understood," replied Tomalon.

"Is the shuttle in position?" Cormac asked.

"In position, yes. It can be with you in five minutes."

"Well, you'll have to wait until we lose that 'ware. There's no telling what else they have in there. Even these autolaser towers are pretty sophisticated, and they're only for the local wildlife. Also, I want Skellor secured before things get . . . frantic."

"I do know what I'm doing," growled Tomalon.

Cormac supposed he must: you didn't get to be the Captain of a ship like the *Occam Razor* without having some grasp of combat realities. He glanced at his two companions.

"Ready?"

Both Gant and Scar gave him affirmative nods.

"Well, let's get in there then," Cormac said.

Scar raised his multigun and aimed at the tower. He did not fire, but merely held the laser sight on-target and transmitted the required information from his gun up to the ship.

"Acquired," Tomalon told them.

"Hit it," said Cormac.

As painful seconds dragged out, Cormac hunkered down, realizing because of the delay that Tomalon must have fired a kinetic missile rather than one of the *Occam*'s beam weapons. He was proved right when fire stabbed down through the tower and it lifted up on a blast. The air-rending sound of the explosion rolled out to them as the tower came apart on the expanding surface of a ball of fire—and disappeared. Globules of molten metal pattered on the ground fifty metres ahead of them, and a dust cloud rolled past them as they rose and ran towards the encampment.

Gant and Scar immediately outdistanced Cormac, as they sped towards the strange object in the centre of the encampment. Now, people were coming out of one of the barracks buildings. Two explosions followed—grenades tossed by Gant—and a man was running and screaming, with most of his suit ripped away. Someone else was turning and pointing a weapon. Observing the shock-absorbing side cylinders and the cable leading down to a belt-mounted power supply,

Cormac realized they were using rail-guns here too, though of primitive design. He fired once and that same someone went over on his back, with vapour jetting from his head. Then Cormac was at the wall of the dome. Not far away he could hear the stuttering fire of Separatist weapons, and the sonic cracking of Gant's and Scar's weapons in reply. Over com he could hear Scar growling with enjoyment. To his right: three people running towards him. Something was punching a line of cavities from the plascrete wall of the dome. He drew Shuriken and hurled it. The throwing star shot away, with its chainglass blades opening out in bloody welcome—through one attacker then another, both of them keeling over, a limb hitting the ground here, blood jetting and vaporizing; then, on its return, the third man losing his head before even knowing his companions were dead. From its holster Cormac sent new instructions: a program he had keyed in earlier. Shuriken swooped away from its three dead victims, then hit the wall of the dome with a circular-saw scream. While it was providing this distraction, Cormac used a smart key on the airlock. As he entered, it was to the welcoming light of the explosion that toppled the 'ware device from its supporting scaffold. And Gant's "All yours, Tomalon," coming over com.

A moment's pause as the lock cycled. When the inner door opened Cormac went through, keeping low, and dived to one side, rolled and came up in a crouch, with his thin-gun aimed and ready. To his right, two men and a woman were struggling into environment suits, to the sound of Shuriken's cutting.

"On the floor!"

One of the men started groping for something at his belt, before toppling over with a hole burned in through the bridge of his nose and out through the back of his head. The woman's eyes flicked towards something on Cormac's left. Turn. Someone on a gantry positioned round a silo, aiming a rifle at him. Four shots slammed the marksman back against the silo, then he followed the rifle to the ground.

"I said on the floor!"

The remaining man and the woman obeyed, and Cormac hit the recall on his shuriken holster. The screaming noise stopped and suddenly Shuriken was hovering above him. From behind it came a thin whistling of pressure differential, through the slot it had cut. Checking a readout at the lower edge of his vision, Cormac saw that the atmospheric pressure here was higher than that outside, so there would be no danger just yet of cyanide poisoning for anyone going unsuited in this dome. He keyed another program from the holster menu, and Shuriken advanced to hang threateningly over the prostrate man and woman.

"If you try to get up, you die," he said, coldly.

The two of them stared up at Shuriken, and showed no inclination to move from where they lay. Meanwhile Cormac scanned around to pick up Skellor's trace just beyond the silo. He ran to the edge of the silo and peered past one of the pipes running down the side of it. A plascrete wall cut across in front of him. Inset in this was a wide observation window, and what appeared to be another airlock. Judging by the equipment he could see through the window, the room beyond was a laboratory, so the lock was probably a clean-lock. Checking to either side as he passed the silo, Cormac slammed into the plascrete wall before peering round through the window again. The room was bright and aseptic. Esoteric equipment cluttered workbenches. Cormac identified a nanoscope, a huge surgical robot, cryostasis vessels, and a surgical table holding what appeared to be the corpse of a calloraptor. Cormac slapped a contact charge against the window and stepped away. The charge blew, and its metal disc went clattering across the floor. The glass remained intact until the decoder molecule began unravelling the tough chain molecules of the glass. After a minute the entire window collapsed into powder, and Cormac leapt through.

"Skellor!"

Cormac hesitated before moving beyond the corpse, as now he saw that he had been mistaken in thinking it a calloraptor. He had never seen anything quite like it: greyish veins seemed raised up from the inside, and had a slightly metallic hue; the face was also distorted—much more flattened than a calloraptor's and of a simian appearance—and the forearms were bigger, the claws more like hands. It had also, obviously, been able to walk more upright, and in its ocular hollows gleamed a line of pinhead eyes. He recognized that there was much of calloraptor in this corpse and also something of human being, and surmised that this creature must be the result of some experiment of Skellor's. He moved on and scanned his surroundings further.

There.

Skellor stepped out from behind the insectile chrome nightmare of the surgical robot. The hologram Cormac had studied earlier had not shown a particularly distinguished-looking individual: he was short, muscular, with brown hair and brown eyes. Fanatical as Skellor was about his *work*, he had apparently never bothered with cosmetic alteration, nor any form of augmentation. The latter situation, Cormac now saw, had changed: a crystalline aug curved from the man's right temple, down behind his right ear, and terminated in three crystalline rods that entered the base of his neck. Recognizing just what this device was, Cormac felt inclined to put numerous holes in him right there and then. He restrained himself.

"Cormac, Earth Central Security. I've come to get you out," he said, going for the less confrontational option.

Skellor snorted a laugh, then shook his head. "You're outside your jurisdiction here," he said.

"You're a Polity citizen and you were kidnapped. That puts anywhere you are found inside Polity jurisdiction," Cormac replied.

"Wrong, citizen, I am here of my own free will, and you are over the Line. But I don't suppose that'll make any difference to your actions. The arrogance of ECS has always been unassailable—hence their insistence on hindering my work."

"If I recall the file correctly, the hindrance was regarding your choice of experimental subjects, not of the work itself. The Polity does not prevent research into anything so long as it doesn't impinge upon another individual's rights."

Skellor gestured to a nearby bench, upon which rested a completely sealed chainglass cylinder supported in a ceramal framework that seemed excessive for the task. Inside the cylinder lay a scattering of pinkish coralline objects.

"Perhaps you should ask your superiors about research into items such as those," Skellor said, "should you survive."

As Skellor turned away, something slammed into Cormac's back and bore him to the floor. Cormac shifted as he went down and fired three shots from under his armpit into the assailant behind him. The only response was a grating hiss—then he was hurtling through the air to crash down onto the equipment lying on one of the benches. The creature from the surgical table. After rolling from the bench, Cormac put three shots into the sharp double keel of its chest. The creature opened its three-cornered mouth and hissed again, as something pinkish welled up to fill the holes the shots had made—and it just kept advancing. This time Cormac shot it in the head, putting out some of those pinhead eyes, which paused it for all of a second or two before it caught hold of the bench, and hurled it to one side. Just then, there came a low sucking boom, and a wind suddenly dragged across the laboratory, towing pieces of cellophane and paper. Dome breach—a large one this time. Cormac leapt over the next bench, turned and concentrated his fire on one of the creature's leg joints. Four shots should have blown away enough of its knees to sever its lower leg, yet the limb clung on as rapidly expanding strands of the pinkish substance filled the gaping wounds.

"Right, point taken," muttered Cormac, slapping the recall on his shuriken holster. Shuriken arrived as Cormac was backed up against the wall of the dome, emptying the last of his thin-gun's charge. It took the creature's head off on the first pass, hesitated when it just remained standing, then—with two hatcheting thumps—cut its torso in half at chest level, then curved back through to take away its legs.

As Shuriken hovered and bobbed, whirring with irritation above the dismembered body, Cormac advanced for a closer look. There was no blood, just pink strands creeping across the floor between body parts, before freezing and fading to a bone white. He prodded at one of these strands with the toe of his boot, and it curled up briefly before shattering into glassy fragments.

"Gant, where are you?"

"Heading your way," came the immediate reply. "The shuttle's down and the unit's clearing up the stragglers."

"There's two inside the dome here. I had Shuriken guarding them, but then I ran into a little trouble."

"Gotcha."

Cormac hit recall again, and held up his arm. Shuriken returned reluctantly to its holster, retracting its chainglass blades at the last moment before snicking itself away. Cormac stepped over his recently demised enemy and trotted over to where he had last seen Skellor. Beyond the surgical robot there was a hole in the wall of the dome, out of which gyred all the loose rubbish sucked from the laboratory. Cormac stepped through it and saw the shuttle—a U-shaped lander twenty metres long—resting at the edge of the encampment to the side where the autolaser tower had stood. A pulse-gun was firing intermittently from one of the shuttle's turrets, bringing down calloraptors that were coming in to see what all the excitement was about. Cormac walked on until the frame in his intensifier closed to a line, and then he peered at the ground. Lying in the dust was the small black button of a memplant—Skellor's implant, the one from which issued the tracer signal. Cormac could only suppose it had been removed some time earlier, and only now—because Skellor had realized what danger it represented—had it been discarded. He picked the object up, then surveyed his surroundings. It seemed to be all over. The Sparkind were herding prisoners out into the open—those of them that had hotsuits—and Cormac could hear no more shooting.

"What happened in there?" Gant asked, coming up behind him.

Cormac glanced round at him—and at Scar, who was following closely behind.

"It would seem that friend Skellor is going to be more of a problem than we thought."

"How so?"

"Well, from what I can gather, he is interfaced with a quartz-matrix AI," said Cormac.

"Shit, that's bad," said Gant.

"Is it?" said Cormac, slipping the memplant into one of his belt pouches. "Would it be as bad as him having got his sticky little fingers on Jain technology too?"

"Double shit," muttered Gant.

The silence of space should have made the destruction seem unreal, but the picture of the station—without atmosphere to spoil the clarity—brought reality home. With kin and clan, Apis Coolant hung in the air before the great screen and watched his world tearing itself apart. As he watched, he picked up snippets of the conversation from the rainbow crowd gathered around him, and they seemed a suitable commentary.

". . . nanomycelium . . ."

". . . too much time. The counteragent too late . . ."

One individual, with emerald skin and pure black eyes, pressed her thin fingers to the chrome aug she wore.

"Miranda just resorbed the subminds. The servers are getting cranky," she said.

"Confirmed . . . Miranda just transported out," said another.

"Where do we go now?" someone whispered.

The Outlink station *Miranda* seemed to be sparkling, but close-up views showed that each glint was either an explosion or where a misaligned gravity field collapsed part of the hull. The stalk of the station was twisting as well, and gaps were appearing in the structure. Debris orbited it in ring-shaped clouds, and beyond this the other ships that had helped take off the last of the survivors were poised like silver vultures.

"Ten minutes to fusion engage," a voice told them.

The clans ignored this and continued to watch the dramatic destruction of their home. For a moment, the screen blanked out. As it came back on, they saw a star-glare going out. Part of the station had disappeared.

"What was that?"

"It's where the runcible was," said someone knowledgeably. "Probably antimatter."

Others felt inclined to argue.

"No, foolish—not antimatter. Collapse of spoon."

"Rubbish. That was flare-off from the buffers. The energy had to go sometime."

An involved argument followed that Apis ignored. What would happen now that his home was gone? Another station? He did not know. All he did know was that he felt a deep anger at what had happened. A nanomycelium had been used, so there must have been forethought. Someone had deliberately destroyed his home. The room jerked and people looked around in confusion, before returning their attention to the screen and continuing their arguments. Talk was a shield against the reality of what had happened.

"Fusion drive engaging in ten seconds. Entering underspace in twenty-two minutes," the voice told them, but was ignored by all but Apis and the woman next him. She seemed confused and kept touching her aug as if probing a sore.

"Don't seem to be receiving anything on this ship," she said.

Apis agreed: there was something strange about this situation—the voice had sounded too mechanical to be the voice of an AI. It sounded more like the voice of a bored human. Peculiar job for a human to have. There was also a slight jerk as the drive engaged, as if something might be functioning a microsecond out—something that should not be.

The picture transmitted by the remotes at the Outlink station remained as good as ever. Apis could see that it had now twisted in half, and that the two halves were starting to revolve in the same direction, like the needles of a dial. They had completed three revolutions, and were upright on the screen and parallel to each other, when the ship entered underspace. The picture then blinked out. When Apis glanced around, he saw that he was one of only a few who remained, everybody else having gone to their allotted hammocks.

*

"Leave your basket here, but bring your pole-grab and net," said Ulat, standing beside the pond with three other pond workers. Eldene glanced at him, then carefully made her way to the edge of the pond, towing her net full of broken deaders behind her. The squerms in this pond were only small ones—less than the length of her arm and only the thickness of her thumb—but you never dared take your eye off them for long. Even ones this size could writhe up the side of a wader to tear holes in a worker's body.

Reaching the bank she climbed out of the water and emptied her net. As Ulat and the others began to move away, she took up her pole-grab then hurried to catch up, falling in beside Fethan. The man was an old hand who had been working the ponds for more than half his life, hence the huge bulge apparent on his chest—over which his ginger beard spread—where his scole lay feeding under his shirt.

"What's happening?" Eldene hissed.

Fethan glanced at her with bloodshot eyes, then twisted his face in a parody of a grin, exposing his lack of front teeth—apparently lost when he had taken a beating from one of the town proctors. "Tricone. Musta been a faulty membrane. Broke through into one of Dent's ponds and drowned—poisoned half the squerms."

Eldene felt fear clenching her gut: that meant half a pondful of deaders to remove. "What size?" she asked.

"Full-grown squerms," Fethan replied, then lowered his voice. "Now'd be a good time to go under. Guarantee one of us'll get scraped today."

Eldene considered that. Fethan had teased her remorselessly about "the Underground"—occasionally saying something to pique her curiosity, then dismissing it all as rumour and myth. Eldene thought it likely that it *was* all myth. She had so far seen no sign of a resistance movement, but plenty of signs of something to resist. She glanced up at the satellites and stations of the Theocracy glinting in the now lavender sky, or across the face of the gas giant, all reflecting the light of the sun that would shortly break from behind the horizon. Then she gazed out across the ponds, to where Proctor Volus was rapidly approaching in his aerofan with its side-mounted rail-gun. What chance did any resistance movement stand with satellite lasers poised overhead, and the Theocracy's religious police below constantly watching the planet-bound population?

It was evident they had reached the pond in question when Ulat halted and stood gazing at the water, with arms akimbo. Dent stood at the foreman's side, wringing his hands, his balding head bowed. That a tricone had broken through the membrane separating the pond's water from the deep planetary soil was not due to any fault on his part. In fact it was more likely due to skimming on Ulat's part—trying to make a membrane last for three seasons, rather than the usual two, and pocketing the consequent saving. But, as Eldene well knew, blame always devolved on the workers, no matter how innocent.

"You checked it before it was filled?" Ulat asked, after hingeing down his mask. Because he used such breather gear showed he was a citizen, rather than just a worker, but it did not raise him to the rank of a true brother. All that could impart that lofty status was the *Gift*, which only those of religious rank above vicar could bestow.

"I did, Ulat," replied Dent.

Ulat flipped his mask back up as he studied the pond again. In the shallow water rested a mollusc the size of a man's torso. This creature consisted of three white cones of shell closely joined, like panpipes, but with nodular fleshy heads resting deep within each shell mouth. All around it the water was discoloured, bluish, and the only squerms anywhere near it were either unmoving or breaking up into individual segments. The rest of the squerms were gathered around the edges of the pond, tangled in the mat of weeds in a hissing and flicking, vicious metallic spaghetti. As Ulat glanced round to where Volus was landing his aerofan, the mask did not conceal an alarmed but furtive expression. Eldene understood that, with the Proctor being here now,

Ulat had no chance to cover up the disaster and put the loss down to the natural wastage entailed by deaders. Someone, she knew, was going to be punished.

"I think not," said Ulat, and abruptly struck Dent across the face. When the man went down, Ulat kicked him in the stomach. Then, as he coiled around this pain, Ulat stamped down on the scole attached to his chest—which soon had Dent gasping for breath as the creature ceased to oxygenate his blood.

"What has happened here, brother?" asked Volus, approaching, his voice echoey behind his tinted visor.

Eldene studied the new arrival, with his stinger resting across one shoulder and his pistol drawn from its recharging holster, and realized that the rumours were true: Volus had received the *Gift* from this work-compound's Vicar. She could see the large bean-shaped object attached behind his ear, scaled and reddish green, and looking alive as any scole. Now he truly was a member of the Theocracy, in his white uniform with sacred words written down the side and down one leg of it, his higher-status visored breather apparatus, and now his *connection* to all brothers and his access to all channels of prayer.

Dent was still gasping for breath as the Proctor glanced unconcernedly down at him, then returned his attention to Ulat.

Ulat gestured down at Dent. "He punctured this pond membrane with his pole-grab, Proctor, and did not bother to report it." He pointed to the pond. "Now you see the result."

"You were required to increase the production of squerms, Ulat. This does not look like any increase to me. The Vicar will not be happy," said Volus.

"What can *I* do?" Ulat whined.

Now Dent slowly began to breathe more easily, as his scole recovered from the blow it had received.

"You can begin by keeping your workers in order. Those of the Hierarchy are not best pleased by the shortfall of trade essence, so their displeasure is focused on the Deacon, the Deacon's displeasure is focused on his vicars, and theirs on us proctors. We have been instructed to take measures. So must I take measures now, or will you get this mess cleaned up!"

Ulat whirled on his workers. "You four, get in there and clear out those deaders!" He kicked Dent until the man stood up, then gave him a shove towards the pond. Eldene caught Dent's arm before he stumbled into it, and got a brief nod of gratitude before he stooped to retrieve his net and pole-grab.

"Work the edge for a moment," Eldene whispered to him, before leaving her own pole and net on the bank and following Fethan into the turbid water. Dent moved off along one side and began using his pole to pull out all those deaders he could reach.

It was back-breaking and dangerous work. Twice Eldene felt the brush of feeding hooks close to her face, as she and Fethan stooped to lift the tricone from the water and carry it to the bank, before returning with their nets to scoop up the swiftly decaying segments of squerm. Cathol, fourth member of their group, swore quietly, and Eldene noticed that he had not been so swift and had lost a piece of his cheek to one of the creatures. The man continued working, though, blood soaking into the collar of his coverall and dripping into the water. After a short time, Volus departed in his aerofan, leaving Ulat nervously patrolling the bank. Hours later, when the team had cleared the pond of deaders, and were mounding them on the bank for collection, the Proctor returned.

"Come here, all of you!" Volus bellowed.

The four workers gathered before him, with Ulat standing at their backs.

"You have done well, brothers, in your labour for the Church of Masada," said the Proctor, strolling along their line. "But it is a shame that it has even been necessary for you to labour like this." He came to stand before Dent, and gestured Ulat to come and stand beside him.

Ulat pulled his mask down. "Yes, Proctor?"

"What do you think is a sufficient punishment for his infringement?" Volus asked.

Ulat took another deep breath from his mask before replying. "I think a few days in a cage should do the trick. We don't want to ruin him completely."

Eldene glanced aside nervously. It was coming now. Volus was bound to suggest a more vicious punishment. Quite likely Dent would soon be dead, and Eldene could see the man knew that: he looked terrified.

Volus nodded slowly. "I see . . . So, that being his punishment, what do you think yours should be, Ulat? Your own crime has been theft from the Church . . . hasn't it?"

Eldene could not help but feel a species of joy at the sudden panic in Ulat's expression.

"I have done nothing, Proctor, I assure you!"

"No, of course not," said Volus, but now his hand snapped out, and he struck Ulat across his legs with the stinger. Ulat shrieked and went down, and Volus immediately stooped over him. Eldene watched in amazement as the Proctor tore away the foreman's breather gear and stepped back.

"Now, brothers," continued Volus. "A new work party will be taking over here from tomorrow. So tomorrow morning you four must report to the ponds on South-side, to join the sprawn harvest. Return to your barracks when you have finished here."

As the Proctor returned to his aerofan, Ulat crawled after him, his breathing heavy at first, then gasping and choking as he tried to summon the breath to beg for the return of his mask. It was a horrible and rare justice, Eldene felt, watching Ulat die, while the Proctor took his aerofan into the air. They loaded Ulat into a basket along with the other deaders—asphyxiated blue under the lurid sky.

2

With the boy on her lap, leaning back against her breast, the woman continued, "And then there was the brother who built his house from grape sticks, and who sat safe while the heroyne ate his friend and clacked its beak in satisfaction. So proud he was of what he had built . . . and don't we know all about pride?"

In all seriousness the little boy said, "Big trouble."

The woman bit her lip trying to keep a straight face, then sat upright. "Yes, 'big trouble,'" she concurred.

In the picture book propped on the console before her, the long-legged bird creature was frozen at the point where it pinched the previous brother's head in the end of its beak. As she clouted the book, the picture continued running through its animation. The creature tilted its head back and swallowed the man whole . . . then the picture clicked back to where it was gripping his head again, and had clearly gone into a loop.

"Bugger," the woman muttered, clouting the book a second time. Now the animation resumed as it should, and proceeded to the house of sticks.

The woman went on, "That very night the heroyne came to stand over his house of sticks. And what did it do?"

Together, woman and child said, "It huffed and it puffed, and it puffed and it huffed, and it blew his house down."

"And what did the brother say when his house was gone?" the woman asked, checking her watch.

"Don't eat me!" was the boy's immediate reply.

"And I'm sure you're eager to tell me what happened."

"It gobbled him all up!"

*

"You can't run, girl. None of us can run." Those had been Fethan's early words to her, shortly after she had crossed the short space from the hover bus that had transported her and five others from the city orphanage to this farming co-operative. Fethan had gone on to explain that euphemism to her: "You *co-operate* on the farm or they kill you."

It seemed Fethan was an old hand. Some time in his youth he had got on the wrong side of some member of the Theocracy, but not far enough on the wrong side to end up dead—only as a virtual slave.

"Why?" she had asked him. "Why all this?"

"Just the way it is, girl. The Theocracy have all the cream, and if we so much as think of licking it, we get trod on well and good."

"It's not fair," she had said. "My parents were executed, but I've done nothing wrong."

"Right and wrong don't come into it. It's a shit situation and y'gotta make the best of it." Later it would be platitudes like this one that would precede Fethan's oblique references to the Underground. "You gotta find an entrance in the mountains first, and no way we'll ever get there with these fellas hanging on us." Fethan slapped at the scole nestling on his chest. "You don't take your pills regular and your body'll reject the bugger. You don't get in the air at night to build up the surplus it feeds to you in the day, it'll die on you and you'll suffocate."

Remembering such past conversations, Eldene finished her meal of nut-potatoes and bread, then went into the chapel adjoining the canteen to say her evening prayers, under the gaze of the Theocracy cameras, before heading for the bunkhouse. Most of the other workers were already asleep, not having had the extra tasks allotted to herself and her three companions, but there were still one or two muted conversations in progress. Seated on her own bunk, as she tiredly removed her boots, Eldene considered her bleak future—if it could even be called a future. Most workers did not last as long as Fethan, since accident, exhaustion, or proctors killed them before they got to enjoy grey hair for long. Escape was not an option, as without their scoles they would suffocate outside in minutes, and the Theocracy rigidly controlled distribution of the anti-rejection pills. Only stowing away on a trader's ship, or rescue by the fabled Underground, offered any chance of getting away, and all that Eldene knew of the latter seemed rumour and myth. There was one other option for her—the same one many female workers chose upon entering puberty. Eldene hoped she would never be so desperate as to take that route, then wondered if she would be given a choice.

"You ever work the sprawn ponds?" Fethan asked her from the bunk above.

"You know I haven't," Eldene replied.

"Yeah . . . right, of course."

Eldene felt a sinking in her belly. Fethan was getting forgetful, slow, old. With horrible certainty she knew that sometime soon she would see the old man die, and would probably have to drag his corpse back for processing into fertilizer—which was the best in the way of a send-off any of them could expect.

"What's it like there?" she asked.

"'Tain't as bad as the squerms. Hard work, but they ain't vicious." Fethan swung his spindly legs over the side of his bunk and dropped down to sit on Eldene's bunk, beside her. "Only trouble is that you gotta wonder why Volus had us moved."

Eldene stared at him. "What do you mean?"

"Well, Ulat was skimming, but you don't get to do that without some help from higher up. Reckon Ulat was paying off Volus, and Volus decided it was time for the arrangement to end once he received his *Gift*. We're trouble for him now 'cause we might have seen things we oughtn't."

"But he could have easily killed us out there . . . claimed we tried to escape," said Eldene.

"Nah, he's smarter than that. He can easily blame any shortfall on Ulat, but if us four got done as well, things might start to look a bit too suspicious to the Vicar."

"So he's just moving us conveniently out of the way."

"Yeah, let's hope so," muttered the old man.

The calloraptors had taken to feeding on their seared brethren, so did not get as far as the guard perimeter set up by the new autogun. Cormac observed the insectile machine as it patrolled its allotted area, swivelling its chromed barrels hopefully, and he swore yet again. He raised his gaze to the incandescent sky, where the iron wing of a heavy-lifter was silhouetted on its way down, and he wondered what the hell Tomalon was playing at. Then he marched over to the shuttle that was now powering up.

"Still no sign of Skellor, and we've got probes out as far as twenty kilometres in every direction," said Gant, over Cormac's comlink.

"What about the stratospheric probes?" Cormac asked.

"No sign of a ship, and they've covered most other possibilities. They've been surveying from the moment we arrived," Gant replied.

"Could be under another chameleonware shield."

"Yes, there is that."

Cormac looked around for Gant, and spotted him over by one of the barracks buildings, where a team was stripping out and crating everything, including those damned coralline fragments. He considered going over and joining the Golem, then rejected the idea. He had to find out what all this was about, why Tomalon was being so difficult. Then he would find out what the hell Skellor had been up to.

Jain . . . Cormac tasted the word as he walked to the shuttle. The name had been that of a member of an ancient Hindu sect believing the material world eternal, and seemed suitable for a race with a seemingly numinous technology. It was also suitably ironic considering the race no longer existed. The first fragmentary coralline artefacts had been discovered before Cormac's birth and had immediately been a sensation, for though alien life was common in the Polity, sentient alien life was rare. Interest had waned when the fragments were dated at over five million years old, then resurged when further examination revealed some of them to be the product of advanced nano- and even pico-technology. That discovery had consequently impelled huge advances in Polity technology. Ever since, the hunt had been on for similar remains, but the sum total of fragments found weighed less than ten kilos. Of the Jain themselves, little more was known than that they had occupied many worlds, had actually rearranged solar systems to suit their requirements, and were now gone. No one knew what a Jain looked like. It was speculated that like humans they had adapted themselves to their worlds when the reverse could not be done. And knowing of what those aliens had been capable, AIs and humans alike expressed the sentiment that perhaps it was a good thing that they were no longer around.

"Tomalon, can't you transmit the message down here to me?" Cormac asked, suddenly feeling frustrated.

"No," replied the Captain of the *Occam Razor*. "It is for your eyes only and it cannot be retransmitted. You have to come *here* to read it."

"You say there's no information as to why we have to pull out so fast?"

"None, unfortunately."

"What about Occam, has it got anything to say?" Cormac asked, as he reached the lock of the shuttle. The lock irised open and he stepped inside. He was removing his breathing gear and goggles when the Captain's reply came through the shuttle's comlink—the craft's hull otherwise being impervious to radio transmissions.

"Occam says that Earth Central is aware of the importance of capturing Skellor."

"That's it?"

"That's it," Tomalon confirmed.

Cormac dropped into the seat next to the pilot, and turned to the woman herself. She was Golem, he realized almost immediately. She watched him enquiringly until he impatiently pointed upwards, before strapping himself in—this being a military craft it did not have the luxury of internal grav-plates. She cursorily scanned the instrumentation then lifted and tilted the joystick. With a deep AC hum the craft rose and turned, the screen polarizing as it partially faced towards the sun. To one side Cormac saw the heavy-lifter coming down to collect, piecemeal, the entire Separatist base. For someone the future would involve a great deal of deep forensic scanning, as they extracted every mote of available information concerning what Skellor had been up to from the material of this base. And the deepest and most rigorous scanning would certainly be concentrated on those small fragments of coralline material.

The sky turned from an inferno to that abrupt blue twilight, as the shuttle outdistanced the sun and continued to ascend. Soon stars became visible, their light punching through the glassy sculpture of a not-so-distant nebula.

"The *Occam*'s coming up," said the pilot, pointing at a distant speck, perhaps emulating discomfort at Cormac's silence.

Cormac felt himself relenting: it wasn't her fault that this mission was being screwed, whether she was Golem or not.

"You know," he said, "when I was first shuttled out to that ship, the pilot pointed it out to me then." She looked at him inquiringly and he went on, "More precisely she said, 'We'll be there soon,' and I suggested the figure of twenty minutes. When she told me forty minutes, I was quite surprised—I hadn't realized just how big the damned thing was."

She nodded her agreement. "The *Occam Razor* is a delta-class dreadnought."

Cormac continued, "You discover, in such situations, that you still have the capacity for awe." He watched the speck as it grew in the screen. Later he discovered his capacity to feel awe was undiminished. The *Occam Razor* hung utterly still in space: a golden lozenge spined with sensor arrays and weapons, four kilometres long, and one and a half wide, and one deep. He felt a moment of disquiet when he remembered that this was not the largest of the Earth Central Security dreadnoughts. It took its place in the Greek alphabet after three other classes.

"You have to wonder how big alpha-class dreadnoughts are," he said, as they passed below a sensor array the size of a cathedral.

"That's something we'd all like to know," said the woman. Cormac glanced at her in surprise: it was not often that a Golem admitted to any lack of knowledge. She went on, "Information on alpha and beta dreadnoughts is restricted. But I know that the gamma dreadnought *Cable Hogue* is not allowed to orbit any world with seas."

Cormac looked at her and waited.

"Tides," she explained. "*Cable Hogue* masses the same as Earth's moon. It's a lot bigger, though."

"Shit."

"Of course, it's only a dreadnought. There are reputed to be others."

"Let me guess: planet breakers? Popular fiction has a lot to answer for."

The Golem woman just stared at him for a moment, before manoeuvring the shuttle into an open bay. A gnat flying into a lion's mouth. And this lion had sharp claws indeed.

Disembarking from the shuttle, Cormac gazed around at the huge cavern of the shuttle bay and at the activity therein. There were other shuttles clamped to the acres of ceramal flooring, and a maintenance team was working on one of these—a team consisting of humans, Golem, and various esoteric designs of robot. As he moved out across the floor, one of these devices—a remote drone—flew an erratic course towards him.

Once the drone was close he said to it, "I want you to take me to the bridge." For he had already experienced disorientation at the shifting of the internal structure of the ship. Occam, the ship's AI, often rearranged that structure for supposed optimum efficiency, though Cormac suspected the intelligence had other reasons.

"Yeah, yeah, yeah," said the drone impatiently, and began its wavering flight away from him. He stared at it in annoyance, and it halted ten metres away. "Come on then," it said, and a clawed arm folded out from its flat body and gestured impatiently for him to follow. He did so, remembering that warship AIs and their various subminds were reputedly cranky. It had something to do with getting a shitty deal as far as employment was concerned. A ship like the *Occam Razor* was effectively its controlling intelligence's body, and was built for wholesale destruction and slaughter. Occam, the AI, spent most of its time twiddling metaphorical thumbs.

The drone led Cormac to a drop-shaft, up which he was propelled at more than usual speed. The drone hovered near him like the carapace of a crab, its metal arms folded underneath. For all that it only had black button eyes evenly spaced round its rim, it seemed to be glaring at him disapprovingly. The irised gravity field slowed him at the requisite level, and the drone led him out into Tomalon's abode.

Sticking out like the head of a thistle from one side of the ship, the bridge was roofed entirely in chainglass, and walled with consoles like compressed masses of fairy lights. Fixed to columns sunk into the black glass floor, in which the spill of optics flickered like synapses, was an arc of command chairs facing the chainglass windows to Cormac's left. The central one of these was the only one occupied.

Tomalon sat there like some ancient king upon his throne, only both king and throne were one. He was a swarthy and thickset man who was utterly hairless—probably because hairs might interfere with the many metallic and crystalline connections all over his body, which in turn made him appear to be suffering from some exotic skin complaint. The surface of Tomalon's body was a plug, and the socket was this crystal and ceramo-composite chair he occupied. It joined him—as closely as it was safe to be joined—to the *Occam Razor*'s AI. From amidst his casings and skeins of optic cable, the Captain glanced at Cormac.

"This message," Cormac said.

"The drone," said Tomalon, tilting his head, "will take you to it."

Cormac glanced aside as the drone slid forward and turned towards him.

"What do you mean take me to it?"

Tomalon explained, "The message you have received is a total-immersion VR package. Beyond that, I know nothing other than its source at EC. Occam knows more, but I am not permitted to tell you what he knows."

Cormac stared at the Captain for a moment, as the man settled back in his chair and his eyes slowly went opaque white—some kind of reaction to direct optical linking—then glared out of the chainglass windows towards the planet below. More pointless delays—why all this unnecessary drama?

"Let's get it done then," he muttered, and turned away.

Cormac moved into a standing position, with his hands arranged as a Pharaoh's and his eyes closed. He held that position for one even expulsion of air, then moved into a sequence of punches, kicks and head-butts to take out five opponents. He finished the kata in the Pharaoh position again, took one steady breath, relaxed.

"You're very fast," someone said.

Oh shit.

The gym was supposedly closed to everyone but Scar and himself, so somehow this man must have got past the dracoman. He appeared young and very fit, which did not mean he was necessarily either, and he wore a gi, so it was clearly not his intention to spectate. Cormac watched him approach, noticing a strong hint of Japanese about him, and something familiar. Five paces away from Cormac, the Japanese bowed in a fighter's fashion—that is, he did not once take his eyes from Cormac, who returned the courtesy.

"Who are you?" Cormac asked.

The man grinned and slid into a fighting stance. Cormac did the same. He felt easy about this: he knew he was good and he was already warmed up, whereas his adversary might only have the benefit of the former. They closed, exchanged a few testing punches, all easily blocked. Out of the corner of his eye Cormac saw Scar step into the gym to stand watching with his arms folded like some paternal sensei. Curiouser and curiouser.

"Scar let you in here?" said Cormac, flicking his foot up at the side of his opponent's head as if to emphasize the point.

"He knows I have nothing but the best intentions," said the man, after successfully ducking the attack. He then countered with three kicks in quick succession, the last of which—a thrust kick turned into a reverse roundhouse at the last moment—nearly taking Cormac's head off. Cormac leapt back, countering the rapidly following punch with a crescent kick. He then himself went into the attack—and meant it. That last kick could have caused him some real damage. This was to be no game. They proceeded to exchange blows too fast for the casual observer to follow. Cormac felt his opponent's rib give under one of his strikes, then felt one of his own go immediately after. The next thing he knew, a foot cracked against his temple, then swept his feet away. He was now on his back, a straight-fingered strike poised, withheld, but ready, over his throat.

"*You* are fast," he admitted, panting.

The "Japanese" stepped back, shrugged, and suddenly appeared a lot older. Cormac immediately recognized him.

"You're not so slow yourself, Ian Cormac. You're the first to manage that in a long time." He pushed his hand against his ribcage and there was a click. He shrugged again and stood upright. That he had a cracked rib showed not at all. Cormac pushed himself laboriously to his feet. His own busted rib was just beginning to hurt.

"Here, let me," said Blegg, and reached out to press his palm against Cormac's chest. A flush of warmth, the pain went away.

"How the hell did you do that?" he asked.

Blegg smiled and waved a hand at their surroundings. "I can do anything here—as can you, should you will it," he said.

Cormac walked to the side of the room and picked up a towel to wipe his face.

He gave the dracoman a calculating look. "Learnt anything interesting?"

Scar showed his teeth.

Cormac turned back to Blegg, who had followed him, and seemed to be sweating not at all. What did he mean, "I can do anything"? Then Cormac suddenly realized what the comment might indicate. He held out the towel and let it drop, then, with a small exertion of will, stopped the fabric in midair.

He glanced at Blegg. "Total immersion?"

Blegg nodded once.

"How much of my memory is repressed?" Cormac asked.

"Enough for the civilities, but now you will remember *where* and *when* you are."

And Cormac did. He remembered his mission on Samarkand—that world devastated by the alien entity calling itself "Dragon"—then his long sojourn on Earth after having spent far too much time trying to find the source of a contract that had been put out on his life—only to discover it was Dragon who wanted him dead. But whether that contract had been put out by the sphere he had killed or another, he did not know—for Dragon was now essentially four entities, each a living sphere a kilometre across. During that sojourn he had, not for the first time, considered retirement, then quickly rejected the idea. Thereafter had come the quick resolution of a problem involving a small group of amphidapt Separatists on Europa, which had then resulted in his pursuit of a biophysicist called Skellor, whom Earth Central Security had been watching for some time. This pursuit had been long but not particularly troublesome—Skellor having a tracer layered in a memplant he had purchased while watched by ECS. Then on to the Line-patrolling dreadnought the *Occam Razor*—and now here . . .

"Get to the point," said Cormac, regaining his impatience.

"As you will," said Blegg, waving a hand.

Instantly a black line split this reality, opened and swept away the entire dojo, and the dracoman along with it. Now Cormac found himself standing on a floor of glass in open space. He gazed down to where Blegg pointed and saw the huge Outlink station *Miranda*, suspended there. Around it, in speeded time, gathered a fleet of ships, and before his eyes the station began to come apart.

"This was Outlink station *Miranda* five solstan days ago. It was destroyed by a mycelium similar to the one used to destroy the Samarkand runcible," said Blegg.

"Deaths?" inquired Cormac, his urgency to find Skellor now seeming childish to him.

"Twenty-three of the Outlinkers refused to leave, but there was time enough to evacuate the rest."

"Did Dragon plant the mycelium? Are we talking outright hostilities with it now?"

"One of the spheres—it is well to remember that they are separate entities now—may have been involved. You will travel to this place in the *Occam Razor*, and you will find out what is happening, then take whatever action you deem necessary."

Cormac stared thoughtfully at the Outlink station as great swathes of its hull unpeeled and explosions sparkled its surface. "If Dragon really is involved, I could do with some assistance out there."

"You are thinking of Mika, the Life-Coven woman from Circe."

"I am," said Cormac.

"You are also thinking of what she might learn from the materials gathered from that base on Callorum," said Blegg. Cormac shrugged, and Blegg went on, "The nearest Polity outpost on your direct route to *Miranda*'s last position is the asteroid smelting station, *Elysium*. Mika will be there when you arrive."

"What about the rest of the Sparkind?"

"Once you are at *Elysium*, copies of Aiden and Cento, having been transmitted through the runcible there, will upload to memory space in the *Occam*'s AI and, should you require them, they can be downloaded into spare Golem bodies that the ship carries. You already have Gant and Scar with you. Thorn, unfortunately, is otherwise engaged."

Cormac nodded, good enough—though working with Golem copies always made him edgy. The minds of Aiden and Cento would be no different from those of their originals, only the bodies would be different, though not visibly, so there was no logical reason for his edginess—just a personal quirk he supposed.

"Anything else I should know?" he asked.

"The nearest inhabited world outside the Line to where *Miranda* was destroyed is one aptly named Masada. It is interesting to note that the theocracy ruling that world ordered, some time ago, the construction of a kinetic missile-launcher, ostensibly to defend Masada against Dragon."

"What might they hope to achieve with it otherwise?" asked Cormac.

"The utter suppression of a rebellion that is, literally, underground."

"Explain."

"The rebels live in caves. And a kinetic missile-launcher of sufficient power can penetrate deep into the ground."

"I see."

Cormac stared at Blegg, trying to see the wheels within. The ancient Japanese was unreadable but then, in Cormac's experience, Blegg was only as readable as he wanted to be. He was named agent Prime Cause. He would perhaps better have been named Prime Manipulator.

"Is this another of your games?" he asked.

Blegg gazed at him with eyes like enamel buttons.

"The *Occam Razor* is not actually the nearest Line patrol dreadnought but, considering the possible involvement of Dragon, you are the most suitable choice of investigator and . . . facilitator." As Blegg spoke, the dojo once again folded in around the two of them, only this time minus the dracoman. "No games, agent Cormac. We have no time for them now." And, with that, Blegg walked to the door of the dojo. Cormac paused for a moment before following him. There were other questions; there always were. When he stepped into the corridor beyond, Blegg was gone: the Cheshire Cat and the Mad Hatter rolled into one. Cormac returned to the dojo, and closed his eyes.

"End program," he said succinctly.

Now he felt his body assume its original pose: the Pharaoh position, as in the kata. The temperature changed abruptly and he felt a tingling stinging at the sides of his head. When that sensation ceased—signifying that the nanofibres had been withdrawn from his cortex—he reached up and pulled aside the auging clamp. Opening his eyes, he saw the ship's drone hovering before him and, glancing around, he once again located himself in the *Occam Razor*'s VR suite.

"We go to *Elysium*, and from what I know of the place, *that* is certainly the most inapt description," he said, stepping from the support frame.

The drone dipped in midair as it, no doubt, relayed this information to Tomalon.

The entire Separatist base lay packaged and strapped down in one small section of one of the huge holds. A shimmer-shield, from ceiling to floor, divided off this section from the rest of the hold, no doubt to prevent wastage of the inert gas that was now being pumped in. Skellor observed the security drone suspended from the ceiling like some art deco light fitting and, whilst sweating in his environment suit and watching in panic the count trickling away on the air-supply indicator displayed in the bottom corner of his visor, called up a specific viral subprogram in his aug. It was getting easier to do this now. No longer did he feel the crystal matrix AI as something separate from himself—it was *he* who was remembering the program, and *he* who was opening the soft link to the security drone.

The link established itself with a click that was almost audible to him. He felt the subprogram uploading through it, and he observed that program draining from the temporary memory spaces in his crystal matrix aug like acid from uncorked carboys. Letting his attention follow it through, he observed the drone's internal defences spiralling out like informational smoke, and in virtual space he erased them. Then he killed the drone and withdrew, subverting its uplink to Occam, to leave only a program to respond to the constant query signal from the ship's AI that the drone was still functional.

Skellor let out a gasp and reached down to fumble for the shut-off button. Around him, the air flickered and he was revealed standing by a stack of crates below the drone. Looking down at the chameleonware generator on his belt—an object like a large white snail shell with a touch-console mounted in its mouth—he noted that he had shut it off just minutes before it would have done so itself. He rested his hand against its glossy surface and felt the heat of it—he had not yet found a way of running a personal generator for longer than a few hours without overloading it, as the power required to run such a device was huge.

He moved away from the crates to stand before the shimmer-shield, still keeping an eye on his air supply. Probing into the walls of the hold, he soft-linked, but was gratified to discover that the shield only linked back to Occam to inform the ship AI that it was functioning, not whether someone had stepped through it. Skellor then stepped through, the shield tugging and pressing against him so that it felt as if he were pushing through thick jelly. Once he was through, another display in the corner of his visor, which heretofore had only read "Argon," now showed that the usual mix of breathable gases surrounded him. He removed his mask and took a deep breath of air redolent of metals and warm electronics, which was always the recognizable taint of ship air. Moving to the wall of the hold, he sat and closed his eyes to more closely explore his relationship with his crystal matrix AI, and found that, of course, it was killing him.

It was a given that direct interfacing with an AI would kill the human participant by blowing each synapse like a fuse in an increasing cascade, and would also drive the AI into its own particular version of insanity. For centuries, researchers had tried to construct AIs more amenable to the joining, but had always failed. This was unsurprising as such a joining was comparable with attempting to weld a lump of steel to a candle—it didn't matter what you did with the steel: the welding process would always be too hot for the candle wax. Skellor's answer to this conundrum was that you didn't weld, you used glue instead. Presently he had yet to use the glue—and the AI had yet to completely burn him out, because it was not fully online. He had also only been directly interfaced for an hour before that bastard Polity agent had turned up.

Now it was time for Skellor to use the glue.

The egg-shaped container he cupped in his hand was as much Jain technology as was its contents, for the contained nanotechnology would overrun even an inert material. Lining the inside were billions of nano-constructs whose sum purpose was to deliver the message "not yet" to the living node they surrounded. Skellor turned the egg so it stood on its end, and linked through to it. Immediately he felt poised at a portal into a vast space crammed with a tangle of glittering and vastly complex shapes. Pulling back, he paused for a moment and considered his options. If he remained linked to the AI, without using this Jain node, he would die within a few hours. If he disconnected from the crystal matrix AI aug, he would return to his previous state, and that was unacceptable. Even with the AI not fully online, he found himself easily capable of working through formulae he had been unable to even begin with before; his memory was now eidetic, and his grasp of his own *work* huge. Disconnection would also lead to his capture, and for some of the things he had done he would most certainly end up being forcibly mind-wiped. His remaining choice rested in the palm of his hand.

Skellor sent the initiation code and watched as the egg opened like the petals of a flower, to expose the Jain node. It was another egg, a smaller version of its container—a metallic egg mottled with complex cubic patterns. It didn't look much, even in this age when a planetary governor could fit into an ashtray, and when a weapon of planetary obliteration was not necessarily much bigger than that. But, in its own way, it was immense. It was still a source of amazement to Skellor that he, of all people, had found this object, when people all across the Polity had been searching for such things for centuries. He knew that corporations spent billions on Jain research, that whole planets had been the subject of archaeological digs, that there were some truly titanic AIs whose only purpose was to find something like this. Yet where had he found it?

The world was wintry, but not killingly cold. Across its mainly oceanless surface grew forests of deciduous trees, none more than fifty years old, as it was only fifty years before that the orbital mirror had been moved into place and the planet heated enough to sustain Terran life-forms. Great canals directed water down from the slowly melting poles to fill up those cavities in the land earmarked as future oceans. It was beside one of these nascent oceans that a spaceport had been established, and where it was rumoured that a runcible facility would soon be installed. Skellor found the market on one of the huge jetties under construction on the yet-to-be-filled ocean's bed. The stall was one of the few not doing very much business, it being cluttered with items that most Polity citizens would discard without a second thought. He had been on the point of heading back to his hotel, for the day was cold and drizzly, and a storm was predicted to drift in from the northern outflow—but a grubby hand reached across and clasped his jacket.

"I got some good stuff that ain't on display, my friend," said the owner of the hand.

Skellor studied her: she looked of a type—those who bought passage to new worlds, then couldn't be bothered to work hard enough to make a decent life for themselves, or to raise enough money to move on. Her cosmetic work was out of date, her clothing shabby, and she had that look of perpetual anger at circumstances she did nothing to correct.

"Like what?" he asked.

Quickly she pulled three plastic cartons from under the table and opened them on its surface. The first carton contained artificial gemstones suitably adulterated to make them look like the real thing, the second contained a selection of augs of the type that would scramble your brains within a week, and the third contained a grey egg and a bag of broken coral.

"See," she said, holding up a Sensic augmentation.

Skellor turned to go, but then allowed his attention to stray back to the third carton.

Where had he seen coral like that before?

"What's that?" he asked, pointing.

She picked up the bag and shook it. "This is real coral, from the Barrier Reef on Earth."

"How interesting," said Skellor, knowing that the chances of stealing coral from that place were equatable with the chances of beating the Earth Central AI at chess. Again about to turn and leave, he remembered where he had before seen coralline objects such as these. In the Tranquillity Museum on Earth's moon: in a chainglass case inside a security chamber everyone was aware could be ejected from the Museum at a moment's notice, to be obliterated in space by CTD—Contra Terrene Device—that euphemistic term for an antimatter weapon.

"All right, how much do you want for them?" he asked.

"You have to buy the whole carton," she replied. "Twenty shillings."

"I don't want that egg thing, so I'll give you ten."

Glancing at the purple swirl of cloud to the north, the woman agreed.

The node was changing colour and there seemed to be movement: interchange within the cubic patterns on its surface. A year of research had revealed to him that the coralline objects were certainly Jain, and certainly useless. Fifteen years of research had revealed perhaps one per cent of the secrets of the node, but enough to put him way ahead of any competitors in his field, and to give him an understanding of what he was dealing with. Tipping the object into the gloved palm of his hand, he raised it to his lips.

Then he pushed it into his mouth.

3

With the slightly bored tone of an adult who knew what was coming, the woman said, "The brother who had built his house from blocks of limestone and roofed it with slabs of the same, already knew the dangers of pride and, hearing that his friends had been eaten by the heroyne, he prayed for them." She glanced at the child in the hope that he had fallen asleep at last, and that she wouldn't have to read the rest. One read-through was enough to get the heavy-handed message and, even though she had been told to persevere, she was contemplating dumping the damned book. The boy, unfortunately, was as wide-eyed as ever.

"For his house was built with the stones of the Satagents, cemented with Faith, and the roof was tiled . . ." She trailed off into silence when she realized that what she was saying bore no relation to the words the book displayed. Thinking that she must be getting ahead of herself, she started again:

"But neither pride nor prayer have influence on the heroyne," she said, then leant forwards to more closely study the text.

"I'm sure it didn't say that yesterday," she muttered. Half closing the book, she was surprised to see that the title of Moral Fables had just acquired a "t" and changed to Mortal Fables.

"Mum?" said the boy impatiently.

"Naughty," she said with a grin, as she opened the book again. The boy gave her a puzzled look, but she continued reading:

"For it came to stand over his house that night, as he prayed to his god. Then it huffed and it puffed, it puffed and it huffed, then it kicked down his walls."

The boy looked even more puzzled at this.

"What do you think the last brother said to the heroyne when his house was gone?"

On more familiar territory now the boy replied, "Don't eat me!"

"And let's see you make a stab at guessing what it did do."

The boy gave the usual reply whilst the heroyne in the picture book repeatedly gobbled down a man in priestly attire . . .

It started after the first sleep period, when the clans came groggily from, in most cases, drugged slumber. Apis had woken before most of the others. Yes, the destruction of the station was terrible, but it was also the most exhilarating thing that had happened to him. His mother woke shortly after, and studied him speculatively as he gazed at the other clan members rising and beginning to move about. No one had an individual cabin. They were in a huge hold, and what privacy they had was provided by plastic sheeting easily suspended in low gee—probably created by slow acceleration of the ship rather than any grav-tech, as Peerswarf informed him.

"Go and find a food dispenser," his mother ordered him, and he quickly went, not being inclined to disobey when her voice took on that tone. Apis soon found a machine set in the wall, and collected a ration of food bars and a container of some sort of hot drink—there had been no labels on the machine. He was on his way back when he heard the uproar. Immediately curious, he went over to investigate.

Two full-gee men stood uncomfortably by doors at the back of the bay. There was something quite odd about their identical dress: they wore white shipsuits that appeared to be padded and armoured, and down one side from armpit to ankle were words in no language Apis understood. They wore visored helmets that armoured one side of their faces, and joined to a ring of the same white metal around their necks. On the exposed sides of their heads they each wore scaled augs with an organic appearance. They both also carried weapons of some kind. Apis realized that these men wore military uniforms—but no Polity uniform that he recognized.

"We want five of you—now," one of the men said, his voice seeming almost disinterested.

The rousing Outlinkers ignored what he had just said, and bombarded him and his comrade with questions. Apis glanced aside and saw that several other Outlinkers were standing back with their heads bowed and fingers pressed to their own augs—none of which had the organic appearance of those worn by the guards. They all bore expressions of puzzlement.

"Nothing," said the old man standing next to him. "I'm getting *nothing*."

As the questioning grew more insistent, the Outlinkers drew closer to the two soldiers, who simply seemed puzzled by this behaviour. Apis did not see or hear what initiated action. All he saw was the soldier—who had not spoken—swing his weapon, and all he heard was the sickening crunch of breaking bone. The crowd parted around a clanswoman falling slow, and foetal, to the floor. Afterwards, there was silence.

"We want five of you," said the speaker, in that same disinterested tone, and the Outlinkers began to move away. "Now," the man added, pointing his weapon at the crowd for emphasis. One of the crowd stepped forward. It was Peerswarf, the man Apis liked to think was his father.

"We demand you let us speak with the ship AI. This is intolerable. Are we animals to be treated like this?" Peerswarf watched as others tended to the woman. There was an expression of disbelief on his face. Apis stared at the woman, and saw that her skull had a cavity and she was not breathing. It seemed that no one wanted to admit she was dead.

The speaker raised his tinted visor and gazed at Peerswarf. Now a sneer twisted the soldier's features.

"We do not allow idiot silicon to order our lives. There is no AI on this ship. Under God, men fly it, men control it, men operate the guns."

Silence of shock, more profound than the assault had caused, met this statement.

"She is dead," said one of those who had stooped down to the woman.

Peerswarf glanced down at him as if he had said something illogical, then he returned his attention to the soldiers.

"You killed her . . ."

"Yes, and more will be killed if five of you do not come with me now."

"What . . . what for?"

"We need five able hands to work in the engine room."

"Engine room?"

Since when had anyone worked in the engine room of a ship? Automatics handled such things. Robots normally did the work in such places.

"Now!" yelled the soldier, and with that raised his weapon upwards and pulled the trigger. There was a low thrumming and something crackled across the ceiling. Apis heard the caroming of ricochets, and noted the line of dents in the metal. Rail-gun, primitive.

Hesitantly at first, several Outlinkers stepped forward, to be directed through the doors. More soldiers waited beyond. Apis turned to hurry back to his mother, but she was already standing at his shoulder. They gazed at each other but they did not speak. Later, when the five returned, dirty, tired, and with the radiation tags on their belts into amber, they exchanged that gaze again. All their lives they'd had information access. They now knew the score: they were in the hands of barbarians.

"I am Deacon Chaisu of the warship *General Patten*," the face on the screen informed them later on. "It is unfortunate that a member of your group was killed today—may she rest in the arms of our Lord—but it must be understood that you are indebted for your lives to the people and planet of Masada and to the God of the Faithful. A small portion of this debt can be cancelled by your work upon this ship, and finally in the yards on Flint . . ." The Deacon went on and on about the wonderful things they could do, and the projects in which they might become involved. He then told them they were the defenders of humanity.

"Perhaps you are unaware of what caused the destruction of Outlink station *Miranda* . . . Some of you may know the story of the system of Aster Colora, some of you may know of the more recent events on the way-station world of Samarkand.

On the latter world, thousands of people were killed by the transgalactic servant of Satan that names itself Dragon. It used a nanomycelium to destroy the buffers of an interstellar runcible so that a man arrived on Samarkand as photonic matter. His arrival was the cause of a fusion explosion that killed many. Many more died in the aftermath, for Samarkand was a cold world heated by energy build-ups from the runcible. The rest of the population froze to death. Know now that the nanomycelium used to destroy *Miranda* was the same one—that Dragon destroyed your home. You must work now to . . ."

So it went on and, each time they thought it had finished with a "God defend the faithful," Deacon Chaisu would start up again.

"Propaganda officer," said someone nearby.

"They're religious," observed Apis's mother.

"So?" asked the speaker.

"They believe their own propaganda. It's where the word originates," she replied knowledgeably.

Apis asked, "What is going on?"

"There is an old word for what we are to become," said the man nearby.

"What is that?" asked Apis.

"Slaves," his mother told him.

The sprawns were the blue of tool steel and over ten centimetres long. Their wings made it necessary for nets to be stretched across their ponds at all times, to prevent them flying off to die in an environment hostile to them. As Eldene understood it, they were another expensive delicacy destined both for the tables of the Theocracy and for them to trade in exchange for luxury goods from other worlds.

"They say these are an adaptation from an Earth creature," Fethan said as he and Eldene laboured at digging a sluice ditch leading to one of the ponds.

"I might like to believe your stories about the Underground, but I don't believe the ones about Earth, old man," Eldene replied.

"Why not?" Fethan sounded hurt, as he shovelled out another clump of black mud.

Eldene watched the nest of green nematodes the old man had uprooted, as they writhed and burrowed back into darkness. "The great mythical empire where everyone is free and everyone has their portion of plenty. I know the difference between what's possible and what's wishful thinking. If this Earth even exists, it's far from here and not doing anything to help us. And as for this Human Polity run by godlike AIs . . ." She snorted and shovelled more mud.

"But it's true," Fethan protested.

"Oh yes, then why aren't there Polity ships amongst the traders?"

"How do you know there are not?" Fethan asked.

"Well, if some of them are Polity, they seem glad enough to buy refined squerm and sprawn essence," Eldene spat, thinking of the buyers the Vicar of Cyprian Compound sometimes brought out on tour, who did not seem overly bothered by the penitential lot of the pond worker.

Fethan said, "Most of 'em are scum of the Line."

"Yes, and I'm a gabbleduck's mother," said Eldene. And there the conversation ended, as it was drowned out by the racket of Volus's aerofan landing nearby. Now silent, the two of them dug their way closer and closer to the heavy iron sluice gate across which they must fit nets before draining the pond. Before they reached the gate, a shriek had them peering over the edge of the ditch.

"That's where Cathol and Dent are digging!" shouted Fethan.

Eldene glanced round and was surprised to see the old man nimbly leap out of the ditch and head in the direction of the sound. Upon tiredly following the old man, she saw Volus standing over by the sluice that the other two had been digging, with Dent sprawled at his feet. The rattling of sprawn wings filled the air, the strange creatures having escaped through the sluice and uncovered ditch. Eldene quickly followed Fethan who seemed, surprisingly, intent on finding out what was going on. Soon they arrived at the side of the ditch, only to see Cathol trapped underwater beneath the collapsed sluice gate, sprawns swarming in the water all around him.

"He's . . . going to . . . kill . . . us," Dent managed to gasp from where he lay at the Proctor's feet.

"Get back to work, brothers," said Volus, turning round from his cold studying of Cathol.

The worker, Cathol, looked dead to Eldene, but it seemed unlikely that the collapsing gate would have killed him or his scole, and his scole would have prevented him from drowning. She could only think, then, about what Fethan had told her the night before, and assume this to be murder. With no idea what she intended, she took a step forward. Volus whipped his stinger across, hitting her arm and then her scole, and she went down with a yell, the entire side of her body feeling as if dipped in acid, and her scole jerking against her. Crawling along the ground, she saw Volus draw his gun, point down, and casually shoot Dent dead. The man slammed face-down, his head opened, and its contents spattered across the black loam. Gasping, and beginning to black out from both pain and oxygen starvation, Eldene stared at Fethan and willed him to run.

Fethan stared straight back at her. "You know," murmured the old man, "there's only so much undercover work I can stand." Then he walked towards the Proctor, jerking but not falling as two shots slammed into his chest, then halted, and speared his hand straight through the man's body.

Twenty of the Outlinkers had their radiation tags into amber when, with a terrifying wrenching feeling of dislocation, the *General Patten* dropped out of U-space. Over the intercom, the speechifying continued, but they had all, after the first repetition, learned to ignore it. The twenty told of the primitive conditions, the lack of automatics, the weaponry openly carried, the radiation leaking into the engine hold.

On the face of it, their situation seemed quite clear, yet some aspects Apis found confusing.

"They called AI 'idiot silicon'—like Separatists would—yet they are auged," he said to his mother.

Peerswarf, who had come over to share food and conversation with them, smiled and nodded at Apis, then said, "Looks like biotech to me, so, as such, it's definitely not silicon. Anyway, they 'do not allow it to govern their lives' which is not to say that they will not govern it."

How plausible all that sounded, yet Apis picked up on the worried look flashed between Peerswarf and Apis's mother, and he knew that plausibility did not make truth. He listened to further discussion of the augs these people wore—how there was absolutely no connection to be made with those the clans wore—but in the end sleep became more important to him than eliciting whatever truth there might be, and he turned towards his hammock. He was just resting his hand on the edge of it, ready to pull himself in when a surge of gee threw him to the floor, then slid him against a wall. There was a crash, followed by pressure on his chest.

"Fast manoeuvring," someone gasped. "An AI would have compensated."

A siren started wailing and red lights strobed in the ceiling above the bay's inner doors. Another crash. The ship shuddered.

"Oh no," someone said, quite simply; there was terror and fatalism in the voice. Apis looked round and realized it was his mother who had spoken. She was staring at the ceiling. He looked up also, and immediately saw how the metal was twisting across its entire length.

"What do we do?" he asked her.

Another crash . . . the ship slewing sideways . . . people's belongings flying through the air. His mother tilted her head to listen to the distant sounds of distorting and shattering metal, screaming, explosions.

"Something's tearing this ship apart," she said, more puzzled now than fearful. "It must be in gee . . . a black hole?

They can't have got too close to a planet. Even they could not be so incompetent."

The ceiling then split, and something surged through: a tentacle as thick as a man's body, and terminating in a flat cobra head with a single blue eye where a mouth might have been.

"Dragon," said his mother. "*Run!*" But where was there to run to? Apis saw it happen, along with many others: the buckling and splitting of the ceiling had pulled open the back doors of the bay. Beside his mother, Apis was one of the first to reach those doors.

"Soldiers," he said, after sticking his head through the gap, and seeing uniformed men half running and half dragging themselves down the corridor by the evenly spaced handrails. Turning to his mother he said, "They don't have grav-plates out there."

"Primitive," she replied as other Outlinkers pushed up behind them. They all turned and looked up, as another pseudopod squirmed through the split in the ceiling. The ship shook once again; emergency lights began flashing in the corridor. Apis checked the corridor once more and saw the last of the soldiers disappearing around a bend in it. Again the ship lurched, sending people floating—observed by the blue eyes of Dragon—towards the broken ceiling.

"We can go through!" Apis yelled, and hauled himself into the corridor.

"No, not yet!" his mother yelled too late.

Apis was halfway to the bend when the others began to follow. His mother reached him ahead of the crowd. Most of them did not reach him. To one side, something distorted and broke, and fire spewed through—flame hanging in the air like layers of fog, with no gravity to give it shape. Apis heard screaming, saw shapes . . .

"Come on." His mother grabbed his shoulder and pulled him onwards. With others, they reached a side shaft that ran through the ship. Uniformed people were floating and propelling themselves up it, aiming for an access way above.

"They'll be heading for craft to escape in," she said. They flung themselves up the shaft, and followed the crowd. No one took any notice of them. Terror had become a taste in the air. Vacuum could claim them all at any moment. The access way opened in another corridor leading to an airlock. Apis and his mother followed the uniformed personnel through it. Three others also in uniform followed them, before a sucking explosion and the sudden slamming of the airlock. One got halfway through, but he did not stop the lock from closing.

The hull of the landing craft clanged as the clamps let go, and all was free-floating chaos as it dropped away from the mother ship. Orders were bellowed and soldiers pulled themselves down into seats and strapped themselves in. Apis and his mother did the same, and only now that the craft was moving away from the ship did they get some strange looks. Glancing back he took in the soldiers there, the mixture of uniforms—in some cases the lack of a uniform, in other cases uniforms soaked with blood. Forward, some sort of commander floated between the passenger area and the cockpit, surveying the cabin. Behind him the pilot and navigator sat at the controls, the curved chainglass screen before them displaying pinpricks of stars and the occasional hurtling pieces of wreckage. Apis stretched himself up to try to get a view of the camera-fed screens below this—those that showed other views. He glimpsed fire, and the hardly recognizable shape of the ship that had ostensibly come to rescue them from *Miranda*, a chaotic tangle of pseudopods, and the dark-scaled moon that was Dragon. When the commander's gaze fixed on him and his mother, he pulled himself back down in his seat.

"Secure those two," said the man, pointing. Heads turned in their direction and soldiers came towards them with plastic ties to bind their hands and feet.

"This is not necessary," said Apis's mother. "We can cause you no harm. We have not the strength—"

A soldier struck her across the face to silence her. It was a blow any normal-gee human could have taken with ease, but it knocked her unconscious. The soldier stared at her in surprise, then turned to his commanding officer, who merely nodded for him to continue. Apis held out his hands to be tied, and looked worriedly at his mother. It was only when he was certain she was breathing that he took any further notice of his surroundings. She needed medical attention, that was all he could think. He had to find a way to get it.

The dark-otter facility sat on the edge of the papyrus-choked bay, before a backdrop of rounded mountains that resembled crouching animals. These slopes were predominantly mottled with heathers, bracken, and other Terran plants that filled the few niches not already occupied by native species. With a few exceptions adapted to a sea full of copper salts, the water beyond the papyrus swarmed with all the strange creatures found on Cheyne III when it had been colonized centuries before. The flatlands that curved back from the bay, on either side of the mountains, grew only papyrus and other native species that could tolerate the poisonous soil.

The killer set up his tripod on a raft of stone protruding from the side of one of the mountains. Bushes lush with cloudberries surrounded him and, up behind him, thick bracken hissed in a constant wind blowing down from the higher slopes.

Sure that the tripod was firmly set and unlikely to rock, the killer—whose name was ostensibly Stiles—stooped down to his case and began to lovingly assemble the weapon it contained. It looked like a hunting rifle, yet the barrel was a metre long and as narrow as a pencil, and the stock and main body were inset with digital displays and touch controls. Stiles mounted the weapon on the tripod and peered through the X10000 image intensifier, before locking the small motion dampers in place. He then scanned the facility.

The perimeter fence stood half a kilometre from the buildings, and he knew the intervening ground was loaded with motion sensors capable of picking up even the breath of any intruder who might penetrate beyond the autogun towers. Guards, and one or two of the new security drones, irregularly patrolled the area outside this fence. But no security was sufficient to prevent someone such as Stiles from taking a four-kilometre distance shot. He grimaced to himself, and directed his weapon towards the facility's back doors.

Now sighted in, Stiles had nothing to do but wait. He lit up a cigarette and gazed out at the adult dark-otters sporting in oily grey water beyond the papyrus. He was well aware of the two watchers hiding in the bracken on the slope, but not worried about them. They would have nothing damning to report to their masters, and he would comment on their presence later to show just how professional he was—all part of the image.

The doors opened and two women in monofilament diving suits wandered out, carrying haemolungs and separate recycling packs for deeper work. They headed for one of the facility's antigravity cars and loaded their stuff up. Not them he was waiting for. John Spader would not be out for another twenty minutes at least. The chief of the facility was very regular in his habits—not a safe way to be for anyone in authority on a world like Cheyne III; it made one a viable target for assassination, kidnapping, whatever the Separatists were into at any particular time. Assassination today, and unusually an outsider was being employed for the hit, but they knew Stiles by reputation and had wanted him signed up.

Spader stepped out of the building precisely to the minute. Stiles sighted on him, got the man's head easily centred in the intensifier, initiated one of the touch-pads on the side of his weapon, and waited until the word "acquired" appeared below the targeting frame. When he fired, there was no sound, and no immediate effect. Stiles kept Spader centred, and waited. It took a long moment for the subsonic bullet to reach its destination and, even though Spader moved in the intervening time, it remained on target. Stiles watched Spader's head gout a cloud of bone and brain, while his scalp and the remaining side of his face spun away. As the target went down, Stiles smiled and scratched at his Van Dyke beard. When he smiled like that, he looked truly evil. Those who were watching from the slope felt a certain amount of fear of him, and hoped he would not spot them. It was rumoured that before he went private he had been Sparkind—not someone to mess with.

After packing away his weapon and folding up its tripod, Stiles trekked back over the mountain, giving every appearance of being an enthusiastic bird-watcher—had there been any birds on Cheyne III. In half an hour he arrived at his antigravity car and, below a sky scudded with sooty clouds, headed back to the city. Police AGCs passed him from the other direction, but he was now one of many, and the police would assume that all AGCs were logged with the AI, so they could easily get a checklist.

Gordonstone consisted mainly of ground-level arcologies seemingly nailed in position with plascrete towers—usually of hotels or the offices of wealthy Polity corporations. Stiles brought his AGC in at high speed, as to travel any slower would betray the fact that it was not under city control. He brought it down in the park next to the swimming pool of his arcology hotel, and was careful to set the vehicle's security device when he climbed out. Should anyone try to break into it, a brief plasma fire in the boot would turn the weapon concealed there into unidentifiable slag.

The man and woman, in appearance members of the runcible culture, watched him from the bar by the pool. Stiles noted the scaled augs they wore as he went directly to the bar counter beside them and ordered himself a cips from the metalskin barman. The ice was astringent on his tongue as the mild narcotic, which gave it its rainbow hue, melted out. After he had paid for the drink and received his chipcard back, he turned to the couple and held the card out to them.

"I believe you have something for me," he said.

The couple glanced at each other. Then the woman removed her sunglasses and turned her attention to Stiles.

She was an attractive sort, but then, any woman could be. It was the ones who did not bother with surgery you had to watch.

"What makes you think that?" she asked.

Stiles put his card on the bar, waving away the chromed hand of the metalskin bartender.

"You work for Brom and you've been watching me for ten days now. Have your two operatives at the otter facility reported in yet?"

The two did not manage to conceal their annoyance. Perhaps they had thought their surveillance invisible. Stiles did not betray the contempt he felt for them. Amateurs— how they had managed to survive for so long was a wonder.

"You think you're really good, don't you?" said the man, his head jutting forward. Stiles considered dropping him there and then, but rejected the idea: he did not have his money yet. He shrugged, keeping his expression blank. The woman shook her head and reached down into her bag to remove another chipcard. She stepped closer to Stiles and pressed her hand against his chest.

"A job well done," she said, before taking his card, pressing her card on it, and tapping an amount across to his account. Stiles finished his cips, retrieved his card.

"Wonderful place," he said after he had checked the amount. He turned to go.

"We'll be in contact. We may have something more . . . challenging for you," said the woman.

Stiles nodded once and continued on his way. Passing the pool, he studied with interest the naked bodies sprawled under the sun-tubes, before sauntering into the arcology hotel and heading to his suite.

Once within, he locked the door and placed a sensor device against it. Any movement outside it and he would have plenty of warning. A quick scan of his rooms revealed five bugs, two of them microscopic. He disabled them all, including the one the woman had placed on his shirt. A small vibrating pad against the window glass prevented any possibility of his speech being read by laser-bounce. Another scan: no optics in the wall. His final precaution was to take a shower, as he was old-fashioned about such things. Under the spray of water he activated his wristcom.

"Thorn here. Has the death been reported?"

"Yes," replied the Cheyne III runcible AI, its voice faint since Cereb, the moon on which it was situated, was now only just above the horizon. Use of a satellite to bounce the signal would have been too risky.

"They'll be in touch. Apparently something more challenging for me."

"Another killing?"

"Maybe. If it is I may have to refuse it, as that gets me no closer to Brom."

"That is your decision," the AI replied—its voice clearer now. "Understand though that your mission is now of limited duration, since you may be required elsewhere."

"Why's that?"

"An Outlink station has recently been destroyed and one of the Dragon spheres may be involved."

"Cormac?"

"Is on his way."

Thorn whistled then said, "Layer upon layer. I wonder if there's some connection to the Dragoncorp augs, or to that other tech?"

"Dracocorp," the AI corrected. "The name of the corporation was changed."

"*Is* there a connection?" Thorn persisted.

"Almost certainly, but your primary mission here is to locate Brom's hideout and call in your team to . . . deal with it. Let others deal with the bigger picture."

"Oh, I won't forget," said Thorn, switching his wristcom to another channel. He smiled to himself, thinking how euphemistic AIs became when discussing these matters. It surprised him that the Cereb AI had not used that other favourite: "field-excision."

"Thorn speaking. Where are you now?" he asked.

"Floor below you," replied the leader of the four-man team that was covering him in the hotel.

"Okay, stay close and wait for my signal. If I do give that signal, I want you to come in hard and fast. None of this 'You are under arrest' bollocks."

"You're the boss," came the reply.

After shutting down com, Thorn finished his shower and, again as Stiles the wealthy killer, went to find some entertainment with one of the bodies lying by the pool. It was not the same as in the old days. It would have been just he and Gant covering each other. But in the old days he had been a soldier, not an undercover agent for Earth Central. He missed Gant, he missed the way things used to be. Samarkand had changed him.

With increasing confusion, Apis listened in to the sporadic talk around him. Who were these people talking to? Did they not have the facility to run silent queries through their biotech augs? His education was broad enough for him to know of prayer, but his experience was narrow and he did not immediately recognize it. He stared at the man seated next to him, who was holding a blood-soaked wad of cloth to his stomach. In his left hand the man held a ring of beads fashioned in the shape of tiny skulls. These were caked with dried blood, and hung still on his fingers. He was muttering to himself in a language Apis did not understand, so he tried to ignore it. Madness. Speaking to gods? It was only real conversation between individuals Apis was prepared to acknowledge:

"How long?" the commander asked another officer, who seemed all efficiency as he ran through some sort of inventory—kneading at his aug as he checked lockers and displays.

"A year, nominally, though there are alternatives."

"Lang, I don't want to hear about alternatives. It is Masada or nothing. How are we for supplies?"

Lang said, "The water we can recycle indefinitely. With fifteen in the cryopods, the food should get us through—just. There will be deficiencies."

"Hardship refines the faithful," said the commander.

His way of speaking confused Apis. The man seemed to use a whole sentence to say one word, when not using a whole sentence to say nothing.

"Yes, I imagine it does, but we have more than hardship," said Lang.

"With prayer no problem is insurmountable."

Lang stared at his commander and it was evident that some silent communication passed between them. After this, the commander swung his attention to the wounded soldiers, then to Apis and his mother. The Outlinker was young and inexperienced, but he immediately knew he was in danger, just as others on that ship knew they also were. The prayers got louder and louder and some men were on their knees working themselves into a frenzy. The commander turned back to Lang and paused for a moment before nodding. Apis shoved at his mother to try to rouse her, but she would not be roused, not then—nor when the four soldiers grabbed them and dragged them to the airlock. Perhaps it was the arrogance of assumed superiority that made Apis speak out, even though he knew a casual blow from them might kill him.

"We mustn't die in bonds," Apis said to the white-faced soldier who held his frangible arms in hands like steel clamps. They were now at the airlock, where another soldier was spinning the wheel. A wheel? A manual airlock! *Madness.* Apis improvised in the pause his words had caused. "Would you have us come before Him in bonds?" It sounded right anyway. With his expression revealing shame, the soldier drew a knife and severed the plastic ties on Apis's wrists and ankles. The same was not done for his mother, though. Together they were shoved into the cramped space, the door wound shut behind them.

Apis hyperventilated at a rate abnormal in any normal human being, and wished his mother could do the same. He was dizzy by the time the air started to be pumped out of the lock—his cells now fully charged with oxygen. He linked one arm round the tie on his mother's wrists and linked the other round one of the bars set in the side wall of the airlock. It was good that those inside were so short of air, otherwise they might have opened the outer lock directly, and nothing would have stopped him being sucked out into void. He allowed the small amount of air in his lungs to eject, then closed his nostrils, ears, rectum. His saliva turned to resin and sealed his mouth. He inflated, and his nictitating membranes closed over his eyes. Against him his mother grew to twice her normal size as her body did those same things unconsciously. She would have forty or fifty minutes. He would have a little longer. Now, as the outer lock opened onto vacuum, he considered what he must do with that time.

Apis wanted to act immediately, but knew that this would gain him nothing. Instead, he thought his way through it. If he and his mother were found still alive inside the airlock, the soldiers would likely make sure they were not alive the next time the lock was opened. Apis studied the interior and noted a storage space set in the wall. He opened it to find inside two emergency suits with small oxygen packs, some lines, and a couple of large canisters of breach sealant. He pulled out the two suits and two lines, and was about to pull one of the suits onto his mother when he saw the outer lock closing. He quickly towed her through it and outside.

With no air to distort distance, the stars shone as bright as arc lamps, and the exterior of the landing craft was revealed in harsh clarity. Apis saw pieces of wreckage floating on a parallel course to it, but the ion engine on this side of the craft blocked his view behind, and he tried not to think about what had happened to the other Outlinkers. To be able to survive vacuum for almost an hour would be no mercy in such a situation. After attaching himself to the hull of the craft with a line, he completed the laborious procedure of pulling one of the suits onto the inflated body of his mother. With everything at full stretch, it only just fitted her. When he turned on the oxygen, the suit mimicked the body it contained and went rigid. Inside, Apis knew, his mother would be returning to normal. Hence, if she became conscious, she would find herself inside a suit much too large for her. He attached her to the hull of the ship with a line, just in time to return to the edge of the outer lock as it began to reopen.

It was the same man who had been sitting next to him, Apis realized, and only because of the skull beads and his injury. The man came out with his arms flailing weakly, propelled by the blood vaporizing from his stomach wound. His eyes were bulging, bloody vapour wreathed him, his mouth was open in a scream no one would hear. Apis caught hold of him for a moment, before sending him on his way, dead already, or in just a moment.

The other corpse was clinging inside the airlock, another man—it seemed that no women wore this uniform, which was another pointer to the primitive culture it had come from. This man was missing one arm, his other arm being linked round one of the bars, and perhaps his face had worn a look of terror before it was blown away from his skull to hang in frozen tatters around his head. Apis saw that he had a weapon and reached in to pull it from his holster, before studying the man. He possessed a laser, yet had not drawn it. Had he gone into the airlock willingly? Or had he been too badly injured to resist? Madness. Apis inspected the weapon then studied the primitive locking mechanisms inside the airlock. He too must join in this madness if he was to survive.

Quickly he pulled himself outside, grabbed the bloated suit containing his mother, and dragged her back inside. Once he had secured her, he pointed the weapon at the autosystems on the wall and pulled the trigger. In eerie silence each box melted, vaporized, fell apart. The outer lock, which had been slowly drawing closed, juddered to a halt. Apis pocketed the weapon and tried the manual control on the outer lock, finding it worked. He turned to the inner lock and inspected the manual controls there, but before he could do anything a glare of light shone in from outside, and gee force dragged him to one side of the lock—the ion engines had been started. Pulling himself back into position, he again eyed the controls, hardening himself against the horror of what he must now do.

Both sets of controls were hydraulically assisted, so it would not take brute force to open or close each lock. There were only a couple of vacuum sensors visible, which he studied for a moment before fusing them. The lack of safety devices did not surprise Apis—obviously these people had a low regard for human life. He pressed the pistol to a stick-pad on his belt, and began to turn the wheel that opened the inner lock . . . while the outer lock still lay open.

She heard a brittle rattling all around her, and was aware of soft earth against her face, before fragments of memory began to intrude into consciousness. Her body felt numb, and she suddenly remembered the agony of being hit by the stinger, of fighting for breath . . . Dent casually blown away while he lay on the ground . . . then Fethan walking towards Proctor Volus, being shot, attacking . . . Eldene just could not make those last images make sense, and felt a horrible sinking terror when she thought about what she must face when she opened her eyes: it would be the cage, or perfunctory execution.

Upon opening her eyes she only felt confusion at what she was seeing.

Before her, the ground was thick with cobbles of blister moss, the occasional empty tricone, and turgid circular pools reflecting Calypse, the gas giant, so they seemed a scattering of coins made from slices of opal. Raising her head slightly she saw now a stand of flute grass—and it was from this came the brittle rattling as the hollow white stems were disturbed by a breeze. At the foot of this stand the ground was heaving up, and she guessed that a live tricone must be near the surface, feeding on soil rich in organics. What the hell was she doing here? This looked like one of the wild areas she had only ever seen when sent in a work party on clearance duty. Then she felt a sudden dread: of course, as punishment Proctor Volus had dumped her out here where she would die without the supplements that kept her scole attached to her. No doubt the Proctor would manufacture some suitable story to transfer blame for her death from himself . . .

Metallic sounds, behind her.

For a moment Eldene dared not move, then she felt an anger and determination to survive building up inside herself, and slowly rolled over to see where the noise was coming from. Immediately her confusion returned. Fethan was squatting beside Volus's aerofan, with its control column in pieces while he worked on the complex tech inside. Fethan was alive, so that meant . . . no, it wasn't possible. All Eldene could assume was that the Proctor had missed, even at that range, and that Fethan had somehow retaliated with a concealed knife. Eldene sat up and the old man glanced at her.

"Feeling a bit more with it now, girl?" said Fethan.

"I've felt better," Eldene replied, her voice catching in her dry throat.

There was something odd about the old man, something out of place. Then Eldene saw that the top of Fethan's coverall did not bulge as it had previously done. His scole was gone! Eldene instantly realized that this was what she could see on the ground beside the pieces of control column. She stared at it in shock, trying to equate its presence there with Fethan's apparently easy breathing—but coming up only with puzzlement. Fethan should be dying. She stared at the old man, hoping for some explanation, but what happened next only increased her perplexity.

"They'll get tracking on this soon," said Fethan, waving at the aerofan with a cylindrical hand tool containing lines of red light. "I want it up in the air by then so that when the hit comes they'll think they got us." With that, the old man glanced at the tool he was holding, then reached down and pressed his finger against the side of his scole, whereupon the baggy insectile thing split and hinged open, revealing itself to be a cleverly camouflaged case. Fethan placed the tool inside and took up another to continue with his work.

"Why are you alive?" Eldene asked.

"Now there's a question that's puzzled philosophers for centuries," quipped Fethan. "Of course, in my case there's many would argue that I ain't."

Eldene contained her annoyance. "Volus shot you twice, and now you do not have a scole." Eldene glanced again at the open case, realizing that Fethan had never possessed a scole. She continued, "You killed him, with your hand . . . just killed him."

"Well, girl, you're gonna find this hard to take, but everything I told you is true: there is a Human Polity, there is an Underground, and there is hope," Fethan replied.

"That doesn't tell me why you are still alive," Eldene persisted.

"True." Fethan shrugged. "Thing is, I ain't completely human. I'm mostly machine, built long ago in that Polity. Right now I'm here to help you people with your revolution."

"Bullshit," said Eldene, which had often previously been her reply to some of Fethan's more outrageous stories.

Fethan stared at her for a long moment, then reached up to grip one of the steel rails of the aerofan. Still staring at Eldene, he twisted until one end of the rail snapped out of its post, and coiled the metal around his hand as if it were wet clay.

"Okay," the old man said, "I ain't mostly machine, but I'm a pretty tough old stick, so you'd better watch your mouth, girl."

Later, when Fethan used another tool from his kit to dig the two small iron slugs out of himself, Eldene became inclined to believe the old man's stories.

First, his mouth turned dry as a sun-baked tile, then it was as if the saliva the node leeched away had been returned to his mouth acidified. Automatically he tried to spit the thing out when the pain became too intense, but it swelled in his mouth and entirely filled it. Drawing deep painful breaths through his nose, he hammered his fist against the wall behind him. His eyes filled with tears. He couldn't scream, he could do nothing about the pain, just as he could do nothing about the horrible sensation that followed it as something oozed down his throat. Gagging now he fought not to vomit, for such a reaction would kill him now. Pain bloomed in his chest, just as it also started to bloom in his sinuses and in the back of his head.

It's going to kill me.

Skellor fought for clarity of vision, and found it in that crystal part of himself, even as pain became suddenly intense around where the aug linked into the side of his head, and where its cooling tubes linked to the arteries in his chest to provide oxygenating and cooling blood to the chemical interfaces within the aug itself. With an all-or-nothing intent, he initiated the start-up package to put the AI aug fully online. A low droning vibrated his skull and glancing down he saw the two chainglass tubes penetrating his chest, fill with blood, and knew that now his aug would be webbed with red veins like something living. And so it was.

His clarity of vision was huge now, and with distant coldness he observed the Jain substructure penetrating and killing his body as it grew. As filaments backtracked the aug connections in his brain and finally penetrated his aug itself, he observed their progress to the chemical interfaces. This Jain technology was subversive: like a parasite it sought to control the system it found itself within and utilize it to its own advantage. It just did not know what was to its advantage, for it was a mindless mechanism. By providing chemical interfaces within his aug, Skellor sought to give it a mind: his own—for Jain technology needed to be tamed.

Finally the Jain substructure began to connect and Skellor began to work at decoding programs and backup systems, to catalogue first trickles of information, then surges of it, in his huge memory. *He*, for Skellor and AI were now both the same being, worked upon the substructure with the capacities of some huge research establishment. The synergy achieved between crystal and organic brain became vast, and questions collapsed like origami sculptures before an avalanche. But the structure grew fast and destructively. Skellor's heart and lungs ceased, on one breath, and his organic brain began to die. Minutes now, only minutes . . . He tried shifting the focus of his attention entirely into his aug as his body died, but he failed. For a moment he was poised on a precipice, then:

Just so.

Skellor halted the random searching growth of the substructure.

Just so.

He cleared it from his mouth, used it to restart his heart and lungs, and set it to repairing the damage it had done to his body.

And thus.

Now he began to improve on nature and grow those devices and biomechanical tools within himself that he knew he would require. Glancing down he observed a tendril break out of his gut and through the fabric of his environment suit, as it sought out the chameleonware generator. It penetrated, deconstructed and read and, as it did so, Skellor built a much improved version of the device inside himself. And whilst all this was occurring, Skellor came to *understand* the Jain.

4

"*Little Molly Redcap walked the plantained path to take potato bread and wine to her grandmother, but unseen by her, with his green and gold stripes, Father Siluroyne stalked the flute grasses,*" said the woman, shaking her head in amazement at the corrupted story. *The picture book showed the girl strolling along, smiling and happy in her sickening piety, then slowly a shape became visible in the long grasses. Previously the creature depicted had born a resemblance to something wolfish, but not now . . . now it was horribly real.*

"*Long before she reached her grandma's compound, she came upon Father Siluroyne lying across her path. 'Where are you going on such a fine day?' he asked her. Showing him the viands she told him, 'I'm taking these to my grandma.'*"

The woman paused and both she and her son leant forwards to more closely study the picture displayed. *So realistic was it that it seemed the monstrosity on the path would surely have the girl as a grandma appetizer there and then—but it looked up at the passing aerofans bearing unlikely-looking axe-wielding proctors, and slunk back into the grasses beside the path. The picture paused in its slow evolution, because the text had not been moved either by touch or voice activation.* The woman continued: "*'Is that all you are taking to her when the flute flowers are blooming?' asked the monster. Little Molly looked about and saw that the flowers were indeed blooming in red and yellow and gold. 'You must gather flowers for your grandma, like a good grand-daughter should.' And Molly went to do as bid, for she had no resistance to these most beautiful creations of God.*"

For a moment, the picture showed the girl gathering flowers, then it quickly clicked to a picture of an archetypal and utterly unlikely cottage in the alien landscape. "Grandma," the text began, "was not having a good day."

"Brom wants to meet you," she said.

Thorn shrugged and continued his meal.

"Now," she said.

"This is excellent fish. You should try some," said Thorn.

"You could get dead, fucking us about," said the man. He leant across the table sticking his chin out. It seemed to be a habit of his. Thorn thought him quite ridiculous and resisted the temptation to break his jaw.

"Calm down, Lutz. Mr. Stiles likes to play hard-to-get. He has his reputation to think about," the woman said, and removed her sunglasses. Thorn looked into eyes with sideways-slotted pupils—they were the latest thing, apparently, and a recent addition for her, since she had not possessed them the last time he had seen her. He smiled. For someone who supposedly hated the Polity she certainly liked the benefits its technology brought.

"When and where?" he asked.

"*Now*, and we take you there."

Thorn nodded and glanced round the restaurant. Three trying not to appear conspicuous while clicking through the menu, at least one outside, waiting by an AGC, probably more. He had a bad feeling. He continued eating.

"Move it, Stiles!" said Lutz and made to shove Thorn's plate away. Reputation at stake, Thorn stuck his fork through the back of Lutz's hand and, before the man had a chance to scream, side-fisted his temple. He caught him before he fell and pulled him so he slumped across the table. A couple of diners looked on in puzzlement, unsure about what they had seen. Nobody but they and the menu clickers seemed to have noticed. The latter three began to rise, until the woman glanced at them and shook her head.

"What do I call you?" Thorn asked her.

"Ternan," she said, staring at her unconscious companion.

"Well, Ternan, you know how I operate. What makes you think I want to meet your boss—and, incidentally, put myself in possible danger."

"Special operation."

Thorn was unmoved.

Ternan added, "Two hundred thousand standard, in any currency, credit, or precious materials."

Thorn dabbed at his mouth with his serviette and stood up.

"Now why didn't you say so?" he said.

As the menu clickers carried Lutz out of the restaurant, the two diners accepted that he had drunk too much. It was that kind of place.

One AGC, no, two. Thorn retained the smile elicited from him when Lutz had revived in the back of this AGC and puked in the lap of a menu clicker. Ternan swore at that point, then chewed at her bottom lip as she drove on—her sunglasses once again covering her fashionable eyes. Thorn secretly kept a watch on the direction indicator. They were heading out over the sea and he wondered just how close his team was and how quickly they could get in. It was comforting to know they would be tracking the underspace transmitter embedded in his pelvis. His body would never be lost, well, at least not that part of it.

"Where is he then?" Thorn asked while, in the back, a menu clicker dressed Lutz's wounded hand.

"You'll see," said Ternan.

He had expected no different. He was about to make some comment about villains' hideaways on remote islands being a cliché, but decided against it. While in training, one of his instructors had warned him about his streak of irreverence, and he had to work continuously to suppress it. Anyway, it was a cliché that villains hid away on remote islands because remote islands were one of the best places for them to hide. Nor did he think Ternan would take kindly to him referring to Brom as a villain. He looked around for such an island as Ternan slowed the AGC. There was no sign of one.

"Where now?"

"You'll see," she repeated.

From the console Ternan flipped up a cover that hid some custom controls and, as she punched in a sequence, small lights ignited along the bottom of the front screen and a grid flashed up, seemingly imbedded in the glass. The whole scene he was seeing, through the screen, flickered and changed. The sea looked somehow different now, and not just because of the huge barge that had suddenly appeared.

Chameleonware. Fuck.

"I'm impressed," he said and Ternan bared her teeth in response.

He studied the barge and estimated it to be nearly half a kilometre long, and a quarter that wide. It was *huge*. It was also liberally scattered with gun turrets and missile launchers, and rested on the sea like some battleship out of ancient history. Brom had to have outside help. No way could he have got all this organized in the few years since the fall of Arian Pelter's Separatist cabal. And chameleonware? That was worryingly sophisticated. Thorn now realized that he needed a damned sight more backup than he presently relied on. If his own team came here, they'd get smeared before they even saw the place.

With practised ease, Ternan brought the AGC in to land on a platform mounted at one end of the barge, and the other AGC followed her down. Four people waited on the platform. Two of them were guards armed with what looked like rail-guns of a manufacture Thorn did not recognize—not Polity because these weapons required a separate belt-mounted power pack. He stepped out and, with Ternan coming to his side and the others coming quickly behind, advanced on the four.

"Ahh . . . Stiles."

Brom.

He wore a loose suit of silky material over his gross frame and seemed indifferent to the chill breeze coming in off the sea. Thin grey hair framed his thickly jowled face and, on seeing it close, Thorn saw the man's skin seemed flecked with small scales. There issued from him a smell reminiscent of a reptile's terrarium. The aug he wore was more than a temporary attachment—it looked like a growth from his body. Thorn recognized him at once from his file, but he was not supposed to know him. He shook the proffered hand.

"You're Brom?" he asked.

Brom nodded and smiled a hard smile as he studied Thorn's face. Thorn glanced past him to the strange individual standing at Brom's shoulder. This man was pale with contrasting flat black hair, and wore a white shipsuit with something written down its side and all down one leg. Around his neck he wore a wide band of white metal, and on the side of his head he sported a scaled aug, the same as everyone else here. His face was lacking in expression, almost dead.

Brom gestured to a stair leading from the platform down to the deck, and began walking in that direction. Thorn, glancing behind to note the others moving off in a different direction, fell in beside him, sticking his hands in his pockets so his wristcom was well away from the itchy forefinger on his other hand. One press and his team would be on their way in—and likely he would have signed their death warrant. He had to just ride this out for the moment, get away safely, then come back in force. No way could he send a message out of this place without being detected. If it came to the worst, he would first use the spring gun concealed in his sleeve.

"You seem well-organized here," he said.

"Due to my friend here: Deacon Aberil Dorth," said Brom.

Thorn glanced at the pale man indicated and got only a flat stare in response.

"Well, your friend has provided you with some sophisticated equipment. That 'ware shield seems almost as good as anything the Polity possesses."

"Ah." Brom raised a pudgy finger. "Now that comes from another source, and you'll understand if I do not feel able to reveal it to you." Brom glanced at him. "You did good work at the study facility. John Spader was beginning to ask some awkward questions about the dark-otter death rate in this area. He had to go."

Was that all?

"And now you have something more for me?"

"Oh yes." Brom led the way down a spiral stair to the lower deck. As he climbed down after the man, Thorn surreptitiously studied the nearest gun turret. Rail-guns again, which confirmed Brom's assertion of there being two sources of technology here, for such weapons were fairly low-tech when compared with the chameleonware shield this barge employed.

Moving across the deck, Thorn now studied a group of people working on a jetty ramp by which was moored a motorized catamaran. Boats like these, he knew, were employed for the illegal hunting of dark-otters for their metals-laden bones, which were used decoratively by those with that kind of taste. The workers were unloading from the vessel plastic crates Thorn immediately identified as the kind that weapons were often packed in. His attention focused on a heavy-set individual, obviously boosted, who was standing next to the woman supervising the unloading. His and Thorn's eyes locked for a moment, then the other turned away as if nothing of moment had occurred. Thorn turned his head so his face was no longer visible to the man.

John Stanton. Jesus!

Stanton was a mercenary often employed by Separatist cabals for his expert knowledge. He'd worked for Arian Pelter, and he'd given himself up on Viridian to betray Pelter, after coming to believe the Separatist leader had killed Stanton's lover—the smuggler woman, Jarvellis. During the resultant battle he had escaped—and no one was really sure how. If Stanton recognized him, then that would be it, all over, for Thorn had been in Ian Cormac's fighting force on Viridian.

Brom led Thorn and the Deacon into a luxurious cabin set right over on the edge of the deck so that the panoramic window on one side of it looked out on nothing but sea. He waved them to a sofa upholstered with dark-otter hide, then played the perfect host with the autobar. He brought over a glass of orange for the Deacon and a cips for Thorn. He himself drank expensive Earth-import whisky—obviously having a taste for wealth, and the luxury it could buy. As the governor of a planet, of course, he could enjoy plenty of both—such was the real aim of many would-be "freedom fighters."

Sitting down in a huge armchair Brom said, "A few years ago this planet lost some of its foremost Separatist leaders—"

"They rest with God," murmured Aberil.

What the hell is he doing here? wondered Thorn. He did not seem Brom's type at all.

With a flicker of a frown Brom went on, "The man responsible for their deaths was an agent of Earth Central, very high up. He is in fact almost as legendary as Horace Blegg. On some worlds they do not even believe he exists. But unlike Blegg, he does exist. His name is Ian Cormac." As he finished speaking, his inspection of Thorn was quite intense.

"Son of Satan," hissed the Deacon.

Thorn ignored Aberil and leant forward. "I've heard of him, of course. Is it him you want me to kill?"

Brom smiled and leant back. "Oh no, I'm just outlining the dangers such people as ourselves need to face, and why we must take the actions we will take."

"Those actions being?" Thorn asked.

Waving a negligent hand Brom said, "Later. Let us finish our drinks and discuss something else. Tell me, *Stiles*"—Thorn did not at all like the emphasis Brom gave the name—"what weapon did you use for that distance shot?"

"Low-speed gas rifle firing an explosive seeker round. Anything above the speed of sound would have been detected, and taken down by antimunitions. I always find the simplest approach is best," Thorn replied.

As Brom mused over this, a chime sounded and he reached out and tapped a touch-console inset in the pedestal table beside him. The door to the suite opened and in stepped Ternan and Lutz, the latter watching Thorn with a sneer of satisfaction. They both held nasty-looking gas-fed pulse-guns. One press on the face of his wristcom would have

Thorn's team coming in—but the team would die if he did this. He curled a finger back to the spring-release concealed in his sleeve, but before he could decide who to go for first, there came a low thunk and something stabbed his chest. He glanced down and saw some sort of dart sticking into him. It had two bulbous sacs that pulsed once, pumping something dark down its glassy stem. Like a ripple on a pool of flesh, deadness spread out from the point of penetration. The gun sprang from Thorn's sleeve and struck a hand already going numb, before clattering to the floor. He stared across at Brom and saw that the man was returning to concealment—under his silk top—something tubular, organic. Brom now waved Ternan and Lutz forward.

"What came up on scan?" Brom asked, as the two caught Thorn under his arms and hauled him to his feet. He managed to get his legs underneath himself and gained a modicum of control over them.

"Underspace beacon in his pelvis, and his wristcom set to transmit a preset signal. We also found two coded frequencies in storage. Got to be Earth Central Security," said Ternan.

Thorn tried to move, but he now felt like a wet rag. Some sort of paralytic in the dart, but what the hell kind of delivery system was that? It was biotech, certainly, but none he recognized. As Brom moved before him, he just had enough strength to lift his head and meet the man's eyes.

"Trooper Thorn, I believe," said Brom. "You know you really should have changed your appearance. Or have you such contempt for us that you can't comprehend that we possess our own information networks?" Brom nodded dismissively to the door and, as his two lieutenants dragged Thorn in that direction, Lutz took great pleasure in twisting the barbed dart from the agent's chest. Thorn wanted to yell out, couldn't even manage that.

Stanton—had to be his doing. The man must have recognized him and passed on this information. The network proscriptions on the identity of ECS agents and soldiers would never have allowed his physical appearance to be recorded or transmitted from either Viridian or Samarkand. Once outside Thorn found that even the dull light of Cheyne's pale sun hurt his eyes. He blinked on tears and managed enough movement from his neck so that he could look around. Stanton was standing there still, watching the unloading of the catamaran. Thorn saw him glance over briefly at him, and turn away. Then he felt a tugging at his arm.

"DNA-keyed I have no doubt," said Brom. "And no doubt it won't work unless still strapped on your wrist. What is it, right forefinger?"

No!

While Ternan gripped his left wrist, Lutz pushed Thorn's right hand across to the wristcom and pressed his right forefinger down on the screen.

"Signal's been sent," confirmed Ternan, and Thorn glanced at her. She had one hand up at the side of her sunglasses, and he realized she must have some sort of screen set into them. "My," she went on, "that was fast. One military carrier coming in from the east. Should be within visual any time now."

"Well, let Mr. Thorn see," ordered Brom.

Lutz grabbed his hair and wrenched his head back. They turned him roughly so he was staring out to sea. And there, immediately, Thorn discerned a black dot on the horizon—growing rapidly as it approached.

"Of course," explained Brom, "they cannot see us."

God no.

The carrier became increasingly visible: like a railway carriage hurled into the sky—all grey armour and hard angles. Four people on board, people he'd eaten with, slept with and worked with for more than a solstan year. He heard the rail-gun turret turn and heard the cycling drone of it powering up.

"Not quite near-c," said Brom.

"At this distance it makes no difference," interjected the voice of the Deacon.

There now came a rushing crackle and Thorn saw the carrier dip in midair, then in silence transform into a plummeting shell spewing fire as it arced towards the waves.

The sound of the explosion came shortly after—the grumble of a distant storm over the sea.

Bastard.

"Right," said Brom, "let's get moving. ECS will soon be all over this area like worms on a turd."

"You'll kill him now?" asked the Deacon.

"Oh no, he's got far too much information in that fine head of his for us to open it so inelegantly. Show Mr. Thorn to his accommodation, Ternan."

As they dragged him, staggering, across the deck, Thorn felt the vibration of engines starting below, and before they took him down inside the barge he saw that it was already moving. The cell they threw him into was a ceramal box containing only a chair and a table on which rested the chromed carapace of a small autodoc. Just for the pleasure of it, Lutz drove his fist three times into Thorn's face, breaking his teeth and nose. Thorn wanted to defend himself, if not with blows then at least with words. All he could do was lie on the floor and bleed, as Lutz then went to pick up the autodoc.

"You know, you can do some real nasty things with these," he said. "Let me tell you: I'm setting it to cut that beacon out of your pelvis without nerve-blocking. But don't worry, I'll also set it to inject the drugs that'll prevent you fainting from shock."

A moment later, Lutz stood over Thorn, holding the doc up for view. The thing was much the same size and shape as a streamlined cycling helmet, and from below his view of it was mainly its chrome gripping legs and the array of surgical cutlery underneath. Grinning nastily, Lutz put it on the floor beside Thorn and stood back. Immediately it scuttled towards him and sliced a hole in the side of his trousers. He felt the tug of it then cutting into his flesh, but the pain arrived only as a probe went in. Thorn closed his eyes and locked his expression—he would give Lutz no satisfaction at all from this. Soon he felt a humming vibration as the doc began to drill into his pelvis. The pain became unbelievably intense for a moment and Thorn felt he might yell out despite himself, but then it began to fade as a bone-welder thrummed, then a cell-welder after it as the probe itself withdrew.

Thorn opened his eyes at last to see Ternan stooping over him. She stood examining something bloody held between her forefinger and thumb. She turned to Lutz. "Go and throw this over the side."

For a moment he appeared set to rebel, but he then took the beacon and left the room.

Ternan returned her attention to Thorn. "You know, we could have done with an emulation of you in which to plant that." She gestured with her thumb to where Lutz had gone. "It would have then taken ECS somewhat longer to get around to genetic testing and therefore discover it wasn't you. We did our own testing very quickly."

Thorn stared at her, puzzled.

"We have people in the facility, you see, and one of them brought us a sample of Spader's so-called corpse." She gave a sneering smile. "It was his ear I think."

Thorn managed a grunt of enlightenment.

"Imagine our surprise," she went on, "upon discovering that the thing you shot was a syntheflesh emulation—no more alive than a wristcom."

With that she left the cell, closing and locking the door on him.

Apis cringed in horror when he saw what he had done, but he did not allow himself to cry. The landing craft was now full of bloated bodies, floating in a fog of their own evaporating juices. He surveyed this human wreckage for only a moment, before selecting one of the bodies and towing it to the airlock to send it tumbling out into space. Quite a crowd was drifting away from the ship when he finally pulled his mother inside and sealed the locks.

It seemed an interminable time passed before his body began to react to the increase in pressure. He felt himself contracting—deflating to a more normal human shape. After a time the resin sealing his lips and nose softened, and he rolled it away before taking his first breath. Inside her suit his mother had also returned to normal, so it was much easier to remove her from the suit than it had been to put her in it. He next installed her in a sleep bag, and was looking for medical equipment when he discovered that what he had at first taken to be lockers lining the walls were in fact cold-coffins. Eventually, locating what he wanted, he returned to his mother with a diagnosticer that seemed primitive to him. It revealed she was unconscious and had a skull fracture, so he administered the drugs it prescribed and left her to recover—hopefully. It was all he could do, and he did not know if the drugs or dosages were right for an Outlinker, but there was no AI to advise him—nothing.

In the cockpit extending across the front of the landing craft, he was in familiar territory again. The controls there were similar to the manual controls on which he had trained. A quick check showed him that the craft was increasing its speed, though that acceleration was still small—the engines having been set for the least wasteful burn. Another quick check showed him that the course keyed in was not to the nearest inhabited world. It was with a cold lack of surprise that he calculated that there would have been quite enough supplies on board to have taken them all there rather than to "Masada or nothing." For a moment he stared at one screen that gave him a view back towards the now distant *General Patten*. Increasing magnification, he saw now only a cloud of floating wreckage dispersing from around its assailant, Dragon. With a cold sick feeling he reckoned how long it would take for him to return to that area, but realized there was only an outside chance that any Outlinkers who had survived the destruction of the ship would be alive by the time he got there. Dare he risk such a rescue mission with Dragon still in the vicinity? He dared not, and surely they were all dead—and sometime soon he knew he would begin to feel that.

Fethan closed the casing on the control column of the aerofan, clicked down a sequence of bright red buttons on the panel below the joystick, and stepped back. Something in the thick floor of the aerofan droned and engaged with a clunk and, starting with a low susurrating whine, its fans began to get up to speed. A second clunk notched up that speed, and from where she stood Eldene felt the blast of air. Upon the third clunk, the machine lurched from the ground like a rock hauled up by elastic and, twenty metres up, it tilted and slid away as if caught in a vicious crosswind. As soon as this happened, Fethan rested his hand on Eldene's shoulder.

"About now, girl, they'll be getting the return signal from this fan. They'll know Volus's *Gift* died, but they won't know for sure about him. We'll soon see if he's been found," he said.

"What do you mean?" Eldene asked.

Fethan did not reply: the sky did. A greenish flash ignited the air, leaving afterimages on Eldene's retinas. Shortly after this there came a thunderclap and, as her vision cleared, she saw that the aerofan was now just falling debris and a drifting cloud of black smoke.

"Guess they found him," said Fethan. "That was the battery EL-41, unless I miss my bet: artificially lased emerald focusing in an argon field-cylinder. It's their oldest array and the only one of that type they have up there."

Eldene stared at him. If Fethan had ever come out with a mouthful like that before recent events, she would have thought the old man's mind going, but now she had to contend with the fact that what was speaking here was not wholly a man. Also, she had to contend with the fact that she now did not have very long to live. Pulling away from Fethan, she stepped to a nearby tricone shell resting on the damp soil and sat down on it.

Fethan gazed at her. "That gives us a breathing space. If we're not seen, we should get to the mountains with no real problems," he said.

Eldene laughed. "*You* don't need to breathe," she pointed out.

"Ah," said Fethan, then quickly moved over to the flute grass near to where he had been working on the aerofan.

Soon he returned, carrying a tangle of equipment it took a moment for Eldene to recognize. "You've got enough in this bottle for a day or so, and the spare should provide you with enough for another two to three days."

Eldene now recognised Proctor Volus's helmet with its tinted visor, lower breather collar against which the visor sealed, and a tangle of pipes leading to a flat square bottle which was worn on the back. For a little while she felt the urge to continue feeling sorry for herself, but Fethan was now offering her a chance at life. She stood up and held out her hands for this equipment.

Fethan withheld it for a moment. "Not yet. You want to get as much as you can out of your scole before it dies and that could be in anything from six to twelve hours—anyway, start direct-breathing oxygen now and it'll just take it out of you to store up," he said. Eldene well understood that, as she knew that the oxygen keeping them alive during the working day was stored up by the scole during the night they spent in the compound bunkhouse. She nodded, and he then allowed her to take the breather.

Eldene inspected the helmet and breather unit—she'd seen proctors wearing these without the helmets and visors, just using a muzzle-shaped mask like Ulat had worn, which hinged up from the collar and sealed over the mouth and nose. After a moment she noticed a pack of such masks—compressed fibre and disposable—clipped to the side of the pack containing the oxygen bottle. She detached the helmet and visor and discarded them, placed the collar around her neck, closing its clip at her nape, then fitted the mask to its hinge below her chin. Hooking her arms through the straps, she hung the oxygen pack on her back—the spare she slung from its straps over her shoulder. With the mask hinged down—for closing it up against her face instantly started the flow of oxygen—she turned back to Fethan.

"You said the mountains?" she said, noting that Fethan now had the Proctor's stinger and pistol at his belt.

"Yeah, we head there and find ourselves an entrance to the Underground. Should take about three days so let's get moving." Fethan led the way across the sodden ground and began tramping a path through the flute grass.

As she followed, Eldene could not help but speculate on how the figure of three days so closely matched the extent of her remaining oxygen supply. Perhaps Fethan was merely humouring her in the last days of her life.

The flute grass was last season's, and consequently dead, dry and brittle. Just by walking into it, Fethan had it breaking and collapsing before him. Each stalk was hollow and the thickness of a human finger, with holes down its length where side shoots had earlier broken away. In gentle breezes, strange music issued from these stands of vegetation, but anything more than a gentle breeze would turn them into snowstorms of papery fragments. Under Eldene's feet, the ground was thick with fragments already trodden down by Fethan, or what had fallen from the plants earlier, and it was this layer, over the plants' rhizomes, that prevented her from sinking into ground that was becoming increasingly boggy. Stabbing up from the rhizomes themselves, she noticed the bright green-and-black tips of this season's new growth poised to explode into the air. When the temperature rose above a certain point—something due to happen soon—the plants would begin growing at a rate that was sometimes visible.

"Ah, Theocracy justice," said Fethan at one point, making a detour around something lying in the stand of grass.

Eldene saw a skeleton pegged out on the sodden ground— grass stalks growing up through its ribcage. With a grimace, she remembered that this was one of the many punishments handed out by the proctors for serious infringements of Theocracy law. Precisely at this time of year the proctors pegged out such criminals, and as the grass grew, its sharp points penetrated flesh and the stalks then just grew straight through. Something like this, she knew, would be her own punishment if they caught her.

The paralysis was easing a bit now, though Thorn was not sure if he could manage to stand. The cold ceramal floor had sucked the heat out of him, and worked its own paralysing effect. His pelvis still ached, but at present the major pain was coming from his shattered teeth and broken nose.

As was his nature, and the nature of his training as Sparkind, he dismissed from his mind the deaths of friends and comrades, and instead concentrated his attention upon his present situation. That Brom intended to use some sort of mind-ream on him, he had no doubt, though he did doubt the man would find anything useful to him by that means, since it was ECS policy to change all relevant codes once an agent disappeared. When they came to inflict that on him, he had to be ready to act—for he either would die during the reaming, or be killed shortly after.

Using a huge effort of will, Thorn rolled over and managed to drag himself to his hands and knees. Just this effort left him dizzy and nauseous, but he pushed himself even further and managed to rock back onto the support of his knees only. His neck felt like it was without bones, his head swollen and aching, and the rest of his body as responsive as a sack of potatoes. Not allowing himself any pause, he flung himself to his feet, nearly went over on his face, staggered to the table, and clung while he vomited over the autodoc.

"Careless," he grated, once he got his nausea under control. He was about to turn the doc over in search of something sharp inside it to use as a weapon when the door opened behind him.

"Oh, up and about already? We'll soon change that."

Thorn glanced over his shoulder as Lutz pulled a baton from his belt and slapped it into the palm of his hand. Behind Lutz, John Stanton drew the door closed. Momentarily Thorn felt despair: he might be able to take on Lutz, but John Stanton? Well, maybe, if he was at the peak of condition.

"John here tells me that Sparkind are trained to resist direct-mind interrogation, but I was delighted when he told me how we should go about softening you up," said Lutz.

Thorn turned fully. Maybe if he threw the autodoc at Stanton he would then have a chance to get to Lutz and take a weapon from the man. While thinking this, it took a moment for it to impinge upon him what Lutz had just said—it was nonsense. Sparkind had no more ability to resist reaming than anyone else did. Something like that could not be trained in; it required substantial alteration of the structure of the brain. He watched as Stanton moved up beside Lutz and looked with bored contempt at the man.

"Yeah," said Stanton, "and because you're so completely stupid, you believed every word."

Lutz had time only to whip his head round. Stanton's straight-fingered strike went into his throat like an axe. Lutz stood there choking for a moment, then went down on his knees, where he tried to retrieve something from his jacket. Stanton stooped down and, with a complete lack of haste, took hold of the man's head and turned it right around.

Thorn winced at the sound of crunching vertebrae and stared as Lutz thudded down on his front and shivered and gargled into death. Then he transferred his gaze to Stanton as the mercenary stood.

"Bloody amateurs," said Stanton at last, rubbing his hands before removing an injector from the pocket of his long coat. He walked over to Thorn and inspected him. "How the hell did they manage to catch you?"

"I got careless," Thorn managed.

Stanton acknowledged this with a snort, then reached out and pressed the injector against Thorn's neck. Immediately something cool suffused Thorn's body and he felt his limbs freeing up.

"It'll take a minute or two. That paralytic of Brom's is a curare derivative. You may find you've received some nerve damage."

"Does this mean you're on my side?" Thorn asked. "I thought you were here selling arms."

Stanton grinned nastily. "That's what they think, too."

Suddenly Thorn found he no longer needed the support of the table. "Some other contract?" he asked.

"You've met Dorth?" Stanton asked, and now there was a hardness in his expression that had not been there even while he had tried to twist Lutz's head off.

"The Deacon? Yes, briefly."

Stanton turned and gazed somewhere distant. "Well he comes from my home world and I have been tracking him for the last year. When I knew him way back, he was just one of the Theocracy's proctors. He was my mother's lover and he had her accuse my father of heresy, supposedly to expedite a divorce. Once she signed the papers, the bastard took my father outside and shot him through the face."

"Your mother?" asked Thorn, studying the man.

"Died under questioning."

"Personal, then," said Thorn, now flexing his torso and wondering if the numbness in the ends of his fingers might ever go away.

With a flat expression, Stanton turned back to him. "I would guess you're here to retire our friend Brom. So, let's be about it. Brom is in his cabin and the Deacon is there as well." He turned and stepped towards the door, drawing a large pulse-gun.

Now more confident in his body, Thorn moved away from the table and stooped down by Lutz, pushing the dead man over onto his back, which incidentally put him onto his face. A quick search yielded a gas-system pulse-gun—not quite as effective as the weapon Stanton carried, firing as it did ionized gas rather than aluminium dust and consequently not having the range, but good enough for close work.

"You don't really need me," Thorn observed, standing. "Why did you risk this?"

Stanton glanced round. "Let's just say that after Viridian I have the greatest respect for Ian Cormac, and that my perspective has changed somewhat."

"Doesn't really answer my question."

"It's all the answer you'll get," Stanton replied, opening the door.

Once they were outside, Stanton removed a small cylinder from under his jacket, twisted the timer on its end, and tossed it back into the cell. Moving on, he led them up the stairs and through a hatch, out onto the deck. It was night, and Thorn realized he must have been out of it for longer than he had thought. Now they moved into the moon-shadows of a tower supporting some odd oblate device.

Stanton pointed at this and whispered, "Ware generator," and placed another cylinder next to the wall of the low building below it.

"What timings?" Thorn whispered.

"Ten minutes. Can't get a low-power signal out while that thing's up, and I'll need to. There's two or three hundred of Brom's people aboard and I can't take them all."

They moved on until Brom's cabin came into sight. Between them and it, all the structures on the deck were well lit. One of these was a long cabin with light glaring through its wide windows. Stanton pointed beyond it. "I've got a nice planar load in their middle hold. That'll go in"—he glanced at his wristcom—"six minutes. The one I have on their pile should go ... shortly." He squatted down and Thorn squatted beside him.

"What's your route out?" Thorn asked.

"Same way as I came in," Stanton replied, gesturing to the right of Brom's cabin, where Thorn had earlier seen him supervising the unloading of the catamaran.

The first of the explosives blew, ripping the side out of the barge, some distance from them. Thorn observed hot metal flung across the sea, then sinking in clouds of steam, next the orange glow of fires lighting the sky as all the lights on the ship went out. He pressed his hand to the deck and felt the vibration of its engines stutter to a halt. Glancing at Stanton, he nodded back at the tower they had just passed.

"Independent power supply—U-charger I think," Stanton explained, rising to his feet.

Some of the crew were now rushing towards the source of the explosion. Others were quite wisely not moving in that direction at all, but arming themselves. The two men broke into a trot to match this frenetic activity.

"Hey, you're—" one man managed, hesitating in his rush to join a group of his comrades. Thorn shot him in the face, then quickly dragged the corpse to a nearby dark hatch and shoved it down below.

Stanton was meanwhile twisting the timer on another explosive, while staring in the direction of the group the dead man had been about to join. He stooped and rolled the cylinder along the deck towards them, then gestured to the nearby long cabin. "We go through here."

Thorn was not sure that was such a good idea, but was not about to argue—his companion certainly seemed to know what he was doing.

Stanton explained anyway. "There's a camera down that side, and you can guarantee Brom'll be watching his screens right now." He kicked open the door, they stepped through. The door closed on explosions and screams from the deck behind them. Inside the cabin were a man at some sort of console, a woman screwing a power pack onto a pulse-rifle, a second man sitting on the side of a bunk, pulling on his boots. Both Stanton and Thorn hit the woman first—the greatest immediate danger—and she toppled back over a bench strewn with weaponry, leaving most of her head on the bench itself. The man at the console was groping for something just to his right when Stanton's shots blew him backwards, still in his swivel chair, then threw him jerking out of the chair, to sprawl beyond it. Thorn meanwhile shot the man on the bunk before he could get his other boot on.

"Back window," urged Stanton, as they ran down the length of the cabin.

To their right, crouching by some lockers, a man still in his underpants, unarmed. Stanton aimed at him, then changed his mind and stepped in, ready to knock the man out. Thorn shot the guy when he made a grab for something in the locker. He went over, clutching a heavy rail-gun, its attached cable and power pack falling on top of him as it fired, taking away half the ceiling and opening the cabin to the night.

"Shit," said Stanton flatly.

Thorn gave him a berating look.

Stanton shrugged. "In his underpants?" he said.

Four shots—not being sufficient to shatter the tough chainglass—blew the window out of its surrounding seal in one piece. Stanton, for such a heavily built man, went through in a graceful swan-dive, rolled, turned, and fired at something Thorn could not see as he stepped through the gap. Soon he spotted the two guards outside the door to Brom's cabin. One of them was down, but the other—boosted like Stanton—was trying to drag his rail-gun round on target, despite having lost his right arm. Stanton and Thorn fired together, repeatedly. The guard went backwards through the door, and the two men followed him through, stepping over what remained of their victim into Brom's so luxurious accommodation. Behind them came two further explosions, the light of which cast their shadows ahead of them as they entered.

"Leave it!" Thorn ordered.

Brom was sunk in his otter-hide armchair, a screen opened up from the pedestal table beside him. His feet were bare and Thorn was fascinated to note that his toenails were painted lavender. His hand was poised over the organic-looking weapon he had used earlier, which was now resting on the arm of the chair. He stared back at them with the intensity of a snake, and slowly moved his hand away from the weapon to his lap.

"Where's the Deacon?" Stanton snapped.

Brom shifted his gaze from Thorn and said not a word. Out of the corner of his eye, Thorn saw Stanton hold out his free hand and as if by magic, a dagger slapped into it. Again, Thorn felt some fascination—the dagger was a Tenkian, and Stanton had summoned it to his hand from somewhere else about his person.

"I won't ask so nicely, next time," said Stanton.

Brom blinked and smiled. "Well, I'm afraid you've missed the fellow. He's on his way home."

"Fuck," said Stanton. He stared at Brom. "When did he go, and by what route?"

Brom shrugged, a hint of a smile on his face as he grew more confident. "He went by AGC about four hours ago. Should be on the shuttle to Cereb even now, if he hasn't already shipped out."

Stanton seemed lost for words for a moment, then flung Thorn a glare of accusation. Thorn looked back from him to Brom, and noted that the Separatist had a slight tilt to his head and an abstracted expression.

"His aug," he said.

Stanton returned his attention to Brom and threw. The dagger entered the seated man below the chin. Brom's eyes grew wide as he choked, then he stood and groped at the dagger with fingers soon bloody. He managed a step before he went over.

Just to make sure, Thorn fired down once, excavating a cavity in the back of the man's head. "Let's get out of here," he then said.

Stanton nodded, held up his hand, and did something with the ring on one of his fingers. Brom's body jerked as the dagger pulled free, arced through the air, and slapped its handle into Stanton's hand. He stooped and wiped it on Brom's clothing. Now there came an explosion that rocked the entire barge.

"Seems like a good idea," Stanton opined, as he stood upright again.

5

Boy and woman bowed over the book as over a very complicated jigsaw puzzle. The text provided the bare bones of the story, but the picture filled out that story to such an extent it had to be studied for some minutes before moving on to the next.

"Presently, little Molly Redcap knocked on the door. 'Who is it?' inquired a gruff voice. At first the voice frightened her, but thinking her grandma might be ill she replied, 'I bring you potato bread and wine from my mother.' Softly the voice replied, 'Come in, come in, you are welcome to come in.' When she entered, Father Siluroyne hid himself under the heat sheet. 'Put the bread and wine in a fridge and come sit on the bed with me.' Molly took off her mask and bottle and skipped over to the bed where she was much surprised at the change in her grandma."

The woman leant back with her hand over her mouth for a moment—already she was beginning to recognize the change of tone. When the boy glanced round at her impatiently, she continued:

"Grandma, what big motion sensors you've got."

"All the better to follow you wherever you go."

"Grandma, what a lot of eyes you've got."

"All the better to see you my little morsel."

"Grandma, what big teeth you've got."

"The very same I used to chew up your friend with the axe."

"Oh, please don't eat me. I'm a God-loving child!"

The woman glanced at the child on her knee, who was staring at the picture of the thing in the bed in wide-eyed fascination.

"I'm beginning to see a pattern here," said the woman.

*

"'Underground' is misleading in a number of ways," Fethan explained as they trudged on out of the stand of flute grass onto drier ground cloaked with mosses, wild rhubarb and black plantains. "It makes you think of a singular secret resistance organization, when in fact it's the aim of most people there merely to survive—not to overthrow the Theocracy. You could also be misled into thinking the word has nothing to do with 'ground' and 'under' when in reality it has everything to do with those words." Fethan stabbed a finger downwards. "Below us there's about ten metres of loose and highly organic soil—the creation of millions of years of tricone burrowing and feeding. Below that is a layer of chalk over fifty metres thick—created by tricone shells sinking through the soil and slowly conglomerating and compressing." Fethan stopped and pointed towards some current movement in the damp ground that was shaking the big purplish leaves of the rhubarb and causing disc molluscs to drop from their undersides like scatterings of silver coins. The ground humped up, and briefly the spiked end of a tricone broke the surface before retracting. "Industrious little soil makers those. The inhabitants here could make a fortune exporting tricones—and the concomitant ecology—to Polity-run terraforming projects. Of course that'll never happen with the Theocracy in control."

"You were saying about the Underground," Eldene reminded him—part machine or not, Fethan did tend to ramble.

"Oh yeah." Fethan looked about himself, then led the way to where the ground rose beyond yet more flute grass. "Underneath the chalk you've got layers of limestone—which is probably the result of the tricone's distant ancestors—with occlusions of basalt and obsidian and other volcanic rocks. You know the geology of this place is fascinating."

"The Underground," Eldene reminded.

"Yeah, well, the water flow of this landmass is also fascinating. As it soaks down, it wears the limestone away, making caverns and underground rivers, till eventually reaching the deeps where it's heated by geothermal energy and pushed out again in hot springs, about fifteen hundred kilometres from here. There are cave systems down there that are thousands of kilometres long, some as big as space habitats—room for cities if you wanted 'em. *That's* the Underground, and that's where, over the last couple of centuries, your people went when they fled the Theocracy."

Through this second stand of flute grass they moved onto higher ground clad in blister mosses and the occasional tricone shell blued by algae. Eldene considered asking what basalt and obsidian were, and how big exactly was a space habitat, but her scole was now shivering against her body, she herself was beginning to pant, and the air tasted like iron in her mouth. They reached a bank, which they climbed, and looked around. To their right a mechanical digger stood tilted into the ground, its windows broken and its entire surface orange with rust. Ahead of them stretched row upon row of low twisted black trees with yellow leaves and a peppering of nodular green fruit, growing out of ground thick with vegetation so green it made Eldene's eyes ache.

"Grape trees," said Fethan.

Eldene already knew about grape trees: those strange plants producing the fist-sized fruits that were turned into wine for the Theocracy. She'd seen pictures of them on the labels of stubby bottles, and once tasted some of the wine stolen by a friend back at the city orphanage. She instead pointed down at the surrounding green vegetation and gasped, "What's that?"

"Grass," Fethan replied.

Eldene glanced back at the flute grass, then eyed the old man with suspicion.

Fethan indicated the flute grass. "That's a native plant so named because of a few similarities to this"—he pointed now at the verdancy below the trees—"which is the real thing. It's one of the plants brought by the fanatics who first came here to set up their colony two hundred years ago. It's *real* grass from Earth."

After negotiating the slope, they entered the orchard of grape trees. Feeling weak and drained, Eldene stumbled to one side and slumped with her back against one of the trees. It was time—she could not go on like this any more. With reluctance, she hinged up the mask of Volus's breather and took a deep breath. The surge of oxygen left her suddenly light-headed, and in a somewhat distracted state she stared down as Fethan squatted before her and pulled open her shirt. For a moment she thought to slap his hand away, as she had with some of the younger male workers who had become a bit too curious about the tightening of her shirt above her scole, but he was an old man—and a machine—and he was helping her.

Her scole was now almost white, and had pushed away from her chest on its eight chitinous legs. Its head was still attached to her: pincers still hooked in and feeding tubules still imbedded in her flesh, but there was now some leakage of blood, and a white pus crusting under her breasts. Below the creature was a neat row of "leaves"—a litter of five baby scoles born to leech blood. Back at the worksheds these would have been carefully removed and transported to the piggeries in the north, where they would be fattened up on pig's blood before being returned to be attached to a new worker.

"About done with, your scole," commented Fethan. "Combination of leafing and Volus hitting it with that stinger of his." While she stared in perplexity, he tugged off each of the leaves and tossed them to one side. "Fucking things," he muttered, then removed his own false scole and opened it up. From within this he removed a small flat pack, which he also opened to expose a sewing kit, and Eldene wondered what the hell he needed that for. She stared at the old man in puzzlement.

"Best we get it done now," said Fethan. "Dying ones sometimes don't detach cleanly, and if they leave bits of 'emselves in you that can cause problems." With that he reached down and took hold of Eldene's scole. Eldene yelled at the horrible ripping sensation, then yelled again when the pain hit her. Through eyes blurred by tears she saw Fethan standing with the scole gripped tightly before him, its legs kicking in the air, its pincers opening and closing, and its three feeding tubules waving like bloody fingers. Then, cast aside, it landed in the grass on its back. Eldene felt a sudden frisson of fear at seeing the thing detached and moving on its own like that. She then stared down in horror at the raw wound welling blood from her chest and, as well as pain, felt embarrassment at her own nakedness—not for exposure of her breasts, but of the area below where the scole had been attached. For more than half her life this thing had lived on her torso and now she felt incomplete without it. After Fethan threaded a needle and stooped to sew together the ragged edges of the wound left by the scole, she turned her head away from such intimate work and wished she could faint from the pain.

"You know," he said as he worked, "scoles are the same old biotech as the squerms and sprawns—brought in by the Theocracy when it first established itself here."

"Really," said Eldene through gritted teeth.

"Yeah. No one uses big ugly symbionts any more, and these things cut your lifespan by half."

Eldene turned and stared at him.

"You didn't know that, did you?" he said.

"I did not."

"It never occurred to you to wonder why proctors and priesthood put up with the inconvenience of breather gear."

"I thought . . . something to do with status . . ."

"You thought wrong."

Through the shuttle screen, Cormac gazed out at *Elysium* and saw neither green fields nor any of the blessed. The station was a morass of linked habitats clustered around the kilometre-long monofilament cables and struts that supported the main catchment mirrors of a sun-smelter facility. Here it was that the more free-wheeling *entrepreneurial* types towed in asteroids for smelting, bought refined metals, ran factories, and generally made large amounts of money—or not—in a grey area where the Line of Polity had simply juddered to a halt and dissolved before the onslaught of the wishes of this place's inhabitants. There was a runcible installed, the reason they had stopped here, but as far as the Polity was concerned this was a place you came to at your own risk. There weren't many complaints made: those who might have wanted to did not usually get much of a chance, being given a brief tour of the inside of one of the smelters.

"There's many feel this place should be broken up," said Cento.

Cormac turned to the Golem, who was piloting the shuttle, and once again was struck by his perfection. This it was that told him he must be dealing with a copy of Cento for, since the events on Viridian, the original Cento had retained the brass arm that he had torn from the killing machine, Mr. Crane, and this Cento possessed no such arm. Aiden appeared no different from how he had looked the last time Cormac had seen him, but the other Golem was yet another copy.

"There are places like this all across the Polity," said Cormac, "and those who object to them don't have to visit them."

"I like this place," said Gant from behind.

Cormac glanced round at him and Aiden. "You would," he said. "Wasn't it to here you and Thorn used to come for your holidays—a bit of relaxing non-lethal violence and enough high-tox cips to dissolve this shuttle?"

"Good days," Gant reminisced.

Cormac snorted and returned his attention to the screen, as Cento brought the shuttle in towards a conglomeration of habitats below the cylindrical tower of a giant refinery. Looking beyond this, he saw an ancient grabship clasping in its huge ceramal claw the single mountain protruding from the asteroid it was hauling in. As he understood it, the asteroid would be brought to one of the many furnace satellites, and then the sunlight from the mirrors would be focused upon it. While it heated, the automated systems on the satellite would draw off materials when they attained their particular melting or volatile temperatures. Nothing would be wasted: this place produced just about everything on the elementary table, and even the asteroidal ash that remained—such as it was—they used to make soil for the habitats. Thereafter, rough ingots and tanks were transported from the furnace satellites to the refineries and factories, there to be turned into bubble-metals, alloys and pure crystal for electronic applications, composites and complex compounds: every substance used by the material technologies of the Polity.

Soon, amongst the habitats, they noticed a structure like a giant octagonal coin around which clustered deep-space and insystem ships. There Cormac saw many of the multi-spherical varieties—ships consisting of any number of conjoined spheres—also ones with the sleek lines of cuttlefish, and those like baroque sculptures, still others that were replicas of vehicles out of human history: aeroplanes, early rockets and shuttles, and even one ship that had the appearance of an ancient sailing vessel.

"You get some *types* here," Gant observed.

Cento navigated the shuttle through this swarm and finally brought it to an open bay in the side of the structure. Cormac glanced back through the rear screen and saw that the *Occam Razor* was still easily visible. The reason given here by the docking control for the dreadnought not being allowed in was that it was just too *large* to be joining this crowd—supposedly just one accidental burst from one of its manoeuvring thrusters could crisp any number of these ships. He doubted this was the true reason and, to be honest, it irked him that some autocrat here could order a Polity battleship to stand off.

As the shuttle drifted slowly into the bay, through the shimmer-shield, Cento made a sound of annoyance.

"Problem?" Cormac asked.

"Not really," muttered the Golem, "but I have just been informed of what we are being charged for the use of this bay."

"Probably ten times the going rate," said Gant. "We're a type that ain't all that welcome here."

There were people coming towards them from every direction as they headed for the ramp leading down to the catamaran, but in the darkness there was no way to easily distinguish friend from foe, or rather, for all those foes to realize that Thorn and Stanton were not friendly. This did not last though, for somewhere on the barge an auxiliary generator or pile cut in. A searchlight beam lit the area around Brom's cabin, and began to traverse the deck. It found them as they were running down the ramp to Stanton's vessel.

"The mooring cables," Stanton instructed almost conversationally, as there rose an outcry from the barge.

Thorn grabbed the nearest cable and unhooked it from its bollard, while Stanton did the same with the other one. Stanton was leaping aboard as Thorn unhooked the final cable. Someone on the barge then decided it was no longer time for just shouting, and something smashed the cable from his hand, while the ramp behind him erupted into jagged twists of metal. He leapt from the ramp onto one of the catamaran's outriders and found himself clinging to a stanchion supporting the suspended cabin as tractor drives engaged in both outriders, and the vessel began to pull away. Thorn ran along the outrider to the steps leading up it into the cabin, but slipped when projectiles slammed holes through the surface next to his feet, and only managed to prevent himself falling into the water by catching hold of the safety rail guarding the steps. With his legs still trailing in the water, he glanced back at the quickly receding barge and saw one of the gun turrets swinging in their direction, before disappearing in an actinic explosion. From the ramp, most of Brom's people started opening up with hand weapons, while a small group of them set up a tripod-mounted missile launcher. Thorn assessed his chances of reaching the cabin at just a little above zero, and his chances of remaining alive, either there or here, as little different. Then a coughing sound from the rear of the cabin, and something cylindrical and black sped back towards the ramp. The explosion that followed sliced the ramp in half and threw those of Brom's people who were still intact into the water.

"Are you coming up here or not?" Stanton shouted.

Thorn finally hauled himself from the water and scrambled up the steps.

The catamaran's cabin was of a standard utile design: cylindrical, with a rear hold and a forward cockpit containing three control chairs. Thorn entered the hold and headed quickly for the cockpit, little comforted to be under cover when he noticed the many bullet holes punched through the walls.

While with his right hand guiding the vessel out to sea using a joystick that had probably, in a previous life, belonged to some kind of nil-AG aircraft, Stanton glanced at Thorn and nodded to the chair next to him. As Thorn strapped himself in, the mercenary swung across the targeting visor he had himself just used to take out the ramp, then kicked across the floor-mounted firing control he had been operating with his left hand. Thorn saw that the hinged beam the control column extended from, as well as the jointed arm supporting the visor, allowed them to be operated from any seat.

"Bit primitive," Stanton explained. "It was connected into this boat's harpoon, but I've replaced that with a weapons carousel. You've got twelve heat-seekers, three chaff, and three antimunition packages back there. Use them wisely."

Thorn pulled the column into position and swung the visor across his face, feeling its skin-stick surfaces adhering to him. Now he had a view straight back to the barge but, thumbing the swing control on the joystick he now gripped, that view swung in increments of ninety degrees, as the launcher on the rear of the catamaran swung round. Tilting his head back, he saw nothing but sky for a moment, before thumbing the launcher round again so the barge was back in the screen.

"We've got AGCs launching," he told Stanton.

"Most'll be running," the mercenary told him bluntly.

"Three are running in this direction."

"That's why I said 'most,'" Stanton replied.

Finding the cursor control under his little finger, Thorn called up the mask's menu and scrolled down through it. The selection buttons Stanton had added—*heat, chaff* and *anti-m*—were red and of an entirely different font from the rest of the menu. He was about to choose one of these when a familiar voice spoke. "That you in there, trooper Thorn?" He quickly made a different menu choice and called up, in the corner of the screen, a mini-display that showed him Ternan's face. Zeroing the targeting box on one of the approaching AGCs, he then selected *heat*, fired off a missile, and had the pleasure of seeing her frantically slapping at controls while the three vehicles broke away. However, anti-munitions took out the missile before it reached its target.

"How long, Jarv?" asked Stanton, speaking into his wristcom.

"Seven minutes," replied a woman's voice.

"Why so slow?" he asked.

"Thousand-kilometre restricted zone. Came on just as you got to the barge—probably something to do with your friend there," she replied.

"Any Polity activity?"

"You bet. When they shot down that military transport, we got a swarm of craft taking off from Gordonstone. As soon as the 'ware generator went offline, two insystem attack boats launched from Cereb. They're about three minutes behind me."

"Great," murmured Stanton.

Thorn absorbed this, but kept his attention mostly focused on the pursuing AGCs. There were seven of them now, and there was no way this catamaran, even with its tractor drive flat out, could outrun them. Observing seven white dots then speeding from the AGCs towards him—quickly highlighted in flashing red boxes on the screen—he selected and fired chaff, shortly followed by antimunitions. Three missiles exploded in the cloud of glittering dust that the remaining four successfully punched through. The antimunitions package flew apart into its hundred component seeker explosives, two of which were detonated by two of the missiles, but the remaining two hammered on in.

"We're not gonna survive seven minutes," Thorn observed, firing one of the last two antimunitions packages.

The explosions were close, shock waves veering the boat in its course and shrapnel clattering against the cabin. Thorn pulled the visor aside in time to see a missile tumbling end over end into the sea beside them, and detonating just under the waves.

"Seven AGCs, and it looks like all of them have launchers." Thorn slapped the targeting visor back into place.

"Jarv," explained Stanton, "we're going to bail out. Thorn, empty that carousel. We're going."

Thorn took the cursor to each missile selection, rattling the firing button on each, then removed the visor and reached for his seat straps. Stanton was already through the door into the hold by the time he had his straps undone. Soon the two of them were moving back to the entry hatch. Thorn glanced to the rear of the hold, where the carousel was clicking round, and heard the missiles launching one after the other. Following Stanton down, he squinted through spray driven up by the outriders chopping through the wave tops. The two men jumped at the same time. Travelling at the same speed as the catamaran, Thorn hit the sea and bounced—the water feeling about as welcoming as concrete. Next, he was into it headfirst, whiteness all around him and copper salts bitter in his mouth. At his first breath on coming to the surface, he saw the catamaran already fifty metres away—missiles still launching from the rear of its cabin. The missile that then hit it, he did not see.

The central cabin just disappeared, like a balloon being burst by an orange explosion. Caught in the blast, one outrider went straight up into the air, then dropped like a dolphin having reached the summit of its leap, and disappeared. The remaining outrider, its tractor drive still functioning, motored on, towing a tangle of smoking wreckage.

"Perfect timing," said John Stanton from behind him.

Thorn sculled round to the mercenary and grinned at him, before looking beyond to where the pursuing AGCs were now coming into sight. Soon the seven vehicles were hovering over the still motoring wreckage of the catamaran. From one of them another missile stabbed down and destroyed even this. Then the attackers nosed out across the area.

"Shit," said Thorn. "You reckon they know we got out?"

"Perhaps," said Stanton.

Thorn shot him a look of annoyance, then began hyper-ventilating, ready to dive under the waves. Stanton seemed amused by this. Thorn was just about to submerge when a double sonic boom shook the sky, and there came a roar as of a giant steel beast. A blast of hot wind hazed the area with sea spray and a shadow blotted out the sky. The AGCs turned and fled, like crows driven away from a road kill, and Thorn gazed up at the trispherical ship as it descended, cables dropping from an underside hatch.

Stepping from the shuttle, Cormac looked around the bay and wondered at why it was so empty. Such a huge area had plenty of space for other shuttles, of which, judging by the number of ships outside, there needed to be many, yet there was none here but their own. He had begun to get an intimation of something not quite right when out of one of the row of drop-shafts to the rear of the bay emerged the welcoming party.

The two men were suited in grey businesswear and wore black intensifier eye-bands and executive polished-chrome augs. They preceded soldiers uniformed in light combat armour, with helmets which extended down one side of their heads—containing military coms and augs no doubt—and carrying pulse-rifles. But all these seemed inconsequential compared with what came up out of the shaft behind them, passed to either side of the group, and swung round in front. Here were two large polished cylinders floating vertically, with weapons mounted at each end. They were heavy-armour AI drones—very new and very dangerous. Even the *Occam Razor* did not have anything like this aboard. Cormac glanced back and noticed that the bay's armoured doors were drawing closed. He initiated Shuriken as the three Golem accompanying him moved out to either side of him.

"Probably come for the docking charges," Gant suggested to Cento.

Cormac glanced at Gant. "Who are these?" he asked.

"Could be anyone," the Sparkind replied. "There's about a hundred private armies here employed by various corporations. More likely though that these are *Elysium* Security—each corporation provides a percentage of its own forces for overall security."

"Got some serious weaponry," noted Cormac, indicating the drones.

"They are ship drones built for Earth Central Security," said Aiden.

Cormac turned to the Golem. "Any communication?"

"They are somewhat . . . terse," Aiden replied.

The drones reached them first and floated out to either side of them, turning to the horizontal as they did so, training their weapons on the four of them. Each drone, Cormac noted, possessed a missile-launcher and an APW—antiphoton weapon—obviously whoever had sent this welcoming committee was taking no chances. The soldiers halted smartly while the two leaders advanced and came to a halt five metres from Cormac. The one on the right, who was bald, quite obviously boosted, and had skin the colour of orange cheese, carefully surveyed Cormac and his companions.

"Welcome to *Elysium*," he said, at last.

"Interesting that you chose those words," said Cormac, eyeing the drones. "I don't *feel* particularly welcome."

"We are always cautious here," the man replied. "And we become especially cautious when paid a visit by an ECS dreadnought. What business do you have here?"

The man's companion, who was shorter, not so heavily built, and had long black hair spilling across his shoulders, showed a set of chrome teeth in a grin. "Lons here is always a little blunt," he said. "But you must understand that many living here have interests that they wish to preserve." He moved forwards, with Lons trailing a step behind him, and held out his hand to Cormac. "Alvor," he said, clasping Cormac's hand in a sweaty grip.

"Ian Cormac."

Both men's expressions abruptly hardened, but Alvor continued: "I'm surprised *you* would want to come here.

But now that you are here, if you would accompany us?" He turned and gestured towards the drop-shafts.

"I think you are misconstruing the purpose of my visit. I'm here solely because *Elysium* is the only place on my present route to possess a runcible facility," said Cormac.

"Unfortunately I am not the one this needs to be explained to." Alvor was now surveying Cormac's companions. He went on, "Also, because of certain security considerations, your friends will unfortunately have to remain here meanwhile."

Cormac raised his hand to silence Gant, who had been about to protest, and asked, "Who do I need to explain this to, and what are these 'security' considerations you mention?"

Lons replied with, "We've no objection to Golem here, except of course when they are Golem Twenty-sevens disembarking from an ECS dreadnought. Then we become suspicious."

Alvor shrugged. "Dreyden is understandably nervous of such company."

"Dreyden?" Cormac asked.

Alvor stared at him for a long moment before going on, "Our employer has been the de facto ruler of *Elysium* for some years now—of which ECS must be well aware?"

"Well, I'm not," said Cormac. "As I said to you, my business here relates only to this place's location—nothing else—and I can't be expected to remember the name of every tinpot autocrat, since hundreds of them rise and fall in every decade around the edge of the Polity." The two men frowned at this, but Cormac continued, "I'll now accompany you to see this Dreyden, but meanwhile my companions will continue with the real purpose of our visit here."

"Are you sure about that, Agent?" Gant asked him.

Cormac glanced at him. "If I'm not back here with you when you're ready to leave, and if I haven't communicated with you . . . then you'll know what to do." He glanced coldly at the two grey-suited men. "I'm sure Captain Tomalon would be more than willing to give his weapons a test run."

"Unfortunately Dreyden does not want ECS Golem running about this place unsupervised, so they *must* remain here," said Alvor.

"And how do you intend to make them remain here?" Cormac asked.

Alvor glanced at the two huge drones, and winced as if it was painful for him to even mention their presence.

"Let me put it another way," Cormac went on. "Is this Dreyden prepared to murder ECS Golem androids out of no justification other than his paranoia? When all they will be doing is going over to the runcible facility to await someone's arrival?"

Alvor put his fingers against his aug, as he obviously received further instruction. "The arrival of whom?" he asked after a moment.

"Not that it concerns you greatly, but a Polity scientist, that's all," Cormac replied, starting to feel irritated now.

Smoothly Alvor went on, "If that is their only purpose here, then you'll have no objection to them being accompanied, then?"

"No objection, just so long as there are no more delays," said Cormac. Then, to his three companions, "No screw-ups. This place is for another day."

Cormac waved a hand in the direction of the drop-shafts, and began heading in towards them. The two grey-suits fell in beside him, and the attendant soldiers parted before him, then closed behind.

Upon reaching the shafts, Cormac glanced back to note that the two drones had remained with the Golem—obviously human soldiers were not considered sufficient accompaniment for those three. Alvor punched a code into the touch-console beside one of the shafts, then stepped out to where the irised gravity field wafted him upwards. Cormac quickly followed. As he was dragged up he felt that familiar slight tugging each time he passed a floor and, counting thirty of such sensations, realized he must be nearing the top of the station. At one point there was a pause in his ascent, before he passed "Restricted Area" signs, and thereafter the sides of the shaft were striped orange and black—the universal colours of danger. At the required level, he stepped out behind Alvor into a vestibule before twin wooden doors. The floor of this space was slabbed with alternate white and translucent-red stones—probably of alabaster and artificial ruby. Suspended from the ceiling by ominously heavy cables was a standard design of security drone, but with an APW bolted underneath. It observed him with matt-black visual receptors and turned to track his progress as he followed Alvor to the door. Glancing back, he saw that only Lons had joined them—the soldiers having departed the shaft somewhere below. No doubt Dreyden considered them unnecessary now Cormac was within his internal security system.

At the doors, Alvor turned and held out his hand. "Your weapons."

Cormac pulled his thin-gun and tossed it across to the man. As Alvor caught and inspected this, Cormac unstrapped his shuriken holster, then handed it across. With raised eyebrows Alvor studied the weapon before pocketing it.

"Interesting," he said, before turning to lead the way in.

Beyond the doors was a glass lock, and through this Cormac saw a huge biodome with a roof constructed from hexagonal panes of chainglass, through which sunlight was reflected from a pylon-mounted mirror on top of the station. Following Alvor through the glass door when it hissed open, he found himself beginning to sweat in the humid atmosphere inside the dome. All around grew tropical plants: cycads, tree ferns, orchids, and other adapted or exotic species. To his right a stand of cyanids reared up into shadow, their sharp blue leaves like huge machete blades, metre-long flower pods open to expose intricate yellow convolutions like the surface of a brain. A low creaking attracted his attention towards his left, where a plasoderm's circular grey seed case slowly opened and oozed the flattened worms of jelly that were its slime-mould spore carriers. Seeing this last plant—a native of Callorum—immediately raised Cormac's suspicions. However, he knew that samples of such plants were always in circulation, and could be easily obtained by an enthusiast. He told himself not to have such a nasty suspicious nature.

"Friend Dreyden has an interest in botany, I take it?" he said.

"Yeah," grunted Lons, revealing even more of his charm now he felt himself to be more in a position of power.

"Donnegal Dreyden was an expert in the fields of biomechanics, botany, linguistics, and political science before he focused his full attention on metallurgy, and subsequently formed Alliance Smelters," said Alvor—quoting straight from the manual, Cormac felt—before gesturing ahead to a building that seemingly acted as a wide pillar supporting the centre of the biodome, and then leading the way over to the metal stairs that spiralled up its side. Lons trudged along behind them, resentment more than obvious in his mien.

At the top of the building, the stairs terminated in a balcony ringing a circular and luxuriously appointed apartment. Entering it, Cormac scanned the fortune in antiques gathered here—there was even what looked like a preruncible computer resting on a replica Louis XIV gate-legged table—then brought his attention to the man rising from a single screen and simple console positioned in one corner. This individual, on cursory inspection, could have passed for one of Alvor's or Lons's associates. Closer inspection revealed that his businesswear was Armani and his aug a Sony 5000. He was thin and his hatchet face looked tired—with shadows under his eyes and those eyes red-rimmed. His movements were jerky, and slightly unsure, as in someone who is withdrawing from some drug. On standing, he took a cigarette from the box on the table beside him and tapped it on his wristcom, before putting it into his mouth. He lit it with a small laser igniter set into a heavy ring on his forefinger.

"Ian Cormac," he said. "I knew a day like this would come, but I did not expect it so soon."

"That day being?" asked Cormac, advancing into the room as Alvor and Lons moved back to stand by the balcony door.

"Drink?" Dreyden asked, gesturing to a nearby cabinet.

Cormac contained his impatience and nodded briefly, watching while Dreyden poured two whiskies from a crystal decanter, then added rainbow spheres of cips ice. Taking the drink proffered, he felt disinclined to sample it.

"You know, it's taken me two years and about a billion New Carth shillings to get this place organized." Dreyden led the way to a seating area and plumped down in an armchair. Cormac perched himself on the edge of a sofa, placing his drink on a coffee table, the top of which was a polished slab of green tourmaline, apparently found on the asteroid that had made Dreyden his first billion, or so said holographic text scrolling round in the mineral.

"And this is relevant to me how?"

Dreyden drew hard on his cigarette. "Because you're Earth Central Security, and don't tell me that ECS doesn't intend to subsume *Elysium*."

"Maybe so, but that has nothing to do with why I'm here," Cormac replied.

Dreyden looked doubtful as he went on, "You know, because of the security service I formed here, crime is down to Polity levels and the standard of living is very high. In fact higher than on many Polity worlds. A lot of people here are making a lot of money."

"Admirable," commented Cormac dryly.

"If ECS come in here then many people will die. They'll fight to keep you out; they like things the way they are," Dreyden told him.

Cormac twirled his glass on the tourmaline and noted that the biggest smelting complex in *Elysium* was Dreyden's property—apparently it could turn a million tonnes of asteroidal steel into foamed-metal construction members in less than a solstan day. Cormac was impressed, but no less irritable and bored.

"You're not listening to me," he said. "I'm not here to conquer your little empire, Dreyden." He looked up. "Though I may yet give the matter some consideration if I'm delayed any longer."

Dreyden stood, and Cormac observed the beads of sweat dotting his brow. The man was twitchy—either angry or scared—as revealed in his sneering tone when next he spoke.

"I have something to show you," he said.

With weary impatience Cormac followed him to the centre of the room, then up yet another spiral stair leading to a platform positioned directly below the chainglass roof. Climbing through the hatch and onto this platform, they came into a smaller glasshouse protruding up from the roof itself. All around, they had a perfect view of *Elysium*. Dreyden gestured to the ships crowding the floating docks, then beyond them to where the *Occam Razor* was clearly visible.

"Big bastard, that ship, but it probably doesn't mass much more than the asteroids we regularly bring in," he said. He now pointed to the habitats and smelting complexes that formed almost a tangled wall in space beside them. "You know, we don't have Separatists here because essentially most of *Elysium* is not actually in the Polity. Though being upon the Line as we are, we share many of the benefits of Polity membership. It's a situation we do not really want to change, either through annoying you people by harbouring criminals or by pushing for full membership."

"Your point?" Cormac asked.

Now Dreyden indicated the huge sun mirrors. "I have complete control over *those* now. The grabship captains have to buy time on them from me, as do those corporations that own the few furnace satellites that I myself do not own," Dreyden said.

Cormac remained silent, waiting for the man to make his point—he now had some intimation of what that might be, but he wanted it clearly stated.

Dreyden went on, "It only takes a minute to shift the focus of those mirrors. You can't see from here, but there is a ring of them, each capable of covering its nearest partner within a matter of seconds. They can also cover all possible approaches to our . . . community."

"Very cosy. So you would be well defended should a stray asteroid head in this direction," said Cormac sarcastically.

Dreyden dropped the butt of his cigarette and ground it out on the platform. After taking a swallow of his drink he glared at Cormac. "You know, we don't even use the tightest focus to melt asteroids. If we tried that on an asteroid it would vaporize and obliterate the furnace satellite it was lodged in. On the tightest focus we can get heat levels—if the conditions are just right—high enough to start a fusion reaction. There's no known substance that can endure that for long, and no field technology that can withstand it."

Cormac wandered over to the glass wall and gazed down at the *Occam Razor*. Dreyden's message was quite clear, but utterly irrelevant considering what he knew of ECS policy concerning this place.

"Last count as I recollect," said Cormac without turning from the glass, "there were two hundred million people living here." He turned now to face Dreyden. "ECS just isn't interested . . . you want the figures? AIs have calculated that with the people here living in such *fragile* circumstances the losses during a takeover would be something in the region of twenty per cent. And to gain what?" He gestured to the nearest giant smelting complex. "The whole infrastructure would probably be destroyed as well, and the Polity would basically end up with a refugee population in the tens of millions. Probably the smelters and mirrors would be destroyed too, so there would be nothing to gain, and anyway most of what is made here is sold to the Polity, and most of the money used to buy it is spent on Polity goods. I'm not here for this, Dreyden."

Dreyden continued to glare and Cormac realized that the man would just never believe what he was being told—he had too much invested here and was evidently too frightened of Earth Central Security to trust any of its agents. In reality his attitude was perfectly understandable: the Polity had without compunction absorbed worlds into itself when that best served the interests of its entire population, and for the same reasons empires like Dreyden's had been undermined, or obliterated.

"I've no time for this," said Cormac, heading for the hatch.

"What do you want with this Asselis Mika, the Life-Coven woman?" Dreyden asked suddenly.

Cormac turned as he began to climb down. "Her expertise. And we will leave with her—understand that."

"So long as you do leave." Dreyden gulped the rest of his drink. "Perhaps, after you are gone, you can pass on the message that Polity battleships are no longer welcome here."

"Oh, I'll pass *that* on," said Cormac, departing.

Jarvellis was probably the most smoulderingly sexy woman Thorn had ever met. She had long straight black hair, a face that seemed perpetually cheeky, as if she was just about to say something quite shocking, and a figure that was well emphasized by the ersatz acceleration suit she wore. Thorn also understood, even on such very brief acquaintance, that she was completely and utterly in love with John Stanton. She did not give a swooning display in his presence, nor did she simper; it was just a sense of connection between the two of them. He had caught it in that one glance exchanged between the two when he and Stanton had entered the bridge sphere of this trispherical ship. It was a personal connection that completely cut anyone else out of the circuit.

After strapping himself in, Stanton gestured back the way they had entered. "That's cargo, as you saw, and the other sphere is the living quarters. We've got a small galley and a machine shop just behind here as well."

As he too strapped himself into one of the two acceleration chairs immediately behind Stanton and Jarvellis, Thorn considered the hold he had just seen. He'd noted the four cryopods fixed upright to one wall and been unable to miss seeing the racked cargo of weapons crates and other less easily identifiable items.

"What I could do with is an autodoc," he said, delicately probing his broken teeth.

"We've got one, but you'll have to wait. All consoles are DNA-keyed to me and Jarv. Also, *Lyric II* is run by an AI, and she tends to trust people even less than I do."

That figured.

Thorn turned his attention to Jarvellis as she piloted *Lyric II* up and away from the planet. The rumbling of acceleration through atmosphere was growing less now, and the middle one of the three screens showed whitish sky diffusing away over starlit space. The right screen displayed a view of the rapidly receding world.

"Ooh, those ECS boys know some dirty words," said Jarvellis, her head tilted towards her earplug.

"And what words are they saying?" asked Stanton.

"Well," said Jarvellis, turning to give Thorn an estimating look, "the gist is 'Stay where you are and wait to be boarded,' but the language is much more colourful."

"They'll think you're escaping Separatists," said Thorn. "Which of course you are not."

Stanton glanced back at him. "No, we are not." He returned his attention to Jarvellis. "What about the 'ware?"

She shook her head. "The runcible AI will be on us now and we'll not hide the AG signature from it."

"Can we outrun them?" Stanton asked.

"Oh, pleeaase," spoke a voice from the console in front of Jarvellis.

Jarvellis patted the console. "I think Lyric can handle a couple of rusty old ECS attack boats—can't you, dear?"

"I should think so," replied the voice of *Lyric II*'s AI.

Just then there came a deep roar from within the ship, and subscreens displaying outside views of the ship whited out. Thorn surmised, by this sound, that a powerful engine had just been put online.

"The language just gets worse and worse," said Jarvellis. "Here we go." She touched a control and the view on one of the main screens changed to show Cheyne III's only moon, Cereb, and two much closer objects—identifiable only as being vaguely wedge-shaped—quickly receding. Jarvellis ran her fingers expertly over some more controls, then pulled her earplug. She turned and again looked back at Thorn. "Now, what do we do with your friend here?" she asked.

Before Stanton could say anything, Thorn asked, "You're going after this Deacon character, I take it?"

"Yes," said Stanton, his face assuming the same hardness that Thorn had earlier seen at any mention of the Deacon.

"Then let me come with you. That barge back there will soon become a reef, if it isn't already, and any mission I had there is over."

"Why would you want to come with us?" asked Jarvellis.

"Because whoever that guy was, he was supplying the Cheyne Separatists and I'd like very much to find out more about *that*."

"We don't work for ECS," said Jarvellis.

"It is also worth bearing in mind," added Stanton, "that ECS has a reward out for our capture."

"I've no intention of trying to claim it," said Thorn. "You saved my life and that might not count for much on a policy level, but it sure as hell means a lot to me."

"Academic, really," said Stanton. "If we try to stop off at any Polity-controlled world or station we'll have ECS over us like worms on a turd—one of Brom's charming expressions, that—so there's no way we'll be dropping you anywhere."

"What about this Deacon—will you be able to track him?" Thorn asked.

"No need," Stanton replied. "He'll head for his rat hole at Masada. That's where we intended to go next anyway, and that's where I'll kill him."

"Masada?" Thorn queried.

"Yes," said Stanton. "Let me tell you about my home world."

The grapes were hard and green and, being a long way from ripeness, only the size of eyeballs. As she chewed on another of the sour fruit, Eldene tried not to think about nut-potatoes and bread and the occasional luxury of meat.

"Do you ever need food?" she asked, after lowering her mask and spitting out a mouthful of green goo.

"Small amounts of nutrients sometimes," replied Fethan, "otherwise my source of energy is somewhat hotter."

Eldene hinged her mask back up into place and spoke through it, having earlier discovered that some device in the collar prevented the muffling of her voice. "Why were you . . . a worker? How did you become a worker?"

"I came here about four solstan years ago at the behest of Earth Central Security, to bring certain devices and make an assessment of the situation down here. Infiltrating the city was not difficult, as to the Theocracy even the citizens are not individuals—just people to be used up. I completed my assessment in two years, by which time I'd found out about the Underground and made contacts there. I've since been working for one Lellan Stanton—the leader of the rebellion—gathering intelligence on the worker situation, and gathering opinions." Fethan shrugged. "It is easy to get defectors from the city, especially from the processing plants, but not so easy out here, and she wanted to find out how best it might be done."

"And have you succeeded?"

Fethan reached into the pocket of his coverall and removed a short plastic tube of pills that Eldene immediately recognized as those used to prevent a scole rejecting and dying.

"Once we've had these analysed," he said, "we have an opening. It seems the only way now. We'll distribute these through those agents we have placed, and when the time is right have a mass breakout."

"Then what?" asked Eldene, looking pointedly up into the lurid sky.

Fethan put away the pills. "You have to understand, girl, I was not sent here by ECS on a purposeless assignment. When the time is right this world will become part of the Human Polity, whether the Theocracy likes it or not."

"When is the time *right*? Why is this injustice allowed to continue?"

"It continues because of politics. The Polity takes control of Line worlds, subsumes them, by consent of eighty per cent of the planetary population—or in cases when there has been a complete breakdown of control and they have been asked for help. If ECS came in here with a shitload of warships and blew the Theocracy to hell, that would cause fear on many other Out-Polity worlds, and that fear might prove a uniting force. Last time ECS got that heavy-handed, it upset the balance on a world that had joined the Polity only a few months before.

That world then seceded from what was described there as 'the rule of AI autocrats,' its government was subverted by Separatists, and the entire planetary population forced into a war they did not want, against their nearest Polity neighbour. So you see; we have to be very careful."

"What happened . . . to the two worlds at war?" Eldene asked.

"Well, ECS had to defend the Polity world. That's the charter."

"The other world?"

"It's still habitable at the poles."

Eldene chewed that over: there had always been a deep streak of cynicism in her—probably induced by her early reading—which was perhaps why Fethan had shown such interest in her. She'd never really believed his stories about the Human Polity, precisely because she wanted so badly for them to be true. Even so, she had taken in much of what he had told her and it was her understanding that the Polity would only have to learn of the injustice here for it to unleash ECS on the Theocracy.

"When will ECS come?" she asked eventually.

"When eighty per cent of the population has voted for such or when there has been a complete breakdown of political control and help is asked for," Fethan replied obdurately.

"How in the name of God are we supposed to vote?" Eldene asked.

Fethan glanced at her. "Do you want the Polity in control here? Would you pledge allegiance to the AIs that run the Human Polity?"

"Damned right I would. Anything has to be better than the Theocracy!"

Fethan halted and turned, gripping her by the shoulder. "Say to me your name and tell me what you want."

Eldene stared back at the man and tried to figure out what he meant. "I'm . . . I'm Eldene and I want the . . . Human Polity running this world. I want to be free. I want . . ."

Fethan released her. "You have just made your deposition. You've just voted for Polity control here." He tilted his head slightly, as if listening to something. "So far that's just over sixty-eight per cent of the population."

"I don't understand."

"The ballots run a limited physiological probe, to make sure the ballotee is not under duress. But because I am what I am, I can collect depositions without it." He gestured behind with his thumb. "Back there I collected fifty-three depositions, which you may be glad to know include Dent's and Cathol's. You were next on my list before circumstances . . . changed."

"Ballots?"

"The Polity has had machines here collecting votes for thirty-eight years, but never managed to get that eighty per cent vote. Your vote, because of your age, has a life of fifty years calculated from average spans here. It's the only way it can work."

"But Dent and Cathol are dead."

"I didn't say the system was perfect, girl."

"I've never seen these ballots," said Eldene, still confused.

"They're machines—they'll be in a ring, an amulet, the button on someone's shirt. Even so, you understand how difficult it would be to get someone to say what you have just said, with proctors and Theocracy cameras watching them at every turn. Most of that sixty-eight per cent is the Underground vote."

Fethan moved on.

"Then how much longer?" Eldene asked.

Fethan was silent for a moment before replying. "I don't think it's gonna be done by vote, girl. I think that the Theocracy will be destabilized. Sometime soon, Earth Central will send certain individuals here, and things will change very quickly."

"Tell me more," said Eldene, excitement twisting her stomach. And Fethan told her much more.

6

"And thus it was that with God's guidance Brother Goodman came at last to the land of the gabbleduck. Hereabouts were trails worn through the grass and the scatterings of the bones of those who had failed the test," the woman told her boy, raising an eyebrow at the picture displayed in the book showing a veritable charnel house.

"The babbleguck, the babbleguck," said the boy impatiently—she had given up trying to get him to pronounce the name correctly and assumed this story would become part of his own personal mythology when he grew up. Scrolling the text down moved the scene along to soon reveal the creature itself: it squatted in the grasses like some monstrously insectile hybrid of Buddha and Kali, with a definite splash of Argus in the ocular region.

"Gabbleduck," said the boy, and the woman looked at him with suspicion before continuing.

"In his right hand Brother Goodman carried the word of God and in his left hand he carried the wisdom of Zelda Smythe. He brought no weapons to the abode of the monster other than these and his Faith. 'Ask me a riddle!' he cried, holding up both books."

At this point, the gabbleduck, with its multiple arms folded on its triple-keeled chest, turned its array of green eyes upon the pious brother.

"'Scubble leather bobble fuck,' said the duck, and in reply Brother Goodman smote the creature with the word, 'Ung?'"

The woman started giggling as the picture book now showed the enormous creature stooping down and opening its large bill to expose an interior lined with something like white holly leaves.

"Then guess . . . what . . . happened?" she managed.

Giggling as well, though not sure why, the boy did not manage a reply. The book showed them both anyway.

The *Occam Razor* was a dark and disturbing ship, made more so because despite its large crew and resident population, it always seemed empty—any crew member possibly being, at any one time, as much as a couple of kilometres away, and that was a disturbing thought. His cabin was large, comfortable, had all the facilities of a plush hotel, and was like a room in an empty house. Standing at the wide screen that served as a window, Cormac sipped a whisky with cubes of normal ice in it, unlike the one he had been poured by Dreyden—whisky with cips ice was a lethal combination—and watched *Elysium*, and the huge sun it orbited, dwindle into invisibility. He felt the need now to be about his business, but there were months yet of ship time to get through before the *Occam Razor* reached its destination. Unable to contain his impatience any longer he swallowed the last of his drink, placed the glass back in the wall dispenser and headed for the door.

The ship was not quiet, yet it had an air of quietude. The sounds Cormac could hear in the corridor were distant and echoey, and as of someone working on things far off: the crackle of a welder, the clang of something dropped, the stutter of a laser drill. He checked the time and, seeing that only an hour had passed since their departure from *Elysium*, he decided not to bother Mika yet—she would hardly have had time to settle in her cabin, let alone establish herself in the ship's forensic laboratory in Medical. He decided he needed to think, and he always thought best while he was walking. There was plenty of room to walk here, so he chose a direction and set off.

In a few minutes it was evident he had left the accommodation area. The walkway soon lost its carpeting—bare gravity plates exposed—then its partition walls, exposing the inner structure of the ship. All around him was an ordered forest of wires and optic cables, ducts and foamed metal beams, and plasma tubes, often intersecting at some bulky wasps' nest of a machine. For a couple of minutes he had a view of something far below him that looked like the Sydney Opera House, but it was soon obscured as some huge deck slid slowly over it. He had been walking for ten minutes when a drone flew waveringly towards him. This particular machine had the smooth shape of an arrowhead with no visible manipulators, and he wondered just what purpose it could possibly serve.

"What's the quickest way to the hull?" he asked quickly, when it became evident the drone was not going to stop. The drone jerked to a halt in midair, turned two ruby eyes towards him, then turned again so it was pointing down the way he was heading.

"First left, about half a klom," it said.

"Thank—"

The drone had already flown off.

Cormac soon came to an intersection of four walkways, and took the one on his immediate left in the hope that he was still going in the right direction. If he was, he would reach his destination in five or ten minutes. After only a couple of minutes it came into sight. The hull of the ship was a steel cliff with neither top nor bottom in sight, just a couple of square kilometres of curving hull-metal. The walkway ended in a circular platform before a shimmer-shield curtaining a rectangular hole piercing the hull. Cormac received an impression of scale it was not often possible to find on a world. This ship was awesome, but it surprised him to have not yet encountered any crewmembers. Strangely, it came as no surprise to him to see a familiar figure awaiting him on the platform, silhouetted against the glitter of stars.

"Now why the hell are *you* here?" he asked as he drew closer.

Blegg was utterly silent until Cormac came to stand beside him, then he gestured to the immensity beyond the shimmer-shield. "Games," he said, while gazing out into the flecked darkness. "Human beings playing at silly games and arguing like children over their toys." He turned to look at Cormac, and Cormac flinched at what he saw in those eyes: a power there, something ineffable.

Blegg went on, "The human race occupies a small fraction of the galaxy, a small sphere at its rim, a hundred star systems at most, but enough that it is beginning to be noticed."

"Yes, I'm sure it is," Cormac replied, fumbling in his pocket and finding a New Carth shilling—the currency used in *Elysium*. He held it out and, remembering the briefing from Blegg he had previously received in VR, tipped his hand and exerted his will to stop the shilling in midair. It bounced off the platform then curved spinning into the space beyond—now obviously outside the influence of the grav-plates he was standing on.

"We are not in VR," Blegg told him.

"Then let me repeat: 'Why the hell are you here?' Did you board at *Elysium*?"

"The human race is beginning to be noticed, Ian Cormac."

"By the likes of the Makers, yes, and we saved the one surviving member of a mission from their race and are now transporting it back. What of that? Its arrival back in its home system is years hence in our terms, and presumably it is now a friend."

"Not just the Makers, Ian, but they illustrate a point—the rogue biological machine of theirs, Dragon, has caused the human race many problems."

Cormac snorted. "You talk of the human race as if you are not a member."

Blegg grinned. "Ye doubt me, Ian?"

"You are capable of things no other human is capable of, at least, to my knowledge."

Blegg allowed that a derisive grunt. "There're others like me, and there'll be more."

Cormac let that ride and instead asked, "Who other than the Makers are beginning to notice us?"

Blegg turned back to the shimmer-shield. It was a moment before he replied. Cormac stamped his feet against the deck plates. He had only just started to notice how cold it was on the platform. A chill blast came up from below, and there were gleaming nodules of ice on the rails.

"They're out there," said Blegg. "They were building starships before humans stood upright. There're star-spanning civilizations that're millions of years old."

"Oh, tell me more, please," said Cormac, his breath visible before his face.

Blegg grinned at him. "Better," he said.

"So what if they are watching us?"

"We have to be ready. Simple examination by such as them could destroy us. Levels of technology—like Dragon. Even now, our astronomers still think that all pulsars and black holes are natural phenomena. They also express amazement at how lucky the human race has been: a moon to prevent Earth's atmosphere becoming as thick as that of Venus, no large asteroid strikes while our kind developed, the aptly timed Ice Age late in our evolution. It also surprises them how abundant are living worlds beyond Earth."

"I presume there is a point to all this?"

"We squabble. We must be unified, strong and as one. Soon we'll be playing grown-up games. As we are we might not survive."

"Masada?"

"Masada. All of them."

Cormac stared at him and waited. He was sure Blegg was bullshitting him again for his own obscure purposes or amusement. *Give the big picture, fine, but what do I do being only a pixel in that picture?* Blegg turned back to watch as a shutter slowly slid down outside the shimmer-shield.

"Entering underspace," said Blegg, and as Cormac felt the strangeness, the dislocation, he saw that for a moment Blegg had gone translucent, flickering like a hologram. He reached out and touched the other man's shoulder, but he was there. His skin felt hot, fevered. As if he had not noticed the touch, Blegg continued to speak.

"Masada is not a heavily populated world but, under the Theocracy there, life is very cheap. The majority of the surface population would rebel, but they do not because they live at a perpetually enforced technological disadvantage. A grid of laser projectors hangs geostationary over their heads and, as I said before, the Theocracy are building a kinetic launcher to suppress what rebellion there is in the planet's Underworld. That religious order controls them all, and most of its members live safely out of the way in satellite cylinder-worlds. The sheep live a hard life on the surface of the planet."

"Sounds idyllic. What do you want me to do?"

"Thirty hours after the *Occam Razor* takes the position of the Outlink station, it will draw the Line of Polity across the Masadan system. It would be useful if the populace rebelled against oppression, then they could be helped. It would be useful if there was a valid reason for the *Occam Razor* to enter the Masadan system."

Cormac noted the sarcasm. "Why not just move in and take over anyway?" he asked, deciding not to make things easy for Blegg.

"Politics."

"Yeah? Explain."

"Masada is held up as something of an icon for Separatists across human space. It would be nice if our intervention was on the behalf of the populace—useful if the Theocracy was made to look villainous."

"I still don't get it," said Cormac, deliberately stubborn.

"All-out war costs. You should know that. It has always been your job to prevent it."

"How very cynical. I can take the Sparkind down . . . to assist?"

"Yes."

"Anything else?"

"Two of the landing craft on this ship are carrying cargoes of high-tech weaponry."

Cormac considered that for a moment.

"What about the lasers? If they are operating we'll never get landing craft down."

"I am sure you can make a malfunction look plausible."

"Fine. So I have my instructions." Cormac turned away, then quickly turned back. "Before you disappear, tell me, are you human?"

"I was when the *Enola Gay* overflew my home city of Hiroshima. I saw my family incinerated about me and I remained untouched. When I walked out of the city I doubted my humanity."

"You don't talk much like a Japanese."

"I lived in Japan for ten years. I've lived in other places for a lot longer than that."

"I'm supposed to believe this?"

"Look at me. Look at my eyes."

Cormac did as instructed; saw that they were black, with a pinpoint of red, advancing. It suddenly seemed to him he was standing on the platform, without the body of the ship to protect him from the hard radiation of the stars and the incomprehensible distortions of underspace. The red came out and filled the gap. Cormac found himself in a furnace and he recognized the character of that fire. He also understood what Blegg meant when he said there would be "others."

Curled foetally, cold and shivering, on the deck plates, alone, Cormac believed in Blegg.

Lying on the surgical table Thorn could not help but cringe as Stanton swung across the autodoc. Though attached to a long jointed arm extending from the pedestal at the head of the table, the doc itself was indistinguishable from the one Lutz had used on him back on the barge.

"They say travel broadens the mind," said Stanton, calling up a program with the touch-console mounted on the pedestal, and initiating the doc. "Whoever says that wants to try spending a few months inside a ship of this size . . . We get into the cold-coffins as soon as possible, and thaw up as near to our destination as possible."

The autodoc hummed as it came towards Thorn's face, opening out its surgical tools and array of legs like a descending spider. He felt something stab into his face, but before he could react to that his face became like dead meat over his living skull. He attempted to speak, but his mouth just did not work, and all he managed was to issue a few grunting sounds. Seeing bloody implements moving about right over his face, he closed his eyes and tried to ignore the tugging sensations and audible crunching as the doc straightened the cartilage in his nose. Next, he felt a tugging lower down and surmised that the doc was pulling his lips apart so it could get to his broken teeth.

"It's measuring up now," said Stanton.

Thorn opened his eyes and glanced aside to see the man watching the procedure with obvious fascination.

Stanton went on, "You should have hung on to your broken teeth. It could have welded them straight back in. As it is, it has to measure everything and match colour and consistency for the synthebone and enamel. You're lucky, in a way: the doc on the first *Lyric* wasn't anywhere near as sophisticated—you'd have got your teeth back, but they'd probably have been the wrong colour."

Thorn wanted to make some sarcastic comment about being too preoccupied at the time to pick up his teeth. By Stanton's grin, he realized that the mercenary probably guessed exactly what he was thinking.

The droning of a cell-welder now ensued as the doc repaired the damage to the soft tissues of his face. While this was done he ruminated on how "cell-welder" was a misnomer, as an autodoc did not actually repair broken, dying, or dead cells—it removed them and reconnected the tissues that had been parted by breaks, splits or cuts. For more substantial damage, the doc used synthetic or regrown tissues to fill in the gaps—in the case of the synthetics, this tissue was subsequently replaced by the natural healing processes of the body. However, he did not think that any such additions, other than his teeth, would be required for him since everything else was still there—if a little squashed.

"Your face looks like it's exploded," said Stanton. "It always fascinates me how they open you up to make even minor internal repairs."

Thorn reckoned Stanton should have been a surgeon—he seemed to enjoy describing to the patient the processes involved.

Now, as well as that of the cell-welder, came the higher-pitched droning of a bone-welder as the doc fixed into place the teeth it had rapidly manufactured inside itself. There came further tuggings as it checked the security of its welds. With the work of the cell-welder still continuing, Thorn was beginning to wonder just how much damage had been done to his face, when suddenly feeling returned to it and the doc withdrew. He sat up and immediately brought his hand up to his face: he now possessed a new set of front teeth and his nose was back to its customary shape, and all he felt was an ache deep in his gums and his sinuses. He took the mirror Stanton proffered him and inspected the repairs—same old face, but with absolutely no sign that it had been broken.

"You say that you now have the greatest respect for Ian Cormac, and that after Viridian your perspective changed completely. But I still don't see why you saved *my* life. You risked a hell of a lot there," said Thorn, handing back the mirror.

"Haven't you realized?" asked the mercenary as he returned the mirror to its rack. "I'm one of the good guys now."

Thorn, who was an expert when it came to "evil grins," felt that Stanton's took some beating.

It was a huge ship, which was convenient as this meant that there were many places to hide—and right then Skellor wanted to hide. This hold-space was old and obviously had been long unused. The ceramal walls were dull, and on the floor were scattered the wing cases of blade beetles that some time in the past must have briefly infested this area. Many of the wing cases, he noticed, had tiny neat holes punched right through them—a sure sign that small ship drones had used their lasers to clear the infestation.

Skellor dropped down with his back to the cold wall and closed his eyes, connecting himself deep into the Jain substructure and assessing the information presented by the devices it was creating within him. Unconsciously he touched a hand to the woody material that had grown from his collarbone and up the side of his neck to cup his chin and cheek, on the opposite side of his head from his aug. This part of the substructure had grown before he had managed to take control of it, and he had yet to find a way to reverse the process. No matter—he'd find a way.

The detector, which was integral to the entire structure inside him, no longer registered Hawking radiation, and from it he no longer experienced the terrible feeling of *threat*. As far as he was aware, the Polity had no interstellar ships capable of carrying working runcibles, since the devices conflicted with the function of the underspace engines, yet Hawking radiation was a byproduct of a black hole—and it was damned unlikely one of those was aboard—or of runcible function, so what had occurred?

Almost on an instinctive level Skellor knew that something had recently paid the *Occam Razor* a visit, and that same something had rung alarm bells in the Jain structure and in himself. That something, he understood, had represented a great danger to him. But fortunately, it had departed the ship shortly after the ship itself had entered underspace, and now it was time for him to make his plans.

He knew that if the AIs that ran the Polity found out about him and what he had achieved, they would not rest until they had tracked him down. How much more severe would their strictures be upon his work now that he had *become* his work? They would throw him into the deepest hole they could find, and fill it in after him. Now, rather than being a researcher who had found the Separatists convenient allies and generous paymasters, he was essentially a Separatist himself. The Polity was now his enemy—it could be no other way.

So first he needed to know where this ship was heading, how many people there were aboard and who they were— and everything else that he was up against. As yet, he did not have the confidence to attempt gleaning that information directly from the ship AI. Yes, in a very short time he had acquired huge capabilities, but he did not yet think himself ready to go up against an AI of *that* level. However, there were other ways of getting the information he needed that would not require him venturing too deeply into the ship's systems: human beings were easily accessible packets of information in themselves. Of course, it would be convenient if, whilst finding out those things he needed to know, he also acquired some allies.

Skellor attempted a smile, but his face felt stiff. Going deeper into his Jain structure he began to build further useful . . . tools.

The corpse was laid out on a table inside the isolation booth while forensic robots, which were complex nearkin of autodocs, swarmed over it like chrome dung beetles as they investigated and catalogued its structure. Cormac observed this process with a feeling of chill that he had brought up with him from the platform on which he had met Blegg. What he had seen down there . . . what had he seen?

"They were rather touchy, down there," said Mika, as she studied screens and, through the touch-consoles below, tapped in further instructions to the robots.

Down there?

After a moment he realized she was referring to *Elysium* and the difficulties the three Golem had experienced extracting her from that place. He smiled then, remembering her inability to ask direct questions. "They thought they were about to suffer a Polity takeover."

"An understandable reaction," Mika replied, as he turned. She made a pushing gesture with her hand, exposing the tattoo on her palm that signified her graduation from the Life-Coven on the planet Circe—a secretive place that produced some of the best analytical minds for biosciences in the entire sector. Cormac studied her. She had changed only a little since the last time he had seen her: her orange hair was now shoulder-length rather than the crop it had been, her eyes were still demonic red and her skin pale, but she had acquired some bulk on her diminutive frame that had not been there before.

"Have you had a chance to look at the artefacts?" he asked her.

"Briefly," she nodded to the nearby case in which they were contained, "but such items require deep and intensive study."

"Then they are Jain?"

"Oh yes, but in all honesty this thing is much more interesting." She indicated the creature Shuriken had killed in the Separatist base on Callorum, as some of the forensic robots now burrowed inside it. "You realize that this was once a human being?"

"I saw the similarities, but I assumed it was just some bio-construct of Skellor's and left it at that. He's had a tendency to come up with some nasty devices: poisonous snakes directed by microminds, birds with planar explosive packed into their bones, and more recently an organic gun that fires darts which are apparently just grossly enlarged bee stings but can inject the poison or drug of your choice."

"It's surprising he was allowed to remain free," Mika opined.

"We never had anything definite on him until he started taking Separatist pay cheques, so we left him alone in the hope he'd lead us to others, which he did." Cormac grimaced. "Though now I suspect that maybe we left him to get on with his work for a little too long." He gestured to the corpse in the isolation booth. "You said this was once a man."

"Or woman," Mika replied. "I'll have it sexed in a little while, though I can't see what there is to be gained from that. Essentially what Skellor created here is a melding of calloraptor and human being, but that's not the most interesting part: this creature has a nanotech structure inside it that worked very quickly to repair its body."

"Yes, quite," said Cormac with irony.

Mika acknowledged his tone and went on, "Only by damaging its body so severely did you manage to take it beyond its ability for self-repair."

"We don't possess anything like that."

"No, I would say its source is Jain, as our own nano-technologies are just nowhere near as advanced." She gestured to the artefacts. "Though I have to wonder if *they* are that source."

"Meaning?"

"From what little I've learnt from them I know that they are Jain, but they're severely corrupted, and I wonder if any more could be discovered from them than we'd learn from a pot shard about the full extent of the Roman civilization."

"Then Skellor has something else."

"One would think so," replied Mika, gazing past his shoulder to the laboratory's door. He glanced back and saw that Scar had entered and now stood waiting with the usual reptilian patience. Mika continued, "Of course you can ask him yourself once he's found."

Cormac snorted at that. "*If* we find him."

"He won't be able to hide down there on Callorum forever, and the remote sensors Occam dropped will pick up any ship that leaves or arrives," said Mika.

"You're forgetting his chameleonware. I guarantee he has a ship stashed somewhere on the surface, which he'll be able to leave on without being detected," opined Cormac. He turned to Scar, "What do you want here, dracoman?"

"It is not a case of what *he* wants," said Mika, standing and moving past Cormac. "Come in, Scar. Let's start where we left off."

Cormac had also not forgotten Mika's fascination with dracomen . . . and Dragon. That, besides her expertise, was the reason he had brought her along.

The *Occam Razor* came out of underspace five hours earlier than expected, some time after most of the crew had gone into cold-sleep, but before Cormac himself felt the inclination. In a pensive mood since his encounter with Blegg and his discussion with Mika, he immediately demanded to know the nature of the problem. Occam took a moment to reply as it was not a very co-operative AI.

"Distress call," was all it said to him.

Cormac tossed aside the note screen he had been studying,

got off his bed and quickly pulled on his shipsuit and exited the cabin. Perhaps Tomalon might have more to say. Reaching the nearest drop-shaft, he keyed in the deck level from which the bridge pod had previously extended, then he stepped in. On the requisite deck, he quickly found one of the ubiquitous drones, and asked it for directions. Luckily, Occam had not shifted the bridge pod, and soon Cormac was there.

"What have you got?"

Tomalon turned towards him blinking to clear his eyes of the views projected through his link with the ship's sensors. Cormac wondered what it was like—flying the ship, being the ship.

"A landing craft. Looks to be of Masadan manufacture. Life signs evident just for one person, though there may be others in cold-sleep." He nodded to one of the windows and up flickered a view of a battered-looking craft with one of the Occam's grabships heading towards it. This unknown craft was a much smaller version of those ships used to tow asteroids to Elysium.

"The distress signal, what format?" Cormac asked.

"Standard Polity."

"Strange."

The grabship closed on the landing craft like some huge metallic tick, its triple claw unfolding spiderish against the actinic glare of the stars. Slowing to match the speed of the craft and adjusting to match its rotation, the grabship closed its claw and gripped before speeding back to the Occam. When it filled the screen, another view was cast up, from one side, of the grabship decelerating into the maw of a hold: a wasp with captured grub, flying into a hole in the wall of a house. As the hold irised shut behind it, Cormac glanced at Tomalon, who lifted a hand almost concealed in linking technology and gestured to the drone that had just entered.

"I'll take you there," he said.

So that was how much he identified with the ship.

"Have Cento and Aiden meet us there, armed," said Cormac, turning to go.

Tomalon nodded and his eyes went opaque again. The drone turned in midair and led Cormac out. Tomalon was leading him, or the AI, or likely an amalgam of the two.

Was I like that? It had been years since Cormac had been gridlinked, and then he had been variously linked with a series of different AIs. Still, it had dehumanized him, hadn't it?

With the gas giant in its position—at this time of year—of leading the sun by only one quarter-day, Eldene knew, when Calypse disappeared behind the far horizon, that darkness was only a few hours away. When workers headed down the rows of grape trees, carrying the backpack sprays they had been working with all day, Fethan changed course to take the two of them away from any encounter. The sky changed from lavender to deep purple then starlit black, and one of the giant's moons hurtled across above wisps of cloud as if late for an appointment with its Jovian father. Shortly they reached another of the tool sheds they had earlier seen, and Fethan broke into it.

"Don't move from here unless you really have to," Fethan instructed her, handing over Volus's stinger. "I'm going to find some supplies." Fethan winked and slipped out of the door.

Eldene was too tired to protest and, pulling the tarpaulin from a dilapidated electric tractor, found the darkest corner, wrapped herself in the material and bedded down. But all her discomforts conspired to keep her awake: the strange lightness she felt without her scole, the sensitivity of her nipples from where, unsupported by the creature, they had been rubbing against her shirt, the itching pain in her chest where its feeding tubules had penetrated, and the discomfort of having to use a breather unit. Instead of sleeping, she lay back and replayed the long question-and-answer session of that day.

Unlike the tutors at the orphanage, Fethan answered her every question succinctly and never lost patience. Eldene now visualized such wonders as runcibles, Polity battleships, wondrous Earth and the heavily populated Sol system, strange environments adapted for human use, and humans adapted to live in strange environments. She contemplated the idea of godlike AI minds wiser and more intelligent than anything she could have possibly imagined before, of medical technologies that seemed capable of extending people's lives indefinitely . . . the strange creatures and stranger technologies and constructs . . . No, sleep just did not seem possible with all these golden visions playing across her retina. Then the next thing she knew she couldn't breathe, and was scrabbling in the darkness of midnight to find the spare oxygen bottle.

"All right, girl," said Fethan from beside her, with swift precision changing the bottle for her.

"Thank you," she said, as soon as her breathing was back to normal.

"You go back to sleep."

She was about to say something else to him, but with seemingly no transition, Fethan was shaking her by the shoulder and light was beaming in through cracks in the grapewood walls of the tool shed.

Eldene lay there for a moment longer, as she felt so warm and comfortable in the tarpaulin, but then habit beaten into her at the orphanage, and further reinforced by the proctors in the work sheds, had her struggling from the tarpaulin and to her feet.

"Were you gone long . . . in the night?" she asked, hinging her mask down in irritation.

"Few hours," Fethan replied, squatting down to open a large pack resting against the wheel of the electric tractor. From this he held up another oxygen bottle and showed it to Eldene before placing it on the floor.

After taking another quick breath from the mask Eldene asked, "Did you get any sleep?" then could have kicked herself for her stupidity, and was grateful when Fethan offered no patronizing reply.

What came out of the pack next, Eldene smelt before Fethan revealed it to her, and, with her mouth watering, she approached almost involuntarily.

"Sausage," she said reverently as Fethan handed her the huge tube of meat, then shortly removed a loaf followed by a four-pack of wine bottles.

"Remember, this has gotta last you four days," said Fethan.

Eldene heard him, but was too busy relishing her first mouthful of meat in something like four months. She followed this with bread, then with a swallow of wine— something she had tasted a couple of times back at the orphanage. Eating was a rather vexing process with the mask, and Eldene could see why the thing was disposable—no doubt it very quickly became quite filthy.

"Where did you get this?" she asked, finally pausing to take the water bottle Fethan handed her.

"There's a lot of Voluses in the world, though this morning there's one less," Fethan replied.

Eldene stared at him in the dim light of the tool shed as she tried to adjust to the casual killing of yet another proctor for oxygen, food and drink. It came as no surprise to her that such adjustment did not require much effort. She took another bite of sausage, another swallow of wine.

Once Eldene had eaten, and recorked the bottle of wine, having only drunk a quarter of it—she well understood how drinking too much would affect her, having never acquired any tolerance of alcohol, and having experienced the effects of Fethan's lethal brew back at the work sheds—they set out into the new day. Calypse was high in the sky, so they were an hour or more beyond the customary starting time for workers, but none were in sight nor came in sight before the pair reached the fringe of the orchards.

"Why did you brew alcohol if you never needed it?" Eldene asked, as heading through flute grass they skirted a wide area of square ponds where workers were scattered like pawns.

"I brewed it because I could, and it gave some of the team there some comfort," Fethan replied.

"They'd have more comfort not still being there."

"Yes, but how many breather masks do you think I could obtain for them?"

Chastened, Eldene now saved her breath for walking. The new growths of grass, like spikes of green metal tipped with blood, were now a hand's length high and it was walking through these that became difficult. The tall growths of last year were becoming increasingly brittle, however, and disintegrated almost at a touch.

By mid-morning, with both the sun and Calypse well up in the sky, they rested upon a huge tricone shell that was buoyed up by the flute grass rhizomes. This monster shell was three metres long and wide enough at its widest end for Eldene to sit on it without her feet touching the ground. Here she sat drinking water and eating a piece of bread while Fethan walked slowly around the shell itself studying the ancient graffiti carved into its nacreous surface.

"I never knew they got to be this big," said Eldene, around a mouthful of bread.

"Neither did I, but then I wouldn't, as the only ecological survey recorded on the AI net is about three hundred years old and was not produced by the most reliable of sources." Fethan paused with arms akimbo and transferred his gaze up to the sky. Then suddenly, moving very fast, he caught Eldene by the arm, half carrying and half shoving her off the end of the shell. "Get inside! Right now!"

Eldene caught a glimpse of things glinting in the sky as she hurriedly obeyed, Fethan diving into the cone next to her. Once safely inside, she tilted her head to the drone of turbines and immediately recognized the source: a military transport was passing right over them. She risked peeking her head out for a look. The transport was just a huge flat rectangular box with windows down each side, one thruster mounted on a rear tail fin, two air rudders depending below the front two corners, and underneath, the two huge turbines that kept it in the air. The blast from these engines raised a wake of fragments from the dead flute grass below, and the noise was deafening. Accompanying this massive vehicle was a veritable swarm of aerofans. She glanced aside to see Fethan watching the sky as well.

"Still no AG on their transports; Lellan's ahead of them on that," he said.

"What's all this about?" Eldene whispered, though she then wondered why she bothered to keep her voice down—the proctors could not have heard her over the racket generated by the transport's engines.

"Might be because two proctors have been killed in as many days, but I doubt that," said Fethan. "The Theocracy don't care so much for their proctors that they'd mobilize a transport. So I'd say Lellan's been stinging their arses—probably with a supply or worker raid. She likes to keep the bastards on their toes."

"Worker raid?" Eldene queried as the flight faded into the distance and she and Fethan finally crawled from cover.

"She'll normally select a work camp, go in with a transport just like that one, and liberate the lot of them. The only ones in the camp who object are usually the proctors, and their objections last only so long as it takes 'em to hit the ground. Lellan's not what you'd call reasonable when it comes to proctors."

"What about the lasers?" Eldene gestured to the sky.

"There are occasional windows of opportunity—when things can be done on the surface unseen. Before now Lellan has also stolen Theocracy transports and their radio identification codes. It's not something she gets away with very often, but when she does she makes the most of it."

They moved on through the flute grass.

Cento, Aiden and Gant met him as he stepped from the drop-shaft nearest the hold containing the craft. This hold was positioned over a kilometre from the bridge pod. Cormac noted that the two original Golem were in uniform and carried their JMC military-issue pulse-guns. Their expressions were unreadable. By contrast, Gant, whom Cormac was still loath to describe as a Golem, was not in uniform—it looked as if he had hurriedly dressed in whatever was to hand—however, he did carry the same weapon as the other two. Cormac made no comment on his presence. If he was out to prove something here, then let him do so.

"Scan shows only one person in there. There may be others in cold-sleep or undetected by scan. Stay alert. I want at least one alive if possible."

"Aren't we a little over-armed for this?" asked Gant.

"Recommend the softer approach when you've got something to lose," Cormac reminded him.

Gant muttered something filthy and fingered his gun. The drone led them through a sliding door into a cavernous hold, where the landing craft rested at the centre of a plain of ceramal deck plates. The grabship had returned to its rack position in a row of ten against the wall—they looked like giant metal insects clinging to a cliff. As he stepped through the door Cormac studied the captured craft.

It was of an old utile design much used before the introduction of cheap antigravity motors. Its body was a flattened cylinder terminating in a chainglass cockpit, behind which, like shoulders, were two ball-mounted thruster motors capable of firing in any direction. At the rear of the craft, behind another pair of thrusters, were two huge ion engines extruding outwards from the craft, these in appearance being simply two large spheres with the rears sliced off them. It had no landing feet let down and so lay flat on the deck.

The drone accelerated away from them to do one circuit of the craft, then hovered above its airlock which lay between the thrusters on one side. When they finally joined it, Cormac directed Cento and Aiden to the lock itself, not daring yet to touch this craft himself for standing before it was like standing before the open door of a freezer. Cento took hold of the manual wheel and turned it easily. There was a slight rush of air as pressures equalized, and when this door was open far enough, Aiden moved into the lock to release the inner door. Cento quickly followed him in with his pulse-gun ready. Cormac followed on with Gant.

Inside the craft, a skinny youth with bright yellow skin lay flat on his back, with Cento bent over him. Cormac took in the situation in a second and shouted to the drone.

"Drop the gravity—to five per cent, now!"

There was a moment's delay, enough for Aiden to step back into the main body of the craft from the cockpit, which he had been checking out. Cormac's stomach lurched as the gravity changed. He glanced round and saw Gant rising slowly into the air, his embarrassment evident, then returned his attention to Cento.

"Outlinker, unconscious, fractured ankle," the Golem announced after a brief pause.

"There's another in one of the cold-coffins: a woman. But the manifest numbers twenty-five on this craft," said Aiden.

"They're not here?" Cormac asked needlessly. He did not see Aiden shake his head. An Outlinker on a Masadan landing craft, now what did that mean?

"How long, do you think, before I can speak to him?" he asked Cento, who was probing the youth's ankle.

"I'll get him up to Medical, and thereafter it will be Mika's decision."

Cormac nodded and stepped back into the airlock. The drone rapidly backed out of his way into the hold.

"Tomalon, I'd like you to hold position until this is sorted. We could then get a better idea of what we're flying into."

The drone said, "You do not command this ship."

"I know," Cormac replied.

"I can give you twenty hours."

Apis Coolant was conscious in three.

Skellor tracked her as she strode along the walkway, then started to move in after she sent about their business the three drones accompanying her. He wondered for a moment just what sort of ship this was that required human maintenance personnel, then understood that the craft had to be old—perhaps something left over from one of the many conflicts during the early expansion of the Polity. That meant that its AI would not be such a godlike entity as the newer Polity AIs and therefore much of the ship was outside its control—hence the human maintenance personnel. It also meant that this ship probably had an interfaced captain, and perhaps even a command crew. Not knowing his own capabilities just yet, Skellor could not judge whether this would make his task more or less difficult.

Walking soft on the ceramal deck plates, he came up behind her. She wore an aug that had the appearance of faceted sapphire behind which she tucked a strand of her long blonde hair as she glanced up from her note screen and gazed about herself. She could not see Skellor with his chameleonware operating, even though he stood only a few paces behind her. Her aug first, he thought, to prevent her broadcasting a cry for help. He reached out, his hand only inches from her face, and paused to relish the thrill of being this close and yet unseen, of having this much power, then he closed his fingers around her aug and tore it from her head.

She shrieked and ducked down in reflex, blood welling from the spot where he had torn the aug's anchors from the bone behind her ear. Skellor tossed the aug from the walkway and watched it continue along in a straight line into the bowels of the ship, now that it was beyond the pull of the grav-plates. The woman pulled herself upright and looked about in terrified bewilderment. Skellor now took offline the Jain boosting of his body, for he had swiftly learnt that with it operating he had no judgement of his own strength. Then, just as he had been taught by one of the Separatist fight trainers, he side-fisted her temple. Catching her as she slumped, he re-initiated boosting and slung her over his shoulder as easily as if she were a sack of polystyrene. Extending the range of his 'ware field to include her he quickly moved off. Had other people been viewing this attack they would have seen her simply rise into the air and disappear.

One of the drones she had sent away approached down the walkway as he marched along it. Pressing himself against the rail, to allow it past, he smiled to himself—utterly invisible, even to machines with a greater spectrum of senses than a human being.

Soon he reached the abandoned hold, where he lowered the woman to the floor before sealing the door behind him.

Now he had to learn how to take exactly what he wanted. Squatting beside her, he pressed his fingers into the raw wound behind her ear and sent filaments from the Jain substructure through her skin and into her skull. Using the same methods the substructure had employed to connect to his crystal matrix AI and to himself, he connected to her and, adopting the same decoding programs he had earlier used on the structure, he read her mind. First he built a model of her brain in one small memory space in his aug, then, decoding the workings of her mind, he began to transfer across everything that was her. Soon he found that he no longer needed the model and erased it. It was a destructive reading, he found: memories, experiences, skills, understanding . . . all those facets of this human mind he absorbed, but by doing so destroyed their intricate source—it was like memorizing a book and burning each page once it was memorized. When he had finished, he withdrew his fingers and observed that she was still living: still functioning on those autonomous impulses that he had not touched. Grimacing, he touched her again, found the relevant area of her brain, and stopped her heart.

Sitting back, Skellor began the process of editing everything that he had taken. He dumped huge amounts of memory he considered irrelevant, and acquired-skills he himself had already far exceeded. In the end, what remained to him was her knowledge of this ship; of the ship's layout and the location of those areas the *Occam* AI could not see; of the function of automatic systems; of the drones, their connections back to the AI, programming languages—a wealth of knowledge that would enable him to travel throughout the ship undetected even without his chameleonware. From her he also learnt why the ship had so quickly departed Callorum, and viewed through her eyes the destruction of *Miranda* as displayed on the viewing screen in her cabin. He discovered too that there was no command crew, but that there was an interfaced captain. He learnt of the army of Golem in storage, of the five-hundred-strong staff of technicians, crew, maintenance, and ECS—mostly now gone into cold-coffins. Finally he learnt where the Separatist prisoners from Callorum were being held, and realized what his next task would be.

Cormac stepped into Medical and quickly caught hold of the doorjamb before he shot up into the air. The youth lay propped up in a cot, his foot in an auto-doc boot, drug patches on his arms. He was eating ravenously from a well-stacked plate. Bright-eyed he glanced up at Cormac. Then, remembering something, his expression became bewildered.

"You're Cormac," he said.

Cormac nodded and moved carefully across the carpeted floor to take a seat by the cot. Abrupt changes in gravity took some getting used to, but any higher than it was at that moment would have been uncomfortable for the youth.

"You're Earth Central Security," Apis added.

"That I am," said Cormac.

"I killed them."

Cormac looked at him carefully. *Twenty-three Masadans?*

"Perhaps you'd better start at the beginning. You are from station *Miranda* I take it?"

"Yes."

"Tell me what happened to you."

Apis did that. When the boy finished, it was Cormac who felt bewildered. So, Dragon definitely was involved—but how? That question would have to wait for the moment.

"It's doubtful you'll be tried for murder. What you did, you did in self-defence, no matter the number killed." Cormac put his hand gently on Apis's shoulder. "If anything, I congratulate you. These Masadan soldiers sound like fanatics and, from what I've heard, seem likely to have been responsible for many deaths." He took his hand away. The youth looked relieved, but that might be because Cormac had not crushed his shoulder. "As for your mother, Mika is having her moved to a cold-coffin up here, where she can more easily make a diagnosis. Mika is good, and I have no doubt your mother will soon be conscious and well. Tell me, do you have any idea why Dragon attacked the ship?" Apis shook his head. "How far did this attack take place from where the station was destroyed?"

"I don't know—we went into U-space. It'll be in the landing craft guidance computer."

Cormac nodded. Occam would have downloaded that information by now.

"Have you any idea why the Masadans took you and your fellows off the station?"

"Not to rescue us . . . though that's what they said. But they made some of us work in the engine room of their ship. Mother said we were to be slaves."

Null-gee construction, thought Cormac: Outlinkers would make excellent station builders.

"That's all for now. I'll leave you to finish your meal."

In the bioscience section adjoining Medical, Cormac found Mika seated with her feet up on a workbench while she studied a portable screen.

"How's the mother?" he asked.

"She'll take a while. She had a fractured skull and a cerebral haemorrhage. I'm leaving her in cold-sleep for the present while I check my files here on Outlinker physiology." She nodded down at the screen she was holding.

Cormac moved further into the room and gazed into the isolation booth containing the thing he had killed on Callorum. Suddenly it just didn't seem as important now.

"Tomalon . . . Ship!" he said.

"What is it?" the ship AI asked abruptly.

"Do you have the co-ordinates of the Dragon attack on the Masadan craft?"

"Of course."

There then came a strange whining muttering sound followed by a sharp snapping. Like a vessel filling from the bottom with flesh, Tomalon appeared in the middle of the room.

"Yes, we have the co-ordinates," he said, taking over from Occam.

"I didn't know you had holojectors on this ship," said Cormac.

"Only in some sections. The *Occam Razor* was being refitted, prior to being called out to Callorum."

Cormac considered that: this ship was an old one and, though powerful, was in many ways far more primitive than other Polity ships.

"Can you take us to the co-ordinates of that attack?" he asked.

A moment's displacement had the room wavering and Tomalon's image flickering on and off, then it stabilized—they had dropped into U-space.

"In transit," said Tomalon, confirming this.

Cormac turned to Mika, who wore a puzzled expression. "Did you ask the boy about what happened to him?" he asked, trying not to put too much irony into his voice.

With a flash of irritation she replied, "I didn't need to ask. He needed to tell someone."

"Then you realize things are starting to get complicated."

"They always do when you are involved," she replied, returning her attention to her screen.

Cormac studied Mika until there came a further feeling of displacement as the *Occam Razor* rose back out of underspace. Returning his attention to the Captain's hologram, he observed it sliding sideways to pause by a console and screen probably used to run research programmes. The screen came on and lights played around the touch-pads of the console, as it no doubt linked into the ship's ubiquitous communications channels.

"We are there now," said Tomalon, his mouth moving but his voice issuing from the console.

Cormac walked over and stared at the screen. It showed him a spreading cloud of twisted lumps of metal tumbling through the void; the hazy glitter of metallic particles and a fog of gases. One large tangle of wreckage contained a dull red glow, and vapour was spilling from this out into space.

"Identify," he said flatly.

"Everything you would expect," said Tomalon. "The remains of a ship torn apart: hull plates, insulation, gas, and corpses."

Now a square isolated the glowing tangle of wreckage and the view closed in on that. Clinging to a twisted structural member projecting from the tangle were two bloated human shapes—one with bright red skin and one with skin of a golden yellow.

"Dead?"

"They are all dead," Tomalon replied. "These two probably died before the others out there, because that glow you see comes from a broken atomic pile."

"Anything else within scanning range?" Cormac asked, glancing behind when Mika came to stand at his shoulder.

"Four hundred kilometres out there is what remains of a landing craft—the twin of the one our friend Apis occupied. Nothing alive there either. I've been close-scanning all debris in the area for survivors, but there are none." Tomalon paused and a strange muttering issued from the console as if he was exchanging a comment or two with someone nearby him—obviously some spillover from his link with Occam. He went on, "Extending the range of scans now."

"A waste of life," said Mika.

"Death always is," Cormac replied.

"Life-form detected," Tomalon said suddenly, his voice containing that rough edge that was something of Occam.

"Where?" Cormac asked.

"Two light days along our projected path."

"Identify."

"Spherical creature one kilometre in diameter. Ninety-eight per cent projection: Dragon."

"Now the shit hits."

Mika had no comment on that. Tomalon merely flickered out of existence.

7

The woman studied instrumentation for a short while and the boy, knowing the importance of those things she did, contained his impatience, and turned his attention to the toys scattered on the floor all about him. Shortly the woman was satisfied with what she was seeing and returned her attention to the book.

"Out of the wilderness Brother Malcolm came at last to the house of the gabbleducks and lifting the latch, he entered said domain. Upon the table were three bowls, and thus Brother Malcolm said, 'I was hungry and so I was fed.' And sampled only a little from each bowl of food, for he was a pious and ungreedy man."

The woman paused as she scanned back through the text. "Ungreedy?" she repeated, whilst the picture in the book showed the great slob of the Brother tucking into a huge mound of food on the table.

"Fatso," said the boy, pointing at the man's picture.

"Just so," said the woman, then went on. "Even after so small a meal, Brother Malcolm found weariness descending upon him, to hook lead weights in his eyelids. Moving then to the other rooms of the house, he found three beds. The largest of these that he tried was too hard, and he could find no rest. The medium bed was too soft, and he could find no rest there either. However, the smallest bed was just right, and he slept the sleep of the just."

In the picture, the great fat Brother had not managed to haul his bulk up onto either of the large beds, and so chose a small bed that sagged under his weight and out of the end of which stuck his feet clad in filthy socks with red and white stripes.

*

The mountains were close enough now for Eldene to discern snow on their upper slopes and dark occlusions of vegetation fingering up from the plains that abutted below. From the slope they stood upon—a rampart of earth that divided croplands from the wilderness of Masada—she gazed out upon this scene with some trepidation. It had taken most of the day to get this far, and as yet there had been little danger of note. However, she wondered if the heavy mesh fence that now stood behind them was there to keep people in or to keep something out—something it was obviously ineffective at doing, as they themselves had scrambled over it in minutes. Her worries increased when Fethan took the stinger from her and handed her Proctor Volus's gun in return, then instructed her in its use.

"It's powered up for one magazine, but that's okay because that's all we've got. There are five rounds in each disc of the magazine, and seven discs in total," Fethan said, displaying the cylinder he had extracted from the butt of the gun before clicking it back into place. "Simple firing mechanism: the trigger's electrical, so it's very light and easy to use. You hold it down on one pull to get continuous fire for each disc—that's the five rounds. One press and release gives you one shot. Double press and hold down, and the gun will empty its entire cylinder—that's thirty-five shots discharged in about five seconds. Be very careful with this. I don't want to be picking bullets out of my syntheskin every time you get a little nervous." He handed the weapon over and Eldene accepted it as if she was taking a poisonous snake.

"Why am I likely to need this now?" Eldene inquired. "Surely I needed it more back there."

Fethan grinned at her. "Oh, it's not exactly a halcyon wilderness out here."

"Any safer than back there?" Eldene asked, gesturing with the gun.

"Safer, mostly—and at least out here there's no chance of you getting trigger-happy and killing innocent workers."

"What am I likely to have to defend myself from, here?" Eldene asked as they descended the slope into head-high flute grass.

"Heroynes, siluroynes and mud snakes," Fethan replied.

Eldene snorted, remembering a book of fairy tales amongst the precious few books the orphanage had possessed. "Yes, and no doubt there's gabbleducks and hooders that I'll need to use one of my precious three wishes against," she said.

Pushing into the grass, Fethan replied, "*Quince Guide* has those last two both listed, along with pictures of them, and Gordon tells of a hooder attack on one of the first survey teams. I myself have only ever seen gabble ducks, though I know of others who have lost friends to hooders, and some who are convinced that they are destined to go the same way."

"You are kidding?" said Eldene.

Fethan glanced back at her. "Oh no, it's all part of the cycle of life here: the tricones feed on decaying matter filtering down through the soil, mud snakes feed on tricones that get too close to the surface, and heroynes feed on them in turn. Gabbleducks, siluroynes and hooders apparently feed on the many different varieties of grazers that eat the flute grass. All the predators I've named, if large enough, will take a stray human if he's careless, though human flesh tends to make them ill."

"You *are* kidding," said Eldene, thinking she really did not ever want to run into anything capable of feeding on that huge tricone they had seen earlier.

"Keep your weapon handy and your eyes open," Fethan replied.

Travelling along gullies and across the occasional flats—in which black plantains and the volvae nodules of rhubarbs sprouted from mats of roots—was easiest, but to remain on course they did have to push their way through stands of flute grass. However, closer to the mountains, the stands became less numerous and they were able to pick up their pace. Twice they crossed flattened trails through the vegetation, and on both occasions Fethan pointed to the ground and said, "Mud snake." By midday the ground began to rise and dry out, and here sparse stands of grass contained sprouts of new growth that were waist-high. Here the blister moss grew in clumps as large as footballs and there were occasional lizard-tail plants curving five metres into the air. These were clad in scales coloured in a clashing combination: purple at the tips, ranging to green, then orange at their roots. Some hours into evening, Fethan called a halt at a rocky outcrop where the ground was at its highest before dropping back into another plain of flute grass.

"Best we stop here," said Fethan. "I can hear if something approaches, but mud snakes tend to hunt at night and one could easily grab you from below."

"Or you," Eldene suggested as she wearily sat down on a contorted stone.

"Or me, yes, but I'd still be in one piece after their attack."

Eldene unstoppered her water bottle, flipped her mask down, and took a drink. Opening and closing the mask was now becoming second nature to her, and curiously, she no longer felt that nakedness at the absence of her scole. She felt free.

Studying the stone she was sitting on, she saw that it was covered with small translucent hemispheres that she at first took to be some sort of mineral. On closer inspection, she saw that something was moving inside each hemisphere, so she quickly stood and moved away.

"They're all right," Fethan assured her, reaching over, snapping one of the things from the rock with his thumb, and showing Eldene the underside. A greenish fleshy sucker clenched at the air for a moment and a single globular palp-eye extruded. When Fethan returned it to its place the creature turned round once as if getting comfortable, sucked its eye back in then pulled down flat against the stone. "If you start to run out of food you can give 'em a go," he added. "They're a delicacy in the Underworld, though they tend to cause flatulence, which is not an admirable condition for someone sharing a cave."

Eldene giggled, then giggled again—then found she could not stop laughing. She sat down with her back against the stone and tried to get herself under control. Looking up at Fethan's puzzled expression, she completely lost it and was laughing so much she had tears running down her face. When finally she got a grip on herself—mostly because her laughter was now hurting the injury her scole had left on her chest—she glanced up to see Fethan squatting on the ground before her.

"You better now, girl?" the old man asked.

Eldene nodded and looked around as night sucked the last dregs of light out of the twilight. Shadow surrounded her, and a touch of a breeze was eliciting faint music from the grasses.

"I never thanked you for saving me," she said.

"It's what I do," Fethan replied, standing and unhooking the pack to drop it beside her. "You get some rest now, and I'll watch over you."

Eldene removed from the pack the tarpaulin she had taken from the tool shed they had stayed in the night before, and wrapped herself in it. Again, sleep seemed to elude her, but then crept up behind her with a brick.

In the Security Area, Cardaff sent two diagnostic programs into the system. One came back with nothing, and the other with a corrupted locking code from one of the outer sections: SA34. Had the corrupted code been in SA1, Cardaff would have been worried, as that was where they held the thirty prisoners. He glanced at the relevant screen and saw that the men and women there, in their ship-issue overalls and security collars, were still in conference. Occam assured him that these people could not link with their biotech augs outside SA1—the walls were so heavily shielded and the augs had no underspace facility.

"Anything on what they're discussing?" he asked Shenan.

The Golem Twenty-seven turned from her console and screen, exposing needle fangs in a smile, and not for the first time he wondered why she had chosen the outer appearance of an ophidapt.

"Their conferencing link is deeply coded and the technology, as we know, alien. Occam estimates it will take two days to crack the codes. Meanwhile we are recording everything," she explained.

"Best guess?" he asked.

"Probably discussing how they might escape, whether or not they will be sentenced to mind-wipe, and how best to retain whatever secrets they have. No doubt fanatics amongst them are putting forward the idea of mass suicide."

"Completely crazy," muttered Cardaff.

"Did you trace that glitch?" Shenan asked.

"Yeah, corrupted code out at 34 . . . shit! I've got another one in SA20." Cardaff punched up views of the relevant section and got nothing but empty corridor, an open security door, and an empty confinement section beyond. "What the fuck is going on here?"

Shenan moved over and stood at his shoulder. Reaching down past him, she punched up a floor plan of the relevant sections and pointed. "The two doors that opened are in a line to the centre here, but SA26 is between. Have you had anything from the security door there?"

Cardaff brought up a view of that door, and checked the readouts before him. "No, nothing. No problem at all," he said.

Shenan tapped a sharp fingernail against the screen. "Except," she said, "that your readout indicates the door as closed and it quite evidently is not."

"Great." Cardaff hit the panic button and the response, rather than the flashing of lights and the squawking of klaxons he had hoped for, was that the console and screens before him went offline. He turned and stared at Shenan.

"I can't transmit out of here," said the Golem. She glanced across to her console, and almost as if in response to this, it too went offline.

Cardaff stood, marched across the room and palmed the touch-plate of the weapons locker. This at least did work and the door sprang open to reveal riot stun-guns, two pulse-rifles, and an assortment of hand weapons. He pulled out one pulse-rifle and tossed it towards Shenan before selecting the same for himself.

"Looks like we got problems," he commented.

"Yes," said Shenan, turning as the door to the room slid open onto the darkened corridor beyond.

Cardaff dropped down behind his console and sighted his rifle on the door. Shenan merely moved back, with her weapon held loosely. It was all right for her, thought Cardaff: Golem Twenty-sevens did not have much to fear in this world. There was a flicker, some sort of distortion in the air, then utter stillness, and Cardaff could feel the hairs prickling on the back of his neck. He had seen nothing come through that door, but this particular nothing certainly had presence.

"Chameleon—" Shenan managed, before something picked her up and slammed her into a wall of screens. She dropped out of their ruin with clothing ripped and syntheskin torn from her cheek. She fanned fire before herself, and her shots must have hit home for there came a bubbling snarl from the air and something searing hot gripped her head and yanked her from the ground.

Cardaff had never heard a Golem scream, and never seen one taken out so quickly. Shenan was discarded and thumped to the floor like a sack of tools—her head a blackened and misshapen thing. Cardaff opened up, fanning his own fire in the area where . . . it had been. There were a few hits, clearly, and again that snarling, then all that was happening was that he was trashing the systems mounted in the wall beyond. Half a second after he ceased firing, something feverishly warm pressed against the side of his head, and that warmth spread into his head, and grew hooks.

Cardaff reached up and slapped his hand against another hand—febrile and slippery to the touch. Suddenly his head felt full of hot wires and he screamed, turning as he did so. Now he saw who was standing behind him.

"Interesting," grated Skellor, tilting his own head as best he could.

Cardaff could feel himself going, draining away through that hot touch. The sight faded from his right eye, then his hearing went. He groped for Skellor's arm with his other hand, tried to bring his pulse-rifle to bear. Skellor shook his hand as if to dislodge an irritating insect. For Cardaff . . . nothing.

"Well, it didn't get away unscathed," said Gant.

They all looked at the view projected on the screen in the bridge pod. The Dragon sphere hung, apparently lifeless, in space—a damaged moon of glittering jade and charcoal. A large segment of it had been charred, and huge black bones protruded into the void like the ruins of some vast cathedral. Around it orbited shed scales and other fragments of its body that had broken away, and this debris was now settling into an orbiting ring. There were no other signs of movement.

"The damaged area is highly radioactive," said Tomalon.

Cormac glanced at him then around at the others seated in the arc of command chairs. The presence of such chairs told him how old the *Occam Razor* was, since obviously it had been built when such ships required pilots, navigators, gunners and the like, and in subsequent refittings the chairs had not been removed. Tomalon's presence told him that the *Occam Razor*'s AI was also old, for the newer battleship AIs did not require human captains to implement or make judgements on their decisions. It was not that AIs were now more trustworthy; it was simply because humans no longer controlled the Human Polity.

"*Only* the damaged area is radioactive," said Mika.

Tomalon did not deem this as a question, so Cormac asked of him, "Is that so?"

"Yes, it would appear to be the case. And that is not normal."

Cormac studied Tomalon. While all of them were looking at the screen, the Captain turned his head aside, his eyes unseeing opaque, and his mind linked to the ship's sensors.

Mika said, "This means it is either dead or has shut down its circulatory system to those areas. Any living creature receiving a radioactive wound soon ends up with the rest of its body contaminated as well."

"It has a circulatory system?" asked Cormac.

"Yes—though what circulates is not blood as we recognize it. Much more complex. Dracomen have the ability to consciously alter what their circulatory system carries, so we can presume Dragon has the same ability. I would very much like a sample of that substance now."

I bet you would.

Cormac turned his attention to the dracoman who had come up with Mika from Medical. Scar stood behind the chairs—he found human seating arrangements difficult—his attention fixed firmly on the screen. Cormac wondered just what was going through his head. Scar possessed curiosity, and the need to survive, but few recognizably human motivations beyond that, and that kilometre-wide sphere of living matter out there was the twin of the one that had created him.

"If your hand was exposed to that level of radioactivity, what would you do?" Cormac asked him. Mika turned and inspected the dracoman with intense curiosity. Scar's gaze slid to Cormac.

"What level?" the dracoman asked.

Cormac nodded to the screen where Tomalon had obligingly supplied the figures.

"Cut it off. Grow another," said Scar after inspecting those figures.

Mika's eyes widened in shock. Cormac hoped she had now learnt just how informative direct questioning could be.

"And if the contamination affected more vital organs?" he asked.

"Isolate organs. Drop to minimal function. Grow more."

"Do you think this is what this Dragon sphere is doing?"

By now, most of those on the bridge were staring at Scar. Even the Captain had come back from the ship's sensors and was watching. Aiden and Cento had turned as one to watch and listen. Gant, moodily slumped in his chair, was the only one with his attention still on the screen. He seemed to be trying to outstare Dragon. Scar was a long time in replying.

"Maybe," he said finally.

"What alternatives are there?"

"Dying," said Scar.

They all turned back to look at the screen, except for Mika, who was fiddling with some instruments in the top pocket of her coverall and gazing speculatively at Scar. No doubt the dracoman was in for another battery of tests, and it was lucky for Mika that he did not seem to mind.

"What does deep scan of the undamaged areas reveal?" asked Cormac.

Tomalon's eyes went opaque again and he spoke consideringly.

"There are signs of life, but I cannot tell if they are normal or not."

"The temperature would be a good indicator," suggested Mika.

"A range between twenty and thirty Celsius, nominally twenty-two a metre under the skin," said Tomalon.

"I would say it is not dead, or has died only recently," said Mika, checking figures on her laptop. "It would take some time for it to cool, as it is well insulated. But if it had died shortly after its attack on the Masadan ship, its temperature would be well below twenty by now."

"Send an all-radio-band signal to it. See if we get a reaction," said Cormac.

"Is that a good idea?" asked Gant, still staring broodingly at the screen. "Wouldn't it be better to stick a missile in it, then move off?"

Cormac had already considered that, but there were things to learn, and even a fully capable Dragon sphere would not have been much of a problem to the *Occam Razor*.

"Things to learn," he therefore said simply.

"Rise in temperature in a lobular structure at its centre," said Tomalon.

"The brain," explained Mika.

"I'll speak to it," said Cormac. "Send my voice." Tomalon nodded to him and he continued, "Dragon, this is Ian Cormac. Please respond."

On the screen, there were signs of movement. Tomalon brought up another view, this one close to the edge of the damaged area: pseudopodia were breaking from a scaled plain of flesh, blue eyes directed towards the *Occam Razor*.

"Cormac," said Dragon—and that was all it said for some time.

"Dragon?"

"I . . . listen . . . you will kill me now?"

"Not unless that's what you want."

"Vengeance!"

"For what?"

"The engines . . ."

"What about the engines?"

"They turned them on."

"This is how you were damaged?"

Silence.

Cormac asked, "Is there any way we can help you?"

Silence.

"Dragon, why did you attack the Masadan ship?"

"Vengeance!"

"Please explain."

"You will help me?"

"If I can."

"They used it on the station."

"Station *Miranda*?"

Silence.

"Are you talking about the mycelium?"

"They used it on the station."

"Did you provide them with it?"

"Yes."

Cormac looked around at the others in surprise. He had not expected so direct an answer. Dragon was the antithesis of Mika: whereas she disliked asking questions, Dragon disliked answering them.

"Why did you provide them with it?"

Silence.

"How did they tell you they were going to use it?"

"Prevent runcibles on Masada."

"So you attacked their ship because they did not use the mycelium for its intended purpose? Is this what you are saying?"

"Blamed me! Vengeance!"

Cormac glanced at Tomalon and made a cutting gesture with the edge of his hand.

"Communications link cut," said the Captain.

"What a load of bollocks," said Cormac. He looked to the others. "What do you think?"

"It could be true," said Mika. "This is not the same sphere as the one you destroyed at Samarkand. They are not all necessarily hostile. It could be this area is its hideaway and it considered the Masadans its allies."

Cormac made no comment on that. Mika had her reasons for looking as kindly on Dragon as he himself looked unkindly. He glanced to Cento and Aiden.

Aiden said, "It would be interesting to know what Dragon was to receive in exchange for the mycelium—and if it received it."

"Yes." Cormac nodded approvingly: clear thinking is thinking necessarily separated from glands and all the other paraphernalia of humanity. He turned to Gant.

"I agree, grudgingly," said Gant. "Its attack may have been because it received no pay-off. It's doubtful Dragon would care that much about how the mycelium was used. We know human life means nothing to it."

Mika said, "You are still judging this Dragon sphere by the actions of the one at Samarkand. You have to remember that the four of them separated twenty-seven years before."

"Does it matter?" asked Gant. They all looked at him and he shrugged. "The Masadans destroyed the station—all the evidence points that way—and this Dragon sphere had given them the mycelium. If they had used it on a runcible, there would still have been deaths. I say put a missile in it."

A definite point.

"I think you are overreacting," said Mika, staring at Gant analytically. "You have not yet recovered from your death."

Low blow.

Gant took that in good humour, but Cormac could see that he was formulating a slap-down retort. But much as he would have liked to see the results of such a confrontation, there was work to do. He cut in with, "The situation in the Masadan system is my main concern and anything I can learn about that situation, before jumping into it, I will be glad of. For this reason: no missile."

"And what will this 'jumping in' involve?" asked Gant, grinning.

"You will all be briefed when I consider the time right." *And when I know what the fuck I'm going to do.*

The bay was large and crowded with shuttles flown in from the huge conglomeration of ships outside, and with small ships like *Lyric II*. As he walked down the ramp from his ship, with a small flat briefcase held close to his side, Stanton watched another ship—this one a sharp metallic cone—easing in through the huge shimmer-shield that prevented air, people and ships from exploding out into space. Quickly catching up with him, Jarvellis linked her arm through his and gestured back towards *Lyric II*. "You know, friend Thorn will see we've taken on more cargo when we do wake him," she said.

Stanton nodded as he observed the cone-ship swinging into its allocated docking area. "Tough," he said. "I just don't want a Polity agent stepping on my heels—especially here." Gesturing to another ship nosing in through the shimmer-shield—this one a flattened ovoid of red metal with stubby wings terminating in ion engines the shape of caraway seeds—he continued, "Another one. I think about half the ships here I already saw at Huma, running arms for the Separatists."

"As did we too," Jarvellis pointed out.

"As did we," Stanton allowed, "but we learnt better. I don't reckon Dreyden quite realizes just how nasty the Polity can get."

Jarvellis squeezed his arm. "Of course he does, darling. He knows it's just a matter of balance. He knows that somewhere there's an AI comparing the likely loss of life here if there was a Polity takeover against lives lost as a consequence of the illegal arms trade. I would also guarantee that this place is scrutinized very closely—and at least here the Polity can do that quite easily. Out-Polity dealing is a little more difficult to keep track of."

"I'd have gone Out-Polity," said Stanton, "if I didn't know for damned sure the Polity want me to have these particular items." Stanton remembered how the dealer on Huma, after selling him the bulk of *Lyric II*'s cargo, had then told him how the drug manufactories could only be obtained here—and that other special items could also be obtained here. Stanton also remembered the watchers in the streets of Port Lock on Huma—Golem every last one of them.

Jarvellis said, "I think you credit them with far too much deviousness—when you have ships capable of wasting planets, you don't have to be devious, just careful not to step on something you might have wanted to preserve . . . Ah, here come those charmers, Lons and Alvor."

Stanton looked across at the two men making their way towards him. Whatever could be said about their charm or otherwise, Stanton knew that these two men were consummate professionals. As he understood it, Dreyden, having climbed so high, was beginning to realize just how far he could fall, and was becoming a bit twitchy about the possibility of Polity intervention here, and starting to clamp down on the arms trade. These two men maintained the fragile balance despite Dreyden's often idiotic meddling: they allowed enough arms to be passed on to the Separatists to prevent *Elysium* becoming a target, but kept the quantity supplied low enough to keep ECS from doing anything drastic against them.

"Good to see you," he said to Lons, who as always stayed a few paces back from Alvor and acted the silent heavy—a position that led people to make the misguided assumption that he was secondary to Alvor and less intelligent. Stanton, however, knew that they had equal standing below Dreyden, and, if anything, Lons was the sharper of the two. Lons nodded, and Stanton turned to Alvor who always did the talking.

"Alvor," he said.

"Good to see you, John Stanton. And as always it is a pleasure to see you, Captain Jarvellis," said Alvor, grinning his chrome grin.

"I can't say the pleasure's mutual," said Jarvellis. "But I think you are already aware of that."

Stanton knew that these two had a history, but what lay between them was not hate, just a kind of lazy bickering. Had it been hate, he would have wanted to know why, and then would probably have to kill Alvor.

"Do you have my cargo ready?" said Jarvellis.

"Of course. The main package can be loaded right now." Alvor looked pointedly at the briefcase Stanton carried. "And the two extra items you ordered are with Dreyden, who would like to extend his hospitality."

Stanton considered suggesting Jarvellis should stay with the ship, when he saw her expression, but knew she would refuse.

"Then we accept," said Stanton.

Alvor grinned again, and rested his forefinger against his aug in a somewhat effeminate gesture. "And so your main cargo is on its way. Will we require locking codes?" he said.

"Lyric will handle it," said Jarvellis.

The two men turned to keep pace, as the four advanced across the bay.

"Oh yes, you have an AI on this ship," said Alvor. "Do you trust it?"

"More than I'd ever trust you," replied Jarvellis.

"That's nice," said Alvor as they moved on out of the bay.

"I am dying."

Cormac was alone in his cabin when Dragon told him that. He was lying on his bed transmitting through the submind. No doubt Tomalon would be listening in, but there was not much Cormac could do about that, nor wanted to.

"Is there no way we can help you?"

Silence.

"There is a very good xenobiologist on this ship and the bioscience facilities are the best." Cormac thought his offer faintly ridiculous. Got any wound dressing that's a quarter of a kilometre wide? And how about ten thousand gallons of unibiotic?

"Why would you want to help me?"

"Why not?"

"You avoided the contract killers."

Ah.

"It was you then, not your fellow I killed at Samarkand—or the other two?"

"They are far from here."

"Did you organize things through the Masadans?"

Silence.

"How long until you die?"

"I will have vengeance first."

"What are you waiting for, then?"

"Take me there."

Cormac chewed that one over. "You've lost the ability for trans-stellar flight."

"Yes."

"Why should I help you kill people?"

Silence.

"What would you do if we transported you to Masada?"

"Destroy until destroyed."

"And how much damage could you do?"

"Enough."

"I couldn't be a party to such *indiscriminate* destruction."

"Vengeance!"

"You're repeating yourself, but your impulse could serve my purposes."

Silence.

"We could transport you there. In return, I would want you to *only* attack orbital facilities. This we can enforce. You are aware of the capabilities of this dreadnought?"

"I am aware."

"Specifically, then: geostationary over the populated area of Masada are laser arrays. Destroy them—only them. Is it agreed?"

"Agreed."

Cormac cut communication.

"You trust this creature?" asked Tomalon.

Cormac kept his annoyance from his voice. "No. But if it attacks anything other than the laser arrays, we can destroy it and be lauded as saviours."

"And after it has destroyed the arrays?"

"Likewise. The crew of that Masadan ship, I have very little concern about, but I'll not soon forget those Outlinkers that died out there."

Skellor gazed from one to the other of the two individuals he had killed: one Golem and one human. As he subsumed the experience of their lives—their knowledge and understanding, and anything else that might be of relevance to him—he could not help but make comparisons. The heart of the Golem's mind, once he had discarded layers of emulation programs, was all logic and clarity and thoroughly documented storage of life-experience and knowledge. The heart of this Cardaff's mind, however, was something that snarled and had to be immediately erased—life-experience and acquired knowledge sitting in layers over this primal animal. As—in the quartz-matrix AI that was an *extension* to his own mind—he sorted all that he had acquired, he began to feel disappointment. Increasingly he found himself discarding irrelevancies until very little was left. All that remained were a few experiences, all that these two knew about the *Occam Razor*, and memories of places to which he had never been. So much dross stored by both Golem and human mind alike.

Moving to the nearest console, Skellor pressed one grey hand down on it and let the filaments flow down into its workings. Soon he found what he was searching for and the console came back online. He gazed at the screen showing the thirty Separatist prisoners. They were *conferencing* through their augs: probably trying now to decide what best to do for the cause. Skellor berated himself for the surge of contempt he felt—they had been useful to him, and would be useful again. With a thought he initiated the program that downloaded the information virus he had been working on into the Jain substructure that interpenetrated his body and was also an extension of himself. The Dracocorp augs had been a very useful tool for the Separatists and now for himself they would become a useful tool. Having an organic basis made them so much more *accessible*.

Moving out of the control area Skellor marched down the corridor just as the lights came back on. Soon reaching the armoured door into SA1, he punched in the code he had stripped from Cardaff's mind, before pressing his hand against the palm-lock. Now the DNA he had stripped from the man's body enabled him to cause enough of a delay in which to shoot in filaments and subvert the lock's security program. The lock thunked and the door slid open.

"Skellor," gasped Aphran, groping for where she usually kept her QC laser. She didn't trust him—none of them did after he had moved back from the development of chameleonware for them to his own *work*.

"Glad to see me?" Skellor smiled.

Aphran was a number of paces away from him, but a boy called Danny stood close enough. Skellor recalled all their names since his change. Nothing he had viewed or known previously was now inaccessible to him. Being direct-linked into the quartz-matrix AI had given him perfect recall as well as huge processing capabilities. Being extended by the Jain substructure enabled him to use those capabilities to devastating effect in the real world. He reached out and caught hold of Danny's shoulder. The boy froze—at first in fear, then because Skellor reached inside him and blocked the relevant nerves.

"Now," Skellor said. "You'll be glad to know that you are going to help me to take over this ship." Taking his hand from Danny's shoulder, he transferred it to the Dracocorp aug behind the boy's ear, and cupped the device in his hand. It felt cold to him, but then very little didn't now.

"Take over an ECS dreadnought?" Aphran sneered.

Skellor nodded as the filaments flowed into the aug and sought out the right connections. Once he found them and connected, he loaded the virus. The boy grunted as if he had been punched. Aphran, her face pale with fear, slapped her hand against her own aug, but the virus was transmitting now and she could do nothing. Skellor folded his arms and watched as she lost her balance and went over. All around the others started to fall over as well. The convulsions hit shortly after, and many of them now were showing the whites of their eyes. Three of them started screaming, which confirmed for him his calculation of a seven to thirteen per cent loss. Stepping further into the Security Area he watched those three die, then waited for the others to recover.

"What have you done?" Aphran asked him as she recovered enough to pull herself to her knees. One of her eyes was bloodshot, the other entirely red. Blood was also seeping from her right ear.

"Just ensuring that you do as you're told," he said. "Now, stand up."

The remaining twenty-seven stood as one, then stared at each other in confusion. Aphran was noticeably grimacing.

"Fight it," warned Skellor, "and it will cause you increasing pain until it kills you. Now, come with me." They followed.

After collecting a meal and a small bottle of wine from his room's dispenser, Cormac sat down to enjoy them while the room's screen displayed an image of Dragon before him. First pouring out a glass of wine, he then peeled back the meal's wrapper and stared for a moment at what might laughingly be described as a roast dinner, then took up a fork and started stabbing at the odd item of food.

Gant's suggestion that they should put a missile into the creature was perfectly understandable, but how perfect a situation they could manufacture instead by having Dragon attack the Masadan laser arrays. Now having accessed the files transmitted by ECS, Cormac had more of a grasp of what was going on there. There was a special neatness about using Dragon, because of the Theocracy's claim that they were building the launcher to protect themselves from this creature. Cormac was not entirely sure what agreements had been broken, but he very much suspected the Masadans of being terrified of Polity subsumption, and of gaining what allies they could—those including both Separatist groups and Dragon. With their arrays being attacked, the *Occam Razor* would of course have to go and *assist* the Masadans—after a suitable delay—and then . . . Then perhaps ECS could learn, very *loudly*, of the oppression of Masada's surface populace and their wish to become part of the Polity.

"Show me the Masadan solar system," he said.

The screen changed to show him precisely what he had requested: Masada itself orbiting within the so-called green belt which supposedly made it habitable for humans. Not very much further out from it orbited a gas giant named Calypse that must loom large in its sky. Numerous moons surrounded both planet and giant in complex intersecting orbits. All these bodies were numbered, but he doubted very much if the Masadans used such numbers; for them no doubt the moons had names out of some religious work.

"Give me the Masadan names for those moons," he therefore instructed.

The submind he was dealing with was prompt in its reply, though it gave no verbal response. Down the side of the same display, it now showed him each of the numbers with a name and a brief description. Cormac snorted with surprise as he read through it.

Around Masada itself orbited two moons, Thom and Lok, both indistinguishable from each other in their irregularity of shape and complex orbits. The last of these were sent into different sequences on each close pass of Calypse's moons, of which four were named:

Amok was small and irregular; the severed testicles of some titan spiralling round the gas giant Calypse. Dante was the largest moon, and the one closest to the giant. It was a sulphurous hell with volcanic activity continually encouraged by the wrenching tides of the giant and its close passes of Masada. Torch was a ball of ice with a slight cometary tail when it was at perihelion; this was due to the flaring of complex ices lighting a tail of ice crystals when tidal forces heated the moon. At aphelion the moon cooled enough for the ices to stop flaring. This was a common phenomenon in comets, but not often seen in moons. Flint was cratered, near geologically dead, and furthest out from Calypse, but was hence the giant's moon that passed closest to Masada on the sunward side of its orbit. It was the kind of moon on which the Polity normally established runcible facilities, but here instead was the base for a shipyard—frameworks and buildings stretching out into space from its surface.

This entire system of moons was named—so the screen notes informed Cormac—by their discoverer, one Braemar Padesh. Cormac felt the man must have used some strange random search in their naming process. He was already ruminating on whatever preparations were now being made on Flint, and how costly they might prove in human life, when his door chime sounded. Immediately, in the corner of the screen he was gazing at, a view into the corridor outside flicked up.

"Enter," he said, and the door opened behind him.

"There's something you should know," said Mika, walking quickly into the room and perching herself on the edge of his sofa.

"That is?" he asked, after washing down another mouthful of food with a sip of wine.

"There has been some kind of communication between Scar and Dragon."

"Specifically?"

"Just before the sphere was detected Scar showed . . . signs of distress, collapsed, then went into convulsions."

"Communication?"

"It seems the most likely explanation. I would conjecture some kind of link."

"Why that conjecture?"

"Because dracomen are tough and as far as I can tell there is very little that can cause them distress; because Dragon is here and it has happened now," she replied.

He studied her for a long moment and wondered if she had bothered to ask Scar what had happened to him.

"Where is Scar right now?" he asked.

"With the Golem—Gant." Cormac noted she had no problem describing Gant as such. "They've got to put your prisoners into cold-sleep. Apparently there are communication problems."

Cormac raised an eyebrow, then turned towards his screen. "AI, can you establish a communications link for me with the dracoman, Scar?"

"Drone present," grated the voice of the submind of Occam's he had been using. Immediately the view on the screen changed to show internal structures of the ship swinging past, and finally it drew to a halt on Scar walking along a gangway beside Gant.

"Scar, does Dragon speak to you?" Cormac asked.

Still moving, Scar lifted his head and gazed at the drone that had to be hovering only a couple of metres in front of him, blinked, showed his teeth, but said nothing. Cormac snorted in annoyance: just like his creator—keeping his cards close to his chest.

"Scar, I want you to return here now. You'll join me in the bridge pod when Tomalon is ready, understood?"

Scar gave a sharp nod and halted. Cormac's last view was of Gant slapping the dracoman once on the shoulder, as Scar turned to head back.

"You hope to learn something," Mika stated, clearly uncomfortable with this near-question.

"I like to keep potential dangers close, where I can watch them, and if necessary, deal with them quickly," Cormac replied, spearing a carrot.

Cormac, Scar and Tomalon stood in the retracted bridge pod and watched as ten grabships approached Dragon. Every now and again Cormac glanced at the dracoman. Only when he was turning back to see the first of the grabships positioning itself against the surface of Dragon did he see some sign of what Mika had reported. Scar flinched—then flinched again as the second ship took position. He bared his teeth as the third moved in.

"You can feel it," Cormac said.

Scar nodded.

"What do you feel?"

"Pain."

"As do we all. I thought you could blank it out."

Silence.

"It's not just the pain, is it?"

"It tries to control me."

"Will it succeed?"

"No. But I will."

Succeed at what?

Cormac was about to voice this question when a change in Scar's expression alerted him to something happening on the screen. He instantly looked up. All the grabships were now in position, most of them out of sight from their point of view, and scalpels of fire were probing the night. Dragon was being pushed towards the *Occam Razor*.

"How will you secure it to the ship?" he asked Tomalon.

"It will secure itself with its pseudopods."

"Any problems?"

"None that are insurmountable. A portion of its body will remain outside U-field, but it informs me that it intends to position itself so as that portion will be part of the radioactive area. That portion will then be left here—cut away."

How to perform surgery with a U-space field generator.

Dragon grew large in the screen. On other screens were views from the various grabships. Cormac saw forests of pseudopodia reaching towards monolithic devices on the dreadnought's hull. He saw the *Occam Razor* growing larger, and was able to compare the size of the creature with the size of the ship. A Dragon sphere had twice almost destroyed the *Hubris*, the ship on which he had travelled to Samarkand. But this sphere came like a supplicant to an iron god.

"Are all the scanners operating?" he asked Tomalon.

"They are all operating. The slightest sign of attempted entry, or the slightest sign of nano-attack, and we will know."

"What can be done with it this close?"

"Many things. We can electrocute it, slice it with particle beams or laser, even detonate a thermo nuke between it and the ship."

"And that won't harm the ship?"

Tomalon came back from his sensor to give Cormac a pitying look. "The hull of this ship is half a metre of Thadium s-con ceramal. There are few energy weapons that can touch it, and it can take a surface blast of up to forty megatons."

Cormac wondered if the people inside could. He also knew of one energy weapon that could touch this ship's hull, and wondered how Tomalon would react to being told that the *Occam Razor* could be destroyed by sunlight. Glancing at the Captain, it also occurred to him that the man looked very much like a creature of myth that could also be destroyed by sunlight, but reckoned Tomalon would not appreciate the humour, and so Cormac continued to watch the show.

There was no feeling of impact as the Dragon sphere took hold where it could and drew itself against the ship. The view of Dragon that Cormac now watched—from one of the grabships as it released—reminded him of a child hugging the legs of a parent. Soon all the grab-ships had returned to their hold.

"Going under now," said Tomalon.

They went.

8

The gabbleduck was his favourite toy. Once initiated, it just would not stop until it had found all of the toy Brothers he had concealed in the area, then chomped them down, and burped after every one. It made him giggle every time when it did that and, even though she tried to conceal it, he knew his mother was amused as well.

"Let's get back to it," she said to him, turning away from the instrumentation that had absorbed her attention for some time now. "Where was I?"

"Babbleguck come home," the boy said without turning from his toy, which had just found a Brother shoved under the edge of the carpet but was having difficulty in pulling the man out by his feet—the victim seemed to have got a grip on the underlay.

"Gabbleduck," the woman corrected, then frowned when she saw her son grin.

"Daddy Duck said, 'Who's been eating from my bowl?' and Mummy Duck, finding the soup in her bowl had been supped too, said, 'And who's been eating from mine?' Baby Duck, not wanting to be left out, looked in its bowl and said, 'Some bugger's et me soup.'"

The picture in the book now showed the room much expanded, the table piled with chewed bones and other detritus from some huge feast. The three gabbleducks were monoliths of alien flesh, bone and muscle that almost filled the rest of the room.

Somebody was talking really fast in a foreign language and she really wished that person would shut up. As she ascended through various levels of awareness, Eldene acknowledged to herself that though she knew what a "foreign language" was, she had never actually heard one spoken. Obviously it was someone else jabbering away in the orphanage dormitory . . . no, in the workers' bunkhouse. She'd have to tell them to shut up in a moment. It was quite enough that she was cold and her bed felt slightly damp and lumpy . . .

As Eldene finally woke up, Fethan whispered in her ear, "Say nothing and make no sudden movements."

Eldene opened her eyes and stared at him. Fethan was crouching right next to her, holding the stinger across his lap. He was clearly visible in the silver-blue light of Amok—one of the larger Braemar moons—and as he glanced at Eldene, his eyes reflected that argent light. With delicate precision, he pointed out into the night.

Carefully Eldene eased herself upright, confused about what had woken her, but wary enough to obey Fethan's instructions. A breeze was evident and for a moment she thought she had been disturbed by the fluting of the grass. Then that other sound repeated, and she froze.

It was just like someone speaking utter nonsense very fast and affirmatively.

"Y'scabbleubber fleeble lobber nabix chope!"

Easing herself higher, Eldene peered in the direction Fethan was pointing. In the moonlight, it did not take her long to discern that something was nosing along the edge of the grasses. All she could see for a moment was a body like a boulder and a long duck bill swinging from side to side, then the creature reared onto its hind legs, opened out its sets of forepaws from the wide triple keel of its chest, and blinked its tiara of greenish eyes as it prepared for its latest oration.

"Y'floggerdabble uber bazz zup zupper," it stated portentously.

"God in Heaven," Eldene whispered, groping for her gun.

Fethan reached out and caught her wrist. "Still and quiet," he hissed. "Gabbleducks are only dangerous when not making any noise."

Gabbleduck!

Eldene had not really believed in them, but now the truth confronted her. She watched as the creature dropped back down and nosed back out into the flute grass, crushing a trail away from them and muttering as it went. When Fethan released her wrist, Eldene let out a suppressed breath and relaxed back against the rock.

"They eat grazers, you said?"

"Yeah, though you'll be unlikely to see any of *them*, as they run before you can get too close."

Eldene reached for her water bottle, but Fethan tapped her on the shoulder and stood up. "There's something else."

Eldene watched him climb up onto the outcrop, then unwrapped herself from her tarpaulin and followed when he gestured her to do so.

"Lot of activity out there tonight," said Fethan as Eldene joined him, failing to not crush the hemispherical molluscs under her feet no matter how carefully she trod. Fethan pointed over the flute grass, in the direction they had come.

The thing stood on two long thin legs that raised it high above the grass itself. Its body had the shape of a thick bucket seat, its long curved neck extending from what would have been the backrest. Below this neck, Eldene could just make out numerous sets of forearms folded as if in prayer. It had no head as such; the neck just terminated in a long serrated spear of a beak. While she watched, it took one delicate arching step that must have carried it over five metres. She noticed its foot was four-toed and webbed.

"Heroyne?" Eldene guessed.

"Yeah, a small one," Fethan affirmed.

As she watched the heroyne, Eldene felt tears filling her eyes—her recent experiences had been frightening, these creatures were frightening, yet both in their way were wonderful and in utter contrast to her grey toil under the Theocracy.

"Thank you," she said.

Fethan acknowledged this with a nod, and the both of them stood there for some time watching the heroyne as it strode on, occasionally spearing writhing shapes, occasionally shaking its beak at the jabbering of the gabbleduck. The rest of the night Eldene slept only intermittently, woken in turn by the increased fluting from the grasses, the momentary return of the gabble duck, by nightmares of a heroyne towering over her and tilting its head while it decided if she might be good to eat—and by a tight ball of something in her stomach that she could only describe as happiness.

Gant smelt burning and just knew there was something wrong. He wondered if this knowledge could be put down to instinct, then he wondered if such an abstraction could have survived the copying process that had resulted in his present self.

"Aiden? Cento?" he said into his wristcom, while drawing his pulse-gun. Then he damned his own stupidity—he was in a security area so radio signals could not penetrate the shielding incorporated in the walls. All communications from here had to be via direct line wires or optic cables. Moving to one of the coms set in the wall itself, he spoke the same words. His voice should have activated the device and his words caused it to relay them to the required recipient, but there was no response. He tried the touch-pads and found them dead.

Of course, his next action should have been to get the hell out of there, then return with a shitload of backup. But Gant was Sparkind and a Golem android now, and utterly confident that there was little he could not squash on his own. He ran to the door and flung himself through it, rolled, and came up into a crouch to spot potential targets. No movement. The guy sitting at the console looked wasted, and the other . . .

Gant suddenly had one of those moments of revelation that in others often necessitate a change of underwear. *Golem.* He tried to communicate with it on the same level as Cento and Aiden did with himself—direct radio transmission, mind to mind—but got nil response. Someone had *killed* this Golem. The head was a blackened ruin, which did not necessarily mean much as the mind was contained in an armoured case in the chest. But the lack of movement or communication did signify. Swinging round, Gant quickly moved back to the door and headed for SA1. He was only a few paces down the corridor when the blast from a riot gun lifted him into the air and deposited him on his back.

"The ship you were on, the *General Patten*, was completely destroyed by Dragon," explained Cormac.

Apis stood in a gravity of one gee. The exoskeletal suit that the Golem, Aiden, had earlier found in the *Occam*'s stores, bulked him out so he now looked to have the musculature to withstand this gravity. The thick grey material covered him from his feet to under his chin, where it flared to cup his head. There was also a coms helmet that went with the suit, but they told him he would have no need of it, just as he would be unlikely to need the hood that folded up from the back, or the visor that could rise to meet it from the chin rest, or the weapon-system connection ports. For this was a suit specifically manufactured for military use.

"Yes, I knew that," he said, staring straight back at Cormac.

"Did you know many of those aboard?" Cormac asked, sitting. Apis moved carefully to another chair and sat down. He would be all politeness, but he wondered what this grim man wanted from him. The Cormac of *The Dragon in the Flower*—the book detailing the events preceding Dragon's supposed suicide on the planet Aster Colora—did not strike him as the kind to waste time on socializing, especially with a teenage Outlinker. They were now heading into a potential war zone, with a titanic dying alien clinging to the outside of the ship. Surely there were more important things that required his visitor's attention?

"My probable father, Peerswarf, also others I'd known in the tech section for a few months, my teachers . . ."

"Friends?"

"They were all in the communal areas. I was in the tech section," said Apis bluntly.

Cormac looked around the room. "Why one gee?" he asked.

That isn't it, thought Apis.

"I want to get used to using this suit. I don't want to be helpless again. If soldiers . . ."

Apis suddenly lost track of what he was saying. It was fear, he realized. With this exoskeleton on, he could fight back.

"You weren't exactly helpless. A brain beats physical strength every time."

You're watching me, thought Apis, *gauging my reactions*.

Cormac said, "Now, I don't want to aggravate your grief, but there are details I need from you. I want you to tell me the entire story."

Ah . . .

"From when?" Apis asked.

"From a relevant point."

Apis stared at him for a long moment. "I discovered the mycelium," he said, and was gratified to see a flash of reaction in Cormac's face.

"Then start from there."

Apis did so, frequently being stopped for questions about various points, some of which struck him as utterly irrelevant. Why did Cormac want to know precisely where the mycelium was found, and at exactly what time? Why did he need to know all the technical parameters of its growth through *Miranda*? Why did he push so hard to learn the wording of Masadan prayer?

When Cormac finally left, Apis felt tired and frustrated, but as he headed for his zero-gee hammock, replaying the conversation in his head, he realized that the agent had missed very little, that it had been a very *thorough* interrogation.

Stanton sipped his drink very carefully, as he did not have Dreyden's tolerance of scotch with lumps of hallucinogenic cips ice in it. Already the man's collection of tropical plants had taken on a slight halo of glowing blue, and there seemed suspect movement just at the edges of his vision.

"The more I look at those things, the more I sympathize with the Separatist cause," said Dreyden as he lit up yet another cigarette. Stanton studied the man: with his feet up on the balcony rail of his apartment in the geodesic dome, which also housed his plant collection, the man was trying to impress with his relaxed urbanity. But Stanton was not impressed. Dreyden was actually gaunt with worry, and eaten away by drugs and the constant medical treatments that kept them from killing him. Though he had reached the top here in *Elysium*, it seemed he was having trouble maintaining his foothold there. Stanton turned from him and looked up at what elicited the man's sympathies.

Outside the dome, the two war drones hovered where they had finished their brief demonstration—all their targets now so much metallic vapour. Dreyden pressed the two yellowed fingers clamping his cigarette against the expensive aug he wore, as if he really needed to concentrate to operate it. One of the segments of the dome slid aside onto vacuum, but trailing the nacreous meniscus of a shimmer-shield behind it to fill the gap. With small jets of thruster flame, the drones manoeuvred towards this gap and one after the other oozed into the dome to then drop down and hover over the cyanids and plasoderms.

"Separatism will eventually lose unless it is prepared to accept and use AI," said Jarvellis. "There's always been a bit of an arms race, but now the Polity is winning."

"Yes," said Dreyden, "the Polity is winning."

Stanton glanced at him and recognized a look in his face that he had only seen previously in Arian Pelter's, from the moment just after agent Ian Cormac had nearly killed him, right up to the point when Cormac actually did kill him. He glanced at Jarvellis sitting in a lounger on the other side of Dreyden and knew her expression: she had opined that this man was, as she put it, "out with the fairies" for some time before Stanton himself had seen it. He had been as slow seeing the same in Pelter as well.

"It depends what you mean by 'winning,'" he replied. "It's suppressing any rebellion against it, and expanding, but there's an awful lot of space out there that isn't Polity-controlled."

"All very well if you want to keep on moving," said Dreyden, drawing heavily on his cigarette before flicking the glowing butt over the balcony. "Now, on to money."

Smiling easily, as if unaware of the man's sudden abruptness, Stanton placed his briefcase on the table between them. Opening the case, he removed a card holding ten cut blue gems, each the size of someone's eye, and each containing square flaws which on close inspection would reveal intricate patterns as of an old integrated circuit. Closing the case, he dropped the strip of gems on the lid for Dreyden's inspection.

Dreyden spun the card with his finger. "Etched sapphires ... interesting." He looked up at Stanton. "Are they scan-enabled?"

Stanton nodded. "Each is a unit representing a hundred thousand New Carth shillings—the price we agreed, yes?"

Dreyden sat back, pulling yet another cigarette from the dispenser and lighting it with his fancy ring. He drew deep and waved one hand airily through the smoke. "Oh, it's agreed."

Opposite them the two war drones, obviously instructed through Dreyden's aug, began to rise back towards the shimmer-shield door in the roof of the biodome—since through there lay no doubt the most direct route to the bay containing *Lyric II*.

"I'll take it on trust that they are genuine," Dreyden added.

Stanton kept a smile on his face, knowing that also through his aug, Dreyden could control the orientation of every mirror out there. He was aware that any who had crossed this man and thought to then escape by ship were now so much drifting ash. Apparently a ship the size of *Lyric II* would last for slightly less time than a fly in a blast furnace if even a single one of the mirrors was directed at it.

There was something horrible about the way Skellor moved, as if something chitinous was heaving along under his skin, but with movements not quite in consonance with his own. Studying him, Aphran wondered at the strange outgrowth that extended up the side of his neck and cupped his chin, at the grey veins that ran across his face and the backs of his hands. What the hell was all that about? And why was there blood flowing in his crystal matrix AI? She could only assume that he had now put it fully online, and that somehow he must have used that weird shit he had been playing with on his off-time from doing work for the group, to prevent it from killing him. Had she been able to, Aphran would have opened up on him with the pulse-rifle she had picked up in the Security Area but, judging by the burnt-out Golem she had seen in there, such action would not have availed her much. Anyway, she was unable to act against him: her aug felt like the body of some vicious insect with its sharp legs clawed inside her brain, and she *knew* that all his orders must be obeyed—the consequences of disobedience would be agony and death.

Glancing aside, she studied Danny, and to a certain extent considered herself lucky. Her own aug, though somehow subverted and now being used to control her, was at least the same Dracocorp item that had been provided by the Masadans. The boy's aug, where Skellor had touched it, now sprouted the same greyish material that inhabited Skellor's body, and roots of it were spreading across the boy's neck and his head. Now, whenever she looked into Danny's face, all she got in return was the expression of an imbecile, but one who obeyed Skellor without hesitation.

Finally finding the courage to speak, Aphran asked, "What about the others?"

"They'll cause sufficient disruption. My 'ware field wouldn't extend to cover you all," Skellor replied.

Aphran glanced about herself—she had not even been aware that they were covered. She glanced to Skellor's belt and saw that he was now not wearing the generator he had spent so much time on. What was he talking about?

"Ah, here," he said, halting and turning to face a door. He reached out and pressed his hand against the touch-panel, and for a moment Aphran expected klaxons to start blaring. Then she chided herself for being obtuse—if he could break into a Polity Security Area, then closed doors were obviously no problem to him.

The door slid aside and as Skellor pulled his hand away from the panel, Aphran saw that it was as if he had just pressed it down in some tar—long strands stretched and attenuated, then snapped back into his palm. Useful ability maybe, but she was not sure it was one *she* wanted to own.

"Cold store," she said, stepping into the room beyond and surveying the rows of cold-coffins either side of a single aisle.

"There are only fifty people here," said Skellor, "but the system that watches this room is the same system that watches all the other sleep rooms on this ship, so I can access it here." So saying he headed down the aisle to a space in one row of coffins, finding an instrument wall. Here he slapped his hand against a touch-console. This time the task for him appeared much more difficult as, after a few seconds, he closed his eyes and bowed his head. Aphran watched the blood pulsing faster in his aug, and noted how the greyish veins on his face seemed to be moving: sliding under his skin like lizard tails.

A series of sucking thumps sent her into a crouch with her pulse-rifle held at the ready, then she realized that the noise came from cold-coffins hingeing open—all of them. Inside each was exposed the naked body of a man or a woman, their concave impressions mirrored in the lids.

Opening his eyes and glancing round, Skellor said flatly, "Damn."

"What happened?" Aphran asked, standing again. She noted that Danny had moved not at all.

"Vascular control," Skellor explained. "I was trying to get the system to pump them dry, then return their blood before they'd reached thaw-up, which would have killed them all rather neatly. Unfortunately, I overlooked a subroutine that isolates the coffins, which in turn then revive their occupants. But don't worry, this was only a test run, so it's only happening in here."

"They're waking up?" Aphran asked.

Skellor surveyed the room as if that had not occurred to him. "Oh, yes," he said. "You've got about six minutes yet, so you'd best hurry and kill them all."

Aphran stared at him in horror, and immediately felt the claw inside her head closing when she made no move to obey. Suddenly she found herself walking towards the head of a row. It was not as if she was being forced, for it was *her* doing the walking; it was rather as if at the wholly animal level she had made the choice to stay alive, for by obeying was the only way she could.

"You take that other row," she instructed Danny, the words tasting foul to her.

Upon reaching the cold-coffin at the end of her own row, she placed the snout of the pulse-rifle against the temple of its occupant, and pulled the trigger. The man's head lifted to the side, blooming open like a flower on the blue flash of energy. However, as he settled back, what ran out of the ugly wound was not blood but the complex antifreeze that had been pumped into his body whilst his blood had been pumped out. The next coffin occupant was a woman, and seeing a tattoo on her arm that branded her as Earth Central Security, gave Aphran no comfort. This was bloody work. She was a soldier in the Separatist cause, not a murderer. Her tenth victim leaked blood, and her fifteenth sprayed it across the metal floor. Her last one of twenty-five opened his eyes and sat upright before she shot him twice in the chest, knocking him out of his coffin. Perhaps she should not have been so tardy; Danny had killed all his lot long before.

Carrying her laptop, Mika entered the cold-sleep area and glanced around. Everything looked as it should be; anything wrong in any of the ten or more of these areas, and the *Occam*'s AI would have registered it immediately. This particular area, though it had room for many more of them, had only eight occupied coffins. Seven contained some of the

Occam's technicians—overspill from another area a quarter of a kilometre to port of the ship—and the eighth one held Apis Coolant's mother.

It had been Mika's intention to leave her in cold-sleep until she could be returned to an Outlinker medical facility, as the injuries she had sustained though easy enough to deal with in a normal human, in an Outlinker were not so amenable to the medical technologies at Mika's disposal. Even the boy's broken ankle had caused her some problems—normal bone welding not being sufficient to the task of repairing fragile Outlinker bone—and she'd needed to fabricate an autodoc boot to monitor the slow process of repair.

But in the end it came down to convenience. Though it would not be easy for Mika to repair this woman's fractured skull and the consequent thrombosis, it was by no means impossible. If Mika was perfectly honest with herself, the only reason she had been avoiding the chore was so she could spend more time studying the human/calloraptor hybrid Cormac had killed. However, this choice was unfair on the boy Apis as, though he might seem rather advanced for a teenager, he'd had some hideous experiences and was now amongst strangers. He needed his mother.

Plugging the optic cable of her laptop into the woman's coffin, Mika waited impatiently for the status list to come up on the screen. After a moment, she looked about herself to make sure she had not overlooked the presence of anyone, then began to speak out loud.

"Who are you?" she asked. "What is that? Why is this? How do you do that?" It was so easy for normal Polity citizens to ask direct questions, yet for Life-Coven graduates it seemed so difficult and unnatural. The ideal was that you used all the resources at your disposal to discover answers—including your own reasoning abilities—and that to have to ask a question was a kind of defeat. In cases where there were no other options available the Life-Coven taught that you should then feel free to ask, which was all very well if the concept of not asking had not been as deeply inculcated from birth as potty training. In this respect Mika was discovering just how wrong her early training had been, so was attempting to retrain herself.

"Where is this item? Do you have this ability? Are you ...?" She trailed off, realizing that the status list was taking an awful long time to come up on her screen. Quickly she started the laptop's self-diagnostic program, and immediately got a response that assured her there was nothing wrong with the device. Now she sent a search engine through the console's memory space to try to find the optic connection. Briefly there came a flash of some very odd code across the screen, then the words "Nil Return Signal." Frowning, Mika rested the device on top of the cold-coffin and headed down the aisle to the instrument wall. Here the same strange code was scrolling across all of four different screens. She tried the touch-controls and the code disappeared, but beyond that there was no response.

Running back to the cold-coffin, Mika felt a horrible sinking sensation. Problems with cold-sleep coffins? They did not have problems—it was unheard of. Grabbing up her laptop she quickly detached it, fed its own optic cable back into it, and laid it on the cold-coffin behind her. Now she tried the touch-plate lock on the lid of the coffin: nil response. Nothing else for it but to use the manual lever—no matter how many alarms this caused to go off. She gripped the cold metal and drew it back towards her, and with a thunk the lock disengaged and the coffin lid sighed open. Gazing at the Outlinker woman, Mika immediately knew something was terribly wrong: the woman's skin had been light lavender when Mika had transferred her from the landing craft, but now it was dark. It was always the case that people in cold-sleep looked colourless, pallid, simply because the blood had been withdrawn from them and replaced by clear fluid. This woman should be bloodless and she was not. Mika placed her hands on the woman's chest. Nothing. With sudden fierce strength, she got hold of her and pulled her onto her side. Stiff with rigor mortis. Her underside was also deep purple where the blood had pooled in the lower portions of the corpse—for this was what she was now dealing with: a corpse. Mika let the woman drop back into place in her aptly named box.

"AI . . . Occam, this is Asselis Mika reporting a malfunction in Cold-sleep Room One." After no response from the intercom set into the control wall, she rushed out into the corridor and tried the intercom there.

"There is no malfunction in Cold-sleep Room One," one of the AI's subminds informed her.

"The Outlinker woman who we recently placed in a coffin there is dead," Mika replied, trying to keep her voice from getting shrill.

"System function return is optimal. There is no problem in Cold-sleep Room One," repeated the sub-mind in a somewhat annoyed tone. Clearly, even though only a submind, it did not like having to point out the obvious to idiots.

"I suggest you send a drone here as fast as you damned well can, because I don't think that rigor mortis and postmortem lividity are particularly healthy symptoms even for someone in cold-sleep! Also, I'm standing out in the corridor at the moment since the com in there does not work either."

"System function return for com is optimal. There is no problem with the com in Cold-sleep Room One. Asselis Mika, do you require medical assistance?"

"I want a direct link with Tomalon or Occam itself," she demanded.

"You have a problem," immediately stated the voice of Tomalon. "Occam is gearing for a full diagnostic check and I have sent Aiden and Cento to assist you."

"Good," said Mika. "I must go back in now to check the other coffins."

"If you do," said the Captain, "do not use your console, as it may be infected."

"You suspect a computer virus," Mika stated.

"Virus or worm, whatever. There are too many safety backups in the cold-sleep control system for it to be anything other than deliberate subversion of programs."

"Murder," muttered Mika, heading back into the room and instantly thinking, like so many of those who have sought to do the best for a patient and failed: *How do I tell her son?* And there was no one who could answer that question for her, dared she even to ask it.

Every com-unit howled, whether it was mounted on a wall, integrated in a wristcom, or part of the device built inside a Golem's head. Cormac exited his room and broke into a run. Halfway down the corridor he felt something lurch through his body as he passed over a fluxing grav-plate. He immediately halted and stepped over to a nearby handle affixed to the wall and gripped it for support.

"Tomalon? Occam?"

From his wristcom issued a sound that could have been interference but sounded more like a steady keening.

"Aiden? Cento?"

"Online," came the twinned reply.

"What's happening?" he asked.

"All the people in Cold-sleep Room One are dead," replied Aiden flatly.

"Oh God, no . . ." Tomalon intruded, his voice fading into then out of audibility. Nothing useful there.

"Aiden, get yourself and Mika back up to Medical. I advise you to use the shaft ladders, as the drop-shafts may not be functioning correctly. Do we know who else hasn't gone into cold-sleep yet?"

"There is no one else," replied the Golem.

"Okay." Cormac paused, not wanting to examine too closely what that might mean. "Is Gant still in the Security Area?" he finished.

"He is."

"And still no response from there?"

"None."

"Right, that seems one likely source of our problem. Cento, I want you to join me there."

"Will do," replied Cento. Then, "There is another probable source."

"Yes," replied Cormac, thinking about the millions of tonnes of alien attached to the outside of the ship. "But would Dragon attack like this from such a vulnerable position? It knows that the *Occam* could turn it to space-borne ash in a few seconds, and anyway every system on that side of the ship is isolated." He believed this was nothing to do with the alien—so it was something else.

"Tomalon?" Cormac asked again.

Again that keening sound, then eventually Tomalon spoke. "They're all dead," he said dully.

"We know that," spat Cormac. "Let's now find out why and prevent any more deaths."

"They are *all* dead," Tomalon groaned.

"What precisely do you mean?" asked Cormac, suddenly all cold function.

"All of them! *All* of them!" The voice was Tomalon's *and* it was also Occam's.

"Do you mean *everyone* who went into cold-sleep?" It was a question Cormac did not want to ask, but had to.

"Yes," the reply, echoed from intercoms all down the corridor. Almost unconsciously, Cormac reached back with his finger and initiated his shuriken holster. Underneath his sudden frigidity of thought, he felt a ball of anger growing.

"Listen to me carefully, Tomalon. I can understand your and Occam's grief, and feelings of guilt, but you are merely feeding each other's dysfunction. I need you to stabilize ship control and go to maximum internal security alert."

"Initiate Golem?" returned the voice of Tomalon, echoed a fraction of a second later by the voice of Occam.

"No. With this level of subversion we cannot guarantee that they won't be under someone else's control. They are just as much in storage as the people in cold-sleep. Get your drones searching the ship, especially in and around the Security Area. I'll be there soon."

"I . . . will," the Captain managed.

Now Cormac altered settings on his wristcom and opened a channel that had been isolated for this single purpose.

"Dragon?"

For a long moment there was no reply, then a grudging "Yes."

"Are you attacking us?" he asked.

There came a roaring, as from a vast crowd-filled auditorium in response to some momentous event. "I am legion," Dragon replied, as this sound slowly died.

"If you do not give direct answers to direct questions, I will send the code to detonate the CTD that presently sits between you and this ship. Perhaps you would survive the blast, but I think it unlikely you would survive being shoved out of the underspace field and being smeared across a few light years."

"I am not attacking. I cannot attack," Dragon immediately replied.

Cormac considered that: how easily it could be a lie. With his finger poised over his wristcom he still considered sending the code that would detonate the CTD, as even if Dragon was not the source of the present danger it would be best to detonate to curtail future dangers. The creature's next words stopped him, however.

"I can see it," said Dragon.

"What can you see?"

"I can see *the enemy*. It is on your ship and it will take your ship. It is what it does and it is what it is."

"This enemy, what is it?"

"Ancient," said Dragon. "The eater. The body that continues to kill and consume after its mind is burnt. You must return to realspace. I must leave this ship."

"You know your words are opaque to me," said Cormac. "Get pellucid or you'll be leaving this ship in pieces."

"You usually call it 'the Jain,' and assume you talk of a dead race of individuals," Dragon replied.

It was all Cormac needed to now understand what was happening.

Skellor.

How so very confident they had been in their superiority, and how so very sure they had been that he had made his escape. Skellor had not escaped; he had begun, from that very moment when they had nearly captured him, to attack. Cormac switched channels back, as he headed for the nearest drop-shaft, so he could address the others.

"We are really in it now: looks like the source of our problems is Skellor, interfaced—as we know—and now possessing active Jain technology," he said. At the shaft itself, he reached in to test that the field was operating, before punching his destination and stepping beyond the threshold. The gravity field dragged in down through the ship, in a curve, so that—without reference to the floor he had stepped from—there was neither up nor down.

"Where's Scar?" he asked of his wristcom as he had to upend himself to walk out of the drop-shaft near the Security Area.

Through Aiden's ears he heard Mika reply, "Scar is still in Medical. He was helping me with one or two things there."

Cormac wondered just what experiments she had been doing on Scar this time, then he spun—with Shuriken ready to throw—as Cento came trotting from the side corridor.

"Firing—down there," said the Golem, pointing down a corridor ahead of him and to Cormac's right. Cormac immediately matched the Golem's pace and, as he ran, he pulled his thin-gun from his jacket pocket. He could not yet hear any shooting, but then he did not have a Golem's superb hearing. Their pace increased when they both heard Gant shout, "Give it up!"

Rounding a corner, they had to leap the corpses of two Separatist prisoners. Beyond these, they came to where someone had blown out the walls, and where insulation and wiring were hanging from gaping holes in the ceiling or blasted up from gaps in the floor. Ahead of them was a figure that turned and showed itself to be Gant, and most certainly Golem: between his neck and his groin, his clothing had been blasted away, as had his syntheflesh covering. The column of his spine and the solid node of his chest, with its rib indentations, were exposed; also shielded optic cables that looked more like water pipes than anything else, and the smooth gleaming movement of his pelvis. Ahead of him, two figures were fleeing, and he was about to give chase; but then he turned, obviously now in direct-line communication with Cento.

"What have you got here?" Cormac asked as he and Cento closed.

"Four prisoners. They already got Cardaff and Shenan— though Christ knows how they got her. Their only weapons are a couple of pulse-rifles and a riot gun. I want to take at least one of them alive, but every time I get close they knock me over with that damned gun." With a degree of puzzlement he looked down at the damage those blasts had done to him.

"Okay," said Cormac. "They won't be able to keep both of you off." He glanced at Cento. "The two of you go in fast and grab at least one of them." Both Gant and Cento moved off at his instructions—accelerating away faster than any man could move. Cormac trotted along behind, scanning about himself as he went, utterly aware that there could be another twenty or so Separatists waiting somewhere in ambush. However, there came no yells and no sudden fusillade. The riot gun blasted once, and there was a brief stuttering of pulse-gun fire, before he came upon the scene of Cento holding a man and woman above the floor by the backs of their necks, disarmed and kicking, and of Gant swearing vehemently and climbing to his feet. Soon Gant had rejoined Cento and taken charge of the woman. As Cormac approached, both Golem were holding their prisoners by the biceps, in front of themselves.

"Where are the rest of you?" Cormac immediately demanded, surprised to note that the two were still fighting against the adamantine grip of the Golem—surely they knew they had no chance to escape, so why did they continue to fight?

"About," said the man, through gritted teeth.

Cormac studied the two of them for a moment. "Where's Skellor?" he asked, but the pair just glared at him with a kind of grim desperation, and still they struggled to escape.

"You know, you can either live or die," Cormac warned them, coldly studying their response.

"We're dead already," the man replied, then went rigid, his eyes rolling up inside his head. Cormac saw that he had bitten right through his bottom lip, and observed the blood running out of his ear as his head slumped to one side. Reaching out he tilted the man's head to more closely observe the Dracocorp aug: the thing appeared deflated—like the desiccated corpse of some strange mollusc. He turned to the woman and saw that she was staring at him with a slightly contemptuous twist to her mouth.

"You survived then," she said. "But that's something I can soon enough change."

"What do you mean?" asked Cormac.

The woman continued, "I told you, on Callorum, that you were over the Line, but being arrogant ECS you just had to push too far. Well, you've pushed me to this, and you'll pay for it."

"Skellor?" Cormac asked.

"Oh yes, I control every one of these prisoners and I'll soon control this ship. It'll be interesting to see what the Polity can do about a subverted AI dreadnought nicely filled with a technology that's about a million years ahead of its own . . . I'll be seeing you, Ian Cormac."

With that, the woman convulsed in the same way as the man, and died.

Skellor smiled a triumphant smile to himself as he stood before this newest door. It was with some relish that he contemplated getting his hands on that ECS bastard and doing something really drastic: maybe rewiring his nervous system so that everything he felt caused him pain, and rewiring his head so he could never faint or die of shock. But that was for the future, when he had complete control of this ship. Right now, he must get complete control. He turned to the door and placed his hand against the palm lock.

He now found that he did not require a sample of the specific DNA for those doors that were DNA-locked, as he had discovered that the locking codes only keyed to a thousand or so specific and short base sequences. Having discovered the positioning of these sequences in the polynucleotide chains enabled him to create a skeleton key in his right hand—actually altering the genetic structure in the skin of that hand to suit. Of course, this did not work without him sending filaments into the locking system to subvert security routines and listen, like a safebreaker, while he changed over to specific sequences to suit the lock. The door he now stood before opened after a few seconds, and he strode through, quickly followed by Aphran and Danny.

"My God," said Aphran, her dull tone belying the words.

This entire room was a storehouse of Golem. Skellor surveyed the racks of skinless androids for a moment before moving on—these were not for him, not yet.

With Cento and Gant at his back, Cormac stepped into Medical and studied the scene. Mika now stood over Apis, who was slumped in a chair. Scar stood to one side, watching the boy intently—perhaps now learning more about human grief than he had ever known before. When the boy looked up, Cormac met his gaze for a moment then turned away. He could offer him no comfort: the boy's mother was dead—murdered by Skellor almost by default, while the man had been killing five hundred other people aboard this ship.

Cormac switched his gaze to the ceiling. "Tomalon, are you listening in?" he asked.

"I hear you," replied the familiar grating voice that was an amalgam of both Tomalon and Occam.

"Okay, I want you to use all the subminds and stored personalities at your disposal to initiate those of the ship's Golem you consider safe. How quickly can you do that, and how many can you provide us with?"

"I can have *all* the Golem with you in one hour—they have not been subverted. From the subminds and personalities I have, I can run as many copies as required."

Cormac glanced at the two Sparkind Golem. "Do you still have copies of Aiden and Cento?"

"I do."

"Run copies from them: they're Sparkind so they'll probably be more useful in this situation than technicians or researchers."

"Understood."

"What about Skellor: any sign of him?"

"None."

"The escaped prisoners?"

"I have located fifteen of them, and have that matter under control."

Cormac now turned his attention to those gathered in the room with him.

It was like a raw bloody wound in his side, where part of his flesh had been excised, but neither that, not the damage to Occam, nor the excision and destruction of a whole internal system, caused him the greatest pain. That was caused by guilt. They had been his responsibility. Five hundred human beings had given themselves over to his care and his infallibility, and now they were all dead. Tomalon had screamed and raged earlier, but the cold machinery of the bridge pod sucked away his cries, and they were as ineffectual as the dead themselves. Grief was not the answer: vengeance was. While, with one facet of himself and Occam combined, he watched Cormac's briefing, he hunted with the rest of himself.

The four he'd located hiding in hold LS-45 had not moved, and shortly the high-speed surveillance drones would reach them. Tomalon considered also sending the hull-repair robot from LS-33, but a diagnostic probe revealed that it had discharged its laminar batteries. Looking through the same robot's two normal and two tracking eyes, he saw through the clearing smoke that the two Separatists were most definitely dead: teeth broken and internal organs shattered, skin blistered where it was not charred. He'd known that, during the long game of hide-and-seek, the two would at some point make the mistake of trying to get past the slow-moving robot, not realizing that though the robot was slow, the wire-feed to its seam-welder was not. It had electrocuted them both when they made that mistake.

The drones were nearly there now. Another thirty seconds would see the four Separatists in LS-45 dealt with. Though shaped like arrowheads, the drones had no sharp edges, but that was of no consequence when they could accelerate to Mach II within only a few tens of metres.

With tears running from his whitened eyes Tomalon now turned his attention to the nine escaped prisoners he had located in LS-26. Four of them were in an outer hold space that possessed an external hatch. They'd panicked when he'd shut them in, but they carried nothing with them they could use to cut through the ceramal door. Their five fellows were coming to their aid with all speed—obviously summoned via the Dracocorp augs they all wore—but it seemed unlikely they would get there before the second hull-repair robot, which was trundling round the hull, reached the hatch. With a kind of horrible glee, Tomalon felt the Occam part of himself calculating vectors from the four—trying to work out which of them would first be sucked out of the fifteen-centimetre-square hatch.

Ah, LS-45, now.

One of the Separatists there had stepped outside, perhaps hearing something. He turned, horror writ clear in his features. Through six red eyes Tomalon saw this, then transferred his attention to the pinhead camera set high in the corridor. He watched as one of the drones hurtled forwards and slammed straight through the man, exploding away most of his torso and spinning the remainder against the wall where it smeared blood and intestines before collapsing. The two other drones turned into the hold to be greeted by screams and yells. Then the stuttering of a pulse-rifle hitting one of the drones before it slammed into the possessor of the weapon in white-hot fragments. The woman next to that man staggering away, groping at where a stray fragment of metal had torn away half her face. The other one, pushed back against the wall by the second drone—it not penetrating because it had not room to build up sufficient speed—screaming as it crushed his chest, blood spraying from his lips. The drone backing off to let him drop, turning to the woman who is now down and crawling, coming down on her head like a stamping iron boot . . .

LS-26 again. The robot connects its key-plug, turns it, inserts it further, turns it three more revolutions, retracts it and trundles back on its hull-grip treads. Initiated now, the hatch motor draws power and begins to lift from its seals. The five other Separatists have now reached the inner door to the hold and one of them fires at the lock with a pulse-gun. This does no more than fuse the mechanism and reduce the possibility of them getting the door open. Tomalon observes this, just as he observes the white mist of vapour-laden air blasting from the opening outer hatch and ice crystals condensing on the hull-repair robot. Inside the hold, he observes the four scrabbling at the inner door as the outer hatch reaches its slide point and slams aside. Suddenly a miniature hurricane drains the hold. The woman who slams against the hatch-hole does not have time to scream before the huge pressure differential snaps her spine and folds her in half—ejecting her into space. The man who hits directly behind her is jammed in place—the differential no longer enough to break him up sufficiently to push him through. Air continues to escape past him. Through the robot, Tomalon watches him—his arm and head through the hatch, eyes bulging and vapour jetting from his mouth, veins breaking and reddening his face like a drunkard's. Soon all the air is gone and he falls back inside to join his fellows, who are on the floor gasping at nothing, and dying.

The surveillance drones have nearly reached the other five who have now stepped back from the inner door—no doubt having received some last communication from their fellows inside. Tomalon turns the drones and sends them in search of the other escaped prisoners. He considers that the evacuation of further air will be no great loss, for the *Occam Razor* is now less five hundred souls who would need to breathe. All around these five Separatists, he closes doors and seals and hatches, then he opens the inner door to hold LS-26. This is a show he wants to see again. He watches the five try to run, fighting the hurricane that wants to snatch them away. He sees one hurtling down the corridor and slamming into the doorjamb of LS-26 before being dragged through, yet knows in his heart that this is not enough vengeance; there will never be enough.

"Hello, Captain."

The voice is close and he feels breath on his face. He slides aside the two nictitating screens that cover his eyes and behind his eyes he stands down the extra optic-nerve linkages. All views external to the bridge pod fade and he gazes at the face before him.

"Hello, Skellor."

The hand that touches his face is hot and feverish, then suddenly scalding. He feels linkages blinking out, subprograms collapsing or being isolated. He feels the *invasion*. Pain in his right arm. He looks down and sees Skellor's other hand on the engine-control vambrace, then that being levered up and tearing from Tomalon's flesh, trailing strands like tar. Engine control gone. Dropping out of U-space. In horror he watches Skellor finally pull it away from him, skeining optic cable behind, then pressing the vambrace into place on his own arm. Security protocols come online, grope for the invasive presence—become that presence.

Tomalon. Tomalon. Tomalon. Like a child mimicking the galloping of a horse, but, behind this, Occam is screaming.

Access codes!

He tries to dump them, but the system-backup protocols will not allow them to go unless he orders it again. *Too late.* System backup slides into black isolation. Tearing. The second vambrace has gone, and now Skellor has his fingers under the Captain's heart plate, his grasp coming near to life-support; and on Tomalon's head the primary connections to Occam are loosening.

Someone is screaming, Tomalon realizes it is himself.

Perhaps this is enough?

Tomalon accesses a system long unused in the Polity, and Occam gladly consents.

It was fun, Occam says.

Goodbye, Tomalon replies.

The unused system comes online like a guillotine slamming down: hard-wired and not easily amenable to subversion; it was built in when humans ran the Polity and AIs were not to be completely trusted. Occam dies, its mind fragmenting under a huge power surge, crystal layers ablating away, perfect logic and stacked memory becoming a searing explosion of static. Throughout the ship, surveillance drones drop from the air, their minds bleeding away and single power-surges scrambling the silicon matrices in which those minds were contained. The hull-repair robot outside LS-26 closes the hatch, shearing in half a corpse still caught in it, before locking down against the hull itself and dying. Other drones either freeze or lock into a repetition of their most recent task. One of these, which is welding a hull member, continues the task long after it has run out of welding wire; and another, deep in the ship, continues polishing an area of floor it will wear its way through some time hence. Control panels shut down for a moment, then come back on in isolated function. And finally, twenty-eight skinless Golem bow their heads as one, dots of white heat appearing on polished ceramal skulls as internal components fuse and burn away. A further twenty-two stand up as one, and step out of their bracing frames.

"Fuck you!" Skellor rages, his hand closing on Tomalon's throat.

9

The image of the room and all its contents, excepting the creatures, faded away, to then be replaced with an image of a bedroom with three beds, and Brother Malcolm, hugely asleep. The woman glanced at her son, perhaps considering showing him this, herself certainly understanding where the story was now going. The boy was busy playing with his macabre toys and probably wouldn't notice if she stopped reading. However, she wanted to carry on because she was enjoying the story herself.

"'Who's been sleeping in my bed?' asked Daddy Duck, upon finding the sheets of his bed rumpled and crumpled," she said—over-egging the self-parody.

Her son glanced up at her and frowned. She continued in a more normal tone, "'Who's been sleeping in my bed?' asked Mummy Duck, finding her sheets all rumpled and crumpled too. 'Mffuful coffle foofle ,' said Baby Duck."

The woman stared at the picture of the smallest of the three gabbleducks—that is to say one that was only about three metres tall—as it ground its jaws from side to side, two feet clad in filthy red and white striped bedsocks sticking out the side of its bill, and blood running in rivulets down its breast. The boy would like this picture, but was too intent on his toy, which had now pulled its victim out from underneath the carpet and was using it in the same way as Brother Malcolm had been used. As, on the final gulp, the two feet disappeared, she finished the text of the story:

"'Don't speak with your mouth full,' said Mummy and Daddy Duck together."

*

In the morning, they pushed through the flute grass for only an hour before coming to a crushed-down clearing in which something had obviously pounced on and devoured a grazer. Old grass and new, the latter being now even in these wetter areas up to waist-high, was spattered with a treacly substance that Fethan told her was grazer blood. Also scattered all around were regurgitated piles of white bone flakes and chewed skin, and stinking worms of excrement—whether this last was from the grazer or the thing that had eaten it was debatable. The most eye-catching item left was the grazer's skull, which sat at the precise centre of the clearing as if carefully placed there. This object was as large as a man's torso, and possessed a jaw set with three rows of flat grinding teeth that worked against a flat bony plate. There were four eye-sockets on either side of the long skull—one still holding an eye that was the colour of iron and contained a double black pupil.

Eldene noticed movement amid the treacly blood and dark flesh still clinging to white bone, and on closer inspection saw this was due to small black crustaceans similar in shape to sprawns—but without the wings—that had come to feed. Stepping back, she realized that the entire clearing was swarming with these creatures. Wordlessly she hurried after Fethan, who now took the track that led from the clearing towards the mountains.

By mid-morning they were on high ground yet again, and the going became much easier. As they drew closer to the mountains, the landscape and vegetation began to change drastically. Lizard tails grew in big clumps encircling some kind of huge flower or fruit with the appearance of a mound of raw liver; stubby flute grasses grew in hollows, but the rest of the ground was covered by blister mosses ranging from blue to green, with the occasional red pod-spike rearing up to a metre in the air; plants like giant thistles encroached, as neatly ranked as marching armies, clad in finger-length thorns and bearing furred heads of deepest purple over bodies of pale green; rocky outcroppings became commonplace and a wider variety of molluscs clung to them. And the ground sloped ever upwards.

"I've never seen this, any of this before, not even in a book," Eldene commented, after she had stopped to inspect some of the rock-clinging molluscs gathered on a large flat stone. Their shells were seemingly enamelled in Euclidian patterns of black and yellow, as if someone had spilt a jewellery box there.

"How many books have you actually seen?" Fethan asked her. Eldene began to count them up, but before she could answer Fethan continued, "If you can even count them, then you haven't seen enough. The Theocracy doesn't allow many anyway, and the only ones you will have seen will be copies of the few brought here by the first settlers, or else the subversive versions smuggled in by the Polity. I'm surprised you've seen any at all."

"They had some at the orphanage," Eldene said.

"Then they are probably a well-kept secret which, if revealed, would get someone into a lot of trouble," Fethan replied. Then, as if this had only just occurred to him: "Were these paper books?"

Eldene stared at him in confusion. "Paper books? They were memory fabric, just like any other book."

Fethan shook his head. "Damn, I'm getting old."

Soon they were high enough to look back across the sweep of grasslands, and the settlement areas beyond. Through the mist of distance, Eldene could just make out the city and, still further, something glinting in the sunlight as it rose from the spaceport. She gazed up at the stations silhouetted against the face of Calypse, and supposed that what she had witnessed was either a trader's ship taking essence of squerm to some faraway port, or a Theocracy transport taking the same luxury protein, in its unrefined form, to the tables of the Theocracy. Much, she knew, was grown up there, in crop cylinders, but the religious hierarchy that ruled their lives had a special taste for such products resulting from the killing labour of the surface dwellers.

"I've often wondered what kind of lives they lead up there," Eldene said.

"Oh, they do very nicely. They wear the trappings of theism and they violently debate the tenets of their faith, but meanwhile they live like primitive kings." Fethan turned to her. "Do you believe in this god your Theocracy has you worship?"

Eldene nearly gave the automatic: "I believe in the one true God whose prophet is Zelda Smythe. I believe in the Creation and the truth of Human Ascendance. I believe . . ." The entire list usually took fifteen minutes to recite, and Eldene remembered how on only one or two occasions had she been made to go right the way through it. Anyway, a proctor usually demanded such recitations as a prelude to some punishment, and would usually find a mistake within the first twenty lines as an excuse to inflict a beating. For the first time Eldene actually stopped to consider her own belief. All it had ever been to her was the memorizing of religious texts, morning and evening prayers recited below the Theocracy cameras, beatings for infringements she did not understand: all a framework that tied her to the grinding toil and misery of her life.

"Yes, I do," she replied, because she could think of no other answer.

"Of course you do—it's been ground into you since you were born. But do you then believe in the god-given right of the Theocracy to rule your life?"

After a pause Eldene replied, "No, I do not. There has to be something better."

"Yeah, there is," said Fethan, turning to continue climbing the slope.

"Do you believe?" Eldene asked, following him.

"I believe only in those things that can be proven empirically. There has never been any proof that a god exists, and if such proof was found why the hell should we worship him? Organized religions are just elaborate con-tricks. Take the Christian religion from which yours is an offshoot: 'Obey me throughout your life, give me the product of your labour, and you will go to Paradise when you die. Disobey me and you will go to Hell and burn forever. Of course I cannot prove that this is what will actually happen—you just have to have *faith*.' That was a good one, and it worked well enough in a society that still believed the Earth was flat."

"But . . . what happened here?"

"An isolated group of fanatics, with sophisticated psychological programming techniques . . . This place would never have survived in the Polity, and it is breaking down even now as the Polity gets closer and information filters through."

"But the universe . . . how do you explain it? When did it begin? What existed before it? Where does it end, and what lies beyond it?"

Fethan glanced at her. "Questions that might similarly be asked about this god of yours?"

Eldene considered that. Of course: what was before God and what lies beyond God?

Fethan continued, "The greatest admission a human can make is that perhaps he does not have the intelligence, the vision, the grasp to fully understand the universe, and that perhaps no human ever will. To put it all down to some omnipotent deity is a cop-out. Factor in fairy tales of an afterlife and it becomes a *comforting* cop-out."

Eldene had always been clever—it had been her ability to memorize and understand things that had enabled her to avoid many of the punishments her fellow workers had received, except when that punishment came from a proctor or orphanage administrator who had taken exception to her very cleverness. Now she sank into deep contemplation of the issues raised. Fethan had quite bluntly just stated things that she had never before heard stated. Surface dwellers hated the Theocracy and the yoke they laboured under with vehemence, but belief in God or the necessity of worship never came into question. With discomfort she realized that since their escape she had not prayed once, nor thought about God, and that discomfort increased when it struck her she had never felt happier. She was deep in thought when Fethan gripped her arm.

"Believe what you want, girl," said the old man, "but don't let it master your life. Do you think that if there is a god who created the universe he would be the petty vindictive god of your Theocracy? They're just people like you or me. Life's precious and short, girl. Just enjoy it."

Eldene looked around at the weird plants, the molluscs clinging to the rocks. She thought about the heroyne and gabbleduck she had seen in the night. Halting, she pointed at a hemispherical shell patterned with beautiful green, yellow, and white geometric shapes.

"Life," she said, "it's so complex—someone must have made it?"

"Ah, Creationism," said Fethan. "Let me tell you about evolution and a blind watchmaker . . ."

Eldene listened and grew angry. It seemed that everything Fethan said was empirically true, yet that all that had been beaten into her was also true—if you had faith. She grew angry because at her core she did have faith, and she was coming to realize just how that crippled her, and she envied Fethan's freedom of thought.

For a moment the grav in Medical went off, then it came back on and climbed to what felt to Cormac about one and a half gees, before dropping back down to about half a gee.

"What the hell?" he asked of the air. "Tomalon?"

He looked around at the others and saw that both Aiden and Cento had collapsed, and were showing no sign of getting up. Stepping over to Aiden, he looked down and saw that something had charred the syntheflesh of the Golem's forehead, burning and blistering it away to expose heat-tarnished metal. Gant quickly joined him in a crouch and helped him turn Cento over onto his back—the same was found there.

Gant gazed at him in bewilderment. "They just went out. I *felt* them go out."

"Tomalon!" Cormac bellowed.

In answer, Tomalon's hologram appeared in the middle of the room, cut in half by a surgical table, faint images of complex systems etching the air all around it. "This is recorded, so attempt no communication," said the Captain's voice.

Cormac buttoned down the question he had been about to ask.

The Captain went on, "Skellor is subverting the *Occam Razor* with Jain technology. It is an old ship and, in the event of attempted AI takeover, has the system facility for complete AI burn, which I initiated. This burn has not been wholly successful and he now has control of twenty-two ship's Golem, as well as life-support and the U-space engines."

Tomalon's mouth opened as if he was screaming, but no sound could be heard. His eyes suddenly became blackened pits and a complex grid-work of black lines traversed his holographic body from head to foot. "You must escape. You must escape," came his grating whisper. Then, "Occam . . . Occam . . . Occam . . ."

The Captain flickered and went out.

"What's happening? What's going on?" asked the Outlinker boy as Mika assisted him to his feet.

Cormac stared at Gant, then nodded towards the fallen Golem. "They were all downloaded, but their bodies were ship Golem so the burn program would have been hardwired. They're dead," he said, wondering if it was correct to have described those two recordings of Aiden and Cento as alive, but deciding that would not be the best thing to say to Gant. Standing up again, he went on, "Well, you heard the man: let's get the hell out of here."

Standing also, Gant said, "All the *Occam*'s shuttles will be in storage, and it takes the ship AI to get them out of it."

"Fuck," said Cormac.

Relentlessly Gant went on, "They'll also be mindless. You'd have manual control, but no automated systems."

"Your point, if one needs to be made?" said Cormac.

"No navigation," Gant replied.

"Double fuck," said Cormac succinctly. He considered for a moment, then gazed at Apis. "The Masadan landing craft. It's our only option."

"No U-space engines," said Gant. "It'd be years before we reached anywhere."

"Our main concern at present is staying alive," Cormac replied.

"Perhaps we should pay the bridge pod a visit?" suggested Gant.

"Much as I feel that we have made a most effective team," said Cormac, gesturing to include Scar in this statement, "I do not think we stand much chance against twenty-two Golem. We go, *now*." He headed for the door.

"Wait!" Mika yelled, grabbing up some equipment and throwing it into a case.

Turning, Cormac said, "Is that irreplaceable?"

"Yes," she said firmly, knowing precisely what he would have said next if she'd said otherwise.

Cormac turned to Gant. "How long would it take the Golem to get here from the bridge pod?" he asked, Gant being an expert on Golem capabilities.

"Ten minutes if the drop-shafts are working." Gant shrugged. "Ten to fifteen minutes longer if they're not."

Cormac stomped a foot against the floor. "Well, if the shafts are operating as well as these grav-plates, it's more likely the latter—the safeties would have cut in. I want you to hit the weapons locker on this level, then join us by my own and Mika's cabins. Bring as much armament as you can, and make sure that includes APWs. Go!" Only anti-photon weapons were truly effective against Golem—so at least they would have that edge.

Gant proceeded to demonstrate just how fast a Golem could move.

"You ready?" Cormac asked Mika.

She nodded, dragging a heavy case along the floor until Scar very kindly took it off her and tucked it under his arm as if it weighed no more than a polystyrene block.

Cormac studied Apis. The boy looked bewildered—no sooner had he learnt that his mother was dead than this chaos had hit.

"You have to stay with us, Apis," said Cormac. "We have to get off this ship, otherwise we're dead. I have no time to explain to you what is happening now."

Apis nodded. "Yes, I understand," he said, which was the best Cormac could hope for.

The grav-plates outside Medical were fluxing, and navigating their way down the corridor was no easy task, but this made it more likely the drop-shafts were in fact out. The drop-shaft at the end of this corridor confirmed Cormac's supposition, so they climbed a side ladder leading up to the residential level. It was only as they were exiting this that Cormac wondered how Scar was managing with that case tucked under his arm. Glancing down he saw that the dracoman was managing just fine one-handed—with his legs hingeing in the opposite direction to humans, he almost did not need to use hands at all. Within a few minutes, they reached their first intended destination, and soon Gant was hurtling towards them loaded down with an assortment of weaponry, and concomitant power packs and other consumables. He skidded to a halt and dumped the weapons on the floor.

As Cormac stooped to see what had been acquired, he was annoyed to see Mika diving into her cabin—no doubt to collect more *essential* items. He handed Apis one of the APWs, and was about to point out to him how to operate the weapon when Apis shook his head.

"I know how this works," the boy informed him. "Are those who are coming against us responsible for my mother's death?"

"Sort of," Cormac replied, realizing the boy had obviously not taken in much of what had occurred so far.

Apis's expression hardened and Cormac was gratified to see that though the lad might be a physically weak Outlinker, he had some steel in him. Glancing over to Scar, he saw that the dracoman had managed to find a pull-out strap on Mika's large case and had now slung it across his back. The dracoman was stooping to make his selection from the mound of weapons.

Gant handed Cormac a pack. "I brought these along too. I can't use them myself as they're coded, but you're an ECS agent."

Cormac opened the pack and grinned. Inside, along with extra power cells for the weapons, were two small polished cylinders with twist timers set into the touch-consoles affixed to their ends. He took one out, pressed his thumb against the largest touch-pad, and a micro-screen lit up displaying seven zeros. Using two further touch-pads—one to advance each digit and one to move that control on to the next—he punched in a seven-digit number, then pressed once more with his thumb. The screen now displayed "PRIMED."

"Probably take them about ten minutes to get here. It's only a demolition charge but that should be enough to gut this part of the ship—should slow them up a little." He twisted the dial round then tossed the cylinder past Mika into her cabin, as she stepped out with a carry-pack slung over her shoulder. "Let's go," he said, as the door slid shut.

Now, as they travelled the convoluted corridors through the ship, they heard sounds as of distant objects falling, the drone of motors starting intermittently, and an occasional resounding boom that shook the vessel's entire structure. At the next shaft that would take them up towards the shuttle bay that contained the landing craft, Cormac held out his hand to Gant. "APW," he demanded.

Gant unslung one of the weapons and handed it across.

Cormac inspected the weapon. The APW had a folding stock of some light plastic, and a wide but short barrel with a polished interior. Its main body was fashioned of chainglass, and inside it gleamed pinhead green lights and a chamber apparently filled with swirling fire.

"One G canister," Cormac now demanded, holding out his hand again.

Gant rooted around in the pack and handed across a squat cylinder the size of a coffee mug, which Cormac screwed into place just before the two triggers. Manipulating switches and buttons on the side of the weapon—touch-pads were not an option on a weapon that might require resetting in darkness—he switched it to stealth mode, thus darkening the glass to hide the gleam of its lights. Further manipulation caused the weapon to emit a cycling whine.

"That a good idea?" asked Gant.

"Yeah," Cormac replied. "I'll save the other CTD for the shuttle bay." He tossed the weapon into the shaft and it dropped out of sight. As he stepped in after it and began to climb the side ladder, he heard the boy Apis ask, "What did he do?"

Gant's reply was a terse, "Set it to dump its load. Should take out most of this shaft."

They climbed quickly, gravity waves fluxing up and down the shaft so that one moment they weighed nothing and the next they were hanging on under two gees. Cormac glanced down to see how Apis was handling this and saw that the boy, in his exoskeletal suit, was perhaps doing better than the rest of them. Moving into a wide service area, Cormac checked the time on his wristcom and hurried the others out of the shaft.

"Back against the wall," he ordered, as soon as they were all out. He was about to check the time again, but there was no need. From below, there came a hollow roar, then a sudden rushing sound. The blast wave came up out of the drop-shaft, carrying with it glittering metallic fragments and a smell like that from a forge.

"That was the CTD," he said. "Come on, the APW will go soon and we don't want to be here then."

They hurried through the maintenance area where various shuttle engines and other heavy equipment were awaiting repair. Halfway through they had to pull themselves along wall bars, where a huge thruster motor was dangerously drifting above negated grav-plates. Soon they reached the end of this area, then entered a tunnel that led to the shuttle bay. The tunnel was wide—for the transportation of engine parts—with sealed double doors at its end. Reaching these, Cormac thumped the palm lock, but nothing happened.

He glanced at Gant. "Vacuum?"

Gant stepped close to the edge of the doors and peered closely at where they met the jamb. After a moment, he stepped back shaking his head. "No, the seals aren't down." Then he turned and faced back the way they had come, and tilted his head to listen. "They're coming," he said. Just then, there was another explosion behind them as the APW dumped its load.

Cormac stepped back. "Scar, the door!"

With the others hurrying to get safely behind him, the dracoman moved back from the doors and fired. Purple flame ignited the air between his weapon and the obdurate surface. The explosion was deafening and blasted a hole perhaps a metre across. The second explosion took out a similar amount of material above this, blasting metallic smoke and fragments into the shuttle bay beyond.

Meanwhile, with cold precision, Cormac primed the second CTD and set the timer for five minutes. Then came further flashes and explosions as Gant fired back the way they had come. Cormac glanced in that direction as he propped the CTD above a console set into the wall. Back at the further edge of the maintenance bay a gleaming skeletal shape flew apart in proton fire—gleaming bones and a polished skull clanging across the floor plates—just as another one came swiftly in behind it. Himself firing in short bursts, Cormac glanced to the doors and saw that Mika and Apis were through them and that Scar was on his way.

"You go on through," said Gant, then abruptly fired up at the ceiling as one of the ship's Golem came scuttling across it like a spider. The explosion took out ceiling panels and caused sparking cables, insulation, and structural members to rain down. Half the lighting panels went out. Cormac did not hesitate—Gant could move a damned sight faster than he could, so it was logical he should come through last. Cormac was already running for the landing craft when to his horror he saw that blast doors were slowly drawing across the shimmer-shield maintained over the mouth of the bay.

"Move it, Gant!"

Behind him there were further explosions. He reached the craft just behind the others and looked back just as Gant dived through the doors, rolled, came upright and turned and fired at the ship's Golem following close behind him. Then Gant was running for the landing craft. Cormac went down on one knee and took careful aim at the doors—subliminally seeing Scar doing the same beside him. At his back he heard thrusters starting on the landing craft and felt a side-wash as the grav-plates underneath it disengaged. Two Golem came through the doors, both of them with pulse-rifles. Scar and Cormac's fire intersected on one and blew it to scrap. The second one fired at Gant, and had him stumbling with smoke exploding from his back. But Gant was Golem too and soon regained his balance and continued. Scar now hit the second Golem, while Cormac tracked other movement to his right. More Golem over there, and he felt a sinking in his stomach when he saw what they were carrying.

"Into the ship, now!" he bellowed, Gant being close enough.

They piled into the landing craft even as it began to lift and turn. Cormac glanced ahead, saw Apis at the controls, and thought it superfluous to urge him to get them out of there. He hurried forward, dropped into the seat beside the Outlinker, strapped himself in, and glanced down at the screen giving a rear view, as the craft tilted nose-down and headed for the shimmer-shield. But there were Golem back there, aiming APWs, so this was not fast enough. Purple flashes igniting the bay, the craft lurched as if a giant hand had slapped its back end.

"Use the ion drive," Cormac instructed—calm and cold.

Apis hit the control for ion drive but, obviously damaged, it blew out its grids and hot metal exploded back into the bay—straight into the faces of the Golem. There was some satisfaction in that, but now nothing but the thrusters operated, and it seemed to be taking forever to reach the shimmer-shield. Cormac noticed that the outer doors had ceased to close, it now being evident that they would not close in time to prevent the landing craft getting out of the bay. Behind, more Golem with APWs were gathering. Skellor did not want those doors now closed between themselves and the Golem. Purple flares again, and again the ship lurched, pieces of it blasting forward, away past the cockpit, in a glittering shower out into space. Then white light filled the bay behind them as the second CTD detonated, and the craft tumbled out through the shimmer-shield on a plume of fire.

"Perfect timing," opined Gant, as he grabbed Scar and pulled the dracoman down into a seat, before strapping himself in. Scar dropped his seat back as far as it would go, for only like this would it accommodate him, and he snarled as he too strapped himself in. Mika muttered something, turned pale, then grabbed up a sick-bag from the compartment on one side of her seat—with grav-plates being so common in Polity ships, there were not many who'd had the microsurgical alteration to their inner ear that prevented motion sickness. Apis, of course, was now in his element.

"Yeah," said Cormac, glancing back at Gant. "But Skellor got control of the doors, so how long before he gets control of the weapons systems?"

All of them gazed at the screens as the craft's thrusters propelled it with painful slowness from the vast ship, so that they rose almost like a drifting balloon from a metal plain. Cormac wondered how long it would take. Tomalon had said Skellor now controlled the *Occam*'s engines, so he could trundle along behind them while he got the dreadnought's weapons online. In fact he probably wouldn't even need to move the *Occam*—they weren't exactly escaping at any great speed.

"Perhaps we should have stayed in there?" Gant suggested.

Difficult call: if they had stayed, the Golem would have killed them; escaping like this the *Occam*'s weapons would kill them. With his emotions under a mental boot heel, Cormac realized he had lost, and that he and these people with him were soon to die.

Then something occluded their horizon: a moonlet of scaled flesh rolled down on them and engulfed them in wombish blackness. Momentarily they were slammed from side to side, and the landing craft groaned as if it might break. Then there was that familiar dislocation, that strange sideways pull into the ineffable, and Cormac knew they had entered U-space. He reached out to the console before Apis, and clicked down the button for external com.

"I thought you'd lost your ability for trans-stellar flight," he said.

"I lied," Dragon replied.

Enough of what it was to be human remained in him for the need to verbalize orders rather than assume complete control of their recipients. He gazed down at the *Occam Razor*'s Captain and saw that the man had managed to crawl as far as the door since being dethroned, leaving a snail trail of blood and plasma.

"Kill that," Skellor instructed, and both Aphran and Danny walked across to the man and fired into his body simultaneously. Tomalon hardly moved—perhaps he had died already.

Skellor now gazed down at himself and realized that he would have to be permanently enthroned so long as he wanted to control this ship. Initially the Jain substructure had sent filaments into the connections, and down the optic cables and ducts that spread from this point, to control the disparate elements of the *Occam Razor*. But as he had sought to refill those spaces where the burn program had taken out essential AI subsystems, it had been necessary for him to thicken those filaments for the transference of information and power—to grow outwards into the ship. Now he sat enfolded in thick ligneous growths, like some woodland statue long abandoned in the roots of an oak. With every effort he made to take control of a system, this structure grew and thickened.

He looked up at Aphran and Danny. The boy wore no expression as, even though not directly linked, he was now a part of the structure—of Skellor. Aphran, however, bore an expression of barely contained horror.

"Go and find those of your group who have survived, and return with them here," he instructed, then silently watched as they turned to the doors. With a microscopic part of himself, he opened those doors ahead of them. That had been one victory, one small system he had overcome. But not enough.

Still Skellor struggled to worm through the hardwired security that remained in place throughout the ship—integral to the control of the weapons systems—and still he was not quite there. So Cormac and his companions had escaped— just when he thought he had them, they had slipped from his grasp. And that both angered and scared him.

Skellor understood that no one must ever know of what he had done. ECS would hunt him down *forever*, and thus he would never be able to settle and find his strength. All those who had escaped must die—including Dragon. But before he killed them, he must first gain full control here. Connecting to cameras one after the other, he tracked the progress of Aphran and Danny through the ship, just as he tracked them from the inside through their augs. It occurred to him then that the two Separatists were operating like submind-directed ship's drones, and that this was a much more efficient option than him trying to *completely* control everything. He could have called the remaining Separatists to himself, but that would have required him to personally direct each one here, which used up processing space. Yes, a certain amount of self-determination in those units underneath him was a good thing; that would free him up to concentrate on other tasks. He understood that there was a limit to just how much he could be *aware* of. It was not so much a case of processing power and memory space, but almost one of having some sort of emotional investment in every situation or system he controlled or viewed.

Turning his head as much as the Jain structure allowed, Skellor viewed the other chairs in this bridge pod, and understood what he must do—there was a rightness to it, almost as if preordained. Seven chairs—and through Aphran and Danny's augs he sensed that—including themselves—seven of the Separatists remained alive.

With an effort that momentarily blinded him to the continuous input of information from that part of the ship he did control, he grew spurs from those roots of Jain structure below the floor. He felt them rapidly growing, feeding on and converting the surrounding material as they did so—insulation, plastics, metals, chainglass. From the skein of optics he was already tracking out to the navigational instruments scattered about the surface of the ship, he sent a spur to one of those chairs. From the monitoring systems for the engines, another. From weapons control, life-support, internal security, ship's maintenance, and shield control. Other smaller systems he attached where appropriate—structural integrity to ship's maintenance, a split spur for control of the ship's reactors to all of them . . . Command was totally his own, but each of the others would possess what autonomy he allowed them. Glancing down he watched these growths breaking through the floor below the seven seats and spreading underneath them. Then he stared at the doors and waited for his command crew to appear.

The utter stillness was familiar and Thorn immediately became aware that he was waking from cold-sleep. Running through mental routines inculcated into him over the many years of his training, he tried to remember just what his and Gant's assignment was this time and, as had happened before, he remembered that Gant was dead. Confusion reigned for a moment as he tried to place himself—to remember where he was and what he was doing. Moving forward from the moment of Gant's death, he remembered his return to Earth and the attempts by a Sparkind general to dissuade him from transferring out, next the retraining in both VR and the field for undercover duties in ECS, and a couple of infiltration missions in the Sol system before shipping out to Cheyne III. Then he remembered what had happened there.

There came a buzzing click, then a crack, and a pale line of light cut down to the left of him. Knowing what came next in no way ameliorated the sudden feeling of pins and needles as the nerve-blocker detached from his neck—it felt as if someone had been rolling him in cactus spines. The lid of the cold-coffin swung away from him—a man-shaped impression in hoared metal. This being a coffin that was upright in relation to ship's gravity, handles extruded from the metal on either side of him and he grabbed them as soon as he was able to move his arms. The needles retracted, to be replaced by the sensation of his skin having been rubbed raw—burnt even. He gasped his first breath, fluid bubbled in his lungs, and he coughed and swallowed. Looking to his left, he saw John Stanton step out of his own coffin and begin isometric exercises—obviously the man was a veteran of travelling this way. It took Thorn a while longer, as he lifted each leg alternately and flexed it, stretched his back and neck, then stepped out as if onto ice, with one hand still gripping a handle for support.

"It never gets any better," he commented.

After touching his toes a couple of times, then running on the spot for a moment with his breath gouting in the cold air of the hold, Stanton replied, "Never really bothered me. Sometimes you welcome the oblivion on long hauls." Stanton moved down past Thorn and headed towards the entry to the ship's living quarters. Over his shoulder he said, "Only one shower here, so you'll have to wait."

Thorn now tried a few exercises himself. Even though normal sensation had mostly returned, the ends of his fingers were still numb from the nerve damage done by the toxin Brom had used on him. Another session with this ship's autodoc seemed likely, he realized, as he went to a locker beside the coffins to find himself disposable overalls to wear while he awaited his turn in the shower. Donning the compressed paper fabric, he glanced round as Jarvellis stepped out of the flight cabin, heading for the living quarters.

"Where are we?" he asked her.

She halted and studied him. "Just coming insystem. The gas giant Calypse sits between Masada and us at the moment. It'll take about six days." She gestured towards the flight cabin. "By all means go and take a look. John and I need a little privacy for a while."

Closing the stick-strip of his coverall, Thorn nodded and, after slipping on the deck shoes that came in the same packet, headed towards the flight cabin. He understood her perfectly: obviously she had come out of cold-sleep some time before himself and Stanton, and he well knew how the body's normal function kicked in over a very short period of time—he himself had often felt unbearably horny in the hour after thaw-up. What he did not understand was why the two of them hadn't left him on ice for a while longer. Looking around, he was suddenly aware of how cramped the cargo area now was. With only small chagrin, he realized that Stanton and Jarvellis had been out of cold-sleep at least once since he himself had gone into it.

In the flight cabin, Thorn dropped into one of the command chairs and gazed at the main screen. Displayed there was the gas giant Calypse, with the corona of the sun glaring to the right of it—its main light muted by a black reactant disc. As Stanton had explained before they had gone into cold-sleep, Masada was surrounded by the laser arrays and cylinder worlds of the Theocracy, with the planetary population held in constant thrall by the ruling caste's technological advantage. This being the case he wondered how his colleagues intended to get *Lyric II* down to the surface. Admittedly, there were often holes through which a small ship could slip, since in any space-borne civilization there had to be a lot of traffic. But this ship, though it could be mistaken for an insystem hauler, was not exactly small. He thought he might as well experiment.

"Lyric, are you able to respond to me?" he asked.

"I *can* respond, though you might not like the response," the ship AI replied.

"I'm a little puzzled about how Stanton intends to get this ship down to the planet's surface undetected. He told me that there's just one spaceport and that's only for Theocracy military or cargo traffic, and I've every reason to suspect that the cargo on board here is not for them."

"And what was your question?" Lyric asked him.

"How does he intend to get this ship down to the surface of Masada undetected?"

"Sorry, can't tell you that."

"Do you have Theocracy security codes?"

"Didn't last time I looked."

Sitting back Thorn grimaced to himself: only the terminally naive believed that AIs did not lie. In fact, in his own experience AIs made better liars than human beings.

"What's your cargo?" he asked bluntly.

"Do get real, Mr. Polity agent."

"Okay, what can you tell me about Masada?"

"I've got about ten thousand hours on the subject. What do you want to know? Political system, ecosystem, symbiotic adaptation, religion? About half of what I have covers *that* last subject alone."

"How about half an hour's eclectic selection? I should think I'll be able to get use of the shower by then."

"All right, I'll begin with the planetary ecosystem prior to the arrival of human beings, findings of the first surveys, then subsequent occupation, and then the history of the Theocracy. Would that be sufficient?"

"Yes, thank you."

With Thorn asking questions, the film show lasted an hour. The two items that most fascinated him were the natural ecosystem and the odd life system introduced by the Theocracy: in the former case the tricones, heroynes, gabbleducks and terrifying hooders; and in the latter the adapted crops and protein sources that were a product of the toil of most of the surface inhabitants. Also the symbiotic life-forms created as a cheaper alternative to breathers and environment suits, as well as being more dogmatically acceptable to the Theocracy than any adaptation of the God-given human form. He was just asking about the Underground when Stanton entered the flight cabin.

"Not a very stable situation," Thorn observed to him.

"No, but stable enough to last for another fifty years, without a sufficient push to topple it meanwhile," Stanton replied.

Thorn gestured to the cargo hold. "And all that stuff's part of the 'push'?"

"It is," said Stanton. "And, do you know, when I bought the main bulk of this cargo on Huma, that planet was undergoing Polity subsumption."

"That normally takes some time, but obviously you found an opening?"

Stanton shrugged. "So I thought. Things were chaotic there, but not very much so. When I found out how tight the security was, I was tempted to go somewhere else, but then a dealer approached me."

"But you risked the deal anyway?" Thorn asked.

"I had a way out but, strangely, I didn't need it. The Polity agents I could see watching my every move did not even attempt to intervene."

"You're saying you have Polity sanction?"

"It was known who I was buying this cargo for. What I am saying is that it's in the interest of the Polity for things to become as unstable as possible on Masada. ECS intends to draw the Line across the world, and most of its population will welcome them gladly."

"Will you?"

Stanton stared at the screen, now showing a lurid but almost rustic scene on the surface of the planet—except for the proctors watching over all from their aerofans, with rail-guns trained on the people below.

"As a child here I always felt there had to be something better than Theocracy rule, but while here, and for some time after, I never saw how you could get beyond the sordid facts of human nature. I've since learnt that the way you do get beyond is by removing human nature from the equation."

"So you are a reformed Separatist?" said Thorn.

Stanton glared at him. "I have never been a Separatist. I'm a mercenary, and that's all."

"Why this, then?" Thorn gestured first at the screen, then at the hold.

"Because I have scores to settle and debts to repay."

Thorn stood and moved to the door, and Stanton walked with him to the ship's living quarters. They entered an area laid out like any planetary house, with a kitchen and eating area, and for the second time Thorn studied his surroundings with some surprise. Most ships possessed automatic food dispensers, yet *Lyric II* had both this and a small galley, which was an expensive option. He felt a surge of nostalgia at the smell of grilling bacon, and also had to swallow a surge of saliva.

"How do you get down to the surface of the planet without being detected?" he tried.

Stanton went over to check the grilling bacon. Jarvellis, who was going through the complicated process of grinding real beans for a filter coffee maker, glanced at her man with interest—no doubt wondering how much he was prepared to tell this ECS agent.

"Take your shower now, then we'll talk while we have breakfast. Your clothes are in there." Stanton pointed.

Thorn moved through into the bathroom of this thoroughly domestic section of the ship, and was further surprised to find luxuries more commonly associated with the huge holiday cruisers found in populous systems like Sol's. There was a shower set over a wide tub big enough to take two people comfortably, and though the shower itself had the usual ultrasound settings and air-drying heads, there were big fluffy white towels on a heated rail nearby. Obviously these two enjoyed their comforts, but comforts like these on a spaceship cost a lot of money.

He pondered the probable source of that money, and recalled the findings of the investigation on planet Viridian. They had revealed that, though the Separatist mercenary Pelter had destroyed the original *Lyric*, Jarvellis had escaped and managed to rejoin her lover Stanton on Viridian itself. But Pelter's money—some millions in the form of etched sapphires—had never been recovered. It would now seem there had been enough for them to buy a larger trispherical ship like this one, and have it fitted out to their requirements. Thorn found he could not resent them their windfall, for Stanton's betrayal of Pelter had enabled agent Cormac to kill the rogue Separatist and concentrate on the larger mission in hand—which was investigating the Samarkand disaster. It was then that Cormac had encountered the alien called the Maker, and finally learnt of the legendary Dragon's responsibility for the destruction of all life on Samarkand.

With the Maker he had connived in inflicting a suitable punishment for this crime—one which reduced the first Dragon sphere to orbital debris.

When he stepped into the shower, Thorn was further surprised when a shimmer-shield came on around the edge of the bath. As he luxuriated in needle jets of hot water, soaping himself down with a rough bar of real soap, he was puzzled to note a couple of toys sitting on the edge of the bath: a small submarine, of the type used in the strange sea inside Europa, and a dark-otter—both obviously operated by a small remote affixed to the porcelain-effect tiling along the adjacent wall. Neither Stanton nor Jarvellis struck him as the type to play with these sorts of toys; he imagined their toys would be of either the erotic or the lethal kind.

After his shower, he found his clothes waiting in an automatic cleaner inset in the wall. All the blood and filth had been removed, and rips invisibly repaired. It was almost a relief to recognize that this had been entirely done by machine—he could not stand the mental image of either of the other two sewing up his trousers with a needle and thread, since it would mean they were entirely insane. Over disposable underwear, he donned the same fatigues, white shirt, and denim jacket he had been wearing when Lutz and Ternan had taken him to meet Brom. Then he pulled on his favoured leather boots—special issue to ECS, and so hard-wearing that they normally only required replacement for the same reason their possessor might require the replacement of a foot. Suitably clad he moved out into the eating area to be presented with a plate of bacon, egg, garlic-fried mushrooms and a large mug of real coffee. Stanton and Jarvellis, he suddenly decided, had made the successful transition from criminals into saints.

"You asked me how we intend to get down to the surface of the planet undetected," Stanton said. "We'll tell you this, and anything else you want to know, if you're prepared to throw in with us—to help." Before Thorn could reply, Stanton held up an eggy fork to silence him and went on, "Before you answer that, there's some things you need to know. You already know what the situation is on Masada, but what you perhaps don't realize is that Polity agents have already been distributing the electronic ballot, and filtering in what technical support they can for the rebellion. Masada is probably no more than a few years away from subsumption."

"How have they been getting stuff in?" Thorn asked.

"It's not entirely closed there," Stanton replied. "The Theocracy manufacturing base is not efficient, so they trade luxury proteins and food essences in exchange for tools and equipment—and wherever there's trade there's smuggling."

"I see," said Thorn—and he did see. If the Polity supported this rebellion, then it was his duty to do the same. He would first have to confirm what Stanton was telling him, but otherwise saw no problem about throwing in his lot with them. In fact he quite looked forward to the prospect as, from what he knew about Stanton, the man was a consummate professional. "If what you say is true, then I'm with you. It is in fact my job."

"Well, that's nice," said Jarvellis, staring directly at Thorn. "Of course, if you betray us in any way, one of us will kill you."

"Likewise," said Thorn, grinning at her.

She tilted her head in acknowledgement, then with a glance at Stanton went on, "We have chameleonware."

"That won't cover an AG reading," Thorn observed.

"Not quite," she said. "But it can blur it for over a quarter of a kilometre, and the Theocracy don't have anything sophisticated enough to pick that up. Our only problem really is the braking burn, as this 'ware isn't sufficient to cover the heat signature and ionic trail that leaves."

Thorn considered what she had just told him. Polity chameleonware could never cover AG readings, which was why, for a hidden descent onto a planet's surface, ECS used stealthed dropbirds to glide on in.

"Is this the same 'ware as they used on Brom's barge?" he asked.

"It is," Stanton replied. "I was there making the second payment for it, which was why there was no tight security around me, and why I could do what I did."

"I thought you were there after Deacon Aberil Dorth?"

"Coincidental. I'd intended to get him on Masada all along."

"I guess I was lucky he was there, then. Perhaps if you hadn't been intent on demolishing Brom's barge, you wouldn't have released me."

"Oh, I intended to fuck Brom over anyway. Poisonous insects like him are best stamped on quickly," Stanton replied.

Thorn studied him for a long moment. What were this man's motivations now? Before the events on Viridian, his only apparent motivation had been money. Why had he changed so much since then? Thorn let the thought go—he never felt inclined to analyse too closely someone else's character, just as he never felt inclined to ask similar questions of himself.

"Do you know the original source of this chameleon-ware? Brom was a little reticent about it and, as you know, I never really got a chance to ask him about it later."

"Separatist research base—and before you ask, no, I don't know where it is. They apparently have a topflight biophysicist working for them. He was also the one who made Brom's poisonous little toy. I only got a name: Skellor."

Thorn vaguely recalled something about that name— something in connection with another operation. That being the case, he supposed ECS had—or were about to—put a terminal brake on the man's activities.

Thorn turned to Jarvellis. "You were telling me about the heat signature and ionic trail."

Having finished her breakfast, Jarvellis sat back with her mug cradled in her hands before her. "Well, most of it we are doing now, shielded by Calypse. The rest we do in atmosphere over Masada itself."

"How the hell do you cover that?"

When she told him, Thorn thought perhaps these two *were* a little insane.

10

With methodical determination and without much resort to the use of knives and forks, the boy munched his way through his dinner. Sitting at the table beside him the woman sipped distractedly at a cup of coffee and studied the open book propped on her knee.

"And thus it was," she said, "that Brother Serendipity was sent out to find his fortune amongst the compounds, but by the evil of the morlocks was driven out into the wilderness." The woman snorted and muttered, "Morlocks, my arse." Then continued with, "Upon the first day of those three numbered by his oxygen supply, he came upon the young heroyne starving in the flute grass."

The woman glanced across and saw that her audience was more intent on trying to spear a broiled shellfish than on the story. She continued anyway, "'Please feed me for I have been abandoned and I am hungry,' the creature begged. 'Why should I feed you when, with strength, you could eat me?' asked Brother Serendipity. 'I give my word,' the heroyne replied. 'Swear your word in the name of God and in the name of his prophet Zelda Smythe,' the Brother demanded. So the heroyne swore and Brother Serendipity gave it one third of the meat cake the old woman by the . . ." The woman stopped and closed the book to check the front cover. It still read Mortal Tales and still bore a picture of a gabbleduck eating a priest, just like her son was tucking into his bread soldiers.

She shrugged and went on: "Thus it was that the heroyne followed him into the night and no other creature attacked him. The Brother's piety and goodness of heart had saved him."

The woman made a gagging sound and scrolled the text down further.

The Reverend Epthirieth Loman Dorth stood in the viewing room of his tower, gazing out upon the canted ceiling of the Up Mirror of *Faith*, and thought that this must be how God felt. Stepping closer to the bulging windows of Polity chainglass, he stared down into the vast well of the *Faith* cylinder world into which the Up Mirror reflected sunlight, and observed the swirls of cloud over the wondrous buildings and vast gardens contained therein, which blurred and faded down to the bright eye of the Down Mirror at the far end of the world. With a light touch through his aug—his *Gift*—he received the impression of thousands of communications being conducted against the strong background swell of prayer throughout the upper channels from the Friars of the Septarchies: this being the way they had found, at last, to prevent the mind of Behemoth from invading their own. When the creature had first come with the gift of its augs, it had seemed an envoy of God, but they had soon seen the ambivalence of its generosity. The biotech devices gave them great power to communicate, to control, to understand, but enabled the creature itself to slowly assert its will over them through the upper channels. Now the Friars prayed, day and night in shifts, thousands of them, to keep the mind of Behemoth at bay.

When he heard the door hissing open behind him and the stamp of feet as the soldiers halted and came to attention, he did not turn. A brief probe told him who was there, and why they were there.

"Is he ready?" he asked, seeking verbal confirmation as, even with the protection of prayer, the *Gift* was not to be trusted.

"He is, Hierarch," said one of the men.

Loman turned, relishing that title, but also wondering if Major Claus was seeking advancement. The man stood with two subordinates, all three of them well armed and armoured. Claus was immaculate but for blood spattered up one leg; however, the others wore filthy and torn uniforms.

All three of the men looked bone weary, but at least they could still stand upright, and in that had the advantage over many of their fellows. It had been a long hard struggle, but well worth the prize.

"Claus, do not call me Hierarch until after my investiture. It would be best to let the Council continue with the illusion that they have retained some power. "Now, let's go and see to Amoloran's . . . disinvestiture."

The three fell in behind him as he exited the tower room. Loman glanced sideways and noted how Claus had moved in close to his left—the position of an advisor and one who shared in the ultimate position. He considered sending the man a pace or two back, then rejected the idea. The reality of the power game was that you needed the army on your side and, thus far, Claus had served a purpose, though he would be removed when the time was right.

"Reverend, I should also let you know that your brother has returned from Cheyne III with bad news: Brom has been killed and his organization is broken," said Claus.

Loman hesitated at the head of the spiral staircase which wound down beside one glass wall of the tower, as he checked this news through his aug. "No matter, there will always be others to fight the Polity on our behalf and they will never have sufficient reason to come here once Ragnorak has done its work." Glancing at the Major, Loman saw that the man looked dubious and wanted to make some comment on that. Loman went on, "It is all planned for. We are the Chosen, and we will not fail."

"As you will, Reverend," said Claus, which was not entirely the wholehearted response Loman would have liked, but that was probably due to the Major's weariness.

Feeling generous Loman went on, "After Ragnorak, I feel that you will have much work to do on the surface, *Commander* Claus."

They descended the stairs to the large chamber Loman had chosen for his own investiture later, and as they did so, he could not help but speculate on how much this tower of Amoloran's had cost in precious resources. Every step was a grav-plate, every one of the tower's fifty floors was tiled with them, and the security system—as he well knew—was particularly advanced. Of course that system had not proved sufficient when the power lines leading from solar panels mounted below the Up Mirror had been severed. It had been remiss of Amoloran to rely too heavily on the *Gift*—the men he, Loman, had sent to cut the power had been recruited from the surface, so were without augs to be detected; and, with a sufficient promise of future influence, the Septarchy Friars had clogged other channels that might have given things away.

Only half of the Council were present: those others who had supported the previous hierarch either taking their own lives maybe at that very moment, or, if they had the wealth to possess such, fleeing in their own crafts. The four hundred soldiers Claus had led in here were currently arrayed around the walls, or scattered through the crowd that was now, very quickly, growing silent. Loman moved out into the open space rapidly cleared at the foot of the stairs and gazed around. Many private channels were open, but he did not feel inclined to force his way in to them, as he knew what most of these people would be thinking. In the end it did not matter what they thought or discussed, just so long as they obeyed.

Set up at the back of the room was the pillar and the frame and he noticed how many Council members of questionable loyalty were glancing at this device nervously. After a moment, one member of the crowd broke away and approached to drop on one knee and take up Loman's hand. The Reverend Loman gazed down into the expressionless face of his brother.

"You return at an opportune time," said Loman.

"I would have come sooner, Reverend, but Brom was cowardly and was hesitating to send his people against the Cereb runcible. And he hesitated too long," Aberil replied.

Loman beckoned him to rise to his feet and opened a private link with him. *"You were sent on a fool's errand anyway. Supplying Separatists gives the Polity an opening through which they can reach us. We must not overextend ourselves and we must be patient."*

Aberil replied, "*Amoloran was without focus or sufficient faith, and he would have destroyed us with his foolishness. You have done the right thing, brother.*"

"*I have done what is required of me by God.*"

"*As do we all.*"

Loman waved Aberil behind him, to his right side—a position Aberil took with some alacrity. Now Loman turned to Claus. "Let it be done," he said.

Claus gave the signal to his men at the back of the chamber, and the crowd parted as Amoloran was marched out, guards supporting him on either side as his legs kept giving way. The old man looked bewildered and terrified—as was only right. Loman noted with some distaste the bright yellow urine stains down the front of the disposable coverall he had earlier been dressed in. The guards dragged him to the frame and began tearing away his coverall as Loman advanced to stand before him. Amoloran resisted them, but to no avail, and soon he was naked and fighting only the obdurate metal that held him cruciform before the crowd.

Tilting his head towards Claus, Loman asked, "Did he have a way out?"

Claus held out his hand, in the palm of which rested three small translucent capsules. "Implanted under his fingernails. He also had a nerve jammer concealed in his neck jewel—and this." Claus held out a beautiful tool of old stainless steel—a spoon with its edges honed sharp.

"You think he would kill himself with a sculping tool?" asked Loman. "I think that gouging out his own eyes would not have been the way he would like to go."

Claus shook his head and pointed at the tool. "Neurotoxin in the handle, to be pumped through micropores in the edges, your reverence. Primarily used to cause pain, but there's the option to pump out the full amount, so one cut would cause instant death."

As he hung the tool on one of his own belt hooks, Loman nodded to himself: this was always how it happened—those of high rank always had a way to kill themselves should the situation require it, and always realized too late when that situation occurred. Himself, he had similar nerve-poison capsules implanted under his fingernails, and he would use them before it ever came to this for him.

"You left him his *Gift*, I see," he said.

Claus looked momentarily worried. "I thought it best to leave that decision to you."

"Remove it now."

Claus fisted his own chest then strode over to the old man in the frame.

"No . . . no, you can't," Amoloran gasped as Claus closed his fingers around the scaled aug behind the old man's ear. Amoloran screeched when Claus tore it off and cast it on the floor. There came an ominous muttering from the crowd, quickly stilled as Loman glanced around at them.

To all, through his aug, he broadcast, "*He loved the* Gift *more than God. Will anyone here listen to his spoken confession?*"

No one stepped forward.

"Have you chosen the program?" Aberil asked.

Loman glanced at him. "No, brother. Do you have any suggestions?"

"I have, and with a healthy individual it can last for eight hours." Aberil stared at the aged Hierarch, his expression now containing more animation than was customary. "Let me."

Loman waved him to go ahead and Aberil quickly went over to a console at the side of the pillar and started tapping away with relish. The frame began to rise, and all around it the knives and bone saws, electric probes and injectors began to sprout and revolve. Amoloran let out a yell, then bowed his head and began the prayer of the Fifth Satagent—the choice of many who faced this fate.

Loman gazed around at the crowd again. They were all watching with avid and in some cases slightly sick expressions—but they were all watching. Aberil's torture programs were legendary, so perhaps many of them hoped to learn something here.

"See the betrayer of God's word," said Loman out loud, holding up one admonitory finger. "He would have had us attack each other while our enemy encroached upon our world. He would allow Behemoth back amongst us. And in the end he would have had us sacrifice love of God for love of technology." Amoloran was now babbling quickly through the last verses of his prayer, which was somewhat distracting. Loman raised his voice. "See, this is what will happen to any who would undermine our destiny. Ragnorak comes now to lance the infection on the planet below us, and as it heals we can turn outward to face our enemy. We are—"

The low thud perfectly punctuated the last verse of Amoloran's prayer. Loman glared upwards and gobbets of flesh spattered his face, just as they did with many of those who stood about him. He pulled something lumpy from his forehead and stared with disgust at the piece of bone and brain he held between his forefinger and thumb. Amoloran hung quivering in the frame. He retained his jaw, but the rest of his head had disappeared. Loman turned and marched angrily away—Claus, then Aberil, hurrying to catch up with him.

"I'm sorry," said Claus. "I'll punish that idiot on the scanner."

"Interesting one," admitted Loman. "Explosive grafts in the bone of his skull. Detonated, apparently, by a recitation of the Fifth Satagent."

Upon reaching the stairs, he turned once again to face the vast room. Studying face after face in turn, he detected only blank or sympathetic expressions—no one in sight dared show any amusement at his embarrassment. Glancing at Aberil he sent, *"I think you know."*

Aberil's knife was out and slicing across Claus's throat before the man had a chance to realize he was in danger, then Aberil tripped him and sent him flying face-down to the floor, to prevent him spraying too much blood over Loman.

Wiping a few spatters from his robe, Loman said, "It's good to have family with one in such situations. Welcome home, *First Commander* Aberil."

Scar was behaving quite strangely, but then perhaps that was understandable considering he was now inside the twin of the vast entity that might have been described as his mother. The dracoman, rather than holding himself to his customary stillness, had released himself from his seat and was pushing his way round the craft in agitation. Cormac was also agitated—they had survived, but it seemed debatable how much longer they might do so. The clonks and slitherings had centred on the airlock and now he could hear a low ratcheting sound.

"Dragon, what are you doing?" he asked, his finger pressed down on the com button.

"I am coming in," Dragon replied, which was not exactly a comfort.

Cormac noticed the Outlinker's head come up at this, and how the boy reached his hand up to the hood of his exoskeleton.

Noticing Cormac's attention, Apis said, "Both airlocks can be opened from outside."

Of course—this was a fact of which Apis was well aware.

"I wouldn't bother with your hood or mask," said Cormac. "If Dragon wants to kill us now, there's not a lot we can do about it." He glanced towards Gant, noticing that, even though the Golem cradled an APW as he undid his seat straps, his expression was resigned.

"It seems to me that Dragon must have some purpose for us," opined Mika, her attention focused on Scar. She still looked ill, but the inhaler she had just used seemed to be having some effect; at least she hadn't yet required another sick-bag.

"But *what* purpose?" asked Cormac. "We know it's pissed off at the Masadans and intends some damage there, but in my experience when Dragon intends to do some damage it usually involves large smoking craters. I can't see why it wants us at all, unless it intends to throw this landing craft at one of the Theocracy cylinder worlds."

Now there came sounds from the inner door of the lock, and as a group they pushed themselves up from their seats and moved over to the opposite side of the craft. As the wheel of the lock spun, Cormac sensed something of what the previous occupants of this craft must have felt when Apis had opened it to vacuum. The door cracked open, and all down its edge fleshy fingers intruded, dark red and covered with scales. Slowly, working on its hydraulics, the door continued to open, and in this Cormac felt some comfort. Knowing Dragon's capabilities he felt it a good sign that the door was being allowed to open at its own rate and had not been already ripped off its hinges. This meant it likely Dragon wanted to keep this landing craft in a usable condition. He just hoped it wanted the same for its occupants.

Fully open, the door revealed fleshy chaos: a pit of ophidian pseudopods terminating in flat cobra heads, each containing a single pupilless blue eye where a mouth should have been; tangles of thinner red tentacles; fleshy webs as of those between the toes of an aquatic reptile binding much of this mass together; and visual flashes of cavernous life beyond. The craft filled with the smell of cloves, of burnt meat, and of a terrarium. The mass oozed its way in, pseudopods hooking up into the air with their blue eyes darting in every direction; then a new addition forced its way through, and rose above them. This had a ribbed snakelike body, pterosaur head and sapphire eyes. Cormac experienced definite déjà vu and wondered what opaque conversation would now ensue.

"I am dying, Ian Cormac," said the pterosaur head.

Cormac pushed himself away from the wall towards the centre of the craft, hooking the toe of his boot on the seat back and folding his arms across his chest. "I've heard that one before."

The head turned so that its eyes focused on Scar. "But I will live," it added.

This was more like the Dragon of old: conversations that were like a sorting of wheat from chaff and discovering potatoes.

"What do you mean?"

The head swung back towards Cormac, spraying milky saliva across the rows of seats below him. Not for the first time Cormac wondered how many heads like this each Dragon sphere possessed, or if they could manufacture them at will—as they did dracomen.

"I will destroy the laser arrays," it said.

"Well, that's . . . helpful."

"They have five ships equivalent to Polity mu-class battleships."

"Of the type you've already encountered?" suggested Cormac.

"That one did not survive the encounter."

Cormac noticed Apis flinch.

"You didn't exactly get off lightly," Cormac said.

"I will not get off at all this time."

Now, despite not intending to be dragged into one of those circular and somewhat pointless conversations Dragon seemed to specialize in, Cormac could not help but yield to his own confusion. "So why the hell are you going there?"

"To live again."

It figured.

"What do you want with us?" Cormac asked.

"As I destroy their laser arrays and satellites, your descent will be unhindered. Rebellion will then come to the Theocracy, and my legions will arise."

"What the fuck are you talking about? Did that mu-class battleship fry part of your brain?"

The head swung once more towards Scar.

"I name thee Cadmus," it said, and withdrew as it had come, the lock closing behind it.

"What was that all about?" asked Mika, and all that had just occurred had sufficiently bemused Cormac so that it took him a moment to realize that she had actually asked a question.

He turned to her. "Shame you chose *that* question for your initiation into the world of normal conversation. I haven't a clue."

"Seems things are going our way . . . sort of," said Gant, easing his grip on his APW when he found that he had crushed the stock.

"Yeah, and that worries me," Cormac replied, then turned to Scar. "What was that Cadmus stuff about?"

Staring fixedly at the airlock, Scar replied, "I do not know."

"I know who Cadmus was," Apis suddenly said, and they all turned to gaze at him. He went on, "He is a man from Greek myth—on Earth. We were learning about Greek myths in our history lessons, as Farins, our teacher, says that a general knowledge of humanity is necessary even if your intended career is only in metallurgy." Apis paused and took a breath, and Cormac wondered if this same Farins had been on the destroyed Masadan ship. Apis continued, "Cadmus was a man who killed a dragon then pulled out its teeth and sowed them in the ground. From the teeth grew men who were going to kill him, until he threw a precious stone amongst them. They started killing each other as they sought to possess this stone. Those that remained alive joined him, and helped him build something . . . a city I think . . ." Apis ran out of words.

"I remember now," said Mika. "There's something else: a Cadmean victory is a victory purchased at great loss."

This was a discussion Cormac no longer wanted to pursue. "Let's get those cold-coffins ready," he said.

Soil had often become displaced by slippery stone and spills of scree descending from above, and now there were very few lizard tails—those they did see appearing stunted—and no sign of any flute grass. The molluscs she had earlier seen lower down were here flatter to the rock, duller in colour, and more chaotic in their patterning. Coming to a steep rocky cliff face, Fethan led the way to the right, cutting across the slope.

"How much further?" Eldene gasped, stopping to remove her oxygen pack and change to her last air bottle.

Fethan stopped to observe her. "We'll need to find some shelter for the night, and with luck we'll be there sometime tomorrow. You've got more than enough to suffice, girl."

Was he just saying that to comfort her, perhaps hoping that her remaining oxygen might stretch to their destination? She gazed around her as she stood to hoist her pack back into place. Well, if she was to die, then this was a better place than keeling over in a sluice ditch down by the ponds. She resolved that on her last breath, when the breather's display tag on its oxygen tube clicked down to zero—as it had just then with the previous bottle—she would remove the mask and put the barrel of Volus's gun in her mouth.

Fethan led the way around the side of the mountain, onto a narrow path that—Eldene noted by the imprints—must have been made by some animal. A grazer of some kind? Or something more sinister? She was about to pose this question when they rounded a promontory on which something stood observing them.

The animal squatting on its hindquarters had the same double sets of forelimbs folded across its triple-keeled chest as a gabbleduck. Its head was not beaked though: below its tiara of green eyes, it had a pendulous snoutlike protrusion that must serve it as a mouth.

Fethan gestured at it dismissively. "Grazer. They suck a fungal slime from the underside of rocks. Completely harmless."

Hurrying to catch up with him, Eldene was not so sure—she did not like the way it was watching her as it contemplatively scratched its snout with one of the hooked foreclaws.

"And what eats them up here?" she asked.

"Hooders and siluroynes," Fethan stated briefly.

After the promontory, they came upon a vista of valley cutting through the mountains, and began to descend by natural stony steps. On the flat stone Eldene saw the rain-etched shapes of fossilized worms glinting with iron pyrites, and she suddenly felt the huge injustice of it all: she had been born on this planet, raised on it and now, as she entered womanhood, was the first time she had really seen or experienced it. For generations there had been surface dwellers who had lived and died without seeing a fraction of what she had seen over the last few days. Was this fair? Was this what any God would intend?

As they descended, Eldene heard the rumble of a river, and gazing down could see it glinting between stands of flute grass, but slowly this view was becoming obscured by waves of mist rolling down the valley. The path began to get slippery and she almost fell twice, so rapt was she in studying the odd, brightly coloured outgrowths on the rocky slopes to either side of her. These things were something like blister moss, but smoother and flatter, and grew in pure colours of blue, orange and red. Set in the ground between them ran strands like inlaid silver.

"That's what the grazers up here feed on," Fethan explained, noting the focus of her attention. "Watch your footing now: that's sporulated slime on the rocks, and it'll get worse."

It did get worse, and Eldene went down twice on her backside—the second time sliding down right behind Fethan. However, she did not manage to knock him over—colliding with him was like running into a deep-rooted tree. He himself did not slip once on the way down.

Soon they were walking up again, through cold mist beside the river, mountain slopes on their left and long grass rustling on their right. Despite all the exertion, Eldene found herself getting colder and colder as now, closely following Calypse, the sun dropped from sight behind the mountains and afternoon slid into twilight. In this poor light Eldene could only just discern the squarish things that flapped overhead and honked mournfully.

"What are those?" she asked.

"Kite-bats—harmless again," Fethan replied.

As it got darker, the bats moved higher up and further away, their cries echoing in the mountains. When something emitted a gasping hiss in the flute grasses behind her, she jumped, then suddenly found herself shivering. For a time she kept silent, not wanting to keep asking about every strange sound, but when the same sound came again she could not stop herself.

"What was that?" she asked of Fethan, who had stopped and was peering back in the direction of the noise.

"I haven't a clue," he replied, then waved her on past him. "Just keep going."

She did that thing, feeling her flesh crawling as she remembered the old man's mention of "siluroynes" and "hooders."
She even considered drawing the gun, but her hands were
shaking so badly now she'd probably shoot her own foot off.

"About another two hours and we cut back up the slope,"
Fethan told her. "There's a cave there where we can shelter
for the night."

Great: a nice cold, damp cave—just what she needed.

As night descended the sound was heard again, as if
whatever made it was keeping pace with them. Now they
distinctly heard something pushing through the flute grass,
its passage followed by a clicking sigh. Eldene wondered if
she would feel so frightened if she knew what that sound
issued from.

"Let's move back up the slope," Fethan suggested. "We're
a bit too close to the grass here."

Eldene quickly obeyed him, with images of something like
that gabbleduck or the heroyne lunging out at her, clamping
down and dragging her screaming back into the flute grasses
to be consumed. She laboured on up the slippery slope,
spilling rocks and dislodging fungi, slipping and grazing her
knees. That didn't matter—she just wanted to get higher.
Glancing back she experienced a sudden terror—Fethan had
vanished. She moved faster, fell hard, got up and kept going.
The slope finally levelled and she found a flat stretch where
she could pick up her pace. Down below, more movement,
and she could just about discern something huge thrashing
about in the grasses. Next thing, Fethan was running along
beside her . . . She did a double take: it wasn't Fethan. It was a
big heavy-boned man dressed in combat gear, breather mask
and helmet. He caught her arm and dragged her off course.

"This way. He's leading it off."

She considered fighting him off, but was just too
frightened. He certainly did not look like a proctor. So she
ran with him, sometimes supported by him, sometimes
supporting him when he stumbled. Gasping for breath, she
was wondering how much further she could manage to run
when he tugged her by the arm towards a tumble of massive

boulders. Rounding the first boulder, two other people appeared and shoved her past them into a cave in which a fire was burning. Standing amid equipment stacked on the floor, she stared at the three now crouching at the cave mouth, heavy rifles clutched in readiness.

"What was it?" asked the only woman of the three: her hair and one side of her face concealed under a military-issue coms helmet.

"Didn't see it clearly," said the man she addressed. "I'd just eye-balled Fethan and this one heading our way when it started to come out of the valley after them. It was big."

The woman studied him for a moment then turned to Eldene. "Did *you* see it?"

Eldene shook her head in bewilderment.

"Whoa," said the woman, now speaking into her helmet mike. "That you, Fethan?" She listened for a moment then her expression paled. "Fuck," she said succinctly and stared out again into the night.

"What is it, Lellan?" the second man asked her.

"He's leading it away," she replied. "Says he'll be back with us by morning."

"Lellan . . ." the man said warningly.

"Seems we got ourselves a hooder out there."

Eldene studied the sick expressions worn by these three heavily armed individuals and wondered just how terrible a hooder could be.

"You're Lellan Stanton," she said at last.

"Yeah," replied the woman. "Welcome to the Underworld." Then she faced back out into the night.

As the ship drew away, Hierarch Loman gazed into the mouth of *Faith* and contemplated his work. It had been said that on Amoloran's ascension a red mist had swept through the cylinder world from the bodies of the thousands who had been tortured and killed. Not wishing to be outdone, Loman had ordered the Up Mirror to be painted with the blood of traitors, to cast a red light into the world, for a thousand days.

His technical advisors had nervously informed him of the impracticality of doing this in vacuum, but then quickly told him how the reflective surfaces did allow for an amount of tunable refraction—usually to prevent too much ultraviolet being reflected in. So now the light of *Faith* was red, though only for a maximum of ten days—anything beyond that would start killing the plants in the gardens.

"A jewel in your crown," Aberil commented.

Loman turned to him and nodded, before scanning the rather cramped cabin in which he and his brother had been installed.

"Amoloran should not have sent the *General Patten*. What was he thinking?" he asked.

Sitting on the edge of the sofa as if distrustful of its comfort, Aberil replied, "He had the ridiculous idea that Outlinkers might serve as hostages should the Polity decide to come in; also the idea that in their gratitude at being rescued they might help upgrade the laser arrays and close some of the gaps in coverage. Had he spent a little less time killing off those technicians who disagreed with him, that would not have become necessary."

Loman winced and briefly wondered if he himself had been a bit hasty in having the chief mirror technician thrown out of the upper tower window into vacuum. Then he dismissed the idea: the man had been impertinent, and could have at least attempted the blood-painting idea.

"Reverend Hierarch, we are ready to U-jump upon your order," spoke a voice from a console set into one wall.

"Then do so," said Loman, waving his hand dismissively.

After a short delay, the viewing screen turned black and engines thrummed deep within the ship. Loman grimaced, well aware that Polity ships did not need to warm up like this before dropping into underspace, and that grav-plates were used throughout their ships, not just in one luxury suite like this. He looked around it contemptuously.

"Now all our plans mesh," he said. "You are sure that no possible connection can be made between the mycelium and us?"

Aberil shook his head. "Our agent entered the Polity at Cheyne III, and travelled via many worlds before finally coming to *Miranda*, and even he did not know what he was taking there. He thought he was taking a listening device to install on a communications array, and anyway the virus we also gave him before he set out killed him shortly after he delivered the mycelium. Our only problem will be Behemoth himself, should he inform the Polity he gave us the mycelium twenty years ago."

"Ah, but would the Polity believe him? I think not. They will assume he has done the same as his twin did on Samarkand, and so seek to destroy him. Behemoth will flee them," said Loman. "Soon we will be utterly free of this Tempter."

"God willing," added Aberil.

Loman walked away from the screen and dropped into the sofa beside his brother. "And once free of him, we can at last excise this cancer that grows at the heart of our civilization." He paused and reached up to touch his aug, discomfited by this much-needed *Gift*. "How long until Ragnorak is ready?" He picked up the inhaler provided to prevent U-space sickness—another aspect of space travel that Polity citizens supposedly did not have to suffer.

"Construction is completed. It will just take another month to move it into position. If Amoloran had started moving it after the construction of the initial framework, it would have been there by now. For some reason he wanted it ready before it was moved."

Loman thought that he understood Amoloran's motivations: having Ragnorak already working whilst it was towed past the cylinder worlds to its orbital position would certainly terrify any aspiring usurpers on *Hope*, *Faith* and *Charity*. He stared at the black screen for a long moment before taking a pull on his inhaler.

Aberil did the same before saying, "You called my mission to supply the Cheyne III Separatists a 'fool's errand' . . ."

"Amoloran was too unsubtle, and not sufficiently ruthless when the situation required it," Loman replied. "He would never have made so decisive a move as we in planting that mycelium. Yet he wanted us to risk supplying Separatist groups on the Line—an action that gains us very little. We must get our own house in order. It is the Polity way that they never take over a stable system, as that would seem unacceptably militaristic to many of its member worlds. We will rid ourselves of the Underworld, and thereafter give the Polity no reason to attempt to seize control of us." He paused as the whole cabin seemed to distort, and he experienced the sensation of weightlessness even though the grav-plates in the cabin held him firm. Feeling slightly nauseous despite the inhaler, he went on, "The Polity cannot continue to expand, and without the guiding morality of God it will eventually be torn apart by internecine conflict. We will assist it along that course, but subtly—keeping ourselves distant and safe."

"You believe this . . . Hierarch?" asked Aberil.

"How can I doubt? A civilization run by soulless machines cannot succeed. God will not allow it to succeed."

"Yes, that is true," said Aberil. "God would not allow it."

"You have to understand our destiny, Aberil. You have to see the larger picture. We are an outpost of the truth, and when the Polity falls, as it must, we will bring that truth back to *its* worlds."

"I try not to doubt, Reverend, but sometimes it is hard when one considers the Polity. It contains thousands of colonized worlds, between which its citizens can travel in an instant. It has hundreds of thousands of ships, many of them the size of Calypse's moons, and many of them capable of destroying planets . . ."

Loman snorted. "Have you been away so long that you have come to believe Polity propaganda?"

"No, Hierarch."

Loman stood and took yet another pull on his inhaler before marching up again to the black viewing screen. This was the sort of thing he should instantly quell: the inflation of rumour and myth about the omnipotent Polity. Now to hear such idiocy from the mouth of his own brother. He slapped his hand against the screen and turned.

"Perhaps I do not do you justice. The Polity does have wonderful technologies, but you must never forget that it does not have our *heart.* Remember that no matter how large or powerful it is, we have already manipulated it to our own ends. Behemoth has fled and, like our hunting dog unleashed, the Polity will hunt him down."

Aberil nodded, his face expressionless. "Yes, Hierarch."

As if to punctuate this conversation, the ship now dropped out of underspace and the atmosphere of the cabin returned to some form of normality. Loman pocketed his inhaler then turned and rested his hands against the bottom rim of the screen, which now showed only starlit space. After a moment, he reached out and adjusted the view on the screen to show a massive structure out in vacuum. For a long time he had been puzzled as to why the appearance of Ragnorak bothered him so. It was only after searching databanks that he discovered a similar shape in the image files used to teach ancient history. There he found what he had been reminded of: the lethal device they were constructing was the Eiffel Tower displaced into orbit above Calypse.

"I didn't understand what you said about Polity field technology," he said, turning back to observe his brother, completely unaware that what he was asking made his previous haughty pronouncements laughable.

Aberil picked up an incendiary bullet he had earlier been using as a model. He held it up before his face. "Each kinetic missile weighs one tonne. If we fired them at Masada, at the velocities Ragnorak is capable of generating, they would explode in upper atmosphere. What we're using is a Polity shimmer-shield over the nose cone of each. It reduces friction sufficiently for the missiles to reach the surface. During penetration they'll turn to plasma, which will burn downwards up to a kilometre. Each of their caves will be filled with this—it will be as if a fusion bomb had been detonated down there."

"Losses on the surface?" asked Loman.

"About thirty per cent," Aberil replied.

"A price we have to pay," Loman said, wondering how long, after these kinetic missile strikes, it would take before the trade in luxury proteins could recommence.

11

The boy had finished his supper and was now listening goggle-eyed to the story in the hope of the usual denouement. The woman pursed her lips as she scanned the next bit of text before reading it out.

"Upon the morning of the second day Brother Serendipity came upon the siluroyne coiled on its bed of grasses. 'Please feed me,' begged the creature, 'for I am old and cannot hunt so well, and I am hungry.' 'Why should I feed you when, given strength by my food, you might rise up and strike me down?' he asked it. 'I give you my word,' said the siluroyne. 'Swear your word in the name of God and in the name of his prophet Zelda Smythe,' the good Brother demanded. The siluroyne so swore, and he gave it the second third of the meat cake given to him by the old woman by the boundary stone."

The boy started playing with the bits left on his plate, his attention wandering.

"Into the night the creature followed him, companion to the heroyne, and so, doubly warded, did he survive to come closer to the compounds."

"Mum's boring," the boy interrupted.

"You must stay with stories like this, my dear, for through them you will receive great instruction, and great understanding of God," said the woman.

The boy gave her a look—young he might be but he had the innate intelligence of both his parents, and the extra intelligence of the genetic tweaks he had received before being born, and he knew when his mother was taking the piss.

*

With no little trepidation, Thorn watched while Jarvellis flew *Lyric II* in towards a large lump of tumbling asteroidal rock. Once she was close enough, the ship's AI took over and, with exact bursts of manoeuvring thrusters, apparently brought the rock to stillness. It wasn't until he looked beyond this piece of asteroidal debris that Thorn felt a touch of nausea to see Calypse and the stars beyond mirroring the tumble he had earlier seen—*Lyric II* now perfectly matching the rock's motion.

Jarvellis now thrust her right hand into a telefactor glove, closed a viewing visor across her eyes, and began to work the loading grab from the centre of the trispherical ship. On various screens Thorn and Stanton watched the multi-jointed arm rise up towards the rock, with its five-fingered grab opening like a hand, then fingers telescoping out so this hand became large enough to get a sufficient grip.

"You say you've done this before?" Thorn asked.

"Four times," replied Jarvellis. She glanced at him. "Don't worry. I've dealt with heavier loads than this."

"That wasn't so much my worry," said Thorn. "I was just wondering if the Theocracy would be getting suspicious about all the meteor activity."

"They don't care unless it's near their cylinder worlds, and it never is," said Stanton. "And any large enough to reach the surface and cause deaths, they'd view as the hand of God—just so long as it went nowhere near themselves."

The grab closed on the rock and began to draw it down to the deck area extending between the three spheres that made up the ship. As it touched down, Thorn felt a faint vibration through the structure of *Lyric II*. With the rock now in position, metal arms folded in from the edges of the deck area and Thorn wondered what their purpose could be; they were not long enough to hold the rock down against the metal. The question he had been about to pose was answered for him when jets of vapour issued from cylindrical objects mounted on the ends of these arms as soon as they touched the surface of the rock.

"Explosive bolts," Thorn said.

"Uhuh," agreed Jarvellis, as she now detached the grab and folded it away.

"Not standard fittings on such a ship," he said.

"As Jarv said, we've done this before," said Stanton.

The ship's thrusters were again firing, this time to correct its tumble. The views on the screens began to settle down, and soon Calypse itself was centred on the main screen.

"We take a sling around Calypse, and from here on in it'll take us five solstan days to reach Masada," said Jarvellis.

Stanton said, "Lyric, start the chameleonware generator."

Thorn kept his attention focused on the screens showing various outside views of the ship. He watched as cowlings split and slid aside from three devices positioned just in from each of the connecting tunnels between spheres. These things had the appearance of huge metallic ammonites, intersecting with something like an ancient combustion engine. For a second every image shimmered, then stabilized.

"How far out is the interface?" Thorn asked.

"About twenty metres, but beyond that the field is ten metres deep," Stanton replied.

That meant that outside that distance there would be no sign at all of *Lyric II*. They were invisible.

The five days ground past like cripples at a funeral, and Thorn came to agree with Stanton that staying in cold-sleep was the best thing to do whilst travelling on a ship this size. On the second day he decided to take the plunge and have the autodoc assess the damage to the nerves in his fingertips, then later had the pleasure of sitting watching it opening the ends of his fingers—folding up the nails like little hatches—as it repaired the damage it found. Thereafter some hours passed before not everything he touched felt scalding hot or searingly cold. The bed set up for him in the hold was comfortable enough, and in an insulation sheet he had no trouble sleeping despite the constant cold. It was the periods *between* sleep that almost had him screaming. It was nice for the other two that they were always so wrapped up in each other, but their intimacy made Thorn uncomfortable, so he had to keep avoiding them. He spent most of his time viewing lectures about Masada, put together by the ship's AI. In this electronic intelligence he found company more to his liking, with its abrasive personality and constant sarcasm. It probably knew how he felt and was doing the best it could to keep him from going mad with boredom.

On the third day, *Lyric II* closely passed the Theocracy's cylinder worlds. Close by extended a structure two kilometres long and half a kilometre in diameter, with a huge mirror mounted at one end to reflect sunlight inside, and at the other end a chaos of loading docks around which various ships hovered like bees round a hole in a log. Further out was another such cylinder with mirrors at *both* ends, but one of those mirrors forming a ring penetrated centrally by a strangely displaced Gothic tower. And distantly there lay yet another such world, shadowed against starlit space and only just visible.

"How many of these orbitals are there?" he asked Stanton and Jarvellis who, for this dangerous flyby, were both back at the flight and weapons controls.

"Just the three," Stanton replied. "With a population of over a few hundred thousand in each."

"I'd have expected more."

"Remember, they don't have Polity technology here, as that's difficult to maintain without using AI—and AI to them is a product of Satan." Stanton pointed at the cylinder world. "The shielding from cosmic radiation and solar flares is not the best, and that causes a high incidence of infertility. They like it that way—keeps the whole thing exclusive."

"Why cylinders?"

"Again: the technology. AG motors and grav-plates are manufactured, but not on any scale. It would take a major industrial upgrade for them to produce enough for these worlds. Then again, why bother? The centrifugal system works well enough."

"Lyric tells me there's something of an imbalance between planetary and orbital populations."

Stanton glanced at him. "Only the usual one existing between the rulers and the ruled. How many major AIs would you say there are in the Polity? One to ten for each planet?"

"But they don't rule, as such," said Thorn.

Stanton grinned. "Yeah, I know, they 'direct.' You have to remember, I've often witnessed what happens to people who don't take the AI's considered advice."

"Thinking of becoming a Separatist?" Thorn sniped.

"Oh no, I've no objection to the Polity. The way I see it is that if you don't like it then there's plenty of places to go where it isn't present. It would be an eye-opener for some of those soft objectors to the 'AI autocrat' of Earth to come out *here* and see how they'd get on."

The cylinder world slid behind them and Masada itself grew large on the central screen. Some time later, Thorn was in a position to ask Jarvellis her opinion of Polity AIs. She replied, "Stone Age men broke flint and found it cut things better than their own teeth did. We've created methods of transportation that work better than legs, and often do things we could only dream of, like flying. A hydraulic grip clamps on things better than a human hand. They're all tools and nobody objects to them, so why should anyone object to creating minds that are better at thinking than our own, and rulers that are better at their job than those humans who would aspire to rule?"

"Tools?" Thorn repeated.

"All extensions of ourselves." She shrugged. "And probably not even that for much longer. With augs and gridlinks and the like, we're seeing them become ourselves. There'll come a time when humans and AIs are indistinguishable. What's a memcording of a human mind? Is it, strictly speaking, AI or human? And when they did that experiment, way back, of downloading an AI mind into a vat-grown human body, what did they make then?"

"So what do you think of the Separatist cause?"

"Anachronisms, throwbacks. AIs are just larger and more efficient versions of ourselves. Those people are fighting for a past that never existed—and they'll lose."

"Why did you run arms for them, then?"

"Money," she replied succinctly, bringing their conversation down to earth.

On the second day, Thorn tried to learn some more about the Theocracy: its aims, its teachings, its structure, and what its members actually believed in. It seemed for them there was a god whose rules for the existence of his children were little different from those posited by the Islamic or Christian religions. And, as was the case with those old religions, the higher up you were in the hierarchy, the more freedom you enjoyed to interpret those rules. In the end, brute force maintained the whole thing, and those who lived in the cylinder worlds spent most of their time utterly wrapped up in power struggles. It would seem they had other methods of population control to "keep the whole thing exclusive," as Stanton had opined, and were often crueller to the losers in this continual struggle than they were to the surface dwellers of Masada. Given the courage and the opportunity, such losers often took the option of suicide, as the alternatives were far from pleasant. They consisted of a device similar to an autodoc but which could be programmed to inflict things the Inquisition never thought of; the aptly named "steamer" in one of the world's rendering plants; and a veritable cornucopia of viral and bacterial agents.

"Do you believe in this god?" he asked Stanton.

"No," came the flat reply. "But if he does exist, I'd like to give him a CTD suppository."

Their exchange of greetings had been brief, and the other three seemed intent on staying at the cave mouth. Eldene crouched alone by the fire, which issued from blocks of some brownish organic matter. It was nevertheless welcome. Slowly the chill began to leave her, and before she knew it she had dozed off then woken again. After a time Lellan entered the cave, crouched beside Eldene, and poked at the embers with a length of flute grass.

"Did he get the ajectant?" the rebel woman asked.

Eldene peered at her. "What's that?"

Lellan looked up. "Did he get a sample of the pills you must take to prevent your scoles from dying?"

Eldene nodded.

Lellan went on, "Then let's hope he gets back in one piece. But then, if anyone could survive a hooder attack it would be him. I haven't yet witnessed anything he can't survive."

"He told me he's part machine and part human."

Lellan grimaced. "Yeah, you could say that, though I'd challenge him to point out which part is human."

"You don't believe him?" Eldene asked.

"It doesn't matter. I'm glad to have him on my side." Lellan stood up and, from amongst the packs, found another rifle like the one she was carrying, and handed it to Eldene. "In there"—Lellan pointed to another of the packs—"you'll find spare oxygen and food, if you need them. I suspect we'll be facing a long night here."

"You suspect wrong," said a voice out of the darkness.

"Fethan!" said Eldene, shooting up.

The old man walked into the middle of the cave followed by the other two. They were called Beckle and Carl—the latter being the one who had run alongside her.

Fethan glanced around. "Very cosy."

"So what happened out there?" Lellan asked.

"Don't think I smelt right, so it stopped chasing me. I tracked it for a while, but it seemed intent on going after a herd of grazers up at the other end of the valley." He shook his head and grinned. "That was some experience. I've always wanted to actually see one of them."

Everyone in the cave stared at him as if he was quite mad.

"You get to my age," he explained, "and you come to relish experiences like that. It's what makes life worth living."

"It's also the kind of thing that can make life shorter," opined Beckle.

Fethan shrugged, then winked at Eldene.

"We all been introduced?" he asked.

"Yeah," said Lellan. "But we can save the getting-to-know-you routine until we've got some decent stone overhead. Let's move out now. I don't fancy hanging around here in case our friend comes back, having worked up an appetite chasing grazers. *That* is not an experience I'd relish."

Quickly the three began gathering their equipment and hoisting bulky packs onto their backs. After passing his own pack to Eldene, Fethan took up one of the bulky ones as well. Carl, who was now the one without a pack, exchanged his heavy rifle for an even more lethal ugly-looking weapon.

"You still got the ajectant?" Lellan asked when they were nearly ready to go.

Fethan pretended to search his pockets in panic before finding the tube of pills and tossing it to her. She studied them for a moment then carefully buttoned them into her top pocket.

"A more important question to ask is, 'Have the manufactories arrived yet?'" he said.

"Not yet," Lellan replied. "But they're on their way—along with some arms, more ballots, and a U-space transmitter."

"A lot," said Fethan, puzzled.

"There, old man: you don't know everything. We've got a ship coming in soon, with enough maybe for us to tilt the balance down here."

"How the hell will you get something that big past the arrays?" Fethan asked.

Lellan turned to Eldene and grinned at her. "Wouldn't he like to know?"

Eldene smiled back uncertainly—she just did not know her own position here. These people behaved as if she was one of them, yet they discussed things that were beyond her. She realized she had a great deal to learn.

They all headed to the cave mouth, Lellan and her two comrades moving some sort of apparently opaque visors across their eyes. Fethan took the lead out into the night, followed by Lellan and Beckle. Before waving her ahead, Carl passed Eldene a pair of glasses of a similar material to the visor he himself wore. She at least understood enough to know that these must provide night vision, but she let out a sound of startlement when she discovered just how effectively—it was as if day had descended instantly. Carl moved in behind her, his head moving from side to side with almost robotic vigilance—his heavy gun hanging from a strap over his shoulder.

It gave her a weird sense of dislocation, this sudden daylight, and walking out into it while realizing that if she raised these glasses she wore it would be night again was weirder still. Trudging along with her new companions, Eldene wondered just how much her life was about to change. She felt trepidation at this, but also a growing excitement at the feeling that she might be taking part in major events. With a sense of irony she realized that just about *anything* might appear "major" to someone who had spent a dull five seasons managing squerm ponds. However, a grinding weariness—with which she was all too familiar—soon extinguished excitement. One of the few benefits of her previous employment had been that you got to go to bed at night.

As the trek went on and on, Eldene found herself slipping into a state of fugue. Even seeing three grazers—of the type she had seen earlier—close by on a slope, worming their snouts between the rocks, did not arouse in her any curiosity this time, and later, when something flew overhead making a strange whickering, she didn't even look up at it.

"Watch your footing," warned Carl from behind her, and she gazed down at her boots as if they were somehow disconnected from her. Nevertheless, the boots trudged on, without any intercession from her brain.

How long this continued she had no idea, until Beckle glanced back towards her, his visor raised, and informed her, "Calypse is up."

Eldene removed her night glasses and blinked in the twilight of early morning. Placing the glasses in her pocket, she felt herself coming out of her stupor, as if they had disconnected her from reality. The gas giant had breached the horizon and, in this stage of the cycle, the sun would not be far behind it.

"Not much further," said Carl in a more affable tone, slapping her on the shoulder as he moved past her.

"Well, that'll be one to tell the kiddies," said Beckle.

From all of them there now seemed a relaxing of tension. When Fethan slipped back to walk at her side, Eldene asked him, "The hooder?"

"From what I gather they only hunt in the full dark. Best stay alert, though—they might be wrong about that," Fethan replied. "Be a bit of a bastard to get hit when we're this close."

"Close to what?" she asked.

"The real Underworld," he replied.

Soon they were walking along under a rocky overhang that resembled a breaking wave. The further along this they proceeded, the further it overhung them, until soon it closed over completely on their right and they were entering a perfectly circular tunnel. Seeing the others push their visors back into place, Eldene took out her night glasses and put them back on. Here the effect of them was even stranger, for the inside of a cave was not a place one ever expected to be as bright as day. She found it weird that it could be so light in here without any apparent source of illumination.

The cave curved off to the left then began to drop. Before the floor became too steep to negotiate easily it became stepped. Staring down at these steps, Eldene realized that they were not natural, and had obviously been specially cut.

"What if proctors ever found this place?" she asked Fethan. "They could march straight in."

"Pin-head cameras," Fethan explained, gesturing to the curving walls. "If they did find this place and tried to go down lower they'd find themselves at the hot end of a pulse-cannon."

Before they had descended much further, Lellan held up her hand and the party came to a halt while she unreeled a thin optic cable from her coms helmet and plugged it into a hidden socket in the wall. She then stood frowning with her hand up against the speaking side of her helmet.

"It here yet?" Carl asked.

She detached the cable, then shook her head. "Nothing yet. The dishes are out to track Ragnorak, but they've picked up nothing else."

"Ragnorak?" Eldene whispered to Fethan.

"A weapon powerful enough to destroy what you're just about to see," he replied.

After a time they came down to a level tunnel lit by wall panels, where they all removed their visual aids. Eldene was already thinking how grim an existence it must be to live constantly under the earth in tunnels like this one, when the tunnel itself opened out into a circular chamber. At the centre of this gaped the mouth of a wide shaft, and poised over this stood a steel framework containing a cable mechanism, electric motor, and lift cage. Lellan led the way over, throwing the locks on the cage's wire door with a remote control she took from her pocket. Inside, Eldene noted a more visible camera that moved on its little stem up in the corner of the cage to inspect each of them in turn. Without any of them touching another control, the lift jerked and began to descend, the motor droning.

Against the sides of the shaft clung square light panels like crystals of some exotic mineral, and at one point an encircling ring of what could be mistaken for nothing other than heavy weapons. The deeper down they went, the whiter the calcite glittered in runnels down the walls; and, as the shaft curved, this calcite formed stalactites and stalagmites, so it seemed they were flying between the teeth of some underground monster. Finally reaching the bottom of the shaft, they exited the lift into another tunnel, curving round towards a huge armoured door with another smaller door inset in it.

"A lot of lights," Eldene observed, gazing at the numerous light panels set on faces of stone, their glow reflecting in rainbow hues from the crystalline surfaces of a forest of calcite above.

"Geothermal and hydroelectric energy," said Carl—answering a question she had not asked. "No shortage of that down here."

Eldene noticed then that he had removed his mask and was breathing easily. Feeling gauche, she hinged her mask down and breathed clear air. It was cold and tasted of iron, but sweet.

Lellan pointed her remote control at the smaller, centre door and it opened with a tearing sound as they approached. Inside was a space the same size as the lift cage, with yet another door at the opposite end. Eldene recognized this was an airlock, but wondered at its purpose when they had walked into breathable air before reaching it. She looked questioningly towards Fethan, but it was Carl who answered that question too:

"The main cavern haemorrhages air all the time, but we can produce it faster than we lose it. This lock is about a century old—from a time when we didn't have much oxygen to spare," he said.

Main cavern? Eldene wondered.

As the inner door opened, Eldene thought for one moment that they had returned to the surface—so bright was the vision before her. Following the others through, she looked about herself in wonder.

The cavern was so huge and so well lit that its lofty ceiling had the appearance of lowering cloud rather than stone. Across it ran webworks of metal, and in places it was supported by huge many-windowed buildings, formed like a collection of bulging discs of distinctly varied sizes stacked haphazardly one upon the other until reaching the ceiling. Running down the centre of this cavern, with arched bridges spanning it, was a foaming torrent, whose source was a dark hollow in one wall, warded at its sides by two slowly turning water-wheels. Alongside this river, Eldene recognized the same pattern of square ponds used on the surface to grow food crustaceans, and their presence helped give a further indication of the sheer scale of this place. Beyond the ponds lay fields in varying shades of green and gold, or the black of recently turned earth. On the floor of this cavern were not many low-rise buildings—it seemed space was at a premium, hence the design of the pillar-townships. However, as they advanced further into this underground idyll, Eldene did spot some recently erected prefabs around which many people busied themselves at many tasks. They too all wore uniforms the colour of old flute grass—like Lellan and her two comrades—and their labour seemed mainly to concern maintenance and preparation of weapons.

On the last of the five days, they were all together in the flight cabin as the ship hurtled towards the atmosphere of Masada. Glancing at one of the subscreens, Thorn watched the explosive bolts detaching themselves from the lump of asteroidal rock, and the arms they were fixed to folding back out of sight. A few blasts from the manoeuvring thrusters were enough to have the rock apparently rising from *Lyric II*, though it would be more correct to say that the rock now hurtled towards atmosphere at a speed slightly faster than that of the ship.

"What about it outpacing you?" Thorn asked.

"It's angled so it'll explode and fragment, rather than burn up. We'll be one of those fragments," said Jarvellis.

Stanton picked up with, "Believe me, no one watching will call attention to the dissimilarity of velocities. Up here, reporting anything to your superiors that you are unsure about gains you no credit, and the best way for the lower echelons to keep out of trouble is to keep out of notice."

"A fatal lack of vigilance," Thorn observed.

"Yes, it's why the Underworld now possesses a more advanced technology than the Theocracy itself. Their only disadvantage is in numbers and position." He called up an image on one of the side screens and gestured to it. Satellites hung stationary around the curve of the horizon, the nearest one bearing an uncanny resemblance to a huge curved machine-gun magazine. "What advantage the Underground does have, it must be prepared to use soon, before the Theocracy finishes building something with greater punch than that." He indicated the satellite.

"And what is that?" Thorn nodded to the displayed picture.

"Laser array—but it's only effective on the surface of the planet. It can't reach into the real Underground."

"They're building something that will?"

"Near-c coil-gun. Should have enough power to penetrate right down to the caverns."

"And the people on the surface?"

"It'll kill millions, but the Theocracy doesn't care about them—down on the surface they breed easily enough."

"If the ECS knew about this, *then* you'd get some action."

Stanton turned to gaze at him. "The Polity just lost an Outlink station out here, supposedly to Dragon. The Theocracy is building things like that," Stanton stabbed a finger at the screen, "supposedly as a defence against Dragon. All nice and innocent, so if the Polity came in heavy-handed now, it'd cause big problems with its members and potential for rebellion inside its own borders. They'll need a damned good reason to intrude here; like an open rebellion, or a cry for help."

"I see," said Thorn.

Now *Lyric II* was vibrating, and a couple of hundred metres ahead of it the rock was producing contrails and small pieces of it were ablating away. All around—ahead of the rock—the surface of the planet filled the screen. Thorn glanced at Jarvellis's profile as she now manoeuvred the ship down out of the contrail and below the rock itself. She looked rapt and beatific—this was what she was all about.

"About two minutes. Stress readings are way up," she said.

Thorn glanced with alarm at Stanton.

"On the rock," explained the mercenary laconically. "We've got a sensor on it."

The rock began to glow and, like a stuttering gas torch with the pressure too high, its contrail kept igniting and going out, until suddenly it ignited completely on full blast. Larger pieces began to break off from the rock, coiling away, sparkling with burning iron.

"We're on it!" shouted Jarvellis, and slammed her hand down on the controls. All at once, the rock broke into four large pieces and many smaller ones, those pieces themselves rapidly parting, driven asunder by gaseous explosions. *Lyric II*'s ion engines roared, for a moment internal AG did not correct, and Thorn felt himself coming out of his seat. On the screen, the breaking-up rock rapidly receded, as *Lyric II* slowed and dropped through atmosphere behind it, underneath a trail of smoke and vapour dispersing across the sky. It occurred to Thorn that on a Polity world this scenario would never have been allowed, not so much because of the superior detectors possessed but because the AIs would have long since mapped the solar system concerned, therefore knowing in advance what asteroidal debris posed a threat, so would have been very suspicious of finding one out of place. Also, no Polity AI would have allowed a rock of that size into inhabited space.

Soon Jarvellis switched the view on the main screen to encompass the planet's surface. Under cloud like swirled sugar, the main inhabited continent soon became visible amid seas of a dark purplish blue. This continent was roughly rectangular, with its four corners stretched out so it bore some resemblance to the sail on an old galleon. Mountain chains spread from one of the corners, as if this was the point where a cannon-ball had holed the sail and it had subsequently been roughly stitched together—the material rucked up in the process. Huge areas extending beyond these mountains were dark greenish blue, whilst other wide areas were khaki or Sahara beige.

"Desert?" Thorn pointed at the last of these.

"No desert here," Stanton replied. "What you're seeing there is old flute grass—where it's not yet been flattened by spring storms or the new is yet to come through like it has elsewhere."

"It's all flute grass?"

"Not all. There's other kinds of native vegetation, and of course there's the agricultural areas—mostly crop fields and ponds—but when you're in the wild it seems like nothing but flute grass. It's said that there were once trees here."

Thorn remembered something from one of Lyric's little lectures. "The tricones?" he suggested. "They disturb the soil so much that nothing large can root, but flute grass survives because it sprouts from rhizomes that sit on the surface."

"You *have* done your homework," quipped Jarvellis.

"Trees *are* grown," said Stanton. "But to grow them requires a major excavation, lined with plascrete then refilled with soil. Even then, the tricones manage to grind their way through. They go through plascrete at a rate of about a centimetre every five solstan years."

"Surely there are better ways?"

"There are: use Polity composites, use genetic splicings from flute grass, build hydroponics facilities, float platforms on the sea. But the Theocracy is not prepared to inject the level of financial resources required for change. If there are shortages of any of the crops they require, they simply attribute blame and innocent people are punished."

"Very short-sighted of them."

"They don't care. Aren't they all going to Heaven?" Stanton spat.

The screen now contained the whole of the continent—the edges of its surrounding world hidden from sight. Jarvellis checked her instrumentation and made some adjustments. The roar of the ion engines, which had been growing increasingly muted for some time, now cut out.

"We're fully on AG now," she explained.

For a short time they found themselves flying through cloud. On one of the subscreens giving a view of the ship itself, Thorn noticed that ice was building up on all its surfaces, then breaking away in thin flat flakes. They emerged from this cloud above the mountains: guts of stone pushed up through the plains and rucked together in tight folds and twisted pinnacles, scree slopes and slanted boulder-fields, the white scars of rivers slashing through dark valleys, and waterfalls cutting down from the heights. Jarvellis now folded her viewing visor across and firmly gripped the complex joystick before her. Obviously flying her ship was a great source of pleasure for her, as the AI could have done the job just as well, if not better. Soon they were hurtling along a riverine valley, grey faces of stone looming over them on either side, as if inspecting this impertinent intrusion into their realm.

"You got the beacon?" Stanton asked.

"I traced that an hour back," she replied. "Though no one's talking to us yet."

Lyric II slowed to negotiate a curve in the valley, then descended further. Thorn could see vegetation blown flat by the wind of their passage, and papery fragments clouding the air behind. At the end of the valley was a small lake surrounded on all sides by precipitous slopes. Jarvellis brought the ship down onto its stony shore, next to a cliff formed by the collapse of one of the mountainous slopes, on an area between boulders that had once formed part of that slope. Thorn heard hydraulics operating as *Lyric II* lowered its feet. Along the bottom of the main screen, six subscreens appeared showing a view of each of the ship's six feet with its spread of four toes. Five of the feet came down flat on the shore, but one of them descended on a small boulder, and Thorn was amused to see the obstructed foot close on it and shove it to one side as if in irritation, before planting itself down firmly—it seemed the AI did still control some things.

Manoeuvring thrusters cut out and various motors and generators wound down throughout the craft. He heard the tick of cooling metal, the occasional loud clunk or hissing crunch as its weight settled. Jarvellis operated a ball control to slide from view to view around the ship, giving the effect of a single camera panning slowly round 360 degrees to survey their surroundings. For a moment she paused at a view showing one of the partially submerged boulders, where something large and insectile squatted, its mantis head tilted towards them while its mandibles fed something wriggling into its mouth, as if without the insectile creature's consent or apparent notice.

"Harmless," said Stanton, "unless you feel inclined to go swimming."

After a moment, the creature raised its snaky body from the stone on rows of centipedal legs, and dived into the water in one smooth motion. Jarvellis snorted and continued on round, until she came back to the original view.

"You'd have thought they would have been here to meet us," she said.

"We gave them a window of two months," Stanton replied. "They couldn't wait out in the open for that length of time without attracting unwanted notice—and I don't just mean from the Theocracy."

"Gabbleducks, heroynes and hooders?" suggested Thorn.

Stanton shook his head. "Not so many heroynes or gabbleducks in these mountains. Siluroynes and hooders cause the most problems, and in the latter case any weapon heavy enough to deal with the problem might attract the notice of the Theocracy."

"Hard to kill?" Thorn's curiosity was piqued.

"Never seen one myself, but I'm told that nothing less than an APW or missile launcher will do the job. Their chitin is something like a carbon composite, and they're mainly made up of that substance and fibrous muscle as dense as antique wood. Small arms just make a lot of holes that do nothing to slow them down, and the heat from lasers quickly disperses through their chitin. Also, for something so large, they move very fast."

"How large and how fast?" Thorn asked.

"I'm told that a hooder once grabbed a proctor, plus his aerofan, from a hundred metres up in the air. As to how fast they move—faster than a man can run, and they hunt grazers that move at a similar rate to the grazers on Earth."

"Like gazelle?"

Stanton glanced at him. "If that's a grazer on Earth, then yes."

"This is all very interesting," said Jarvellis, "but what do we do now?"

Standing up, Stanton replied, "I'm for stretching my legs outside. Anyone coming?" He looked from Thorn to Jarvellis. "Lyric can listen for any signals coming in from them."

As he headed away through the entrance tunnel, Jarvellis turned to Thorn. "You know, every time I land here it confirms for me that the Theocracy has the right idea."

"Living safe in their cylinder worlds?"

"Safe anywhere you're not likely to get eaten," she replied.

Aphran and Danny entered the bridge pod first, soon followed by five other Separatists who looked both tired and frightened. Skellor observed them as they halted just inside the doors and showed no inclination to come further in, and through their augs he sensed the gritty taste of their fear and their confusion at what they were seeing.

Nodding to the command-crew chairs he said, "Take your places."

With their eyes widening in horror, they stared at the chairs with the growths poised underneath them like grasping claws. Through most of them, he sensed continued fear and confusion, but from Aphran he felt sudden panic at her partial understanding of what he wanted. He reinforced the order with something like a mental slap that jerked them all into motion. Inevitably it was Danny who responded first, and was soon in the seat nearest to Skellor.

"You don't need to do this," said Aphran tightly, fighting all the way but unable to stop herself from sitting down.

Skellor did not bother to reply. Whether or not he actually needed to do what he was doing was irrelevant—he was doing what he *wanted* to do, and because he could. With the seven now seated, he started the Jain structure growing again, observing it climbing around the backs of each chair, fingering over the arms, and fumbling at the clothing of the seven Separatists. At the first penetration of his skin, the man on the end groaned in pain, then his groan was cut off as the filaments penetrated his spine and rapidly made connections as they sped up to his brain. Skellor then shunted over programs to run the man and programs for him to run. Where the man's own experience or memory or skill conflicted with what was now required of him, it was erased—chalk wiped from black slate. Drooling in his chair, the Separatist took control of the almost irrelevant systems of life-support.

Aphran, Skellor noted, was making weak whimpering sounds as an extension of the structure slid over her shoulder and rose up by the side of her face and hung poised there like a cobra. She showed the whites of her eyes as she tried to peer round at it, but was unable to turn her head. She yelled once when it struck, and thereafter lost herself as she unwillingly gained control of the weapons systems of the *Occam Razor*. But she did not control them as a human being—she controlled them as a submind of Skellor, an extension, a useful tool that possessed as little self-determination as a trigger. Aphran did not drool; she just slumped in her seat and her face lost any vividness of expression it had once possessed.

The others followed, one after the other, and as he delegated control of systems, Skellor freed up much processing power within himself in which to more fully view and understand his conquest. The *Occam Razor* was a formidable ship, but it was not yet entirely his. Such had been the destructiveness of the burn Tomalon had initiated, there were huge sections of the vessel that Skellor could not yet even see, let alone control. He realized now that he needed a breathing space in which to grow the Jain structure throughout the whole ship, and he understood that here was not the best place to initiate that chore. Using another member of his crew as a sophisticated search-engine—an informational bloodhound—soon revealed to him a simple recording of a conversation that gave him all the information he required. He smiled nastily to himself: so Dragon was going there, outside the Polity, to a world that was utterly primitive by comparison—a place where it would be easy to still the wagging of tongues. With a half-nod to that member of his crew who controlled the U-space engines, he had the *Occam* taken under, and away. Then, when—through the Jain substructure—he experienced underspace utterly unshielded, he screamed. And one second after, his command crew mimicked him exactly.

12

As she read she could see it would soon be time for the boy to go to bed, for his expression was becoming increasingly glazed. Checking ahead she saw that there wasn't all that much more to read and realized that the boy would soon be taking a greater interest.

"On the third day he came into the realm of the gabble duck, and found that many years had passed since the faithless had come to test themselves, and it had also been many years since the creature had fed, and to Brother Serendipity it seemed but a mound of skin and bone." The woman bit her lip, then pulled her chair round beside her son's, so he could see the picture in the book. The gabbleduck appeared as a pyramidal monstrosity looking down on the little man. Behind the man the heroyne towered hugely, and coiled on the ground behind it rested the siluroyne, picking at its hatchet teeth with one claw. All three creatures had in their expressions something like suppressed amusement. The boy indeed started to pay more attention now.

"'Please feed me for I have not eaten in many a year and am fading away,' spake the gabbleduck. 'Why should I feed you when, strengthened by my food, you might riddle me to my doom?' asked the good Brother. 'You have my promise that it will be otherwise,' the gabbleduck replied. 'Swear in the name of God and in the name of his prophet Zelda Smythe,' the Brother demanded. And so swore the gabble duck, and in recompense ate the last third of the meat cake gifted by the old woman. That night none dared approach Brother Serendipity and his three protectors as they came at last in sight of the boundary stone of Agatha Compound."

*

As the cold-coffin opened, Cormac saw a pterodactyl head poised over him, as if contemplating the opening of a can of food. For a second he felt utterly vulnerable, but his previous assessment of their current situation inside the landing craft—inside Dragon—had not changed. If Dragon wanted to kill them, then there was nothing they could do about it. Ignoring the head, he pushed himself up from the coffin and to one side. Turning in midair, he also ignored the always painful return of feeling as he reached over to the adjacent locker and removed his clothing. Only when he was dressed, and with Shuriken strapped to his arm and his thin-gun in his pocket, did he turn to observe Dragon.

"You interfered with the timings on the coffins," he said.

A mass of tentacles once again filled the airlock, but some of them, he now saw, snaked through the air to penetrate much of the craft's instrumentation.

"Your timings were wrong. We are already off Calypse and you would otherwise have slept for one solstan week more," Dragon replied.

Cormac rubbed his arms and, after pulling himself down to the floor with one of the many wall handles, he stamped his feet on the deck. Glancing around the inside of the craft, he thought for a moment that Apis had also thawed up, then realized that what he was seeing was the boy's exoskeletal suit strapped upright to a handle right by his coffin. He next saw Gant sitting utterly still in the co-pilot's chair: he too had shut himself down for the duration of the journey, but it seemed strange that he had not roused by now, for surely any unexpected sounds or movements would have woken him instantly. Cormac noticed that one of the draconic tentacles had snaked up the side of the chair and penetrated the Golem's side.

"Why have you woken me alone, then?" Cormac asked.

"The only way to win is to become."

Ah, it was going to be one of those conversations—a kind of verbal chess in which he did not know the value of the pieces played. Cormac decided not to dignify such an opaque comment with a reply.

"You referred to 'the enemy' being aboard the *Occam Razor*, and I presumed that to mean the Jain. Were the Makers—your makers—once at war with them?" he asked.

"It is not *they* any more."

"You mean the Jain are a dead race?"

"I mean it is not a race."

"Is the rumour true that you enjoy speaking a lot and saying nothing?" Cormac asked, getting irritated.

The head turned towards the cockpit, where a mass of something with the consistency of raw liver darkened the front screen. However, one of the lower screens came on, to display a view *outside* Dragon. It revealed the swirled opal face of the gas giant Calypse, with two moons poised nearby. From the nearest of these moons, some sort of structure feathered out into space, small ships moving about it like beetles over a pile of twigs.

"That's Flint—and that structure some sort of shipyard, I would guess. Why did you come into realspace out here? Surely closer in would have been better? You could have hit the laser arrays and been out before they had a chance to respond."

"I am not planning to leave."

Great.

"That still doesn't tell me why you're this far out."

"Let them tremble at my presence. Let them see!"

Its final bellow had Cormac clapping his hands over his ears. He saw tentacles retracting; Gant jerking, then abruptly whipping his head round. Behind him, the cold-coffins began to open.

"What the hell?" asked Gant.

"I begin," said Dragon, quietly now, and suddenly the very air in the craft seemed taut with energy. Behind him, Cormac heard Mika groan, then Apis asking a question—but he could not distinguish the words because they became so distorted. Huge pressure built, so it felt to him as if his head must implode. Then there came an immense sound, as of two seconds broadcast from inside a hurricane, and in this vast exhalation the tension and pressure drained away. The screen became a distorting lens showing the view down a long tunnel towards the shipyard. As it settled back to a normal view, the yard disappeared inside a pillar of fire, ships tumbling out into space, some burning and some breaking apart, a crater now glowing in the face of the moon.

Then they were moving, Calypse and its moons dropping behind.

"Vengeance is mine, saith Dragon," the head intoned.

The shaking of her room had been enough to bring Eldene to the surface of slumber, but not enough to hold her there. It was the constantly increasing cacophony in Pillartown One that finally dragged her back to the surface and held her there. She had been lying awake, but just too comfortable to move for quite some time, when the door opened and the lights came on.

"Come on, slugabed, you've slept long enough I think," said Fethan.

Feeling a sudden flushing of guilt at her unaccustomed laziness, Eldene quickly sat up in bed and observed the old man unshouldering first a rifle then a heavy backpack and depositing them on the floor. Now finding she was completely naked, she realized Fethan must have undressed her after she had collapsed into this bed last night. Embarrassment added to her discomfort.

"How long have I been asleep?" she asked, clasping the clean pale blue sheets about herself, and noticing how filthy were her hands in comparison.

"About half as long again as you're used to."

Wiping a hand over her face Eldene studied her surroundings with somewhat more attention than previously. That this—the largest and most airy room she had ever slept in—should be found underground was a constant surprise.

Fethan pointed to an arched entrance over to one side. "There's a shower in there with hot water and other luxuries you could easily get accustomed to. You've got an hour before we set out again, so you'd best get moving, girl."

Eldene glanced in the direction he indicated, but felt little inclination to get out of bed naked—even if the old man had undressed her last night.

"Where are my clothes?" she asked at last.

"Threw 'em away," he replied. "There's some new kit in this pack for you."

"What's the hurry? And where are we going?"

Fethan stepped over and sat on the edge of her bed. "A ship's just come in with new supplies, and I thought you'd like to see it. It's not far to go, but Lellan's limiting the number of trips out to visit it in case the activity is spotted, so this'll be our only opportunity." He then abruptly stood up, perhaps finally realizing why Eldene seemed uncomfortable. "Did you get all that Carl was telling you when we arrived here?" he asked.

"Some of it," Eldene replied, for she had been almost dead on her feet whilst Carl lectured her.

"So do you remember where tunnel seventeen is?"

"Where the river comes in?"

"That's it," said Fethan. "If you're interested, be there in one hour." He grinned slyly and headed for the door. As soon as he was gone, Eldene kicked the covers back and went to use the shower. She had to stay with Fethan, for without him she just did not know what to do—this was perhaps the most difficult aspect of going from a life of virtual slavery to one that offered choices. In the shower, she was delighted to discover the hot water, scented soap, and large warm towels, though she could not spare the time to luxuriate. She washed quickly and methodically, dried herself thoroughly, then hurried over to the backpack he had delivered. Before opening it, she picked up the rifle—the same sort as those carried by Lellan and the others—and inspected the thing. She doubted this was Fethan's own, and left here by mistake—she was coming to realize that Fethan did not often do anything without purpose—so he must have specially left it for her. She dropped the weapon on the bed, and tried not to wonder what the provision of this object might mean about her life from now on.

Inside the pack she found underwear and fatigues that she quickly donned, noting how no allowance had been made in the dimensions of the shirt for a scole, and felt fiercely glad of that fact. Also in the pack were a quilted jacket, oxygen pack and mask, cooking equipment, a sleeping bag, and various other items of survival—some of which she did not recognize. Fethan had said the ship was not far away, so taking up the breather gear and jacket only, she left the rest of the pack's contents and set out. She also left the rifle where it was.

The pillartown was a source of greater wonder to Eldene than the familiar ponds and fields on the floor of the cavern. Vaguely she had memories of several-storied buildings, from her orphanage childhood in the capital, but those were memories of dismal grey boxes stacked one upon the other, and joined by toll-tunnels where you must pay to breathe the air. She knew that there were parks and larger spaces, but they were the province of high Theocracy—the proctors, soldiers and priests—not gutter trash like herself. Here the buildings were so utterly different: every floor had wide viewing galleries and balconies open to the cavern air, plants grew in every available niche and were obviously carefully nurtured, the floors everywhere felt soft—and always there was light.

Eldene headed for one of the high-speed lifts Fethan had earlier demonstrated to her, and was soon walking out through the pillartown's lobby. Here was where food and domestic goods were distributed, and she could see stalls stretching endlessly in every direction. All around her there were people—uncowed people who were not waiting for the discovery of some minor infraction of Theocracy rules and the consequent punishment. Outside the building, Eldene covered the short distance down to the river, and then followed a path along the bank to the entrance to tunnel seventeen. She broke into a run once she saw that Fethan, Carl and Lellan were already waiting there, so arrived amongst them panting.

"Let's go," said Lellan, as soon as Eldene arrived, and led the way through an armoured door, then along similar tunnels to those they had arrived through. As they ascended, and breath became short, Eldene shuddered as for a second she felt she was returning to her old life. Realization that this was not so came as a flush of joy.

Tunnel seventeen opened out onto a narrow path cutting across a scree slope, then down a trail etched between platforms of stone that almost seemed to have been placed on purpose—though for what purpose was unknowable—into a valley that might have been the continuation of the one where she had fled the hooder yesterday. However, this path made her feel very much safer as it was cut into stone rising twenty metres above the rustling flute grasses.

Soon the valley turned a corner, and the river glimpsed through greenery terminated in a lake—whether flowing into or out of it was not clear, the river being glassily still.

Lellan, who had been speaking quietly into her mike, glanced back towards Fethan as they approached the lake. "Well—she's down on that further shore." She wore an amused expression as she pointed vaguely.

"Chameleonware," said Fethan. "Risky."

Lellan's amusement evaporated. "Sometimes you are just no fun at all." She continued leading the way.

Eventually their path descended in long steps to the point where the lake connected to the river. They had to walk a short way through flute grass that was chest-high and now throwing out dark red side-shoots, creating a tangle that required some effort to push through, then came to a shoreline of flaky shale scattered with pieces of white bone, like driftwood. There was a tide-line of empty jewel-like mollusc shells, and the shore hissed underfoot when they stepped on it.

"What is that noise?" Eldene whispered to Fethan, subsequently wondering why she was keeping her voice low.

"Small water lice. They feed on animalcules washed down the river to here." This also answered her question about which direction the river flowed.

As they reached the boulder-strewn further shore of the lake, Eldene turned her attention, only momentarily, to a nasty-looking creature squatting on a half-submerged rock. As she turned back to look where she was going she let out a yelp of surprise and abruptly stepped back into Fethan. Suddenly, where there had been only empty shore, there now stood two men and a woman, standing before what seemed to her a huge trispherical spaceship. She felt nothing but confusion, and would have run if Fethan had not held on to her.

"The ship was hidden," he said close to her ear. "It projects a field that, amongst other things, bends light around it and makes it invisible. We just walked inside that field."

Eldene calmed herself and studied the three individuals who stood waiting. They did not wear face-masks, so either they were like Fethan, or some other fabulous Polity technology was at work here. Lellan walked up to one of the men—a thickset ginger-haired individual who appeared to be quite capable of tearing someone's head off—and with her arms akimbo, glared at him.

"We'd almost given up on you. What the hell have you been playing at, John?"

The man rubbed his face, causing the field that contained air over his nose and mouth to shimmer.

"Dorth was on Cheyne III, so I paid my last visit to friend Brom, who was hosting him," explained Stanton.

"Did you get him?" asked Lellan, her tone suddenly avid.

"No, he's back here. But Brom's out of the picture now."

Lellan bowed her head in disappointment.

Meanwhile, Fethan had sidled up to the other man. "ECS?" asked the old man, and Thorn nodded in reply. Fethan went on, "Thought so—it's the company you keep."

Eldene could not help but feel an outsider in all this. She resolved to not remain so for very long.

It was howling in his head, trying to penetrate the now frantic shouting of the Septarchy Friars—a looming hot ophidian presence. He did not need Aberil to announce, "Behemoth is here."

Through the wide chainglass window extending across the front bridge of the lead Ragnorak tug, they could only see Calypse and a distant feeble glow on the moonlet called *Flint* where, only minutes ago, there had been a shipyard and a population of thousands. In front of the pilot and navigator—in the tank displaying the relative positions of just about every object in the Masadan system—a new object, outlined in red, was moving away from the devastated shipyard. Seated in the couch especially provided for him, on a recently installed grav-plate floor, Loman leaned forwards to peer more closely at this tank.

"What is it doing?" he asked through gritted teeth.

"It's coming insystem on a realspace drive of some kind," Aberil replied, gazing at the instrumentation before the seated navigator, where he floated at the man's shoulder—outside the influence of those few plates provided for Loman. "The fleet is embarking from *Hope*, and preparing to U-jump on your order to attack."

"How long before they can jump?" Loman asked.

Aberil closed his eyes for a moment and, when he opened them, said, "Thirty-eight minutes."

"Tell them to only prepare."

Aberil glanced at him. "We cannot allow Behemoth to get close to our cylinder worlds. It must be destroyed." Loman stared at him until he added, "Hierarch."

Loman continued to stare, feeling panic rise up inside himself. It had always been accepted that Behemoth would run, after *Miranda* had been destroyed. Had it not come out here to hide from the Polity in the first place?

"The *General Patten* was the biggest and most advanced ship we had, yet Behemoth tore it apart without using the weapon it's just used to destroy the *Flint* complex. What do you think the fleet could do against it?" he asked.

"They could slow it, Hierarch," suggested Aberil.

Loman stood up, walked to the edge of his grav-plates, and stared up at the chainglass screen. He placed his fingers against his aug and tried to find something amid the racket blocking or obliterating the channels. It did not take him long.

"*Amoloran! Amoloran!*" something bellowed over the ether.

"*Listen to me,*" Loman sent back. "*I am the Reverend Epthirieth Loman Dorth, Hierarch of Masada. Amoloran is dead. What do you want here, Behemoth?*"

Suddenly the static faded and Loman felt himself to be standing in a vast chamber. The screen he gazed up at now seemed to have translucent scales all across its surface; a sharp astringent smell filled his nostrils, and he felt uncomfortably warm.

"*You closed me out with prayer, and I could have destroyed you then. You destroy an Outlink station, and for this the Polity blames me. Now you have hurt me, and for this you will pay,*" Dragon told him.

"*You were not hurt by any order of mine,*" Loman replied. "*You attacked a ship sent on a mission by Amoloran. Those in that ship turned on its engines and burnt you, and for that you killed them all. There is no payment to be made.*"

"*Oh you will pay,*" Dragon replied.

"Hierarch, it's turned towards us," said Aberil.

With some difficulty Loman severed the link, blinking away the strange after-effects from his vision, and turned to his brother. "What?"

"It just changed course. It's heading towards us."

Loman felt his mouth turn dry and a brass hand clench in his guts. "Send the fleet," he said, and unsteadily returned to his couch.

"*Would it be possible to hit Behemoth with Ragnorak?*" he silently asked Aberil.

"*No, Hierarch. Ragnorak is designed for static targets, and Behemoth would just move out of the way.*"

Aloud, Aberil continued, "It's accelerating."

In silence, Loman watched the display unfolding in the tank, then a display on one of the control screens fed through from the targeting gear on Ragnorak. There all he saw was a small, slightly distorted sphere growing slowly larger against a background of blackness.

"How long will it take to reach us?" he asked.

"At this rate, just over the hour," Aberil replied.

"So the fleet will get to it first?"

"Yes."

But then what? Loman considered how brief would be his reign as Hierarch. There had been briefer ones, but never with such possibilities of great achievement. He closed his eyes and thought that perhaps this was their reward for dealing with one who had obviously been an emissary of Satan, not God—this was their punishment for not recognizing the difference. Members of the crew at the instrumentation around him were now mumbling prayers. In his mind, he slowly began to recite all the Satagents—but now with his eyes open, and all expression erased from his face. He was on the fifth one, just like Amoloran, when Aberil broke the gloom on the bridge.

"The fleet has gone into underspace."

Loman groped for some sort of reply. They might succeed in stopping the creature, but it seemed very unlikely—something that could tear apart a warship like the *General Patten* and could destroy something as huge as the *Flint* complex in a matter of seconds would take some stopping.

He was about to speak again when something slammed into him through his aug—tearing open a link in a way he'd always thought impossible.

"*How so obviously you are not Polity AIs, and how slowly your ships enter underspace. With your pathetic fleet all around you, Reverend Epthirieth Loman Dorth, look to your world!*"

"What . . . what do you mean?"

The only reply was fading gargantuan laughter.

"Behemoth has dropped into underspace. It has gone," said Aberil.

Loman sat back and very carefully closed down the channels that linked him to the U-space transmitter on this ship, and thus through to the cylinder worlds. He did not want to listen to the millions dying.

It was a brief U-space jump, yet it seemed interminable.

"Not too bright, are they?" opined Gant, staring at the console out of which had been relayed Dragon's exchange with the Hierarch.

Cormac shrugged and was about to make some comment, but Apis intervened, "Dragon seemed about to attack that device. What happened?"

Cormac explained, "It looks like their ships need to get up speed first to drop into underspace . . . they can't do a standing jump. But Dragon can."

Apis looked thoughtful for a moment as he closed the clasps down the front of his exoskeleton. "Perhaps they are not used to making war on something that fights back."

"Perhaps," said Cormac, now gazing up at the pterodactyl head that was still hovering above them. "You lied about your ability to drop into underspace, so am I now to believe your story about these people using the mycelium you provided to destroy *Miranda*?"

"It is true," Dragon replied briefly.

"Okay, I'll accept that for now, but do you suppose for one minute that the Polity would ever forgive you the slaughter of the population on Masada or in those cylinder worlds?"

"I am dying."

"I see, so you intend to go out in bloody style."

"I will live."

"Any remote possibility of a straight answer?"

"I will destroy only their laser arrays."

Cormac glanced around at his companions. It was with a total lack of surprise that he saw Mika holding some sort of instrument up to one of the draconic tentacles. Scar was poised in the air—a reptilian statue. Gant had his foot hooked under the back of one of the seats and once again clutched his APW to his chest.

Cormac returned his attention to Dragon. "What about us? What do you intend for us?"

The head suddenly dropped down so that it was poised right before Cormac. "If I kill and destroy, your Polity will kill and destroy me. You will let me live, Ian Cormac. For how I will now help you, you will let me live."

"I might when I figure out what the hell you mean when you say you are 'dying' and 'will live.' I'd have thought a creature of your capabilities would have learnt how to communicate clearly by now."

The head swung so that it was directed towards Scar. In response the dracoman hissed and seemed ready to attack. Dragon merely said, "He will know—when it is time." With that it abruptly withdrew towards the airlock, tentacles detaching and slithering away after it; the great plug of tangled flesh drew back into a living cavern beyond, and the airlock began to close. The screen they had been observing now showed only something dark and organic, which shifted slowly.

Cormac paused for a moment, then said, "Get strapped in. I think the shit's about to hit."

Seconds later they felt Dragon surface from underspace and, ahead of the lander, curtains of skin began to part. Cormac hunted across the controls until he managed to adjust the setting of one of the lower screens to infrared, to obtain the view he required. Now they could all see a tunnel opening ahead, and going into huge peristalsis. The craft slid forwards twenty metres, and slammed to a halt with a dull boom—then again, as another stretch of tunnel opened. Five times this happened, until through the main screen they saw a vague circle of luminescence. With competent precision, Apis reached down and reset the screen Cormac had previously adjusted—back to its normal view overlooking one side. Then they were out, and falling towards the gleaming arc of a world, starlit space fading to blue on that arc, and hanging nearby a huge machine-gun-magazine satellite, gleaming in bright sunlight. In the rear-view screen Dragon loomed huge against the stars, a distorted sphere across which now passed ripples of light, as over a pool of water containing fluorescing bacteria into which a stone has been cast.

"Shit! Get us out of here!" Cormac shouted.

Apis, who had strapped himself in at the controls before anyone else could object—though Cormac wouldn't, as the boy probably knew them better than anyone else on board—ran at high speed through a start-up sequence and grabbed the joystick. Thrusters roared and the craft tilted to one side, the view of the planet swinging round by a hundred and eighty degrees. There came a thunderous crash, and light flooded the cockpit as from a lightning strike. Now the satellite was behind them, and blowing apart, huge fragments hurtling outwards ahead of a wave of fire.

"Hold us here," ordered Cormac. "I want to see this."

Manipulating thrusters, Apis swung the craft around so the main screen showed a view of Dragon rolling across the darkness above them, heading towards the horizon of Masada—following a line of gleaming shapes suspended above atmosphere like a bracelet of charms for the planet. The creature remained in sight as they descended into atmosphere, and they watched it pause by another satellite and spit an actinic bar down onto it—another satellite gone in a fiercely bright explosion against the blue-black of space.

"Take us further in," said Cormac, then he looked round when the boy seemed disinclined to respond. Apis looked pale and slightly sick.

"The Golem, on the *Occam Razor* . . . they hit the ion engines," he stammered, as the landing craft began its brick-like descent. "We've only got manoeuvring thrusters."

Cormac closed his eyes and massaged his temples with his forefingers—he was getting a headache.

"Of course," he said. "This craft hasn't got AG, so we're going to need a flat area at least two or three kilometres long. How much can you slow us with the thrusters?"

Now asked technical questions, Apis lost his sick expression and shrugged himself into a businesslike frame of mind. He checked his instrumentation. "Enough to prevent us burning up, though I calculate . . . we will be going in at between five hundred and a thousand kilometres per hour."

Cormac glanced round at the other three. "This could prove interesting," he observed.

"You have a strange idea of what constitutes interesting," Mika replied.

"Normally something that involves an explosion, unfortunately," added Gant.

Scar merely bared his teeth.

Cormac went on, "If any of us survive this, it's going to be you, Gant. Your primary mission has to be to get news of what happened on the *Occam* to the Polity. ECS has to know about Skellor—he could be more dangerous than anything we've ever faced before."

"You *are* a cold bastard," said Gant.

"Whatever gets the job done," Mika commented sarcastically. Cormac ignored them both.

The craft was soon shaking, and what had earlier been merely a low droning outside was now growing into a constant roar. Cormac gazed ahead as they punched through stratospheric cloud, above purplish ocean with a scattering of islands like black scabs. Apis manipulated the thruster controls, lifting the lander's nose for the further horizon. Soon they noticed the ocean below was scattered with icebergs.

"Will we make it to the main continent?" Cormac asked almost conversationally.

Apis gave a tight nod in reply.

Separate bergs started knitting below them into an ice sheet, which then started to break apart again. The line of a landmass rose over the horizon, with thick cloud tangled above it. When it became evident that this terrain ahead was mountainous, Apis used the thrusters to take them higher. The roaring was now deafening, the craft shaking alarmingly. Across the main screen rolled motes of something molten, and along its edges a hot glow encroached. Valleys and tors rolled underneath the craft, and it punched through cloud masses—losing vision for long seconds. Spearing down through a final cloud bank, they came out over flat plains, with a glimpse of chequered ponds and a wider spread of agriculture surrounding them. To their right a city loomed out of haze, then rapidly receded.

"Dragon!" Cormac yelled, pointing up to the sky where blooms of light ignited behind cloud, as from a distant thunderstorm.

Signs of civilization receded and they were now plummeting onto an uncultivated plain. The roar doubled as Apis initiated the thrusters to slow the craft, and kept them full on. As he fought to keep its nose up, the craft continued to descend, blurs of beige, dark red and green flashing by beneath them. There came a loud vicious hissing and, glancing at the rear-view screen, Cormac saw a cloud boiling up behind a track hammered through the vegetation below. Apis hit boosters and the cloud was shot through with sheets of flame. Suddenly they were all pressed hard against their straps, and their craft was bouncing and breaking. In the rear-view screen, a thruster nacelle, still jetting flame, curved into the cloud and disappeared. The craft itself began to slew, but Apis managed to correct for this. When Cormac glanced at him, the boy looked terrified but determined. This state of affairs seemed to just go on and on, then, as the din lessened, the craft abruptly, tilted, then flipped. There followed a chaos of rending crashes and bone-jarring jolts, as they rolled over and over, with pieces of the lander breaking away, and cold acidic air rushing in through the gaps torn in the hull, along with a haze of papery fragments. Then they were sliding along, tilted to one side, with wet black mud spraying up through gaping holes.

Cormac found himself fighting for breath as the oxygenated air inside the craft poured away. A roaring in his ears soon drowned out the chaos of the crash. With his vision tunnelling, he saw that Apis had managed to close over the hood of his exoskeleton and the suit, detecting the lack of oxygen, had automatically raised the visor. Behind, Mika was fighting for breath, while Gant was undoing his safety straps. Then Cormac lost it—he blacked out completely.

Thorn could not help but be impressed by the set-up they had here. Studying his companions in the elevator, as it rapidly accelerated up into the building, he wondered what their story might be. The girl looked a little bewildered by events around her, but utterly determined to stick with the old Golem, Fethan. Lellan Stanton . . . now here was an intriguing woman. She had little of her brother's brutish appearance, but obviously a shitload of his innate intelligence.

She and Jarvellis were of a kind—clever, forceful, and not to be crossed. Yes, Thorn rather liked her already.

"What was it?" John Stanton asked.

Lellan replied, "Some sort of explosion." She listened to her helmet's earphone. "I'm not getting much sense out of them up there—there's a lot of yelling."

Thorn reflected on their frantic journey across the floor of the cavern in the jury-rigged AGC. Something big was happening, and there might ensue some kind of reaction from those down here—this place was wound up tight and seemed ready to explode. He'd seen it in the faces of the soldiers and technicians, and he'd seen the armament they'd built up. Through the glass side of the elevator Thorn saw that they had now reached the ceiling of the cavern, but that they were not slowing. Up and through—dark stone speeding past lit eerily by the elevator's internal light.

"Could be something to do with that rock you dragged in with us?" he suggested.

Jarvellis shook her head. "That fragmented and burned up without their notice, but maybe *we* were detected. That might explain all the activity," she said, her expression worried.

"No, that," said Lellan, tapping the side of her helmet. "That was Polas I was listening to. As far as I can gather, there's been an explosion on or near EL-41, and the possibility of explosions at 40 and 39. They're putting up the big dish and refractor now." She paused, listening again, then: "Seems that was 38."

Finally the elevator drew to a halt and its doors slid open onto a chamber crammed with equipment. One side of this chamber was walled by a window of tinted chainglass giving a view of mountains and sky, so it seemed evident they were located inside some high peak.

As soon as Lellan stepped out of the elevator, a thin weasel of a man began to gesture to her frantically. He sat in a half-circle console with a number of screens jury-rigged before him. Other people throughout this chamber were operating other machines, babbling into microphones, or frantically tapping instructions into consoles of antiquated design. Removing her helmet, Lellan trotted over to the beckoning man. Thorn took his time following along behind, as he once again studied the set-up around him—they had obviously had to do the best they could with whatever they could lay their hands on, but this was as good an operations room as any. It surprised him to see that it even had an old military projection tank—a holojector showing the entire Masadan system. However, he doubted that it displayed real-time—that would have bespoken a sophistication they definitely did not possess here.

"It's gone," the man called Polas was saying. "It's fucking well just gone."

"Show me," said Lellan.

Polas gestured at the screens. One of these showed a radio picture of the black dots of stars on a white background, cut off to one side by the black arc of Calypse. Another showed an empty grid, while another showed just empty blue. On a ring of lower screens, mathematical symbols and graph representations clicked on and off, flickering and changing as if some primitive AI were trying to justify the impossible.

"What about the recording?" Lellan asked.

Polas grimaced. "The machine dumped it as being out of parameters—thought it had made a mistake." He shouted across to one of his fellows, "Dale, you managed to retrieve it yet?"

The woman Dale shook her head as she continued clattering away at her keypad—chasing down something on her screen.

"The rest?" asked Lellan. "Have they gone as well?"

"So the equipment tells us. There's also that." Polas pointed to the chainglass window. Outside in daylight sky, a smoky disc was dissipating—one edge of it silhouetted against Calypse.

"Okay, it's time to send up the probe," said Lellan.

"Might be software, glitched by whatever that was," Polas pointed out.

"Just do it."

"A probe?" Thorn turned to Jarvellis, who was standing beside him.

"We brought it for them on our last trip. They only have the one," she replied.

"Won't its launch be detected?"

"Dispensable probe, and a separate and dispensable site."

Polas swung a side console across his lap—one with touch-controls rather than the buttons and ball controls of most of the consoles here—and with his fingertips expertly traced out a sequence. The radio screen's view changed to the same one they were seeing through the chainglass window. This view then vibrated as somewhere a rocket probe blasted from its hidden silo and headed into the sky.

"I've got it!" Dale yelled, while they all watched this scene, and she came running over with a software disc. Polas snatched it from her, swung the touch-console back out of the way, and inserted the disc into a slot in one of the more primitive consoles. He quickly rattled over the buttons while gazing at the gridded screen, then triumphantly hit the last button with his forefinger, and sat back.

"About a minute beforehand," he explained.

The screen image changed to show the curved satellite laser array Thorn had earlier seen from *Lyric II*, except that this view was from below, and he could clearly see the reflective throats of laser tubes open before him. They watched this unchanging scene for slow drawn-out seconds, then abruptly Polas leant forwards and stabbed his finger at one of the smaller screens, showing a tangle of signal waves.

"That's what made it dump the recording. No way can we set this system to accept a U-space signature—it screws everything," he said.

"U-space?" Lellan repeated. "They don't jump this close ... what is that?"

On the screen, something gigantic loomed behind the laser array. As they watched, it rolled closer—a vast and incomprehensible shape. From it, off to one side of the screen, a black fleck fell away, then the screen whited out for a second. When it came back on, the laser array was a spreading cloud of debris laced with fire, and the vast shape rolled on.

"What the fucking hell was that?" asked Lellan.

Polas wiped his hand down his face to cover his mouth. Almost as if he didn't want what he was going to say next to be heard, he muttered, "There was something about it. Something out at the cylinder worlds . . . Behemoth . . . just a name."

"There's no mystery," interrupted Thorn.

They all turned to look at him.

"That was Dragon," he told them. "And my guess is that things are just about to start getting very complicated—and very deadly."

The agony and the terror left him, sucked away through the growing Jain architecture inside the *Occam Razor*. Those of his command crew who still had enough of their humanity left to feel their own pain were sobbing, which meant there were only two of them, being Aphran and the man who controlled the U-space engines. Skellor silenced them with a thought and began to analyse what had happened. When he had discovered that, he glared at the corpse of Captain Tomalon and wished he'd not been so hasty in having the man killed. The trouble Tomalon had caused was worth as much punishment as that damned Cormac would receive when Skellor finally got hold of him.

It was the burn again. Through the crew member who now controlled all the *Occam Razor*'s energy shielding and shield generators, he located the huge misalignment. Overall there were eighty-four separate generators that shielded the ship from the hard radiation of space, or attack, and most importantly from the mind-scrambling effects of U-space—which even now were not clearly understood, at least by any human mind. The flat screens—a harder version of the shimmer-shield, and likewise a product of runcible technology—all had to mesh perfectly within a second of the U-space motors dropping the ship into under-space. They also oscillated on and off thereafter—the brief period they were *off* enabling the U-space motors to keep the ship hurtling through that ineffable dimension. But that had not happened: they'd dropped into U-space unshielded; then, within only a few minutes, had been forced out of it again when the shields started operating out of alignment to the motors. Every one of those generators had been connected in a complex net, and every one of them had been run by something that fell somewhere in between a submind and a plain control program.

"You piece of shit," spat Skellor, shutting down the grav-plate below the Captain's corpse. Then, grunting with an effort that had tears of blood forming in the corners of his eyes, he extruded a Jain outgrowth from the wall behind the corpse, which grabbed it around the neck and hauled it upright and back against the wall. Probing inside the man, he found nothing alive. It was not the shots that had killed him—the man's mind was burnt out like everything else on this ship. There would be no satisfaction there.

Skellor closed his eyes, the rage in him growing beyond the proportions of the human part of his mind, cycling into something difficult to contain. Opening his eyes, he fixed his gaze on the man—the thing—he had created, to control the ship's shielding. This man started shaking inside the Jain architecture that enclosed him, then he started screaming as its material closed about him. His bones broke with erratic thuds, and suddenly his screams were choked off. Abruptly all of him that was still visible shrivelled and turned grey. He diminished, drained away as nutrient for . . . Skellor.

With his rage finally under control, Skellor slid into a cold analytical mode. There had been no real satisfaction there because what he had killed possessed less sentience than an animal, and the screams had been little more than an autonomic reaction, utterly disconnected and operating in its own limited circuit. Now Skellor must grow a replacement for this erstwhile member of his command crew. He turned his attention to Aphran and saw that she was watching him with terrified eyes—there was still enough of her left to realize her danger. Skellor turned his attention away from her before further temptation to kill overwhelmed him, and gazed out through the ship's sensors. Taking navigational information from those parts of himself and from the command crew wherein it was contained—already he was finding it increasingly difficult to identify those parts as somewhere outside his own mind—he saw that there was a solar system near enough for the ship to reach in a U-space jump of only minutes' duration. There he would find what he needed: energy from a sun, asteroidal matter—all those things he needed to *fully* control the *Occam Razor*, and to grow.

Cormac returned to consciousness, gasping: lightheaded with the euphoria produced by oxygen flooding a brain starved for long enough to drag him into unconsciousness. He reached up and more firmly clamped the mask over his nose and mouth, then opened his eyes.

His vision was blurred and dark around the edges, and it was a moment before he realized Gant was stooping over him. In another moment, he remembered where he was. He looked at the main screen, saw fire and black smoke, and heard a roaring crackle from outside the craft.

"You all right?" Gant asked.

Cormac removed the mask from his face for a moment. "Bruised, but not broken I think, though somewhat annoyed with myself." He put the mask back on.

"Annoyed?"

Cormac found it easier to speak into the mask, rather than run out of breath while speaking with it pulled away from his face. "I should have remembered about the air mix down here, just as I should have had Apis run a diagnostic on those ion engines."

"As to the air mix, not everyone's perfect," said Gant. "And as to the engines, do you think that knowing they wouldn't work would have helped in some way?"

"Maybe Dragon . . ."

Gant grimaced.

Cormac shrugged, wished he hadn't, then looked to one side. Apis was not in his seat. He tried looking back, but his neck hurt too much. "They okay?" he asked.

"In the back," Gant explained. "Let me help you."

Gant undid his seat straps and, using his supporting arm, Cormac got unsteadily to his feet, then took the oxygen pack Gant was holding and carefully slung its strap over one shoulder.

The back of the craft was in utter chaos—part of the floor was torn open, and seats had come away from their mountings; mud blackened many surfaces, having been sprayed up through this hole; and the air itself was hazy with smoke. Scar was not present; Mika stood, with her face masked, strapping on an oxygen pack; Apis had meanwhile opened a number of lockers, and was hauling out bits of equipment. There seemed to be plenty of it, certainly, but Cormac couldn't see any way they might transport it. He noted that the young Outlinker had an oxygen bottle, similar to Cormac's, clipped on the back of his exoskeleton, its nozzle obviously compatible with the exo's universal adaptor.

"Where's Scar?" he asked.

Gant pointed to the ceiling of the craft. "Up there, having a look."

"That's good, though I suspect he's not going to see a lot. Now, as far as I see it, we've got to get to help before our oxygen supply runs out."

"Help being?" Gant wondered. "I don't think the Theocracy are going to greet us with milk and cookies."

"What help we get from them might not be willingly given, but we'll have it all the same. No, we have to get ourselves to this Underworld and, from what I understand of it, the way to get there is through those mountains we overflew on the way in."

At this Apis spoke up: "Those mountains are now two hundred kilometres away."

"I didn't say it was going to be easy," said Cormac.

"There are also other aspects of this place which may make things difficult," added Mika.

"Delight me with the news," said Cormac.

"Obviously, knowing where we were coming to, I accessed the *Occam*'s files concerning the ecology of this place."

"Let me guess: the full set of flesh-eating monsters?"

"In most cases that is correct," she agreed. "Though in one case the creature concerned is probably capable of eating metal as well." She glanced at Gant. "No offence intended."

"None taken, I'm sure," Gant replied.

Cormac turned to inspect the stuff Apis had pulled out of the lockers. "Okay, let's see what we can take and get moving. Even though the Theocracy currently has enough problems with Dragon, they still might send someone out here to investigate."

Cormac soon had confirmation that they had no shortage of supplies—it was just a question of how much they could carry, and what items to select. When Scar returned inside, and bluntly informed them that the fire—having used up all the air that had spilt like a pool around the lander—was dying, Cormac realized that they would not need oxygen for the dracoman—the lack of it outside obviously not having bothered Scar in the slightest. Slightly puzzled, Cormac asked him, "Why did you need oxygen on Callorum?"

"Didn't," Scar replied. "Just didn't want to change for the cyanide."

Cormac glanced at Mika, and saw her staring with fascination at the dracoman, then looking round for the equipment she had brought.

There were enough large army backpacks for one each. They filled one with oxygen bottles, and Scar hefted this huge weight with ease. In three other packs they distributed food, medical supplies, power packs, heat sheets, and anything else they could think of that might be of use for what lay ahead. In the final pack—taken up by Gant, after he had replaced his clothing with some found in a locker and donned a thick flak jacket that concealed his loss of syntheflesh—they put all of the equipment Mika had transferred from the *Occam*. Cormac was not sure what use it would be, but he was certain the Life-Coven woman would possess some items in there that were at the forefront of Polity technology, and should therefore not be discarded. Only as they were leaving the vessel did it occur to Cormac that it had been more than just a landing craft; most certainly it had been designed for the insertion of ground troops. This was an item of information he filed for future reference.

Outside, the fire had run its brief course, and now only steam was rising from the heated ground. If this had been on Earth, the flames would have become an inferno amid the dry dead stems of the surrounding vegetation. But fire needs oxygen, and here that was a sparse commodity. Walking over to Apis, he had the boy show him the air indicator on the wrist of his exoskeleton. There was oxygen in the atmosphere, but only enough to slow the process of suffocation for a human being. Cormac removed his mask and sniffed at the air, which was redolent with a smell like baked potatoes. Gazing round, he realized this came from the seared tubers of the plants. Reaching the point where the flute grass stood tall again, he turned and led the way back down the swathe the landing craft had cut through it. That way lay habitation, and that way lay the mountains. He wondered if they would get to see either.

Tersely, Thorn told them all what Dragon was—though he knew Stanton and Jarvellis had heard the story before, and Fethan looked unsurprised. What Lellan and Polas had just seen invalidated any disbelief *they* might have felt. There was almost an embarrassed silence after he had finished speaking, until Lellan said, "What does it matter what this thing is, and what . . . some part of itself did in the past? It's destroying the laser arrays, and to my mind that makes it the best ally we have ever had."

"Yes," said Thorn. "But will it stop at the arrays?"

Lellan glanced down at Polas. "That probe in position yet?"

Polas checked his instrumentation. "Few more minutes yet."

Thorn said, "You know, there's obviously a bigger picture here." Lellan gazed at him speculatively, and he went on,

"Back on Cheyne III, I had a brief but intriguing conversation with the Cereb AI. It told me I might be required for another mission, as an Outlink station had been destroyed and one of the Dragon spheres might be involved in that. I wonder if that station was *Miranda*—it being the nearest one to here." Thorn paused, seeing how pale Lellan had suddenly become.

"Did you say *Miranda* might have been destroyed?" she asked.

"Might have been, yes," said Thorn, trying to interpret the looks being exchanged.

Lellan grudgingly explained, "We have a U-space transmitter now." She glanced at Stanton and Jarvellis before going on, "But it's a long haul to broadcast into the Polity from here, and *Miranda* was to be our relay and signal booster. We'll have to scan the carrier signal about, until we find a capital ship close enough to do the same job." She paused and rubbed tiredly at her face. "Go on, tell me more about your bigger picture."

Thorn waited for further explanation, then said, "Before I go on . . . tell me, what exactly are you sending by U-space?"

"A cry for help: including five thousand hours of sealed recording of what goes on here."

Thorn thought about that until Lellan prompted, "Bigger picture?"

Thorn continued, "All I thought was that there are other things to factor in. Your Theocracy uses Dracocorp augs, doesn't it?"

"What?" said Lellan.

Stanton interjected, "I've seen them before, when I was with Pelter—and for some reason they freaked him out—but they're available all across the Polity now. If there was a problem with them, surely they'd be made illegal."

"Dracocorp is an Out-Polity corporation that was set up by Dragon's agents. All augs that come into the Polity, whenever ECS can track them down, are checked for subversion access. As far as I know, nothing has been proven, because their technology is so damned complex."

"So what are you getting at?" Lellan asked.

"I'm just pointing out these things: an Outlink station possibly destroyed by Dragon, a lot of Dracocorp augs around here, and now Dragon up there destroying laser arrays. You may be benefiting now, but I'd guess that what is being done is not specifically for your benefit. Of course"—he fixed his attention on Stanton—"if the station destroyed was *Miranda*, then it's likely someone else might be turning up here."

"Who?" asked the man.

"Ian Cormac—he usually gets called on when there's any shit involving Dragon."

"Yes," said Stanton, his face expressionless.

"That's good, isn't it?" asked Lellan, looking from one to the other of them in confusion.

"For Masada, quite probably, but not necessarily so for me," said Stanton.

Before Lellan could ask anything more, Polas interjected, "I'm getting a picture now." The man was operating a small toggle control, and each of the screens showed views over the curve of Masada, then space, and the face of Calypse. "There," he said, pointing at one of the screens.

Dragon loomed clear on the horizon, and Polas pushed his control forwards to take the probe closer. As it slowly drew in, the picture kept juddering, and when asked about this Polas replied, "Automatic avoidance—it's dodging debris." On two occasions thereafter they saw drifting clumps of titanic wreckage, fires glowing inside them, gases spewing away.

Closer to Dragon, and a flash of light blanked the screen. It then came back on to show a spreading ball of fire and debris—and one less laser array.

"I don't care," said Lellan. "We've lived under those for too long."

"God in Heaven," said Polas. He was operating other controls, calling up views all around as the probe accelerated towards Dragon. Radar images came up, spectral displays—he seemed to be trying every instrument the probe possessed.

He turned to Lellan. "EL-24 and 26 next," he said.

"How much of a hole has it made for us?" she asked.

Polas removed his hands from the controls—perhaps because they were shaking so much.

"Talk to me, Polas," said Lellan.

He turned to her, with a stunned expression, then stared back at the screen when it blanked yet again. "That was EL-26. One more to go, and that's it."

Lellan still hadn't quite grasped what he was telling her. Her expression showed irritation, confusion, then slowly dawning realization.

Polas nodded.

"It's destroyed . . ." He blinked at the screen as it flickered off then back on again. "It's destroyed all forty-six arrays. There's nothing but wreckage up there now."

13

"In the predawn light Brother Serendipity stood at the bounds of Agatha Compound and turned to address his three companions. 'You have served me well these three days, and should know that in that service you have served God and his Prophet: For the great day of his wrath is come; and who shall be able to stand?'"

The woman made a slight whimpering sound as she suppressed a laugh. The Brother stood to one side of the tall boundary stone, with his arms spread wide and a beatific expression on his face. The three creatures looked at each other with expressions that were completely unreadable. The gabbleduck then lifted what could loosely be described as a hand up to the side of its head and, with what could equally loosely be described as a finger, scribed circles in the air.

"As the sun rose over the compound, Brother Serendipity said unto his companions, 'You shall come with me to share in this glorious day!'"

Now the three creatures moved in around the Brother, almost concealing him with walls of flesh, bone, claws and teeth.

"'Here, from my trial in the wilderness, I come to claim my birthright. I shall smite the morlocks in their dank caverns and I shall rise up over my brothers and rule from the sky!' said the Brother. 'That would be a good place to rule from,' said the heroyne, sharpening his beak on the side of the boundary stone. 'This boy could go far,' added the siluroyne, sharpening his claws on the other side of the stone. 'Shame,' concluded the gabbleduck, whose teeth and claws were always sharp."

The boy didn't get it for a moment, until he saw the picture of the creatures pulling apart the Brother like a piece of naan bread. He then grinned with delight and pointed at the picture.

"Gabbleducked," he asserted, not without a degree of craftiness in his expression.

The woman looked at him warningly, then finished the story.

"And thus our story ends with the moral: You can have your cake and give it away, but never turn your back on a gabbleduck."

The night sky was bright with shooting stars that burned long courses through the oxygen-bereft air. Occasionally, distantly, some larger piece of wreckage would make it to the ground, and there then would be a flash and a boom as of gunfire on a distant battleground.

"Dragon is nothing if not thorough when it decides to destroy something," commented Mika.

"It always works on a huge scale," said Cormac, taking a sip from the tea Gant had made out of a packet he'd found amongst their supplies. Cormac and Mika were sitting on their packs whilst watching this display; Apis stood a little apart from them, his head tilted to the sky; and Gant and the dracoman were out "taking a little recce," as Gant put it.

Cormac nodded to the Outlinker boy. "You notice how all his hatreds are directed towards the Theocracy here and against Skellor on the *Occam*. He hasn't had a bad word to say about Dragon, yet the creature destroyed the *General Patten* and killed many of his kin."

"I had not noticed that," agreed Mika, studying the boy.

"It's an attitude prevalent throughout the Polity—since Samarkand, and probably before, Dragon has been viewed as more a force of nature than a being in its own right. It's too huge and unfathomable for most people to see it otherwise. You might just as well hate a hurricane or a volcano."

"I think I understand that: even with scientific objectivity, one cannot help but feel awe. It is godlike in its power and size, and its rather Delphic communications only make it seem more so. There is also its immortality: you once destroyed one Dragon sphere, yet Dragon still lives," Mika replied.

Apis turned towards them now, and walked back over. As he seated himself on his own pack, Cormac thought that behind his visor the boy looked rather unwell.

"How are you doing?" he asked.

"Gravity," confessed Apis. "This exo damps out most of the effects, but I can still feel it pulling on me. I'm tired, even though I'm not working."

That was not actually what Cormac had been asking about, but he let it ride. "We are all tired," he said. "I'd like to stop for sleep, but . . ." He gestured at his oxygen bottle.

"Oh," said Mika, glancing at Cormac. "I thought, being an agent, you would have been . . . adjusted."

Cormac considered that: many people, especially in Earth Central Security, had the function of their bodies adjusted so sleep was, at worst, necessary only for a few hours, and then not every night. When he had been gridlinked, he himself had been such a person. After losing his link, he had then deliberately sacrificed the rest of his augmentations. Blegg, his boss in ECS, had been right about the dehumanizing effects of gridlinking, but had not gone far enough: for in Cormac's opinion *all* augmentations dehumanized. And, furthermore, Cormac found that with human weaknesses he operated more efficiently. This was actually psychological, and he knew that it too could be adjusted, but he felt that in the end people had to draw the line and decide for themselves just how much they wanted to *remain* themselves. Because of his previous experience of gridlinking, Cormac did not want to fool with his own mind, so he drew his line long before many others drew theirs.

"No," he said. "I'm not adjusted—and I'm tired."

Mika reached into one of the pockets of the pack she was sitting on and pulled out a reel of drug patches, each one on the same paper backing strip no more than a centimetre wide. Catching the reel Cormac tore off one section, removed the patch, discarded its backing strip, and reached inside his shirt to press it against his torso. Then, holding up the reel, he nodded his head to indicate Apis.

"No," said Mika.

"Why not?" Apis asked.

"Your system is not used to the constant drag of gravity, especially your heart, so using stimulants might be suicidal. Anyway, you probably will not need any sleep. The nanites building up your musculature and adding density to your bones will also be clearing out toxins."

"But I feel *tired*," Apis protested.

"Psychological," replied Mika, tapping her head with her forefinger.

As the stimulant scoured away the fuzzy coating that seemed to have been thickening over everything for the last few hours, Cormac was glad to have it confirmed that it had, after all, been a good idea to lug along Mika's equipment. He himself had refused to use a nanite booster treatment so that he could handle the higher gravity on Callorum, a treatment that would have required him spending forty hours in a tank. Luckily for Apis, Mika had an interesting device with which she could manufacture nano-machines to her own specifications—a device Cormac was not sure was entirely legal within the Polity—and those specifications, he had since learnt, owed much to her study of the hybrid Skellor had created. The Outlinker himself now had a few varieties of those machines beavering away inside him, building muscle, bone, and all those other structures required for a body to handle gravity. Of course, Mika had to make only one mistake and they might end up having to pour Apis out of his exoskeleton. However, the alternative was that the point eight gee on this planet would kill him over time. Thus far the only detrimental result of this treatment was that the boy was forever hungry. Cormac watched him as he fingered the touch-pad on his neck ring, to draw his visor down into his chin rest so he could begin stuffing another meal bar into his mouth.

"If I'd known there'd be such a celebration of our arrival, I'd have put on my dress uniform," said Gant, striding out of the darkness with Scar at his side.

"I don't think the Theocracy have anything to celebrate at present, and I think they'll find this particular firework display rather costly," said Cormac.

Gant came to a halt with his APW cradled across his chest and nodded at the sky behind them. "You seen that?"

Cormac glanced round but could see nothing else of note, but then the flute grass stood in a tangle two metres tall there, so blocked out most of the starlit sky. He stood up, Mika and Apis also, and they all quickly saw to what Gant referred.

"I think this was what I missed on Samarkand, wasn't it?" said the Golem.

Cormac glanced at him, trying to read something in his expression. Yes, on Samarkand . . . Gant had never got to see this. He'd been ripped apart, underground, less than an hour before Dragon had appeared in the sky—as it had done here.

The latest "moon" of Masada was a small reddish-grey penny in the dark sky, nowhere near as impressive as the descending giant Calypse, or the moon *Amok* that was following it down—that was until you tried to grasp the fact that this was a living creature.

"What, *now*, do you think?" said Gant.

"Indeed," Cormac replied.

Apis looked at the two of them, his expression showing stubborn anger. "You never tell me anything," he protested.

Cormac was pleased at such a reaction—it was better than the kind of dead efficiency the lad had heretofore displayed.

He explained, "Dragon has probably destroyed every laser array up there, but we think it unlikely it's now just going to meekly sail away into the sunset. That creature is a very large imponderable . . . so to speak."

"Perhaps it's going to die . . . like it said," Apis suggested.

"Or live," Gant added.

"Or do both," said Mika. They all turned to look at her, and she went on, "Well, it didn't seem able to make up its mind as to exactly what it was going to do."

"Quite," said Cormac, and was about to go on when suddenly Scar snarled, his eyes fixed on the sky. They all turned back to observe Dragon.

"It's moving," said Gant.

Cormac could not tell for sure, but then he did not have Gant's eyes. He glanced at Scar. "What's happening, Scar—or do I mean Cadmus? What's Dragon going to do next?"

"Dragon is coming," announced Scar.

They gazed back up at it and could now see clearly that it was moving. Dropping lower and lower, it grew larger and larger, clouds of vapour boiling around it, then flashes of orange fire, so that soon it looked like the open circular mouth of a furnace. Distantly, at first, there came to them a steady thunderous grumbling that grew in volume. Cormac gazed around, wondering where they could run for safety, but there was nowhere—if this gigantic sphere was coming down on where they stood then they had no chance at all of getting away. Once again, he resumed the view he had taken aboard the landing craft: if Dragon wanted to kill them, then there was little in these circumstances that they could do about it.

Lower now in the heavens it revealed the vast storm of fire behind it—a wake that continued to boil out in a wide V to cover half the sky.

"It'll come down about fifty kilometres away," said Gant. As a Golem, he possessed the ability to range the creature and work out its angle of descent and its relative velocity.

In the clouds behind and over the surface of the leviathan, forks of lightning flickered, and occasional gunshot discharges hit the ground. The grumbling had become a roar and the ground began to vibrate in sympathy.

"Suicide?" Cormac wondered.

"It's not coming down completely freefall—must be using AG," Gant replied.

At the last it almost seemed to dip, to slam down in the distance, and the fiery cloud of its wake rolled on, blasting up dark clouds and weird vortices of flame.

"On the ground," ordered Cormac.

They flung themselves down with their heads sheltered behind their packs—being the only barrier between themselves and what was coming. The ground shuddered and rocked, and it seemed the whole vast plain dropped a few metres before rising back into position. The roaring increased in volume, then the hurricane was upon them. The flute grass flattened before the blast, and for a short time the air above was filled with long stems and papery fragments, these skirling a hideous dirge as they hurtled past. Then came earth, smoke, and a further rippling of the ground. As this blast-wave passed, it tried to suck them into its wake. After a few minutes, it died and broke into random eddies and the occasional mini-tornado that played strange music with still unbroken stems of grass. In time, they were able to stand up and view the devastation of the flattened plain—and the distant funeral pyre. Scar, tilting his head to the sky, let out a long and mournful howl. Cormac wondered if this was for Dragon . . . or for something Dragon had done.

Soldiers were revving up the engines of the few machines that would be of use on the surface, and checking weapons that seemed in pristine condition. Thorn had slept, despite the cacophony that seemed only to grow since the destruction of the arrays. Then, upon waking to discover Stanton and Jarvellis gone with soldiers to unload *Lyric II*, he made his way to Lellan's control room where, after the guards finally let him through, he found further frenetic activity.

"You have to understand that we are just as unprepared for this as they are," said Lellan, during a brief pause when people weren't approaching her for orders, explanations, even comfort, as the military machine she had built reconfigured itself for these strange circumstances. "There's a few units of the Theocracy military on the surface, but mostly it's the proctors, and they only possess limited armament."

"The arrays," said Thorn. "What else would they have needed?"

"Exactly," said Lellan, nodding. "On the surface they only have hand weapons, aerofans, a few military carriers and armoured cars, and limited antipersonnel weapons. For more than a century they've had no need for heavy armour, missile launchers, or anything with more punch than a hand grenade. Why bother with anything else when in a minute you can summon a satellite laser strike accurate and powerful enough to take out anything bigger than an aerofan?"

Fethan, who had only then arrived, interjected, "About four of the arrays were accurate enough to target and take out *single* individuals, but the Theocracy never bothered—it meant using a huge amount of power, and when was there ever a single individual offering a sufficient threat to 'em?"

Thorn glanced at him, noticed the girl Eldene walking a pace behind him, the pulse-rifle hung from a strap over her shoulder, obviously an unfamiliar weight to her. To Lellan he said, "Surely that makes it all a lot easier for you?" He had already guessed the answers Lellan might give him, but wanted confirmation.

"Well," she said, "we never bothered building any armoured vehicles or any launchers that could not be carried by a man, for the same reasons—the arrays could just take them out. All our forces are kitted essentially for guerrilla warfare, and that kit is limited in quantity—we never expected to be in a position to take all our forces to the surface at once."

"Bastards woulda used the arrays at leisure," said Fethan.

"Can you take the surface with what you have?" Thorn asked.

"Yes, only to lose it again," Lellan replied. Thorn studied her queryingly. "*Charity*," she went on, "is just a great big training camp for the military. It's spun over to one gee, so the fifty thousand active troops there are training in gravity higher than we have down here. So there's them, and they can come down in landers at any time. With the big ships of the fleet down, they can unload launchers and tanks, and in the end, if all else fails, they can bombard us from orbit with atomics."

"Seems no-win," admitted Thorn.

"In the end it's down to Polity intervention, and we've always known that. The guy at the bottom of a well with a bag of rocks is always gonna lose to the guy at the top," said Fethan.

"It's a balancing act," said Lellan. "We want to capture the surface for long enough to get the ballot over eighty per cent, and then to ask for help from the Polity. We need to create enough disorder so that the Polity can justifiably intervene, but not so much that the Theocracy are forced to go nuclear."

"Never clear-cut, is it?" said Thorn.

"No," said Lellan, moving away with the latest group dressed in camouflage fatigues who had demanded her attention. "Always dirty, and infected."

Thorn now turned to Fethan and Eldene. "And probably deeper and dirtier than even she knows," he muttered, stepping past them to Polas, who had been listening in to their conversation whilst keeping half an eye on his consoles and screens. It seemed that most of the tasks required from him at present he was managing to automate.

"I want to see that recording again," Thorn said, resting a hand on the back of Polas's chair.

Polas glanced up from his instrumentation and eyed him dubiously. "They say you're ECS," he said. "Were you sent here to help us, or just make fruitless inquiries?"

"I wasn't sent. I ended up here by accident," Thorn replied.

Polas raised an eyebrow as he opened a box underneath the console and from it removed a computer disc, which he shoved into a slot in the console. Again, on one of the screens before him, the recent events that had occurred above played out.

"Stop it there," said Thorn, and Polas froze on the image of wreckage hurtling away from the dispersing explosion. "Can you move backwards slowly with this set-up?"

"We're not entirely primitive here," said Polas.

Flickering, the image jerked back in frames: wreckage reversed back into a brightening explosion as the laser array re-formed.

"There," said Thorn. "That came out of Dragon."

Polas squinted at the screen, and adjusted the image back, and they saw for certain an object spat from Dragon just before the creature's strike on the laser array. He now moved the image back and forth until the object was at its most visible. "We should be able to close in on that and clean it up a bit," he said. He opened his box of discs and sorted through them. Finally selecting one, he held down two buttons while removing the recording and replacing with the new disc he selected. The image remained in place and a grid flicked up to cover it. Using a ball control, he adjusted the grid to centre the object in one of the grid's squares. Pressing down the control, he called up a target cursor in the corner of the screen, and then zeroed it on that square.

"Here we go," he said, pressing down the control again to select.

The image broke apart, then the one from the selected co-ordinates began to re-form in small squares across the entire screen. After a moment, a blurred and vaguely rectangular shape became evident. With the computer chuntering away, and each of the squares breaking and re-forming into smaller pixels, the image became steadily clearer.

Before it had completely re-formed Polas said, "Military lander."

"Theocracy?" Thorn asked.

Polas nodded.

Thorn studied the image as it continued to clear. "Now what was Dragon doing with that?"

Polas shrugged and, as the computer finished its work, he used the ball control to pull up a menu and save the same image.

"Any idea where it came down?" Thorn asked.

"I might be able to find out," said Polas, gazing down at his open box of discs, "if it crossed any of our viewing stations. It'll take some time, though."

"Please do so—this might be important. I'm sure Lellan would be as interested to know who was in that craft as am I."

Even though it was quite likely Dragon could have snatched a Theocracy craft on the way here, perhaps to seek information, perhaps just for the hell of it, it seemed odd to Thorn that it had then released it in one piece—especially after seeing what Dragon did to the laser arrays.

At last, in a moment of calm, Carl paused while staring at the forward screen display, and tried to absorb the fact that a circumstance more unlikely than the most extreme he had trained for had now come about. This ground tank—like the other nineteen possessed by the Underground, part of an apocalyptic scheme thought up by Lellan's predecessor—had been retained only for use in the tunnels in the event of an underground attack. No one had even considered the possibility that it might be used on the surface, except perhaps that same predecessor. Carl remembered him as a strange little man who, after raising Lellan to the position she now occupied, had shuffled off to hang himself in Pillar-town Two. His scheme back then had apparently been a mass breakout to kidnap the Hierarch during one of his periodic visits, and he had only scrapped it because the said dignitary had ceased to visit the surface.

The tanks to either side of Carl—three in all, since the others had long since gone to other break-out caverns—were already belching steam from their exhausts as hydrogen turbines wound up to speed. On the surface these would cease to function in the oxygen-bereft atmosphere, but by then they would no longer need the huge torque output of the engines, and could go back onto battery drive.

Glancing back, Carl saw that the rest of his crew was ready: Beckle on the heavy pulse-cannon only recently installed; Targon on the medkit, replacement duty, and just about everything else; and Uris on logistics and navigation. After listening to the communication that came direct to his comlink, he announced to them, "Lellan says time to give them their wake-up call."

"I was hoping to put them to bed," said Beckle, fiddling with the adjustments inside his targeting visor.

Carl reached out and clicked over the switches that started the turbines and immediately they began to cycle their way up to speed—the tank vibrating and groaning like some waking monster. Ahead, the first tank turned towards their exit tunnel, its treads flaking up stone from the floor.

"We're still in tunnel seven?" he asked.

"Confirmed, tunnel seven," said Uris. "Gets us into the centre of the coming shit storm."

Gripping the control column, Carl engaged the turbine and eased the tank forwards, as he had earlier done during the infrequent practice sessions with this machine. It still seemed almost insane to him that they were heading for the surface. With the laser arrays functioning, there had always been small windows of opportunity they could use for a surface attack, outside of which their losses immediately soared above ninety per cent. Never, though, had there been a window large enough to drive a tank through, so to speak—it seemed almost unnatural.

"What's our target?" Beckle asked.

"Nothing from Lellan yet on that," Carl replied.

"It'll be either the Agatha or Cyprian compounds," said Uris. "They're the nearest ones with a military presence."

"Both have autogun towers, and both have over three thousand troops *in situ*," said Beckle, probably wondering if the pulse-cannon was enough.

"Confirmed on Agatha compound," said Uris. "Full plan feeding across." He studied his readouts in silence for a moment before continuing with, "Four towers and, at last count, three thousand five hundred troops. We hit this tower at 0.33 from mark time."

Carl glanced at the map screen before him, as the coordinates came up. He then concentrated on where he was going—T-2, 3, and 4 ahead of him now motoring up into the darkness of tunnel seven.

Uris went on, "After we've taken down the tower, we're to hit anything that comes out by air until things get too hot, then head towards Cyprian to rendezvous with Group Two at second co-ordinates, and head north. Holman is even now mining the area underneath second co-ordinates, where it's projected the Theocracy ground troops from both bases will meet."

"How many should that net us?" Carl asked.

"Estimated thirty per cent casualty rate," Uris replied.

"That could mean two thousand dead people," said Targon, who often acted as their conscience as well.

Glancing across at him, Uris said, "More than that when we turn back and hit them again while they're still reeling. With any luck there won't be enough of them left to scrape up with a spade."

The tanks ahead, now going onto the straight upslope, were closing in their two wide treads, which had until then been necessarily apart for steering purposes. Carl operated the control to set his tank doing likewise, turned on the tank's side-lights, and watched as the lead tank hit the earthen wall at which the tunnel terminated. Now with its treads closed to form a continuous belt, that tank opened its tread dips and began to plough its way through. Once up on the surface, the treads opened out again for steering and fast manoeuvring, but Carl had to wonder if, even with their light foamed-metal construction, they would be able to proceed on that surface without sinking.

"What about the infantry? When do they go in?" asked Beckle.

"That old tunnelling machine with the compacter and plascrete spraying arms'll be following us directly, so the tunnel should be ready about an hour after we hit the towers. Infantry'll be coming up then, to take the bases," explained Uris.

"Then where for us?" inquired Beckle.

Uris did not reply—he just looked at Carl, who glanced round at him briefly before replying to the question they all wanted an answer to.

"You know how it is—it depends on exactly what they've got on the surface," he said. "We get proctors or army running around with smart hand-launchers, then we're back to foot-slogging. These bastard lumps of metal make easy targets." He slapped the control console before him, and did not add that Lellan would tell them to abandon only once losses in the tank section grew higher than the gains—and with only twenty tanks to lose, those were odds Carl did not care to study too closely.

Loman did not know whether to feel relief, anger or sadness. Yes, Behemoth had destroyed every one of the laser arrays, killing thousands of good men and breaking the Theocracy's steel grip on the population below, but *Faith*, *Hope* and

Charity were still intact, and the creature had crashed itself into the surface of the planet. And, now it was gone, there was only the unnecessary chanting of the Septarchy Friars filling the upper channels, when those same channels could be so *useful* to him.

"All the traders pulled out as fast as they could. They knew what would happen: breakouts all the way across," said Aberil as, accompanied by a party of armed guards, they disembarked down a grav-plated gantry into the tower of *Faith*. "That godless bitch won't be able to field *all* her forces, but she should have enough."

"It is a time of change," said Loman, not greatly interested in what he was hearing. "We have been given this opportunity to write clean scripture." Noticing the cold assessing look he got from Aberil, he said no more, for he felt very deeply that the said new scripture would not be what any of the Theocracy, including his brother, would expect. Almost like probing the cavity in a tooth, he felt his mind drawn to the place Behemoth had attempted to occupy in the network of augs, but there he found only chanting—always the chanting of the Septarchy Friars. He drew back, and focused on his surroundings, as they finally arrived at the floor containing the previous Hierarch's luxurious apartments. With a thought, Loman instructed the guards to spread out and take position throughout the outer building before he sent the code that opened the grape-wood doors through his aug. Gesturing for Aberil to follow, he entered, instructing the doors to close behind them, then reluctantly returned his thoughts to the immediate and prosaic, as he faced his brother. "What of our forces on the surface?"

"They'll hold for maybe two days. After that, Lellan and her traitors will have control."

"We could use the fleet to bombard them from orbit," Loman suggested.

Aberil shook his head. "Much as the idea appeals, that would mean our effectively losing the surface of the planet. The only weapons the fleet possesses for direct bombardment from orbit are atomics, and Lellan's forces are already well into the croplands and getting near to the city and spaceport." He hesitated. "Though, should circumstances permit . . ."

Loman walked to one of the long overstuffed sofas and sank down upon it. "Then what do you suggest, brother?" he asked.

Aberil replied, "Our soldiers have spent time enough in *Charity*, training for Amoloran's ridiculous schemes. Their purpose has always been military landing and limited ground warfare. So let's use them for that."

"There will be objections," said Loman. "Many would call this a police action and beneath the dignity of soldiers who were essentially trained to attack the Polity."

"Then by their objections they will reveal themselves as showing loyalty to a dead Hierarch rather than to yourself— and to God. The soldiers themselves will not object, and they are the most important factor. Other objectors—perhaps some of the officers coming from the high families—can visit the steamers should they feel their objection strongly enough. But I suspect they won't."

Loman studied his brother as he stood with his hands slack at his sides, and his expression and entire mien without animation. "Very well," said Loman, "I gave you the title First Commander, and now you will use it. Get your men out of *Charity* and down to the surface. Use them to destroy our enemies." Sending to the doors again Loman had them already opening behind his brother. The fleeting expression that crossed Aberil's face was almost like pain, as he turned abruptly and departed. Loman watched the doors close again, and once more reached out across the realms of the *Gift* and wondered how closely he could grasp control of them and make them his own, as he had done in this physical realm.

With something of bemusement, Thorn sat himself down in the rim of a huge balloon tyre belonging to one of the ATVs, and removed the helmet of his uniform, dropping it over the barrel of the pulse-rifle he had already propped against the tyre. The infantry—mustering to follow the four tanks once this nearby tunnel was ready—were similarly armed and uniformed as himself. Thorn was reminded of like occasions in his past, even before his Sparkind days, and before he had removed his uniform and sloughed away some of the apparent clean morality of straight face-to-face combat. Within him was the temptation to just go with these men and women, to shrug at responsibility and just obey orders, but he could not do that. His Sparkind training and his subsequent training as an ECS agent had made him, surprisingly, more moral, and more inclined to look for the really dirty jobs to do. It had also been his experience that they were never too difficult to find.

"Agent Thorn, reply please."

The voice from the helmet was tinny, but recognizably that of Polas, the man in the rebels' operations room. Thorn again donned the helmet, levering its side-shield, with contained transceiver and other military tech, down into position.

"Thorn here," he spoke into the mike just to one side of his mouth.

"I've sent those co-ordinates you required. They'll be in there as message number six. All other messages relate to the ground attack."

"Okay," said Thorn, reaching up and pressing one of the touch-pads on the side-shield. With a low whir, a rose-tinted visor slid down from the rim of the helmet. On one side of this, a menu was displayed in the glass.

"Cursor," Thorn said, and a red dot appeared at the centre of his vision, and tracked with the subsequent movement of his eyes. Looking to the menu he selected *Messages*, and kept one eye closed until the dot flashed into a cross. Upon opening his eye, ten messages were displayed, but rather than go to the one Polas had sent he opened some others at random. The message "Med-tech personnel are reminded that ajectant will be available from the manufactories now being set up in PA fourteen, and that all ATV ambulances must carry at least four cartons for distribution amongst the surface workers" he thought was in amusing counterpoint to

"Second and third hand-assault weapons are now available in PA twelve—these are for distribution amongst those field workers prepared to fight." It seemed that the cargo being unloaded from *Lyric II* had brought succour and death in equal proportions. He now went to message six: "Lander came down at these co-ordinates." Thorn ignored the co-ordinates and went straight to the *Go to Map* prompt below it. The craft had come down in the wilderness two hundred kilometres from this particular cavern, and though the map was detailed, the contour lines, colours, and biblical names gave him no idea of what might lie between him and it.

"Trooper Thorn," said a grating voice.

"Off," said Thorn, and the visor snapped back up into his helmet. He looked up at the old Golem, Fethan, behind whom stood the girl Eldene. Both of them wore the same combat gear as himself. He noted that the girl's fingers were white on her pulse-rifle, as if she was frightened that someone might take it away from her. Thorn doubted this—he had already seen kindergarten infantry troops younger than her.

"That's something I haven't been called in a while," said Thorn at last.

"Something you *were* called, though," said Fethan.

Thorn stood up from the rim of the balloon tyre and inspected him. That Fethan was a machine had been evident from the first—him being the only one of Lellan's party not requiring breathing apparatus—but Thorn was now beginning to wonder just what sort of machine Fethan really was. He did not move with that seemingly obdurate disconnection from his surroundings that was the hallmark of all Golem—even the newer ones. Sometimes it was difficult to spot them but Thorn was trained to it and had been used to working with such constructs for much of his life. Fethan, though, moved with more *connection* to his surroundings—as if he knew what it was to have to breathe, to feel his own heartbeat, to know real pain and real pleasure, and not some emulation of it.

"What are you?" Thorn asked abruptly.

Fethan grinned, exposing the gap in his front teeth.

He held up two fingers. "I'll give you two guesses."

Thorn considered what those two guesses should be. "Either you're a memplant loading to a Golem shell, or you're a cyborg. I would guess at the latter."

"Correct first time," said Fethan, lowering his hand.

"Then," said Thorn hesitantly, "you have been around for a while. I don't think anyone has gone cyborg for the last hundred years."

"Maybe," Fethan replied, obviously reluctant to volunteer further information about his own history. "Now, tell me, you're going to find out what's going on with this lander Dragon was carrying, ain't you?"

"I had considered that," said Thorn cautiously.

Fethan stepped close to one side of Thorn and slapped a hand down onto the thick foamed-neoprene tyre of the ATV.

"Then we'll be needing one of these," he said.

"I don't think Lellan would appreciate one of these vehicles being taken and, incidentally, what's your interest?"

"Lellan's interest, in fact. She took to heart your comments about Dragon, and she wants to be certain it's dead. I'm to head out there to make sure. And where Dragon came down is not far from where that craft came down. Two birds with one stone you might say."

"Yeah, *you* might," Thorn replied.

The autogun tower opened up with a staccato rattling, and Proctor Molat swore unremittingly after jumping up startled and banging his bald pate on the corner of his office cupboard. It took him a moment to realize just what he was hearing, as the last time those guns had fired had been during a test, so long ago, Molat recollected, that he still had thick black hair on his head. Flipping up his breather mask he rounded his desk—his feelings about leaving the stack of paperwork there, and the reasons for leaving it, somewhat ambivalent—yanked open the sealed door, and stepped out into the grey day. Only to have that day turned terribly bright when the autogun tower disintegrated in a ball of light.

"Muster! Muster!" commander Lurn bellowed over aug channels. *"We are under attack!"*

Proctor Molat grimaced at that: how incredibly observant of Lurn. He glanced over to where some soldiers were setting up a gun on the embankment to the right of the burning tower, and observed aerofans spiralling up into the air in the eastern section of the compound, shortly followed by Lurn's two carriers. Arms fire crackled in the air, and other explosions blossomed in the compound as Lurn's forces ran for the embankments, whilst his own armoured vehicles trundled from garages they should have abandoned, in Molat's opinion, as soon as the laser arrays had been destroyed.

"Molat here," he said over the Proctor's channel. *"That you up there, Voten?"*

"It is, sir," replied his lieutenant.

"What do you see?"

"Four heavily armoured tanks coming in from the east."

Molat flinched as a wall blew nearby, and something that might once have been a soldier bounced across the ground. Attempting to retain some dignity, he continued walking to where he had last left his own aerofan. Climbing inside it and initiating the lift control, he went on, *"What kind of armament? Anything we haven't got?"*

"All looks fairly standard to me," replied Voten.

Within a few seconds, Molat was high enough to see for himself. He watched one of the tanks spin on its wide treads and spit out a missile that blasted a hole through the earthen embankment, incidentally burying one of Lurn's armoured cars and the small field-gun it was towing. It had always been Molat's worry that when the rebels finally did do something big, it would be with advanced Polity weapons. He was considering how little different was the armament on these tanks from that of Lurn's own forces, when a pulse-cannon opened up from the lead tank down there. To his right he saw one of Lurn's carriers tilt in the air as one corner of it blew away, then slewed sideways and down to obliterate a barracks building. The blue fire continued to stab upwards, and with merciless accuracy began to nail aerofan after aerofan.

Molat hit rapid descent and watched in horror as the fire tracked across towards himself. There was a flash, a sound that seemed to tear his eardrums, and he was clinging to the rail as his aerofan plummeted, tilted sideways, the motor making a horrible whickering noise as of a horse being led to slaughter, and the fans setting up a teeth-rattling vibration as they went off balance. Black smoke was pouring from under the cowling, and the coils were spitting out tendrils of St. Elmo's fire. He glimpsed a tank right underneath him, then mud, something belching black smoke, then flute grass. It wasn't instinct that made him jump, just the sure knowledge, from long experience of flying those unstable machines, that either a motor or a fan was about to fly apart.

There seemed to him only half a second before he crashed through flute grass, hit the ground, and penetrated the surface. Up to his waist in the mud below the rhizomes, he glanced back just in time to see his aerofan arc up and suddenly slam down nearby. He was congratulating himself on having survived, when one of the abandoned craft's fans went completely out of balance and disintegrated. Something smashed Molat in the back of his head, almost hauling him out of the ground again before depositing him face-first back into it.

"Any activity?" asked Lellan.

Studying the screen showing a picture transmitted by the probe they had initially sent up to observe Dragon, Polas very quickly and coldly replied, "Fleet ships just out from *Charity* and taking on landing craft and troops."

Lellan allowed herself to feel some relief—perhaps, she thought, this was the relief of the condemned upon discovering it would be the cage rather than the spring pinning over the flute-grass rhizomes. Had that fleet come direct to the planet, without stopping to take ground forces and the means to get them down to the surface, she knew that they would have been in for nuclear bombardment. Such a possibility remained, but it was now just that little bit more remote.

"Did you get that, John?" she asked.

From *Lyric II*, it was Jarvellis who replied, "John's already on his way, Lellan. I'd comlink you through to him, but I know he doesn't like any more of a distraction than having me speaking to him."

"Just so long as he does what is required," said Lellan.

"Have you known him to do any less?" Jarvellis asked.

"Very well," Lellan went on, "what about the transmitter?"

"The U-space transmitter is up and running, and you can patch through at any time. What do you want to do: send your megafile?"

"Yes—send it now."

"Okay, it's on its way," Jarvellis replied. "What about the realtime broadcasts?"

"As soon as you get a reply on the megafile, liaise with Polas and go to realtime. Polity AIs will know what's going on and how best to deal with the information. The ballot we won't get up until the compounds have been taken, but we'll send that as soon as possible."

Lellan cut the connection. There had been no real decision to make: the file documenting two hundred years of Theocracy atrocities, with its depositions and sealed tamper-proof holocordings, would go first, to give News Services and Polity AIs something to get their metaphorical teeth into. The viewing time of that file was something in the region of five thousand hours, but it seemed likely that the first viewers of it—being Polity AIs—would not take so long. Then, as soon as it had been safely received, the rebels would go realtime and ask outright for Polity intervention—their request reinforced by the ballot. But that was for the future; right now she had a battle to organize. She turned her attention back to the screens before her.

"Carl, that was quick—or do you have a problem?" she asked, observing the pattern of dots spread across a map showing the inhabited area of the continent.

"All somewhat quicker than expected," Carl replied. "They put their aerofans and carriers up straight away, and we took them down with the pulse-cannon. They're now coming after us with a few ground-cars and infantry."

"Our losses?"

"None. I think we caught them well untrousered—but that won't last."

Lellan studied closely the dots on the maps, the constant readouts and battle stats. One tank had been blown at Cyprian compound, and a further two north of the spaceport. They were doing better than expected but, as expected, were now encountering real resistance from the old fortifications around the city. Lellan swore and stood up.

She turned to Polas. "Take over here, Polas, and keep relaying through to my console on the carrier." Then, before Polas could voice any objections, "What's the minimum time we have before their landers start coming in?"

Polas glanced at his screens. "If the fleet left now, which it shows no sign of doing just yet, then they'd be landing on the day after tomorrow. I'd still reckon on that, as I don't think they'll delay much longer."

Molat hauled himself up out of sticky mud as slowly as he could, wondering if he dared reach round and touch the back of his head—scared he would find broken bone and touch living brain with his filthy fingertips. Even this deliberate slowness was too fast, and the ringing in his ears rolled back down his spine, stamping on every nerve on the way. He vomited into his crumpled mask, choked as he tore it away from his face, and fumbled for another from the container on the side of his oxygen bottle. With the second mask finally in place, he carefully eased himself to his knees then attempted to stand. What had happened meanwhile? Was the battle over? Surrounded by tall flute grass and with the continued ringing in his ears drowning out any other sound, he had no way of telling for sure. Looking at his watch he saw that he'd been unconscious for maybe twenty minutes, and turning in what he hoped was the right direction, he began to trudge for home. The tank which loomed suddenly ahead of him, flattening flute grass, he had no time to identify as friend or enemy before it knocked him backwards, and its foamed titanium tread crushed Molat into the ground. Maybe he screamed—he never got time to hear.

A fine grey mist filtered down from the spraying machine, until the circular airtight door closed behind it. Behind the door, Thorn could hear the machine moving towards the surface, with the thumping of its compacters and the roar of its plascrete sprayers as it consolidated the tunnels—initially opened by the tanks, but prone to collapse—into a more permanent structure. The plascrete smell remained acrid as the chemical reactions took place in the settling mist on his side of the door. If he had not kept his breather mask up, Thorn knew he would be coughing and choking by now, his lungs nicely lined with grey epoxy—perfectly preserved but utterly unable to function.

Stomping back out of the tunnel entrance, he observed the infantry now seated separately in their various squads, ready to head for the surface. Lacking in heavy armour and large transports, the conveyances these troops used were crude antigravity sleds with impeller fans mounted on the back—and not many of those either. He suspected these jury-rigged vehicles were mainly for the rapid transit of troops and equipment to reach a target, whereupon the rest of the battle would entail a footslog.

No one was checking weapons now, he noticed—that had been done enough times already—and most had their visors down whilst they read the updates on the battles that were taking place above. As the troops finally began to stand up and shoulder their packs and weapons, Thorn checked his helmet screen and realized that Lellan had given the order to move out. Shouldering his own weapon, he rejoined Fethan and Eldene at the ATV.

"Let's get moving, shall we?" he suggested.

The girl, he noticed, was still white-knuckling her pulse-rifle, watching the infantry depart with a kind of unfocused determination. He rested a hand on her shoulder.

"You ever driven one of these?" he asked.

She stared at him. "No."

"Then it's time for you to learn." He gestured on ahead of him.

Fethan gave Thorn a nod of acknowledgement before following her inside the ATV. After glancing at the gathered infantry, Thorn followed him on board. She could, he was well aware, have served as mere fodder for the infantry war that was sure to ensue once the imbalance of missiles to flying machines was levelled out and everyone was grounded, since it hardly required much in the way of an education to pull a trigger, whether that trigger was electric or mechanical. But for some reason the cyborg had formed an attachment to this young girl. It was one that Thorn felt he could understand; he'd seen the mess a rail-gun slug made of a human body, and that mess was never proportional to the victim's innocence.

The inside of the ATV was designed without flourish with the same stark utility as its exterior. The raised hump in the middle of the single cabin formed the cowling for the large H and O engine, and it was flat on top to serve as a table, a work-bench, or a surgeon's slab. The front screen consisted of three panes of tough plastic imbedded with a grid of wires, above a simple navigational console, a steering column, and pedals for hydrostatic drive and brakes. There was one seat only in front of this, the seat and targeting visor for the two gun turrets located at the back of the vehicle being set midway down the cabin. Along the other walls were drop-down seats and stowage lockers. It seemed that no space was wasted, and that the interior of this vehicle was designed primarily as a field surgery—the autodoc stowed in a perspex case at the back offering sure proof of this. Thorn felt guilty about Fethan commandeering this vehicle, but felt sure that if it had been truly indispensable Lellan would not have allowed him to have it. He suspected that this particular wheeled vehicle had been superseded by more modern AG transports, built around the grav-motors which the likes of Stanton and Jarvellis had been smuggling in, and also that this vehicle—designed for travelling underground—was now considered too slow.

Demonstrating the use of the controls to Eldene, Thorn noted that they had not been quick enough in heading for the tunnel entrance, as already it was blocked by the infantry on the move in that direction. They advanced in neat lines at a steady jog, towing the grav-sleds along by handles mounted on their sides. No doubt these troops would climb on only when they reached the surface, and only then start up the fans. Glancing back, he observed Fethan checking out the gun turret's control and visor. Soon, after only a couple of lurches to begin with, Eldene had the ATV rolling in behind the departing infantry. It was perhaps twenty minutes later that she actually drove into the tunnel entrance.

With the hydrostatic drive in operation there were no awkward gear changes to make for handling the slope—the vehicle did that automatically—and shortly they were approaching the now open door, which had earlier been closed while the spraycrete machine did its work. This door had been placed across at the dividing line formed by the chalk layer between limestone and soil. Once they were through it, Thorn watched, on the rear-view screen, the three sections of the door irising closed. Two minutes later, they rolled out onto churned mud, green with unearthed nematodes and crushed vegetation, all scattered with torn-up mats of rhizomes. The abandoned spraying and compacting machine lay to one side, its tank empty and its spraying arms locked in an upright position like the forelimbs of a threatened tarantula. All around them, infantry were clambering onto the fan-driven sleds, which were starting up in a concert of roars that filled the air with a haze of grass fragments and a mist of slurry.

"Take us south and get the display map up on that side screen, like I showed you. Polas has already transferred both sets of co-ordinates across, so they should show," said Thorn.

Eldene turned on the side screen and, using a ball control to move the cursor, selected *Maps* from the menu displayed. While she pulled back on the initial map, to bring up the co-ordinates of the area where Dragon and the escape craft had fallen, Thorn gazed through the front windscreen at distant flashes and plumes of dust and smoke. Even here, in this airtight vehicle, he could hear the sounds of distant explosions and feel vibration through the ground. Soon Eldene had the ATV heading in the direction they wanted—into battle, unfortunately, but from the lights everywhere in the sky it seemed there was no direction that took them away from it.

For a second time Molat hauled himself out of sticky mud, and again changed his mask. He turned to watch the tank continue on its way and, with a kind of lunatic logic, was completely unsurprised that this second dunking had somehow restored his hearing. To either side of him there were other vehicles growling through the grasses, and he realized that these were Lurn's force going in pursuit of the enemy's tanks. He considered trudging after them, then decided that two near-death experiences in one day had been quite enough for him, so turned to head back towards Agatha compound. Anyway, he was religious police—leave warmongering to the soldiers.

Trudging through churned mud and broken rhizomes, he observed dead soldiers and splashes of blood across the flute grass. He felt no sympathy with the men who had died—they not being proctors but military—and anyway he found it difficult to sympathize with anyone else at the best of times. But now, with his entire body one great ache, his aerofan destroyed, and his uniform muddy, burnt and ripped, what he needed was to get back to base, get himself washed and changed, and back onto . . . gunfire ahead.

Advancing with more awareness of his surroundings now, Molat reached the embankment and the barrier fence—now flattened by both the enemy tanks and Lurn's forces—and climbed it cautiously to take in the view.

Infantry—quite obviously belonging to the Underground—were attacking the now poorly defended compound. The fighting around the ponds and grape trees was fierce and without quarter, bodies were strewn everywhere like some new and grizzly harvest, and the fire of rail-guns and pulse-rifles was rapidly turning sheds, trees, fences, agricultural vehicles, and people into an evenly mixed morass of wood splinters, metal and plastic fragments, raw earth and shreds of flesh. Lowering himself back out of sight, Molat looked back the way he had come. In his aug he searched for the direct address of Lurn's aug, and sent:

"Lurn, ground forces are taking the compound."

By the tone of Lurn's reply, it became evident the man had other concerns:

"Well, that's real surprising fucking news."

Molat went on:

"Surely the compound is more important than a few tanks."

Lurn relented a little:

"Same problem at Cyprian compound, only they're closer to us now. I'm going to join up with Colas, who has also been out chasing tanks, and together we're going to hit the infantry that's attacking there."

"Agatha compound?" Molat asked.

"May be considered a write-off until new forces come down from Charity. My advice to you is for you to get as many of your people out of there as you can, and head over here."

Molat did not bother taking another look over the bank, but quickly turned back into the flute grass. A few hundred metres in, he came upon three corpses—one of whom he vaguely recognized—wearing army fatigues, and from these obtained a working rail-gun and a knapsack of magazines, a rations pack, and a jacket not too filthy with mud and blood. He was morbidly probing from his aug through to theirs and finding only ghostly networks that were breaking apart as the biotech augs died on their hosts, when someone came crashing through the grass towards him. He turned and fired in that direction.

"No! No! I'm unarmed! I give up!" someone shouted.

"Come forward, Toris," Molat sent.

There was a long silence, then Proctor Toris stumped out into the open, aware that because of the aug connection he could not deny his presence. Molat studied the man: he was short and fat and always seemed to be sweating, even now in a temperature that was not many degrees above zero. Molat gestured to the three corpses.

"Take whatever you need. We're walking to Cyprian compound," he said.

Toris had found himself a working hand laser, and was studying it speculatively, when a huge explosion bucked the ground beneath their feet. Gazing in the direction of Cyprian compound, Molat observed a column of smoke belching into the air and immediately felt a horrible wrenching through his aug—a sudden distancing and almost painful loneliness, as if he had been in a room full of friends and suddenly been instantly dragged many kilometres away.

"May God have mercy on them," he murmured.

Molat knew that you could hardly feel one death through the aug network, unless it was that of a close friend, but he had just felt thousands die. He turned to Toris.

"Best collect their oxygen bottles. I think we may have to walk a bit further."

"Amen," concluded Toris aloud, though Molat was not sure to what.

"The plan is for us to head for the city now—we're needed to hit the old defences," said Uris.

"Yeah," replied Carl, staring out at the mayhem the mines had wrought upon the Theocracy forces from both the Cyprian and Agatha compounds. It seemed not one square metre of the churned ground did not have human body parts randomly commingled. "We won't be able to go into the city itself, though, unless she wants us to abandon the tanks first."

Uris replied, "About half the infantry will be going in to take the city after we've knocked out its defences—the rest of them will stay out here to secure the compounds and organize the distribution of ajectant amongst the workers."

Carl engaged the drive of the tank and took it around a blackened APC, out of which he had earlier seen two soldiers stagger, their clothing on fire until the lack of oxygen outside their vehicle extinguished the flames. The two had by then suffocated.

"What about the initial attack there . . . on the city?" Beckle asked, not taking his face away from his targeting visor.

Carl glanced over at Uris. "Anything on that?"

Uris merely shook his head, so Carl opened his direct channel to Lellan's control room and asked the same question. It was Lellan herself who replied with, "Heavy resistance, Carl. Apparently Deacon Clotus pulled in all the roving forces as soon as Dragon trashed the arrays, and those forces are now screwed in to the old fortifications."

"They care so much about their people in the city?" Carl inquired sarcastically.

"They care about the spaceport, I think," Lellan replied.

"What losses there?"

"We lost five tanks to some big launchers Clotus had set up."

"Now?" asked Carl, as he drove the tank up beside a stand of new flute grass and noted, on the radar traces transferred from Uris's console, that other tanks from other attack points were now converging on his own.

"Most of the launchers are down, apparently, but there are still snipers with rail-guns stuck in the old bastions—like scole leaves, as Polas puts it," Lellan replied.

Carl succinctly relayed this information to his crew.

"Still seems too easy," remarked Beckle, pushing his targeting visor away from his face and glancing tiredly towards Carl.

"It is," said Carl, his face without expression. "All bets changed once the arrays went down." He now stared down at the screen to which Uris was relaying all command signals. "If it makes you feel any better, Polas is keeping me updated on the situation up above: the fleet is now on its way, with forces embarked from *Charity*, so it seems likely we'll have a whole rush of Theocracy troops up our arses any day now."

Into the short silence that followed this announcement Uris interjected, "Then we need to take the spaceport as soon as possible."

"Yes," agreed Carl. "If they can bring down their mu-class ships, then they'll be able to offload heavy armour. Without the port they'll have to use the landers and infantry, and they'll have to come down on the plains, as there aren't enough clear areas around here to land on."

"It'll get bloody," said Paul.

Thinking of the carnage they had so recently wrought, Carl said, "What do you mean, *get*?"

The sun sank close beside Calypse, bouncing light off the gas giant in a brief flood that turned the landscape golden. Within half an hour this odd light was fading, and now the clouds along the horizon, behind which both planet and sun were sinking, had the appearance of stretched marshmallows in pastel shades of green, blue, and red against a rusty orange sky.

"It's because of the dust and smoke," said Cormac. "Pollution makes for the best sunsets."

Apis only half heard what the agent was saying, as pain and anger sat inside him hand in glove, clenched in a fist around his insides—or perhaps the physical pain he felt was due to the constant drag of gravity, of being confined here in this dark well. After all, the words "My mother is dead" seemed to have no real meaning at all, along with phrases like "*Miranda* has been destroyed . . . I am the only survivor from the supposed rescue ship, which was in turn destroyed by Dragon . . . I killed twenty-three of my fellow survivors because they would have killed me . . . the AI dreadnought that then rescued me has been hijacked by a Separatist madman wielding the technology of a five-million-year-dead race—the same technology that is now keeping me alive in gravity that would otherwise kill me."

"How are you doing?" Mika suddenly asked him.

Apis glanced at her. By what he had learnt from Cormac and Gant, the ability to ask questions was something she had only recently acquired, and he could see that just asking a question was an end in itself for her. It was not as if she required any specific answer—the nanomycelium growing in the tissues of his body, which it was currently rebuilding, monitored him at a level far beyond that even of an autodoc; and, as far as he understood, transmitted reports to this suit's CPU which in turn conveyed the information to Mika's laptop.

"I'm alive," replied Apis.

Mika's expression showed some confusion for a moment, then she turned away to observe the other members of their party as they trudged through flute grass that had been grazed down to ankle height. It occurred to him that though Mika was learning to ask questions, she had yet to discover what to do with the answers—it seemed that whole new landscapes of conversation were opening up for her, and that she was still agoraphobic in that respect.

He decided to ask a question himself, more to ease her discomfort than because he wanted answers. At an intellectual level he knew that he should have answers and knowledge of all that was occurring, but on an emotional level he just did not care.

"What makes this Jain nanotechnology you are using better than the Polity version?" he asked her.

Mika turned back to him with her expression relaxing into the comfortable superiority of the didact. "Besides their basic nanomachine units being as far in advance of our own as the AGC is to a horse and cart, it is the structural nanotechnology that is so . . . useful. The technology employs nanomycelia, which enables a powerful support structure for the machines at the business end, and almost instant communication between machines. Essentially it is the linking together of disparate machines: it is the *organization*. A useful analogy would be in the building of a city. With our technology, it would be as if you had sent in a thousand stonemasons each with blueprints and the tools to do the job. The masons would do the job, but get in each other's way, repeat tasks, and make outright mistakes because of the ensuing chaos. Jain nanotechnology is more hierarchical: every unit knows its place, its job, and all inefficiencies are therefore wiped out."

"Jain technology is *social*, then," he said.

Mika appraised him wonderingly. "Yes, you're right. You're absolutely right."

Apis went on, "Perhaps a better view of your masons, in Jain terms, would be them standing on each other's shoulders, passing up tools and stone to build the castle."

"Yes, that is indeed a simplification of the mycelial structures now being built inside you." She glanced at her laptop. "Within two solstan days you will no longer require that suit. Using Polity tech, a similar result could only be obtained in about a month—and you would have spent most of that same month in a tank, along with the nanites, monitored by AI."

"Jain tech is self-monitoring then?"

"Yes, it is," Mika replied, slightly puzzled.

"Does it have inbuilt AI then?"

Mika had no further reply, and Apis noted her expression of worried fascination. That she had not foreseen the possibilities was perhaps some facet of her inability to ask questions. That none of them had understood what Dragon had meant when saying of the Jain, "It is not *they* any more . . . it is not a race," he put down to the fact that they had all been under quite a lot of pressure recently, and that they did not have the Jain growing inside them, like he did.

Skellor gazed down upon the sulphurous moonlet with a vastness of comprehension that was almost godlike, but still with the pettiness of human drives—anger, hate, power-lust—and felt a hint of disappointment when the first missile punched down through its surface. There seemed to be no satisfaction in destroying the inanimate, no satisfaction in destroying something that could not appreciate its own doom, nor feel pain or terror. The second, third and fourth missiles then punched into the moonlet, evenly spaced around its equator, timed to impact to its spin, so they struck all four quarters. The explosions that followed collapsed thousands of square kilometres of surface and raised vast clouds of dust in shades of yellow and chocolate brown that were dragged round in orbital streamers to obscure from the normal human eye much of what followed. Skellor's breadth of vision encompassed nearly every emitted radiation, though, and he enjoyed a grandstand view of the destruction he had wrought.

Each collapsed area was flooded through rapidly opening fumaroles and soon became a lake of molten rock. From these lakes, huge crevasses opened in the surface and spread, separating mountain ranges and swallowing them, turning frozen plains of sulphur into boiling seas, and finally joining in a network that spread across the entire surface. At this point the fifth missile struck and tore the moonlet apart: here an asteroid fifty kilometres long trailing streamers of molten rock, its cold face what had once been a range of mountains; there a vast sheet of sulphurous fire separating out into smaller spheres cooling into something like black glass; an incandescent cloud of gas spreading, turning, already moving—dragging back into the shape of an accretion disc.

Skellor observed all this with the eye of a physicist, before sending out the *Occam*'s grabships in search of suitable chunks of debris. Like wolves cutting through herds of great brown buffalo they sped, selecting the calf-sized chunks to clamp onto and drag back. Whilst this was happening Skellor inwardly focused his attention.

He was all-encompassing, but all his systems did not yet operate to perfection—there was much he still needed to do, and soon he would have the material for the job of extending and expanding the Jain architecture of the ship. Through this architecture he would gain absolute control of all the ship's distant systems, and perhaps enough control to be able to still the intimate mutterings of what remained of the minds of his command crew, or rather have sufficient control that such things were no bother to him. Suddenly overcome with curiosity about the functioning of minds from which he was quickly becoming alienated, he studied their . . . output.

Danny's mind revealed only a low instinctual mutter related to sex and the urge to procreate—something that always functioned most strongly when extinction was close. The man controlling the U-space engines—Skellor did not know his name as that had been something erased as irrelevant—was listening to music as if on a looped tape. Linking through to a library on the *Occam*, which he had only recently subsumed, he identified the tune as a Mozart clarinet concerto—not the usual easy listening indulged in by a Separatist fighter out of Cheyne III. The mutter from Aphran's mind was something of a duologue—a parody of the madwoman speaking to herself.

"There's a limit, there's always a limit. Go beyond this point and the technology you acquire from the enemy shafts you, and you become the enemy."

"But it wasn't acquired from the enemy, it was acquired from wonderful Skellor whom I love who acquired it from the artefacts of a dead race."

"Don't matter, there's still a limit: rail-guns are okay, but anything that starts to think for itself is dodgy. AI is the limit. Jain stuff is AI—almost alive. No, no further."

"What about Mr. Crane? He thought for himself, and he nearly creamed that bastard Cormac."

"Unstable and dangerous. How many of our own did he kill?"

Skellor's curiosity was further piqued, and he immediately raided Aphran's mind for all information concerning this Mr. Crane. In half a second he had all she knew. Encased in Jain architecture, he snorted derisively. "A brass metalskin Golem—a simple machine like that," he said aloud.

"Yeah, and how much closer did you get with Jain tech and a fucking delta-class dreadnought?" said one of the two Aphrans.

The other one tried to drown this with, "I love you I love you I love you Skellor!"

This didn't stop him finding the best way of hurting . . . both of her, and this was more satisfying to him than destroying a moonlet.

14

"And thus it was in the fiftieth year of colonization that the *siluroyne* came to dwell underneath the Bridge of Psalms and sorely troubled the low people of the compounds, and in the fiftieth day of the fiftieth year there came to that bridge the two pond workers, Sober and his wife Judge."

The picture the book displayed was of a mountainously fat couple made even more grotesque by the huge green and red scoles that seemed almost moulded into their bare chests. They wore only breeches and open shirts and were both so bristly and ugly that it was difficult to distinguish male from female.

"Greedy peasants," commented the woman.

The boy looked up at her and waited.

"You'll never see a fat pond worker," she explained to him.

The boy continued staring at her until she continued with the story.

"As the two workers crossed the bridge, the *siluroyne* climbed out before them and said, 'Give me my toll of flesh blood and bone.' Terrified, the two could not say a word as the monster bore down upon them. Then Judge, more quickwitted than her husband, said, 'Let us live, and we shall bring you more flesh blood and bone than you can shake a stick at!' Craftily the monster said, 'One of you will bring it to me whilst I hold the other here.' Judge went and brought first the Brother whose sin was gluttony . . ."

In the picture the *siluroyne* held Sober in one of its multiple hands, whilst with the other it ate, one after the other, the sinning Brothers that Judge led to the bridge. Glancing at her son, the woman was glad he did not seem to notice when she missed reading out some of the sins committed by the Brothers—he *was so busy watching those Brothers being crunched down and the gut of the siluroyne expanding.*

Dawn crept in unnoticed, covered by the flashing of pulse-cannons and detonation after incandescent detonation. Slowly, the ancient walls and bastions surrounding the city became distinct from a purplish sky—gradually revealed in all their repro-medieval glory. In the past these huge limestone and plascrete defences had served the purpose of keeping the somewhat hostile wildlife out of the small inhabited area within. The growth in the population and the spread of crop fields into the wilderness had driven said wildlife back, and for a hundred years the walls had served only to prevent the city itself from spilling out across the land like some kind of poisonous technological froth. Now they once again served a truly medieval purpose, as this morning the enemy was at the gates.

Carl noted the position of the rail-gun in the north tower, as it opened up on one of the remaining tanks, which sped down the causeway between two squerm ponds. The racket of iron slugs impacting armour was horrendous and pieces fell away from the tank as it turned and motored down into one of the ponds, taking itself to cover. Carl hoped, for the sake of the occupants of that tank, that no slugs had penetrated. If the tank had been holed, and those holes were big enough, the occupants wouldn't even have time to either drown or suffocate before the squerms got them.

The transformer hum, followed by a strobe light, signified that the pulse-cannon had cooled down enough for Beckle to fire it once again.

"Got the bastard," he said.

"Are you sure about that this time?" Carl asked, observing the water slopping against the lower edge of their own tank's display screen, and the squerms in that same water scraping their way across the vehicle's surface, perhaps sensing that there was something soft to chew on inside the big tin can in their pond.

"Sure enough," Beckle replied. "It was the same one as before, I reckon they just wheeled it across from the other side."

Carl looked up at this latest burning cavity cut into the limestone, and opined that they would be wheeling nothing nowhere now.

"Let's get out of this hole then," he said, and thrust the steering column forwards and up. The tank's motor droned in response, while squerms and water slewed away from the screen. Immediately there came the rattling clanging of small-arms fire impacting on their armour, and Beckle replied by cutting chunks out of the city wall with his pulse-cannon. On the displays, and by glancing to either side, Carl saw that all the tanks were now advancing.

"Let's take down that gate," ordered Carl, speaking into his comlink. Missiles flashed from right and left, and the ancient grapewood gates disappeared in a cloud of fiery splinters, then the gate towers were soon collapsing into dusty piles of rubble. Carl drove his tank up onto one of these piles and, as the dust cleared, looked down into the city. Before them lay the sealed complexes and towers, the underground tunnels and roofed parks and greenhouses that made up the place—a place that people simply called "the city" and sometimes forgot had once been called "Valour," but then it was easy to forget a name like that in a place where one false step could mean death and where people could get into debt for merely breathing.

"I wish we could just go straight in," said Beckle.

"We'd kill thousands," warned Targon, again acting as their collective conscience. "It cannot be done like that." Carl observed the Theocracy soldiers dodging between the buildings, then swung the viewpoint to behind them. Over the chequerboard of ponds the infantry were now coming in on their grav-sleds, fans kicking up spray behind, and leaving agitated movement in the squerm ponds. He listened to his comlink, then glanced across at Uris who was receiving the same instructions via text and logistic diagram, before reversing his tank down off the pile of rubble.

"I could have hit a few," said Beckle. "I'm not that inaccurate."

"Too much collateral damage," said Carl. "Anyway, Lellan's coming out with a couple of carriers, and we're gonna join the attack on the spaceport now."

Spinning the tank full circle on its treads, he applied full power to send it away and around the city—away from aberrant missile-launchers, be they hand-held or tripod-mounted. He did not mention to his crew that they were one of only three remaining tanks now joining the attack on the spaceport. He didn't think that would be helpful or encouraging.

Listening in to Lellan's battle channels, Stanton raised the Proctor's set of binoculars and observed the first explosions as a heavy pulse-cannon opened up on the spaceport cranes. The response was immediate: armoured vehicles roaring across the huge foamed plascrete slabs to meet the attack; Theocracy carriers rising into the air, surrounded by swarms of aerofans; fire and missiles and explosions and, most importantly, all over there. Lowering the binoculars Stanton glanced down at the man from whom he had taken them. The man was young, inexperienced, had been arrogant in his new position of power, and Stanton had taken less pleasure in snapping his neck than he had in doing the same to the Separatist, Lutz. All the same, Aberil Dorth had been just like this young man all those years back, and look at what he had since become.

Stanton reached down and hauled the man up to the rail of the aerofan, then tipped him over so he fell with a splat onto the damp ground between wide spreads of native rhubarb leaves—his naked skin flecked over with spatters of black mud. Had the man been smaller or thinner, Stanton would have needed to find another proctor of sufficient girth, as the uniform had been his main requirement, though he was happy to have acquired an aerofan to get him into the space-port more quickly. The man should have been less careless in pursuit of what he must have considered a worker gone astray. Things might have turned out differently—strange, the workings of serendipity.

There were no queries as Stanton took the aerofan in over the fences and rail-gun towers on this side of the port, nor when he brought it down by a large bedstead shuttle that was undergoing maintenance—though not one of the maintenance crew was now in sight. Picking up his rucksack Stanton stepped out of the aerofan and moved out across the acres of plascrete, viewing his surroundings with something approaching nostalgia.

Most Polity worlds had outgrown ports like this, what with the spread of the runcible network and the advent of efficient AG technology. This port, built two centuries ago to support the landing of ships without AG, was still in use as such—a vast platform of foamed plascrete slabs that floated on the muddy plain to support the huge ships when they came down, along with the tangled infrastructure of rolling support towers and cranes, refuelling tankers and cars, a whole world of what on many worlds was called "heavy tech." Like so much on this world, this port was an anachronism. The traders coming to buy the squerm essence produced by the refineries in the city did not actually need the infrastructure, but were confined to the port to prevent smuggling and other infractions of Theocracy law. That confinement had not prevented Stanton himself from stowing away as a child, and thus escaping this world. He noted that, like the rats that they were, all the traders were gone now.

"It's pretty nice to have a port like this," he said into his comlink. "But to be utterly dependent on it when there are alternatives is downright stupid."

"Convenient for us, though," Jarvellis replied to him from *Lyric II*.

Stanton grunted noncommittally as he removed an innocuous cylinder the size of a coffee flask from his pack, plugged a miniconsole into the end of it, and punched in the required code. Satisfied with the response, he detached the console, and dropped the cylindrical object down into the narrow channel between the two huge slabs of plascrete. He then looked across to where something detonated, and a huge loading crane twisted with an agonized scream and went down like a falling tree, incidentally cutting a building in half in the process. Beyond this he now saw two carriers rise into view: one hovering protectively above the attacking tanks, and one ahead of them, bombarding troop positions concealed in the warehousing at the edge of the port. It was a bombardment that did not last long, for a missile stabbed up and punched through the second carrier and, trailing fire, it ploughed sideways through buildings as it came down, throwing up a wave of burning wreckage before itself. Stanton thought the Theocracy troops must feel proud of themselves—managing to hold off such a force from such a vulnerable position. He felt almost proud to wear their uniform himself as he dropped another cylinder into the gap between slabs below a huge container that he suspected, by the smell, was full of something wonderfully flammable.

"One more, over nearer the centre, then I think it's time I went away," he said.

He trotted across slab after slab to reach the centre of the landing field—he felt that a casual stroll was not really suited to the occasion—and there he initiated another innocuous-looking cylinder and dropped it between slabs. Looking down he saw it plop into black mud five metres below, then slowly sink, its red LEDs swamped at the last.

"That's it, all done now," he said.

"Tell me when you're on your way out, and I'll inform Lellan. She's swearing already about plausibility," Jarvellis replied.

"Tell her now: I can look after myself, and I don't like the idea of her sacrificing more of her armour," said Stanton.

"I'll only tell her that when you're on your way out," said Jarvellis stubbornly.

Stanton swore, and broke into a run for his abandoned aerofan. Half an hour later, Lellan's forces were driven back by the resolution and fighting spirit of the Theocracy forces. Tragically, Lellan had been unable to take the most essential installation on the planet—and Theocracy commanders even believed that to be her aim.

At first Eldene found huge satisfaction in dozering the ATV through tangled stands of flute grass now turning dark green; accelerating across areas of rhubarb, plantain, and multicoloured blister moss; carefully edging around areas where the fighting was most obvious, then bringing it back on course for the south. But she discovered that operating the simple controls was not exactly demanding and, after the initial novelty had worn off, her actions soon became almost automatic, and in a state of weary fugue she found her mind drifting back to the apartment in Pillartown One, and the conversation there between herself and Fethan:

"How much of that Dragon business did you understand?" Fethan asked, cutting straight to the core of her confusion.

"Some ship attacking one of the arrays. Then there was something about a creature . . ." She trailed off. What she remembered didn't make any sense.

"Dragon is a creature the size of a small moon," Fethan explained. "It came here and it destroyed every single laser array in orbit, before falling to earth in the south."

Eldene nodded, waiting for the punch line that would turn a patently ridiculous statement into some moral epigram, or the explanation that would make clear what Fethan was actually saying. He'd not elaborated.

After a moment Eldene said, "You're saying some mythical creature flew here through space and destroyed the laser arrays—that we are all now free and will live happily ever after?"

"No, I'm saying that an alien creature, but well known in the Polity, and which named itself after a mythical one, came here and destroyed the laser arrays, and that now your people have a chance to fight for their freedom—a fight they still might lose." He held up a finger. "You hear that?"

Eldene listened to the noise coming from the rest of the building. She nodded.

"That's everyone getting ready to move to the surface: civilians, military, the lot. The laser arrays might be gone, but a Theocracy device that could penetrate even down to here is still on its way. At present they control the surface, and we must take that from them, and we must hold it and not allow them to retake it. Staying here, we are dead; if we lose on the surface we are dead; and if we do not collect the rest of the votes required for the ballot and persuade ECS to come here, we are dead. Now, girl, do you understand that I am not telling you sweet fairy tales, but a . . . grimmer kind?"

Eldene said, "What can I do?"

Fethan reached down beside the bed and picked up the pulse-rifle she had abandoned there. He tossed it to her and, catching it, she jerked awake, finding herself again at the controls of the ATV. His reply was a fading whisper in her mind:

"There ain't that many choices going, girl."

Choice?

Here on the surface, choices were limited to two—fight or die—and they were not mutually exclusive. A long day of avoiding ground actions only sometimes to come across the hideous results of such had shown her the consequences of these simple choices; and just seeing such had worn her ragged and almost to the edge of tears. Fethan took over, as the weight of Calypse and the sun dragged night over the land, whilst Eldene found a padded mat and a heat sheet and fell quickly asleep on the vibrating floor. When she awoke, with seemingly no transition, it was to bright daylight in the front screen, and she wondered why she had felt so weak before, and resolved never to feel weak again.

On the other side of the cabin Thorn was also sitting up, having just woken as well.

Fethan looked round at them both. "Ah, at last, the snoring ends," he said.

"Why've you stopped?" Thorn asked, scratching at his beard.

Only when he said this did Eldene realize that there was no vibration from the engine.

Fethan gestured to the door of the ATV. "Be best if I show you, I think," he said.

Thorn opened the door only after he saw that Eldene had copied him in flipping up her mask. The door made a slight whump as it opened, but the pressure differential was such that little breathable air would be lost from the cabin. Eldene followed him out into surroundings little different from those she and Fethan had encountered when first going out into the wilderness. To her left lay flute grass, plantains and native rhubarbs, cut through with a curving path made by the ATV—that path already blurring out of existence as the new grass slowly regained its upright position. The ATV rested in an area strewn with blister moss, the occasional algae-green tricone shell, and flashes of that bright green plant Fethan had identified for her as real grass imported from Earth. To her right there stood an embankment topped with a high mesh fence. When Fethan clambered out of the ATV and led the way up the bank, Thorn and Eldene followed with caution, since the sounds of explosions and gunfire from beyond the fence were almost constant.

Along the base of the embankment, below the fence through which they were gazing, was a muddy track, then a band of grape tree orchards. Beyond these lay squerm and sprawn ponds. On the causeways and embankments between, a running fire-fight was taking place: groups of Theocracy soldiers lay down covering fire for a gradual retreat towards a distant mesh-fenced compound; Underground forces advanced behind grav-sleds on which had been mounted shielded rail-guns. Bodies and wrecked sleds were scattered all across this area. A Theocracy armoured car was burning—the fire fed by its own internal air supply—and some of the ponds were red, and foamed with voracious feeding.

"The rail-guns on the sleds are a recent addition," observed Thorn.

"I was just speaking to their commander," said Fethan. "Because of the resistance here, and the lack of cover, they dismounted what they could salvage from the wrecked towers of the previous compound they took. This fight has been going on since yesterday: every time they drive the Theocracy soldiers back to the compound, they get hit by the towers still working here."

"Then we should go round," said Thorn.

"That'll add three hours to our journey and, from what I understand, the problem's going to be solved anyway in the next hour." Fethan glanced to the sky above the far right of the compound. "In fact, probably in the next ten minutes."

The military carrier with its retinue of aerofans was clearly a welcome sight for the Theocracy soldiers guarding the compound, for they waved as it came racketing in over the ponds. Two minutes later they were burying their faces in the black soil as missiles lanced down from the carrier and turned the two ironwork towers behind the compound fence into glowing wreckage. These men could not hide from Lellan's fighters, who guided the aerofans in above them and opened up with the side-mounted rail-guns. The rebels pounded those trying to hide into slurry, and those who abandoned their weapons and ran out with their hands in the air just made easier targets. Within half an hour the forces of the Underground had taken this more difficult compound.

"Let's get moving," said Thorn, as he observed the carrier and its retinue depart.

Eldene tried to feel some pity for the Theocracy soldiers— as would have been morally right—but all she felt, when they drove down a causeway past smashed and near-obliterated bodies, was annoyance at such waste of equipment. As they passed the compound buildings—Fethan giving a salute to the commander of the rebels—she observed with a deep empathy a group of bewildered and bowed pond workers, their arms clutched protectively around their scoles. Almost with embarrassment she realized she was patting her hand against the itchy area below her breasts where the wound left by her own scole was still healing, then clutched that hand in her other one to still it. To then see that some of the rebels wore the padded overalls of pond workers underneath their flak jackets—bulging with their own scoles—immediately raised her mood. These people—obviously recent recruits—she saw, further on, distributing packs of ajectant and weapons amongst their recently liberated fellows.

Beyond the compound lay more of the carnage of battle, which they drove through for the best part of an hour before seeing another high embankment and mesh fence ahead of them.

"We should reach the first co-ordinates by late afternoon," said Fethan. He glanced at Eldene. "Do you want to take over now?"

Eldene hesitated—she wasn't confident about driving the ATV up the bank and using it to knock down the fence, as Fethan had done upon entering this agricultural area. Before she could formulate a reply, there came a sudden staccato clattering down the side of the ATV, and pieces of something were rattling and pinging around inside the cabin, and yellow breach-foam was oozing from holes in the vehicle's walls as it sealed them.

"Shit! Shit!" Thorn yelled as the ATV lurched, throwing both him and Eldene to the floor. As she grabbed for one of the wall handles to try and pull herself upright, she got a canted view through the front screen as Fethan drove the vehicle down into one of the ponds. Thorn was quickly up into the weapons control seat, the visor across, his left arm stiff at his side and blood trickling down from his torn biceps.

"Where the fuck did that come from?" he asked, whilst manipulating the controls of the weapons turrets, and turning his head from side to side—the visor throwing up views for him in whichever direction he looked. "Got it!" One of the turrets whined round above, and emitted a low thrumming as it emptied part of a magazine. "Fethan, take us up and out. They've just gone down into a pond."

"Sorry, trooper—got a burst tyre," said Fethan.

"Who attacked us?" Eldene asked.

Thorn unstuck the visor from his face and glanced at her, then to Fethan, who looked curious to know the answer as well.

"Small armoured car, bloody fast as well," he replied.

"Running?" suggested Fethan, studying the display that showed the tyre reinflating.

"I'd guess so," replied Thorn, pressing the visor back into place. "Yep, definitely running—they're up and moving now."

Fethan wound up the power in the motor, and slowly eased the ATV out of the pond. With a horripilation, Eldene observed the hooked bouquets that were the mouths of squerms flashing up before the screen and brass segmented bodies whipping through the air and dropping away. The ATV still had a lean-down on the back left corner as that tyre, after auto-repair, slowly inflated. They came up out of the pond and turned, bringing into view a black armoured car running on front steering treads and rear balloon tyres. It had nearly reached the embankment when both turrets on the ATV stuttered and hissed. After a few seconds one of the turrets stopped firing, and from it came mechanical clonks and buzzings as it inserted another magazine. On the bodywork of the car flashes ignited and fragments of metal, from its armour and from ricochets, splashed into the surrounding ponds or flung up small explosions of earth. Then it was up the embankment, flattening the fence before it, then down and gone.

"Fuck," said Thorn succinctly, pulling the visor from his face. "That tyre ready to run yet?"

Fethan shook his head. "Two minutes at least."

"Your arm," said Eldene.

Thorn glanced at the wound, then reached down, pulled an evil-looking knife from his boot, and with practised ease split the material of his sleeve and peeled it back from his leaking flesh.

"Can I help?" Eldene ventured.

"Well, there should be a suitable wound dressing in here somewhere." He gestured with his knife to storage lockers at the back, on either side of the packaged autodoc. "Try in there."

Eldene opened one of the lockers and looked with bewilderment at the packages and equipment it contained. She tried to find bandages, cotton wool, antiseptic, but saw nothing she could identify as such.

"The blue one, there," said Thorn, who had moved up behind her.

She picked up a round flat packet and then tried to open it.
"No," Thorn told her, "just press the darker side against the wound."

She did as instructed, then snatched her hand away when the package seemed to move underneath it. In amazement, she watched the thing deform and spread on his biceps until joining in a ring around his arm.

"It reacts to the blood," said Thorn, raising his fist and opening and closing it.

Eldene stared—he seemed now to be in no way impaired by just the kind of wound that would have had a pond worker's arm in a sling for many days. She looked to Fethan, who was watching her calculatingly.

"Could have done with one of them when you lost your scole. It's Polity tech—available to all for less than the cost of a cup of coffee," the old cyborg explained.

Eldene then truly felt a deep anger at the Theocracy, even though she had no idea what a cup of coffee might be, or how much it might cost. That it came cheap she had no doubt—just like human life down here on the surface, and strangely it was not awareness of this second fact that made her angry, for she had been aware of that all her life. No, it was the growing awareness that such cheapening of human life was not necessary; that this was an economy the Theocracy rulers, for their own ends, must struggle to maintain.

The edge of the crater was a hill of debris: mounded flute grass and its rhizomes, black mud veined with green nematodes, and stranded tricones—some of which had been killed by the impact shock and were giving off a stink it was possible to detect even through a breathing mask. Following Gant and Scar, Cormac climbed the hillock to gaze down into the devastation the fall of Dragon had wrought.

The crater had a teardrop shape, and they stood upon one of its long, banked sides. At the rounded front of this indentation in the landscape, the debris was mounded even higher. Proceeding to the horizon, from the tail of it, was a wide lane of destruction that looked somehow unreal, so neatly had the plain been parted, and so regularly had the growths of flute grass been flattened on either side where the trail cut through stands of that vegetation. Cormac was studying this trail, when Scar hissed and pointed with one clawed finger.

"Yes, it's Dragon," said Cormac, looking again at what remained of the titanic creature.

"Comprehensively wasted, I would suggest," said Gant.

As Apis and Mika joined them on the hillock of debris, Cormac studied the slope down into the heart of the crater. Only a few tens of metres below where they stood, the slope consisted entirely of black mud—at least half a kilometre of it descending to a star-shaped explosion of white chalk that even now was being obliterated as the mud slid back down. What remained of Dragon was slowly being interred, and would perhaps, in a few months, be hidden from sight.

"What are our chances of getting down there without getting buried in mud?" he asked generally.

"Do we need to get down there?" Gant asked.

"We need to get down there," said Mika quickly. Cormac glanced at her avid expression as she studied black bones and broken flesh, the glitter of a million scales, and masses of pseudopods spilt like intestines, beyond real intestines spilt like nacre and brass castings in a broken framework of sickle blades and tangled bare spinal columns.

"Said without any bias at all, of course," he said. Mika glared at him as he turned back to Gant and Scar. "Nevertheless, we do need to get down there. I want to know for sure that this Dragon is dead," he continued.

Gant nodded, then gestured to their left where the mounded debris rose highest at the head of the crater. "Limestone further up the slope there—probably torn up by the impact. I think I can see a way down."

Cormac glanced at the greyish-white smear down the slope he indicated, then gestured for Gant to lead the way. As a group, they trudged round the lip of debris. Here, Cormac found, was the highest elevation they had reached since crashing the lander. And here, gazing round, he saw just how utterly they were isolated in the middle of a bland and boggy wilderness.

The stands of flute grass mostly stood high enough to conceal those areas between. There lay long valleys inhabited by blister mosses, low spreads of purple-leaved native rhubarb, and other growths with no Earthly comparison or name. Travelling them was easier than pushing through the grass stands but, since they had no maps of this wilderness, it was necessary to stick doggedly to a straight-line march so as not to be drawn off course by attempting easier routes. Those areas were also preferable to Cormac, for in them he occasionally got to see some of the native fauna: creatures both reptilian and bovine hurtling away in an odd gliding lope, ubiquitous tricones puncturing the surface and submerging again instantly, groups of creatures that appeared very like terrapins until their spiderish heads protruded and they contemplatively grated together their mandibles. Some of those same shelled creatures roamed the slope close by, and it was reassuring to see them bumbling along feeding on the broken vegetation rather than something more *animate*. In the distance Cormac could see creatures that he at first took to be wading birds, until he gave himself a reality check.

"I've got no sense of scale here," he admitted to Gant. "What do *you* see out there?"

"Creatures standing . . . about four metres above the flute grass. No way of telling their actual height, as there could be a few metres of leg and foot going way down through the grass and mud. They're moving away from us, anyway. It's those other ones that aren't visible which I find more worrying."

"I beg your pardon," said Cormac.

Gant shrugged. "I've led us round some big wormlike things that lie underground—don't know if they're predators or not—and Scar here stung the arse of something that started homing in on us all just before this happened." He gestured towards the crater.

"I'll thank you to keep me informed in future," said Cormac, almost unconsciously bringing his fingers up to the touch control of his shuriken holster as he scanned their surroundings.

"Those are heroynes," said Mika.

Cormac turned to her. "What?"

She pointed at the distant creatures. "Heroynes."

"Dangerous?" Cormac asked.

"As dangerous to a human as a terrestrial heron is to a frog," said Mika. "They might mistake us for food."

"Shouldn't be too much of a problem, then," said Cormac. Mika just stared at him, as he went on with, "Last I heard, terrestrial frogs didn't go around armed."

At this, Apis let out a laugh that sounded almost like a gasp of pain. Perhaps it was the surreal imagery; perhaps he was just losing it. He laughed again, tears in his eyes, then shook his head and made a weak gesture towards Scar, who was now crouching, with his attention still directed down into the crater, as it had been from the first. Cormac nodded, allowing that Scar bore a resemblance to a large and heavily armed frog, then turned his attention to Gant as the Golem gestured beyond the distant heroynes.

"That's not all," he said. "From the direction they and those other things in the grasses are heading, I'm seeing munitions flashes; and from what I've been able to pick up on uncoded frequencies, there's some sort of war going on."

"The Underground," said Cormac. "They'll be taking the surface now. From what I know they would have grabbed the opportunity presented."

They soon reached the area earlier indicated by Gant, where the impact had peeled up a huge slab of limestone from the bedrock and dropped it like a ramp up the slope of mud. Also peeled up with this rock was a mass of chalk and tricone shell conglomerate that lay in boulders half-sunk all around. Chalky water had drained from these and from the slab, and had run down the slope to gather in milky pools. There was movement here as well, as tricones gobbled their way under the surface dragging crushed vegetation down to be munched at their leisure. Gant led the way down into the crater, quickly followed by Mika with instruments, recently taken from the pack Scar carried, clutched in both hands. The dracoman came down last—reluctant and hissing quietly as he stepped delicately down the stone. Broken shell in the chalky slurry across the face of the stone made footing firm and it was only minutes after stepping onto it that they could all step off it to trudge through a chalky morass towards the remains of Dragon.

"Ambient temperature's low. From previous experience, *too* low. And there are no electrochemical signatures . . . nothing out of the ordinary," observed Mika.

"You're saying it's definitely dead?" said Cormac, who had stopped to change his oxygen bottle. "No ambivalence in the readings, like there is in Dragon's conversation?"

"I think . . . yes, I am sure," said Mika.

"Okay, we'll give you an hour here—so find out what you can," he said.

Mika looked round at him. "Only an hour, why?" she asked.

"Now that question sounded almost natural," Cormac replied. "It's a shame that the answer is quite obvious." He held up his empty oxygen bottle, and then tossed it aside. Mika went quickly to work.

Eldene allowed the ATV to roll to a halt as it broke through into the clearing. Thorn, who was inspecting the turret gun magazines from a drop-down ladder, swore then released his hold to land on the floor in a crouch. Fethan had reached the weapons-control chair before him and held the targeting visor ready to press against his own face.

Eldene looked round. "Something's happened to them," she said.

Thorn came smoothly upright and was beside her in a second, one hand leaning on the console as he gazed through the screen.

"Ease us forward," he said. Then with a glance back at Fethan, "Stay on it."

The last of the flute grass parted before the vehicle, to reveal a mossy clearing around a low outcrop of limestone nested amongst black plantains and the nodular volvae of rhubarbs. What lay near this outcrop was identifiable as the armoured car that had fled them, but only just so. It had been torn apart: the back end, along with one axle still bearing shredded balloon tyres, lay to the right, a section containing a torn-open engine and one tread lay in front of them, and the remaining tread, cabin and guns seemed to have been put through a mincer, then pounded into the ground.

"They must have been carrying planar explosives or something," said Thorn. He glanced at Eldene. "Stop us here. I want to have a look at this."

He and Fethan were out through the door, even as Eldene was shutting down the motor and applying the brake. Before following them, she studied the scene a moment longer—such a savage wreck, but no burn marks ... She left the ATV with her pulse-rifle held across her stomach, and with its safety off.

"Has to be a planar load," Thorn was saying. "I can't think of anything else that would make such a mess."

Eldene noted how Fethan scanned the surrounding grasses, his gaze coming to rest at last on an only just visible channel pressed through it. The old cyborg then tilted his head and listened intently.

"Where are they?" Eldene asked.

Thorn glanced round at her. "What?"

"Where are the soldiers?"

With a puzzled expression Thorn stepped closer to the wreckage to study it. He prodded at a shredded tyre with the barrel of the pulse-gun he had drawn, Eldene standing now behind him, nervously surveying their surroundings.

"Not there," said Fethan. "Over here." The cyborg crooked a finger at them.

Eldene and Thorn walked over to him and gazed down at what he indicated on the ground. The moss here was red, as such mosses often were, but this red was wet and glistening and recognizable as human blood—which she'd seen enough examples of quite recently. Also, scattered here and there, were small diamonds of human skin and fragments of bone.

Fethan squatted down, picked up one of these fragments, and held it up to show how one edge had strange concave serrations, as if someone had drilled a line of holes before breaking the bone along them.

"Back to the ATV. I'll drive," he instructed. Then, pointing off to the right, "We go that way."

"What is it, Fethan?" Eldene asked, feeling something crawling up her spine.

"It's almost pointless to run if it comes after us," he replied. "In the mountains I had cover, and that was a small one."

"Quit with the mysterious bullshit," said Thorn.

"Hooder," said Fethan, pointing to their left. "It's about half a klom over there, as far as I can estimate, digesting its meal." Indicating the wreckage, he finished with, "And, judging by what's happened here, that meal was just an entrée."

Standing behind the Captain's chair, Aberil studied with cold satisfaction the screens and readouts in front of the man. Lellan had failed to take the spaceport, and would now be caught between hammer and anvil. The *Lee* and *Portentous* carried two armoured divisions each, and they would provide the hammer. The forces contained in the three remaining ships—*Ducking Stool*, *Gabriel*, and *Witchfire*, the last of which he was presently aboard—were the anvil against which the rebellion would be crushed. It annoyed him now that he had chosen to board one of the ships carrying the fleet of landers, but he had not expected Lellan's failure to take the spaceport, and had not wanted to be stranded in orbit, merely conveying his orders to the attack leaders. Gazing around at his staff officers and orderlies, who were clinging to the rope nets ranged behind the seated command crew of the ship, and who would soon accompany him to the surface, he nodded with satisfaction then sent:

"*God defend the right, only when the right cannot sufficient defence make. Captains of the* Lee *and* Portentous, *take your ships down and begin the attack.*"

Back through his aug he got a wash of approval. General Coban on the *Lee* sent back:

"We'll take the fast-track launchers out first—that'll give them something to chew on while we bring out our tanks. Then they'll know we've arrived. God defend the faithful."

Aberil winced at Coban's abrupt and cursory, "God defend . . ."—the man, like so many other officers in the army, did not have a sufficient fear of his superiors to convey the required sincerity of tone. It was something that, after this present situation was dealt with, he would have to look into. Presently, General Coban was too experienced and useful to alienate.

Now turning fully to his chosen staff Aberil addressed them aloud. "We must allow these fighters their head in the coming battle, but in the future they must be brought back into the fold. Too long, I think, they have forged their own path within the confines of *Charity*."

There was much nodding and grim-faced agreement—he had chosen these people himself, and knew them to be of like mind. He enjoyed their company, and with them knew exactly where he was: on top.

"Now it is time for us to disembark. Our landing will be in the wilderness one hundred kilometres south of Valour, and from there we shall sweep in, our line impenetrable."

"First Commander Dorth, what of those rebels who flee to the caverns?" asked Speelan—a thin and intense individual about whom Aberil sometimes had his doubts also.

"In the end there is always Ragnorak, but Lellan will know about that and therefore not allow her forces to retreat. She'll realize there will be no quarter given, and none expected."

"Should we pursue them down below, if they do flee?" Speelan asked.

"No, we merely seal the entrances and carve RIP on the rocks above."

After the dutiful laughter, Aberil towed himself along the ropes to the exit tube leading from the bridge, his officers and orderlies following close behind. Soon, by the convoluted ways of this mu-class ship, they came to the chaos of the lander bays, where men in white and pale blue uniforms covered in samples of scripture found some relief from cramped landing craft where they were racked as closely in the bays as bullets in a magazine. Many of these men, Aberil noticed, were praying, whilst others found more comfort in checking their weapons and body armour. It irked him that none of them became sufficiently silent and attentive at his approach, and that those who bowed or saluted seemed to do so with nonchalant lack of respect.

The command lander was twice the size of all the others, containing as it did communications equipment, heavy Polity pulse-cannons, as well as the luxury of grav-plates and some civilized space. Aberil was glad to be back aboard and, as he took his seat beside the pilot's—with its screens and logistics displays—he once again felt totally in control. Anyone from outside the Theocracy would immediately have noticed the lack of communications equipment, but then such people would come from a society where wearing an aug was still a matter of choice.

"General Coban, status?"

The General snapped back over the ether, *"Two hours and we'll be down. Lellan's forces seem in disarray: some are heading back to Valour, and some are just rolling back out into the wilderness."*

Aberil checked his screens and saw that this was true. He turned to his command crew, who were seating themselves at their various consoles.

"What is your assessment?" he asked a fat mole of a man called Torthic, who was the logistics officer of the group.

"Seems like a falling out amongst thieves," the man replied as he checked the data he was receiving. "Either that or the head has been cut off. We know a carrier was destroyed in the initial attack."

Aberil linked into the public address channel of his aug: *"All troops return to landers. We begin descent in one half of an hour."* Then he sat back and contemplated the coming obliteration of the Underground. He really hoped Lellan was not dead, as he had been so looking forward to meeting her, in the flesh. But if she were dead, there would be plenty of other prisoners to provide instruction and entertainment back on the cylinder worlds.

The sun set upon the land, bringing the grey hour that served to highlight the flashing of weapons used in sporadic conflicts towards every horizon. After changing his location for the fifth time that day—more out of boredom than any need to elude pursuit—Stanton began to bring his stolen aerofan down into thick flute grass, saw something large thundering towards him with what he felt were not the best intentions, and quickly jerked the column up and away to get out of range. A great flat beak clapped shut with a sound like a mat being beaten on concrete. He caught a glimpse of an array of glowing green eyes below a domed head, the muscled column of a body with more limbs than seemed plausible, and a whiff of quite horrible halitosis. Pulling away, he heard something that sounded like someone swearing in a quite obscure language.

"A bloody gabbleduck!" he exclaimed.

"Say again," said Jarvellis over com.

"Gabbleduck just tried to get me. You don't normally see them around here—the noise from the spaceport scares off their prey, so they don't bother coming in."

"Lellan said something about that earlier: seems the fighting is attracting things in from the wilderness and down from the mountains. There's even been a report of a hooder going into one of the compounds and systematically emptying squerm ponds."

"Perhaps humans dying make similar sounds to those of their normal prey."

"Perhaps—or perhaps they've just decided that enough is enough with these damned squabbling humans."

"Be nice to think that," said Stanton. "But we'll probably find it's some frequency of radio emission or the smell of some explosive or incendiary that attracts them in."

"Aren't you the optimist."

"Yeah," said Stanton, bringing the aerofan down into the middle of an area of low vegetation—wide plates of blister moss and grey thistles, rhubarb volvae just opening to expose leaves like tightly screwed-up black paper—which was well away from any stands of concealing flute grass, so he had a clear view of his surroundings. "It's called experience," he added.

As the motor of the aerofan wound down into silence, a deep thrumming vibration became evident. For a moment, Stanton surveyed the fragmented cloud strewn across the darkening sky, before stooping to open his pack. From this he now removed a square flat package that opened like a small briefcase to reveal a flat screen and miniconsole—a touch-console clustered around a single ball control—as well as a small winged egg. The screen he removed and secured against a rail of the aerofan by means of its rear stickpad. The egg he tossed up into the air and watched flutter away like a sparrow. Soon the flying holocam had given him a perfect view of the spaceport and all the activity there.

"You got this, Jarv?"

"Yeah, busy little soldiers, aren't they? Lellan says it's two of their ships coming down—they should be in view within a few minutes. A swarm of craft are coming down from the remaining three, and should be landing about the same time, probably in the south."

"Shame we can't have a surprise ready for them as well," Stanton opined.

"You wouldn't want that actually, knowing now who's coming down with the landers. Be far too quick for him."

"*Him?*" said Stanton flatly.

"The same."

"Then I guess I'll be joining Lellan when her forces converge."

"And in the meantime what do I do?" she asked.

"As we agreed: you stay safe. Losing a father would be more than enough for the kid."

The *Lee* and *Portentous* dropped through cloud like giant cannon-balls through layers of torn tissue-paper. Partial AG made their descent less bricklike, and took some of the strain from the huge landing thrusters that even now were glowing red-hot in their cowlings. But, even so, the noise was tremendous, a hot wind blasting across the swamps below them, and the ground quaking. Stanton watched them pass overhead, one after the other: conglomerations of black and rust, now less like cannon-balls as their full construction was revealed. Gun turrets, viewing bays, locks, and engine cowlings could now be clearly seen; also visible were areas where their original spherical hulls had been cut away and ugly square or flat-edged extensions grafted on.

Whilst watching these two huge ships slow and turn above the spaceport on huge blasts of thruster fire, Stanton removed from the top pocket of his acquired uniform the miniconsole he had been using earlier. All its five displays were nominal, which meant that there was nothing blocking the U-space signal coming from the five cylinders, and nothing to block the signal pulse he could send at any moment. He watched the ships slowly descending, until they were out of sight behind the taller stands of flute grass, then he transferred his attention to the screen affixed to the rail of the aerofan. With this bird's-eye view he observed the ships come in to land—their weight actually sinking the entire spaceport a couple of metres into the swampy ground—then the subsequent activity as ramps and gantries were moved into place by great caterpillar towing machines, and cranes were rolled in to connect higher gantries.

"Lellan wants to know what the delay is all about," said Jarvellis.

He replied, "The more open doors, connected ramps and gantries, and equipment in the process of being unloaded, the less the likelihood of an emergency takeoff succeeding."

"Cold bastard sometimes, aren't you?"

"And you would do it differently, my love?"

"Har-har-har."

Treaded missile-launchers and armoured cars were at last motoring from both ships when Stanton nodded to himself, laid his thumb across all five buttons, and pressed down. The screen he was watching whited out for a second then came back on to show metal frameworks looking like tinsel under a blowtorch; great slabs of plascrete riding up on arc-fire explosions; one ship tipped over and sliding down canted plascrete, the white-hot hollow of its interior exposed; the second ship trying to lift, but dragged sideways by the attached gantries and ramps, to crash down and bounce amid the growing atomic inferno. Like leaves before a wind, armoured cars, unidentifiable wreckage, whole slabs of plascrete hurtled out on the ensuing blast wave. The sound preceding it did not hit him at once, it just grew like the revving of some huge engine, became titanic, then, in sympathy, the ground began to move like a slow sea. Stanton recalled his holocam, quickly secured it and its screen back in their case, then he crouched, gripping the rails of the aerofan. He observed the cloud of smoke and fire growing alarmingly into view, before all the flute grass was flattened by the sudden wind, to reveal a carnage of fire and a wall of smoke and steam boiling outwards, interpenetrated, led and followed by debris. Crouching even lower, Stanton watched a slab the size of a playing field tumble overhead. To his right what remained of an armoured car bounced once, and spread white-hot fragments hissing through the vegetation. As the smoke and steam hit, he bowed his head and closed his eyes, wondering if perhaps just one CTD might have been adequate—and if it might have been wiser to observe the results from more of a distance.

The glow became a blazing eye on the horizon, ringed round with shades of lurid purple and orange, some tens of seconds before they heard the long drawn-out grumbling of the explosion and saw clouds drawn suddenly into lines and seemingly snuffed from existence.

Standing with his boot resting on one of the gun turrets, Thorn asked, "You knew this was going to happen, so what was it, then?"

Sitting on the other gun turret, Eldene observed the old cyborg as he too watched the distant glow, whilst combing his fingers through his raggedy ginger beard. When he finally did turn to answer Thorn's question, it was with a distracted air.

"Well, unless I miss my bet, that was the spaceport and any military landing there being attempted from the cylinder worlds. Can't confirm that yet, though, as com's all down," he said.

"EM pulse," said Thorn, gazing back at the orange glow. "So that was a nuclear explosion?"

"More than one, I think—small tactical CTDs." Fethan looked down at Eldene and grinned. "*More* wonderful things devised by the Polity."

"Anything that destroys the Theocracy is all right by me," murmured Eldene.

Fethan frowned at her but, before saying anything about that, tilted his head and said, "Ah, seems the Theocracy just lost two of their largest ships, along with any facility to land more of that size." He turned and pointed. "But not the ability to land, however."

A roaring had now grown distinct from the sound of the explosion, and it became evident this had little to do with the blast itself. Like shoals of grey sharks, the landing craft of the Theocracy filled the sky and slid overhead—hundreds of them. The three of them felt an urge to duck out of sight, but where was "out of sight" with such a swarm of craft filling the sky?

"We're only small beer," said Fethan, "but best to get moving anyway. They might send someone out here once they've landed." He leapt down from the roof of the ATV and entered it. Eldene quickly followed him down then inside, but Thorn took a while longer.

"CTDs are not something the Polity hands out like lollipops, you know," he commented, upon finally re-entering the vehicle.

With half an ear to the ensuing exchange, Eldene set the motor to spinning up its flywheel, before engaging the hydrostatic drive and getting them under way.

"Seems John Stanton had no trouble getting hold of them," replied Fethan. "But why am I telling you this? You should know, as you came here aboard his ship."

"Sealed cargo and a hostile ship's AI—so I didn't get

to find out very much. All I was sure about was the drug manufactories and pulse-rifles."

"Ah, so you didn't get a look at the two Polity war drones and the U-space transmitter?" said Fethan.

Thorn's reply to this involved a physically impossible sexual activity in conjunction with the edible but prickly fruit of a bromeliad.

"There is a girl present, you know," Fethan warned, and this time received an even briefer retort.

Eldene tried to suppress it—it seeming so inappropriate in present circumstances, and she had only understood half of what Thorn had suggested—but the giggle escaped her nonetheless.

"Ignore him," said Fethan. "These Earthmen are just foul and uncouth creatures."

That, coming from Fethan, had the tears running from her eyes, and she found that her suppressed laughter only escaped with more force.

"Watch where you're driving," Fethan added.

The little electric heater was an amazing device that folded into a case no larger than the palm of a hand. The grid opened out into a twenty-centimetre square that was suspended just off the ground by two U-shaped telescopic legs; the microtok was a flattened ovoid between these, simply supplied with water from a small filter pipe pushed into the damp ground. It was, Molat suspected, a device intended for cooking upon, but it put out a wonderful blast of warmth, and he could not summon the inclination to damn this piece of Polity technology. Like all proctors, he would have punished its possessor before adding the item to his own collection, but since that earlier possessor was presently rotting down into the thick loam of the planet, there was nothing much to do about him. Holding his hands out towards the square of red-hot metal, Molat looked across them at Toris.

"We'll head out for the landers. I for one will not surrender myself to the Underground in this uniform," he said, rather than relayed through his aug. It was more comforting to speak out loud in this darkness, and there was so much horror coming in over aug channels of late that he was beginning to develop an aversion to using them. Perhaps Toris felt the same, for he too replied aloud:

"They'll be going all out to attack our wonderful First Commander Aberil Dorth. We might be somewhere behind them or caught between the two of them."

Molat didn't like the *tone* he seemed to be getting from Toris ever since the destruction of the spaceport. Most proctors neither liked nor trusted Aberil Dorth—the man was psychotic at best—but that was not an antipathy you allowed yourself to voice aloud, or to even think if you could help it, since mistakes were easy to make over aug channels.

"Nevertheless," he said. "That is the only direction we can head to find safety."

Toris looked up, and seemed about to say something he might regret. However, a rushing rustling in the flute grass stilled further vocal conversation.

Toris: *"What in God's name was that?"*

Molat: *"It sounded big, and I felt the ground move."*

Toris: *"You know there are heroynes and siluroynes out here?"*

Molat: *"Thanks for the reminder. That's made me feel much better."*

Molat turned off the little heater and stood up, blinking to clear the gridded after-images from his vision. Another hissing in the flute grass behind Toris had Molat pointing his rail-gun in that direction. Toris turned, with his own laser pistol gripped two-handed. Something odd about the grasses over there . . .? Then Molat realized what he was seeing: two deep dark eye-pits in which glittered eyes like faceted grey sapphires. Its huge head—which was the most yet to become visible—had the appearance of a bovine skull patterned with flute-grass stripes, and trailed two flat-tipped feelers from its lower jaw. The teeth, when they were exposed, had no camouflage, however, and gleamed like blue hatchets in the moonlight.

"Siluroyne! Siluroyne! Oh fucking hell, I'm dead! A Siluroyne!"

Molat supposed that Toris didn't even realize he was broadcasting, as the man fired his hand laser into that huge face. The monster bellowed and reared, its multiple forepaws opening out in silhouette against the sky like a huge clawed tree. Molat realized that Toris's shooting had only pissed off something that had been intending to eat them anyway. It seemed to him there was only one way for him to escape. He reached out and, as hard as he could, shoved Toris towards the monster—before turning and running.

"Bastard! Bastard! Bastard!"

Glancing back he saw the thing stooping down, its many forepaws closing in like a cage.

"Oh God no! Please no!"

It was upright again now, and in two of its sets of claws it held Toris like a hot dog. Molat shut down his connection as the monster began crunching down the other man's leg like a stick of celery, almost as if it wanted him to continue screaming, and knew that if it bit the human's other end the screaming would stop. Molat ran hard and fast, not caring in what direction, just so long as it was *away*.

The first grabship brought in a chunk of asteroidal rock that was too huge to get in through the doors of the heavy-lifter bay. But such was the original architecture of the *Occam Razor*, Skellor found he could reposition whole floors and compartments, huge generators, ducts, and the numinous devices of the ship, and then actually part its armoured hull to allow such a mass of material inside. In the new bay thus created, Skellor kept the great stone positioned centrally by a balancing of grav-plates, and reached out to it there with an explosion of the ligneous pseudopods that were Jain, and himself.

High-speed analysis which was more like touch and taste soon rendered to him the chemical structure of his prize. He found large quantities of iron, silicates, and sulphur;

lesser quantities of carbon, much of it turned into useful fullerenes by the heat of the explosions that had destroyed the moonlet; rare earths and radioactives—there was in fact very little on the periodic table that was not represented here. Having tasted, he then fed—his pseudopods thickening and hardening, and the asteroid, now laced with webworks of filament, visibly shrinking like a fly being sucked dry by a spider.

Soon there was no need for the grav-plates to hold the rock in position, as his pseudopods had become almost indistinguishable in girth from great oaks. Other asteroids, drawn into other bays, he treated in the same manner, but now almost unconsciously—like a man simply breathing or feeding. With more conscious application he created a superconducting network from the fullerenes to link together the eighty-four flat-screen generators and the U-space engines. The independent controls of these he found burnt beyond the recovery of any Polity technology; however, that recovery was not beyond him. With silicon and rare earths he rebuilt the little controlling subminds, understanding, as he did so, why the system was not centralized; how, with a ship this size, even the high-speed adjustments he could make through the net were not fast enough.

With other materials Skellor strengthened his grip on the structure of the rest of the ship but, having discovered the utility of being able to alter its internal and external structure at will, he did not completely ossify it in the ligneous growth of the Jain architecture—so he kept the movable floors and walls, and the bridge pod that could be expelled from the ship with a thought. Even so, upon taking an external view through the sensors of one of the grabships, he saw that the *Occam Razor* was now very much changed in appearance: its great lozenge of golden metal was now marred by the grey and silver of Jain architecture, patterned like lichen.

It was from these outer structures that Skellor felt the harsh radiation of the nearby sun like a balm, as he sucked it in and converted it to his purposes. In truth, materials were not his greatest requirement here—but the energy to absorb materials, and to extend throughout the ship was. Almost unconscious, again, had been his earlier calculation that he would have drained all the *Occam*'s energy resources by doing what he now did, so would have had none left to drop the ship into U-space. As his work continued, his requirements for energy grew. The radioactive material from the asteroids was quickly refined and burnt away, and soon he was flinging out huge curving spines up to a kilometre long, between which he exuded nacreous sheets that were something like the meniscus of a bubble, which then turned deep black to absorb more of the sun's energy—to grow, to keep on growing . . .

It took one of the grabships, blasted off course by some huge chemical explosion occurring in the load it was bringing in, and then crashing into a growing array of these sun sails, to raise Skellor's awareness out of this incessant *growth*. Abruptly he realized that nothing more was now required; that he was ready to drop himself into U-space. Consciously bringing to a halt the expansion of *himself* throughout the ship, while retracting the sun sails, he found difficult. There was inner resistance from that part of himself that was Jain. It was that same separation of self that an addict experiences, and Skellor realized he must never allow himself to go too far along that way again. It would be so very easy just to lose himself in *growth* for growth's sake, and forget all other purpose. In moments his will had reasserted itself, and he remembered *his work*, which was more important than anything, anything at all.

15

"The monster was as greedy to fill itself as were Sober and Judge, and so, to save her husband from its jaws, Judge stole food from the compound when there was no sinning Brother to be found there."

The picture explicated this with an animation showing Judge tramping a mountain path with a great sack of food slung over one shoulder. As she walked, she dipped a hand into the sack and crammed food into her great jowly face. The woman, just to be sure, closed the book to have a look at the cover, shrugged, then continued:

"On the seventieth day Judge could find no more sinning Brothers in the compound and no more food in the warehouses, so, with much sorrow, chose to lead Brother Evanescent to the bridge."

Brother Evanescent was obviously about half a second away from acquiring a halo and, considering all that had gone before, the woman clearly guessed what was going to happen to him.

"The monster rose up before Brother Evanescent, but he was not afraid. 'I am armoured with my Faith, the Word of God is my whip, and His Grace is my Spear!' he cried and, casting aside his white robe, the good Brother revealed golden armour that glowed in the sun. In his right hand he bore a long golden spear and in his left hand he bore a whip as hot as molten iron."

The woman and the boy observed with some perplexity that the picture was precisely in concurrence with the text.

"And so for one day and one night Brother Evanescent battled the monster from under the bridge," continued the woman. "Ah, now I see."

The Brother kept attempting to spear the siluroyne whilst,

with a bored expression, the creature leant an elbow on the parapet and knocked the point of his spear aside with one claw. In the background Sober and Judge were stacking wood.

"With Faith you cannot come to harm."

When the two workers gave the signal, the siluroyne picked up Evanescent, and plucked away his whip and his spear as if taking away dangerous toys from a child.

"With God's word you will chastise your enemies."

As if preparing a kebab the monster threaded the spear through the back of the Brother's armour, and used the whip to bind his arms and legs in place.

"With God's Grace your enemies will be brought down."

The purpose of the two Y-shaped sticks on either side of the woodpile now became apparent. Once ignited, the wood burned as it never ever burned on Masada.

"With all three, the world will fall at your feet!"

The woman and the boy watched as Brother Evanescent was sufficiently broiled, with implausible speed, then Sober, Judge, and the siluroyne opened up the hot parcel of his armour to enjoy a merry feast.

Loman cupped a blue rose, brought it close to his nose, and closed his eyes as the subtle perfume drew him back to his childhood. The pain of thorns penetrating the flesh of his palm was also a reminder, for at one time he had been destined to join the Septarchy and had briefly experienced their bloody discipline. Opening his eyes he surveyed the ordered beauty that stretched far away from him, and blurred into rainbow hues riding up round the inner arc of *Hope*.

The gardens of the Septarchy were beautiful indeed, which was something Loman always found surprising, considering the gardeners themselves could have little appreciation of the colours; but then perhaps, with the *Gift*, they saw them through the eyes of others? He turned now to the First Friar and studied the man: he was emaciated, almost as if he suffered some wasting illness; his dark robes, tied close to his thin frame with twists of rope made from human hair, were worn thin and losing their dye through too-frequent washing, but of course the First Friar would not know this, since sewn in the place of his eyes were the ancient memory crystals that once contained the truths of the first colonists.

"They say you construct your gardens by scent alone, and that there is a whole landscape of olfactory meaning that those of us with eyes cannot appreciate," said Loman.

"The power of myth must never be underestimated," replied the Friar.

Loman stared beyond the cropped lawns and intricate stone gardens towards the great colonnaded sprawl of the main Septarchy halls. In their white uniforms the platoons of soldiers, marching in to take up positions around the beautiful white buildings, seemed in perfect consonance. The First Friar and the two young acolytes—with their sewn-up eye-sockets—could not see this, but would know soon enough. Loman glanced around at his bodyguard scattered between the borders and neat shrubberies, then at Tholis—who was Claus's replacement and a man thoroughly aware of the precariousness of his position.

"Subtle," he said, returning his attention to the Friar. "But in the end plain power is what must not be underestimated."

"That is something I never do," said the First Friar, at last beginning to sound worried.

"Why then do you persist in occupying the upper channels with your prayers and your chants?" Loman asked.

"They are offered to the glory of God," said the Friar.

"They were intended to keep Behemoth from taking hold of our minds, and now Behemoth is dead they are no longer needed."

"How can you—the Hierarch—say that prayer is no longer needed?"

Loman sighed and, shaking his head, held out his hand towards Tholis. The man did not need the brief instruction Loman sent him via aug. He drew his pistol and placed it into Loman's still-bleeding hand.

The First Friar now tilted his head. "Why have soldiers entered the Septarchy halls?" He turned towards Loman, and the Hierarch could feel the questioning probes coming through so many channels of his aug, his *Gift*. He replied with a simple statement: *"One whole quarter of Hope used for your damned Septarchy halls and damned useless gardens."*

Now he could feel the spreading *noise* as people in the area nearby, so accustomed to bloody pogroms, reacted with panic. The Friars themselves were not panicking, accustomed as they were to being above such pogroms. No one had been killed yet, as the soldiers herding the Friars out of the halls and into their gardens were showing greater restraint than they normally showed with other citizens. This, Loman knew, was not out of any respect, but through fear of the power these Friars had enjoyed under previous Hierarchs. It was time, he decided, for someone to die and, so deciding, pointed the pistol just to the First Friar's right and fired four times. Both acolytes dropped: one of them dead before he hit the ground, the other coughing up blood from shattered lungs until Loman fired again, opening a closed eye-socket and blowing out a froth of brains across the close-cropped grass.

"No! You cannot do this!"

Loman carefully clicked the pistol's safety switch across then tossed it back to Tholis who caught and holstered it in one swift movement. The Hierarch was pleased with this new commander of his guard, for the man so quickly anticipated his orders that it almost seemed unnecessary to give them. Already two of the guard were closing in to take hold of the First Friar, even as Loman unhooked from his belt the sculping tool he had taken from Amoloran. The Friar did not have eyes, but he screamed as if he did when Loman cut and gouged the two memory crystals from his head, then continued screaming as the neurotoxin worked its way through the exposed raw flesh of his eye-sockets.

"Release him, now."

With the two bloody crystals in his right hand, Loman stepped back while the First Friar fell face-down and in his agony seemed to be trying to bite the ground. Glancing down to the Septarchy halls, Loman saw his soldiers now needing to use more brutality to get the blind friars out into the open. He sent instructions to Tholis:

"*Finish it on their lawns and throw their bodies into the flower borders.*"

Aloud, Tholis asked, "What *are* your orders, Hierarch?"

Loman turned and gazed steadily at him, then after a moment relented: it was understandable that the man wanted to hear a direct order witnessed by others.

"I want you to kill all of these Septarchy parasites on their wonderful lawns, and I want you to throw their bodies onto the borders, so that the flowers are fertilized by their blood. Is that clear enough for you?"

"It is clear, Hierarch," Tholis replied.

They first came in high over the inhabited lands: ion thrusters filling the sky with actinic white stars in rectilinear display, on wave after wave of bulky landing craft. Below each wave the flickering of orange lights ignited the sky beyond the edge of the crater, and soon the sound of a distant storm came grumbling down onto them.

"They're bombing something," observed Gant.

"Yes," said Cormac, "let's get our gear together and get out of here."

Out of sight the craft must have turned, because soon the first waves were coming in over their heads—now heading towards the inhabited area of the planet—and Cormac supposed it was too much to hope that the Theocracy would not come to inspect this site where the creature that had destroyed their arrays had come down. As the last line of craft rumbled over, one of them peeled away and descended on the eastern side of the crater.

"Mika, move it!" he shouted, as the Life-Coven woman once again turned on the inspection light she had secured to her temple with a skin-stick pad, and delayed to study some bizarre gory object and cut samples from it. She hurried to catch up, as he stood waiting with his boot resting on the bottom of the slab.

"We could hide here," she suggested half-heartedly, indicating the macabre architecture she had been studying, which now—in the semi-dark which was all of a night this place managed—seemed to be turning into an organo-Gothic monastery. It was a protest really—she just didn't want to leave this place of such reverential interest to her.

Trotting up behind her Gant said, "Not too clever an idea—only one way out, and they'll certainly be coming down here."

"There's so much more to learn—I've hardly scraped the surface," said Mika, looking back regretfully as she stepped onto the slab to follow Apis.

"I promise that when this is all over we'll let you come back here and dig it all up," said Cormac.

"A lot of digging," said Mika. "There is, by my calculation, only fifty per cent of Dragon visible here in this crater."

Cormac caught her arm. "What do you mean?"

She gestured to the slopes on either side. "The rest of it must be buried deeper under here, or it vaporized on impact," she said.

"Remember, a lot was already sheared away from the creature," he reminded her.

She shook off his arm and moved on up the sloping stone. "I have, of course, taken all that into account," she said haughtily.

"Oh damn," said Cormac, surveying the scene in the crater with infinite suspicion, before turning to Gant. "Where's Scar?"

Gant glanced up the slope to Apis and Mika, then quickly scanned all around. Abruptly his expression became puzzled, and he lifted his fingers to touch the side of his head. "He's not responding to his comlink," he announced.

And so it begins, thought Cormac, then instructed, "Go with the others and get them under cover. I'll catch up with you."

Gant looked set to protest, but Cormac didn't give him a chance, quickly turning away and heading back the way they had come. A glance behind showed Gant hesitate, then turn to bound easily up the slab after Mika and Apis.

Cormac quietly initiated Shuriken as he moved into the shadows of the Dragon corpse. Many years ago he had been present when the entirety of this creature had apparently suicided. He'd foolishly believed it then, so to say he was suspicious now would have been an understatement.

"Scar?"

The dracoman was crouched by a charnel hillock of black bone and broken flesh. At first Cormac thought Scar was staring at him, until he moved aside and realized the dracoman was gazing directly at the slope Gant had just climbed. Cormac moved to his side and squatted down next to him, peering in the same direction.

"What do you see?" he asked.

Scar hissed, exposing his teeth—bright white in the moonlight—then turned and just looked at Cormac.

"We have to get out of here," Cormac said.

"I stay," said the dracoman finally.

Cormac shook his head. "You're not stupid, Scar. Theocracy troops will be down here soon to investigate this place. They may find you here, and if they find you they'll certainly kill you."

Scar seemingly did not consider this worthy of a reply, and Cormac understood that perfectly. The dracoman used only such words as were necessary and never bothered formulating replies to the patently obvious. Cormac reached out to touch the dracoman's shoulder, but Scar's hand snapped up and caught Cormac's wrist—that hand was hot, febrile.

"What is happening, Scar?"

"I stay . . . it is soon." Scar released his wrist, then returned his attention to the slope.

Cormac stood up: he had no time to spare, and he knew he would be wasting time trying to get anything further out of the dracoman. He stepped over and picked up the denuded pack of oxygen bottles Scar had discarded.

"Take care," he said, turning to go. The dracoman bared his teeth in what might have been a grin.

The stars were now easing into visibility between ragged strips of cloud—cloud that also parted coyly to reveal the distant baroque and glassy sculpture of a nebula. Glancing at this, Cormac realized it was the same one as filled the sky of Callorum, only there he had seen it from the opposite side. As he scrambled down the sloping debris into the flute grass outside the crater, one of the moons sped across the face of the nebula like a searchlight flung by a catapult—its tumbling light occasionally stabbing through cloud gaps. Gant still waited for him at the edge of the flute grass, then led the way into a dense area where the stalks gathered in a protective wall all around.

"Scar's not coming," Cormac told him.

Gant nodded. "I knew one day it would happen. He's not human, and he's always seemed to me to be marking time—waiting for something."

"I'll let you explain that to Mika, then," said Cormac.

Gant grimaced.

Without an oxidizing atmosphere, the laser worked at almost twenty per cent above expected efficiency, and it took the team only a few hours to knock down a wide enough area of flute grass. Such a clearance was not entirely sufficient to the task at hand, which was why a second team went in—once the laser was shut down—to spread a powder of copper sulphate to poison all the plant roots in that same area. Had they laid the inflatable flooring direct onto still-living rhizomes, new growths of flute grass would have punched up through the tough plastic within a matter of hours. After observing all the outside activity for a while longer, Aberil turned his attention from the infrared screen to his own gathered staff.

"The loss of the *Lee* and the *Portentous* is an object lesson to us all: we must never underestimate the rebels, and we must show not the slightest hesitation, nor mercy, as we prosecute their destruction," he said.

Returning his attention to the screen he observed the troops, now disembarked from the landers, gathering into squads and preparing to move out. They had little in the way of armour or transport—the largest items being balloon-tyred cars on which could be mounted launchers and larger rail-guns, but which were mainly for the moving of supplies—but that was intentional. Though there was always comfort in having armoured vehicles to use, in this kind of war they never lasted very long. Lellan had employed her tanks for a swift assault, their main target being the rail-gun towers of the compounds, but now those tanks were all but obsolete, just as were large airborne carriers. When a single man could easily carry a high-penetration missile-launcher with intelligent tracking, large vehicles soon became more vulnerable than single individuals. In fact, Lellan had quite dramatically proven this point at the spaceport.

He considered what had happened there: obviously she had sacrificed a carrier, and ordered the apparent disarray of her forces thereafter, to fool them into thinking they had killed her. An elaborate trap and an effective one: in one stroke she had wiped out a quarter of the force sent against her. That she had destroyed the heavy armour aboard those ships was irrelevant as such, because Aberil suspected she could easily have taken the spaceport before, rendering such armoured vehicles—perhaps the only ones that could have lasted long enough under hand-held attack and put a dent in her forces—completely useless. No matter, right now he had with him thirty thousand well-armed and thoroughly vicious infantry skirmishers, whereas Lellan's forces numbered per-haps one-third of that even including those she had recruited from the crop fields. And she would pay—he had seen to that.

Bombing from landing craft was not an easy option, as they were not really equipped for the task. They had accomplished this by connecting magnetic mines to the undersides of the craft—mines they could disconnect by radio, and detonate by the same means. Only one craft had been lost, when some fool sent the wrong signal first, but overall Aberil's main aim had been achieved: Lellan could not retreat directly back down into her caverns, now he had destroyed all her breakout tunnels.

"Over this night we'll move our soldiers into position, and in the morning we go in on their left flank," he said.

"Nothing elaborate: we just hit them hard and drive them back from the spaceport towards the mountains."

"The mountains are easily defended," noted Torthic, the logistics officer.

Aberil studied his fingernails. "And utterly useless to us. We cannot establish crop ponds or colonies there, and they are riddled with caves where traitors can hide."

"Your meaning?" Torthic asked, taking the prompt Aberil sent him over a private aug channel.

Aberil shrugged. "The *Witchfire* is aptly named. I should think a scattering of ten- and twenty-megatonne devices should take the backbone out of Lellan's army once she considers it safely ensconced in the mountains."

In bright moonlight, they moved out in squads of twenty into the flute grass. Each squad had its own commander with an open aug link to Aberil's logistics staff, its own car carrying either a heavy rail-gun or a mortar, plus supplies. Each soldier was armed with a rail-gun capable of firing anything from single shots to eight hundred a minute, and carried enough of the small iron slugs to maintain ten minutes at that latter rate of fire; a short-stock grenade-launcher; and curve-bladed commando knives for more intimate work.

They had trained all their lives for this kind of action and were ready and willing for it. They eagerly looked forward to their first encounter with the rebels, who at present were ten kilometres away from them. As squad commander Sastol led his men in a brief prayer, he felt his stomach tight with excitement and his head buzzing with the sometimes contradictory instructions that filtered down from First Commander Aberil. Finishing the prayer with a silent "Amen" over his *Gift*, he found that nevertheless the central order was unchanged. Advance and destroy the rebellion—in the end it was simplistic.

"We march behind the car for the present. The moment any part of the line hits resistance, we spread out and link up with adjacent squads," said Sastol. Then focusing on his lieutenant, Braden, he went on, "You and two others of your choice get to ride on the car. I want you on the heavy gun at all times as I think that when it starts, it'll start fast."

"Don't *you* want to ride?" asked Braden, with a touch of irony.

"Not now. I need to loosen up for . . ." Sastol paused as the order for them to move out came through his aug. He held up his hand for a moment, then raised it above his head, made a circular motion then pointed with two fingers into the flute grass. Hand-signalling—an anachronism from days before the Theocracy had received the *Gift* from Behemoth—was something many military commanders obdurately continued to practise. The precise technology of aug communication not being entirely understood, these men liked to be prepared for the eventuality of its failure in a battle.

As one, the army of the Theocracy moved into the flute grass, each squad cutting a swathe separated from its neighbours by a hundred metres of vegetation on either side. Sastol watched Braden ensconce himself behind the heavy rail-gun, observed Donch and Sodar clamber up behind him, Donch taking up the simple detachable drive handle to set the car in motion. As the rest of their squad moved in behind the car in a loose double column, Sastol moved in behind them. In truth, he preferred walking because he was so charged with adrenalin that it would be almost painful for him to sit still—experiencing action at last after a lifetime of training for it.

Only action came rather sooner than he expected. A hissing crunching sound to the right snapped Sastol's attention in that direction, whence he saw a sharp-edged yellow hook the size of a man's arm cleaving through the ground towards his men. It was such an odd sight that it took him some time to recognize it for what it was.

"Mud snake!" he bellowed, just as the sliced mat of rhizomes parted and the creature heaved its giant caterpillar body into view, clacking its huge beak with appended slicing hook, and emitting horrible coughing barks. Rail-gun fire slammed into it from both sides, and it was beginning to disintegrate even as it surged forwards. Turning its blind head sideways at the last moment, it clashed its beak shut on Dominon and bore him to the ground. Continued fire separated front end from back and leaking blood like molasses, its rear end sank back into the ground. Immediately the squad fell upon the front end with knives and rail-guns, levering the monster's ragged beak open.

"*I'm okay, no need to panic.*"

Finally, by cutting corded muscle at the base of its beak, they were able to wrench the top half of it back—which unfortunately released human arteries that had been pinched shut.

"Really, I'm okay," Dominon reiterated out loud, then, "Oh."

He died before one of the roving med-squads could reach them, but Sastol thought that perhaps for the best, as Dominon—as athletic and libidinous as the rest of them—would not have wanted to continue living in only the top half of his body.

"Gods protect us all," intoned the medic as he bagged and tagged Dominon to be picked up later.

"Not the first?" asked Sastol.

The man looked at him, his face expressionless behind his tinted visor as he sent the statistics across via a private channel. Mud snakes had already killed eight and injured seventeen sufficiently for them to be out of the fight. A siluroyne, disturbed at the eastern end of the line, had taken out an entire squad of twenty. Three were lost to a heroyne before the creature had been brought down. It had apparently swallowed them whole.

"It's not even night yet," Sastol said gloomily.

"They're certainly all stirred up," said the medic, "but let's hope the enemy will be facing the same problem."

A wide area of flute grass had been flattened around the enemy lander, and that area was now lit by arc lights as troops began pulling equipment out into the open.

"Laser," observed Gant, holding up the ends of some of the laid-over grass for inspection. Discarding them he pointed to a heavy device mounted on a flat tray, with one driving wheel behind. "Only for levelling an area of the grass—not really manoeuvrable enough to be used as a weapon."

"Like they need another weapon?" said Cormac, eyeing the rail-guns and grenade-launchers most of the men carried.

"True," said Gant.

How bloody must warfare become when most fighters carried weapons that could turn a human being into steak tartare in a second—and where there was nothing but flat swampy ground and nothing to hide behind? It seemed to him that the fighting Gant had earlier referred to must have been bloody indeed. He glanced aside at the Golem, then back towards the spot where Apis and Mika were concealed. The four of them possessed APWs, so could wreak havoc in this clearing, but it seemed unlikely that they would live long enough to board one of the landers and lift it off. Even Gant with his Golem Twenty-seven chassis would eventually be destroyed by enough rail-gun hits. He caught the trooper's eye and nodded back the way they had come. They crawled back into deep shadow beyond the range of the lights before standing up and returning to join Apis and Mika.

"What do you suggest, Agent?" Gant asked.

"I suggest we find somewhere to bed down for the night, and reassess things in the morning. Maybe they'll send an investigation party down into the crater, and an opportunity may present when there's a few less of them about the lander."

"Scar's still in the crater," said Mika, falling back on her usual technique of not asking the question she really wanted to ask.

"Yes, well spotted," retorted Cormac and, ignoring her pique, turned back to Gant. "Maybe we could get ourselves one or two of their uniforms—reach one of the landers that way?"

Hesitantly Apis asked, "Where would you then take the lander? Hundreds came down between here and where you want to go, and if you steal one, that will soon be broadcast."

Cormac glanced at him and nodded. "I know that. I'm just thinking about our immediate future." He rattled a forefinger against his oxygen bottle. "Anyway, we could fly out and round, and put down in the mountains."

"If not shot down first," said Apis.

Cormac grimaced. "We've gone from an AI dreadnought to creeping around in the undergrowth, so I wouldn't be surprised."

"And there I was thinking you an optimist," said Gant.

"You still haven't—" began Mika, but just then grenades went off to their right.

"Lead!" Cormac shouted to Gant, then he, Mika and Apis hurried after the Golem as he moved swiftly into the flute grass.

"How did they . . .?" Apis did not manage to finish the question, but Cormac answered it anyway.

"They must have put up an infrared detector. We were a bit too close," he said.

More explosions to their right, followed by the distinctive vicious cracking of rail-gun fire. Gant slowed to a halt and held up his hand. Mika swore aloud after stumbling into his back, then fell silent when he glared at her. He made a downward gesture and they quickly squatted low.

"They're not firing at us," he said. "There's something else out there."

They listened as the firing drew further to the right of them, and something moved through the vegetation with a sound like a leaking compressor.

"What the hell is that?" wondered Cormac aloud.

"Big bastard of a hooder," said a voice none of them recognized.

Cormac observed with surprise the old man who stepped into view. He was short, gnarled, had a large ginger beard and a distinct lack of teeth, but most importantly he had managed to get this close to them without being detected by the hearing of a Golem Twenty-seven. Gant himself was gaping in amazement at the oldster, and Cormac grinned to himself—it was well for one such as Gant to be reminded he was not omnipotent.

Casually, Cormac pointed the thin-gun he had drawn at the old man's chest. "And you are?" he asked.

The stranger surveyed the four of them in turn, studying with great curiosity the exoskeleton that Apis wore, before returning his attention to Cormac.

"You came down in the lander—from Dragon," he observed.

"You didn't answer my question," said Cormac, tilting his head to pick up further sounds of rail-gun fire, and the racket of seven or eight grenades going off one after another.

The old man grinned, and spoke over the noise. "You didn't ask the right one. What you meant to ask was, which side am I on?"

"And?" Cormac asked.

The old man lowered his voice to a whisper. "Yours, Agent. Now shall we get the hell out of here? I just led a nightmare over to visit our Theocracy friends, and I don't want to be leading it back again."

Cormac considered for all of half a second, then reholstered his weapon before gesturing to the old man to lead on. He received looks from both Gant and Mika that suggested they were on the edge of questioning his judgement, when suddenly there was a huge crash from far behind them, followed by continuous rail-gun fire and grenade explosion after explosion. Looking back, they saw wreckage fountaining up through the arc lights, then hurtling through the night above them went the engine of one of the landers.

"Fucking hell," Gant suggested.

The lights suddenly went out, but the firing and explosions did not quickly cease—nor did the screams. Something reared up into the night, and there came a sound as of a hundred glass scythes sharpening themselves against each other. Cormac saw something glittering, as of red light reflected from spilt mercury—etched against a background of something wide and black.

"Yeah, hell's about right," said the old man, quickly leading them away.

"That was a hooder," said Mika—again a statement.

"Observant, ain't she?" said the stranger.

A hundred metres further along, where the tall grasses petered out into purplish darknesses of deep rhubarb, Gant caught hold of the old man's arm and halted him.

"Who's that ahead of us?" the Golem asked calmly.

"He's all right, he's just waiting for me," explained the other.

Gant was having none of that—he'd been caught out once that night, and it was enough. He ducked into the dank vegetation, to approach whoever was ahead of them. Behind, there now came only sporadic gunfire, the occasional explosion, but the screaming remained almost constant.

"What the hell is it doing back there?" Cormac asked.

"That's mostly terror you can hear. The screams from the ones it catches would get more muffled."

The three of them stared at him with morbid curiosity.

He shrugged. "They normally eat grazers that have toxic structures layered in their skin, bones and flesh, so of necessity they eat slowly and meticulously. I'm told it takes them a while, so a human victim will die some time after being stripped down to the bone."

"Muffled?" asked Apis, clearly fascinated.

The old man brought a cupped hand down on the palm of his other hand. "By its hood—that's what it traps you under."

It didn't require the superb senses Gant possessed for him to realize there was something decidedly odd about that old man. Even so, Gant reckoned on the stranger not meaning them any immediate harm, else why had he revealed himself? Also, whatever the old man was, it involved some high-level Polity tech—little to do with the hostile Theocracy here. Probably the man who was lurking just on the other side of this small, perfectly circular, mossy clearing offered no immediate harm either. But Gant had heard something, felt something . . .

Was instinct, intuition—or any other of those intangibles humans believed in—recordable? For Gant this was not some rhetorical question to stimulate interesting debate—it was a question that lay at the core of everything he was. If these intangibles did truly exist, then perhaps others like ego, self, soul . . . In the end Gant had to wonder if he was really Gant, and to find the answer to that he needs must pursue things neither solid nor easily defined.

The unseen man was good, very good for a human: he was so still that all Gant could detect was the very slow and easy cyclic breathing, and the even beat of his heart—its rate attesting that though the man knew Gant was present nearby, he wasn't allowing himself to get over-excited about it. Before the others could catch up, Gant stepped out into the clearing.

"You can come out now. I know where you are," he said.

The man's heartbeat suddenly ratcheted up very high. Gant could only presume this meant he himself was about to be attacked. As he leapt forwards directly towards the half-seen figure, a hand shoved him aside and he ducked the folding stock of a pulse-rifle. Turning fast on the boggy ground he caught hold of the weapon, withheld an instinctive strike at the other's momentarily exposed neck, and consequently got the heel of a hand smashing into his nose. But the fight had a foregone conclusion: Gant lived in a Golem Twenty-seven chassis so however brave or skilled was his opponent, it was like matching a lion against a battle tank. Ignoring the blows that rapidly slammed into him, Gant picked the man up and threw him out into the clearing. He was instantly up, and a dagger clanged off Gant's head and went whickering into the flute grass. Light from the tumbling moon then suddenly ignited the tableau.

"What the hell are *you* doing here?" Gant asked. "You know, you never possessed much finesse, even when you were alive," Thorn told him.

The carrier lay where she had brought it down, almost entirely filling a squerm pond. From underneath the vehicle the writhing and scraping of segmented bodies rose and fell in flurries of skittering hissing, as if the creatures were pursuing a long-running argument down there in the darkness. Standing upon the ramp that descended from her carrier to the muddy ground, Lellan surveyed the horizon through her image intensifier, and wondered just how long the pounding would continue before the ground attack began. The presence of the laser arrays had negated for both sides any need to accumulate both armour and air power on the planet's surface—on her side because it would provide too easy a target and be too easily destroyed, and on theirs because the arrays had provided ample firepower. The same rules however did not apply to the Theocracy army on *Charity* because, as she understood it, its purpose was armed insertion on Polity worlds in that mythical time when the godless Polity supposedly collapsed. Stanton's activities had managed to prevent the enemy getting any armoured vehicles down, but some kind of air force had been dropped from one of their capital ships and was heading this way.

Lowering her intensifier, she surveyed those of her forces ranged here behind the embankment. They had a window of some two hours before the fleet of attack ships came in over the Theocracy lines, and were using that time to best advantage.

The commissary was up and running, with huge aluminium pots—that had come from she knew not where—now boiling over a number of those wonderful Polity heaters, and squerms were being dunked, then their cooked and separated segments handed out. She liked the fact that her troops were stuffing themselves with great hunks of meat considered a delicacy up on the cylinder worlds, where it was served only on small sesame seed biscuits; and something more than that on other worlds where it was sold as a bottled food essence. She liked the fact that here and now, so many workers recently freed were for the first time eating the product of their own killing labour.

Beyond this commissary area, the troops had erected many tents, in or around which they were either sleeping or preparing their weapons. Rail-guns had been mounted all the way across the embankment, but only those guns that could not be fitted on some kind of vehicle, because static targets made short-lived targets. The two remaining tanks were still workable, and Lellan was now debating with herself about whether or not they could be used, since they moved slowly and again made easy targets. Perhaps it would be best to leave that decision to each tank's own commander.

In the end her hopes for the coming attack rested mainly with Polity technology. Against an airforce and thirty thousand aug-linked, fresh, highly trained—and also trained in higher gravity—Theocracy troops she could only field a scattered force of ten thousand tired fighters, a few hover-aerofans, and her grounded carrier. Never expecting to be able to come out onto the surface in full force, to fight, the Underworld had never really geared to that eventuality, so, though there was no lack of weapons, they did have a shortage of breather equipment, ration packs, and quite simple things like warm clothing. Lellan cursed the fact that the ten thousand she now had on the surface was one fifth of the number she could have fielded had she possessed the equipment. And she hoped that these two newest additions that were coming had been worth their weight in the breather equipment *Lyric II* could have carried.

Polity technology levelled the playing field a bit by giving her troops communications of an equivalent sophistication to the Dracocorp aug, and weapons either equivalent or better. The pulse-rifle was more sophisticated technologically, but the Theocracy rail-gun performed the same function with an efficiency that was little different: that function being to put holes in people. Her first hope rested with the "hand-helds" that John had brought them in his last smuggling run. These light missile-launchers would be a boon in the coming air attack. With their magazines of five armour-piercing missiles that could run on intelligent targeting, Lellan knew her forces would be able to take down quite a few attack craft—but that wasn't enough. With so little cover for her troops and the impossibility of digging foxholes in the boggy ground, she wanted the air attack over quickly, as she was well aware of the devastation that daisy-cutter and multiple-warhead munitions could wreak, let alone a tactical nuke. She needed more of an edge, and the two who should have arrived here only a little while ago would hopefully provide her with that edge.

"Polas, where the hell are they?" she asked into her helmet comlink.

From the concealed control room in the mountains Polas replied, "It took longer than I thought to upload to them."

"Is there a problem with them?" she asked.

"Not with them, just with our gear. They each received the five-thousand-hour package we sent through the U-space transmitter, and all recent data. They would have sucked it up in seconds, but it was our system here that screwed. It was glitching because we just went realtime on our broadcast to the Polity, and we were also sending the increased ballot figures."

"Someone's replied?" Lellan asked, her previous queries going out of her mind.

"Yes, it's an AI dreadnought and it's boosting our signal into the runcible system for us." Polas could not keep the delight out of his voice. "Also, in preparation for orders from Earth Central Security, it's on its way here—ETA one hundred solstan hours."

Lellan was dumbfounded. It was working, it was actually working . . . but still there was much work to do if they were to survive this.

"Have you now finished with the uploading?"

"Yeah, and our two new friends are on their way with just one diversion, to ferry your brother to you as he's not that far out," Polas replied.

"Then my brother is in for some harsh words here for delaying them. The Theocracy line is only ten kilometres away from us," said Lellan, not yet managing to put as much bile into her words as was her custom.

"It was not your brother's idea," interrupted a voice that was unfamiliar to her.

"Polas? Polas, who is this?"

Polas replied, "That was CED Forty-two. It was its idea to fetch your brother."

"I thought they were supposed to *obey* orders," said Lellan.

"We do obey orders," came back doubled voices. Then one went on, "We have been monitoring the situation. No attack possible from Theocracy forces during our approach time . . . We approach now."

Three dots resolved in the sky. One of them was an aerofan, on which rode John Stanton. On either side of him, flying sideways on, with weapons and detection devices scanning all around, came the cylinders of the two heavy-armour AI drones he had brought from *Elysium*. Observing these objects Lellan well understood now what John meant when he explained that Polity AIs loved their euphemisms: CED stood for Controlled Elimination Device.

During their descent, the drones swung into upright positions on either side of the aerofan, so that when Stanton finally stepped from it, the appearance given was of a man stepping between two pillars—only these pillars advanced with him as he approached Lellan.

"Not a good uniform to wear around here," she said to him when he was close enough for her to see he was dressed as a proctor.

"I'll change in a minute," he replied, nodding towards her carrier. "But first let me introduce to you CEDs Forty-two and Forty-three."

Lellan felt a bit uncomfortable being required to address two armed and armoured cylinders that showed no characteristics of life, but then she was not so well travelled as her brother.

"I don't like that," she said. Then, when her brother gazed at her questioningly, "Forty-two and Forty-three. If these are AI, and accepted as being alive, then they should have names." She stepped forwards. "Which is which?"

The drones had now settled to the ground on either side of Stanton. He glanced at each of them, then shrugged. "I don't rightly know."

Lellan studied the one to her right, trying to find some feature on it to focus on in place of a face. Eventually she focused on a collection of lenses and antennae clustered below the panpipes missile-launcher on its end-cap. "You will henceforth be known as Romulus," she said, then turning to the other drone, "And you will be known as . . ." she hesitated, a twist to her mouth, "Ramus."

"Very funny," muttered Stanton.

Ignoring him, Lellan said, "Welcome, Ram and Rom," wondering if she *should* be welcoming what looked to be the future of warfare.

Disgusted at his own excess—at his uncontrolled feeding and growth—Skellor concentrated on organizing his resources and properly preparing himself. The underspace package the ship's automatic systems had intercepted whilst he had been growing, and to which he had given his dissembling reply, he metaphorically put to one side. Thereafter he refined his internal structures and created storage like giant fat cells for excess materials; he burnt out waste and honed down systems to their optimum efficiency. It was while he was collating and cataloguing all useful sources of information inside the ship, to incorporate them into himself, that he found Mika's database and inspected it with fascination. Gazing through Jain structure, he then recognized the corpse of his calloraptor/human hybrid and immediately knew what to do with some of the excess he now contained—and plunged Jain filaments into the hybrid corpse.

Incorporating human DNA had been a mistake brought about by lack of imagination and resources, but now, utilizing the complex calloraptor trihelix, he knew he could make something much more useful. Isolating what he required was the work of a moment, as were the subsequent processes of meiosis and recombination. Almost with a shrug he tore out the walls of Medical, and expanded the space there to take a huge polyhedral framework of Jain structural members. To the junctures of polyhedra he pumped raw materials and, in their passage through nanotubes and nanofactories, they knitted into complex organic molecules. Small pearls sprouted and grew as they were pumped full of the required nutrients. Then, at the last, Skellor opened nanotubes into microtubes to transfer the already well-developed zygotes he had grown into the awaiting eggs. Raptly watching the growth of this army of his creatures, he found himself more reluctant to disengage from the process than he had been before. With slow grinding force of will he forced his awareness out from the warm internals of the ship and himself, out to his interface with the harshness of space. Here he observed the system and what he had done.

The planet itself could have been the twin of Neptune, and now would bear a closer resemblance as the debris from the shattered moonlet spread as it followed the moonlet's original orbit. Coldly, Skellor calculated that this debris would form a complete ring in one hundred and twenty years solstan—the five largest surviving chunks of the moonlet acting as its shepherds. But what did any of that matter? With that same grinding strength of will he forced himself into a higher awareness of the present, and realized it was time for him to stop playing with the power he now possessed, and to use it. Employing the conventional ion manoeuvring thrusters, he drew the *Occam Razor* away from the debris and closer into the sun itself. For a time he felt as one great beast wallowing in the harsh radiation, then he forced his attention back to the underspace package he had earlier put aside. Once again he felt something like dry laughter echoing inside himself—knowing where this communication was from.

Five thousand hours of secret holocording, filming, and depositions—in fact recordings in every medium available to humanity. Those same hours, which he viewed in less than one hour realtime, told him a lot about his destination, but it took him a while to understand the purpose of the transmission. Subsequent communications from someone called Lellan, and transmissions of realtime events on the surface of the planet, brought home to him what it was all about. As did the meticulously recorded ballot of the indigenous population, which clearly made their wishes known. The five thousand hours detailed *atrocities* and the *unjust* rule of a Theocracy. This was a cry for help directed towards the Polity. These people *wanted* Polity intervention.

Annoyingly, the signal might already have got through to the Polity—but no more. His reply to it and his offer to act as a signal-boosting station had been immediately accepted, and someone called Polas was grateful in the belief that the signal was now being relayed into the heart worlds of the Polity. This would all give Skellor time to get a lot closer, where he could more easily employ the signal-blocking technology of this ship. Chuckling to himself—inside, for his face no longer had the ability to show expression—Skellor gave his instructions, and smooth as a snake the *Occam Razor* slid into underspace. They would certainly get intervention on this world called Masada—but he didn't think they would like it.

16

Certain now that the boy was deeply asleep, the woman tiptoed away to her seat in front of the screen and reopened the book. She did not like to act the censor, but this picture book was definitely now out of the realm of Disney and into that of some psychotic relative of the brothers Grimm, and she suspected that some of the later stories had a greater potential for bloody distortion. The one she chose now was entitled "Four Brothers in the Valley" and the initial picture was far from ominous, displaying as it did the four good Brothers themselves making ready for their journey.

"Yeah, right," said the woman, wondering if there might be a hint of AI to this book. She reached out and touched the top of the text column, and the Brothers moved now—talking to each other and laughing. The woman cleared her throat—slightly embarrassed to be speaking to herself—and began to read.

"Four good Brothers set out upon a journey to find and bring finally to justice the Hooded One. Brother Stenophalis wore armour of aluminium and carried a thrower of iron. Brother Pegrum wore armour of brass and carried a sword of light. Brother Egris wore armour of iron and carried the caster of thunderbolts. And Brother Nebbish wore his armour of faith and carried in his right hand the Word of God and His Prophet."

The woman paused as the book clad each of the brothers in the required garb, and set them on their way. It all seemed like a happy scene from some wonderful tale in which right and justice would triumph. She tried fast-forwarding the text but it just wouldn't move.

"I see," she said, then read on.

*

Three of them came over in the first pass, and turned the entire area occupied by the rebel tents into a brief morass of fire and flying dirt. Lellan guessed that this was just a probing attack, however. The pulse-cannon, on the one remaining tank, spat up from its place of concealment close beside the embankment. One of the fighters—a wedge-shaped, one-man craft with swing wings, and enough weapons pods to give it the appearance of a tern with a very bad fungal infection—flared briefly and then became a line of white-hot fragments tumbling across the sky. Another of the fighters bucked as if an invisible hand had slapped its back end, then overcorrected and nosed straight into the ground—the following explosion sleeting mud even as far as where she and her brother were dug into the embankment.

"I'd get out of there, Carl. They'll have you spotted now," said Lellan.

Stanton lowered the intensifier and glanced round at his sister, as he listened in on the man's reply.

"It'll be the carrier they hit next," Carl replied. "We'll take a second shot at them, then leave the pulse-cannon on automatic."

Stanton nodded to her his agreement with Carl—the Theocracy fighters would take out preselected targets to begin with, before raining down the real shitstorm.

In the second pass came five of the fighters, low this time—then turning away from the swarm of missiles released. The carrier leapt out of its pond on the first scattering of explosions, and came apart on the next. Only small fragments reached the ground, as was the similar fate of another of the fighters.

"Now we get our heads down," advised Lellan.

The fighters came in low again, flying directly along the embankment this time, high-powered rail-cannons opening up to create a long swarm of explosions that wiped out every weapon the rebels had mounted there. Still more fighters came hurtling in low over the flute grass, into the face of pulse-cannon fire from Carl's tank. A row of explosions stepped through the grasses towards the tank, and on the final explosion it ceased to fire. Lellan hoped the pulse-cannon had been on automatic—hoped that Carl was still alive.

"Polas, speak to me," she said.

"Main body is coming in right now with the big bastards behind—three of them," came the reply.

"Remember, everybody." Lellan addressed her troops scattered through the flute grass. "When I give the order, you cease firing and let our friends deal with the bombers."

A full wave of attack aircraft came in only shortly after she spoke, and their numbers darkened the sky.

"Kill them," she hissed.

All through the long grasses, troops cast aside the flak blankets they had been lying under, shouldered their handhelds, and began firing. Soon there was more light in the sky than the predawn sun had managed, and a constant rain of wreckage. Stanton led the way out of their foxhole, brought his hand-held to his shoulder, and just held its trigger down. There were enough targets for each of his five missiles to find one. Amid the grasses there came explosion after explosion, as cluster shells dropped, and even though a counter in the corner of her visor was ticking up just how many of her people were dying, she knew it could be a whole lot worse. On the big bombers following, there would be daisy-cutters—wide-area antipersonnel weapons—and probably enough of them to kill off most of her little army.

"Ram and Rom, are you ready?" she asked.

"We were *created* ready," came the ironic reply.

Gazing at the chaos filling the sky, the wreckage and burning fighters falling to earth, Lellan decided that now was the time.

"Cease firing and go for cover," she ordered her troops, knowing that the only cover they had out there was under the Kevlar-filled blankets. She continued, "Drones, the sky is now yours."

The two cylindrical war drones burst from where they had buried themselves in the soft ground far to the right flank of Lellan's army. Immediately they performed a strange ballet around each other as they hurtled up into the sky. Then suddenly lines of violet fire began spewing from one end of each drone, so that they seemed tumbling torches. Unseen through this, their missiles speared out with horrifying accuracy, and all across the sky the fighters were disintegrating. Lellan observed some fighters turning to attack the two rising cylinders, but they were nowhere near as manoeuvrable as the drones, which simply slid aside and obliterated their assailants as they went past. It wasn't all one-sided though; the two drones were jerked about by the occasional hits they suffered, then one of them lost its APW in a brief flare. But they continued to rise, their course coming to intersect perfectly that of the first bomber. The lumbering giant did not stand a chance, and the explosion that cut the sky was twinned by the flare of sunrise, which heralded the sudden attack of the Theocracy infantry.

Suddenly their ATV was full of people, and Eldene felt angry at her space being invaded—then suddenly confused about why she felt thus.

"Slow and easy," Thorn advised her. "Take us round the other side of the crater."

"Did it work?" she asked, almost too shy to look round at the intruders as she spun up the vehicle's turbine.

"Spectacularly," said Thorn, but she could tell he was angry about something. She watched him as he turned to the four newcomers. "Let me introduce some old comrades," he said to her. "Ian, Mika, and my old friend Gant—who is dead."

Eldene was busy wondering about the yellow-faced boy in the big suit, before Thorn's final words impacted. She did not react, however, merely turned her attention back to the screen and set the vehicle in motion. That she felt confused again came as no surprise to her—she'd been in a state of confusion right from the moment she had seen Fethan ram his hand into Proctor Volus. As Thorn returned to the back of the ATV, the strange boy moved up beside her and studied the controls she was operating. She gave him a tentative smile and he returned it tiredly, as he took hold of one of the support handles fixed above the screen. She could sense he felt more comfortable here.

"Dead or not, he looks mighty well to me," commented Fethan in reply to Thorn's brief acerbic introduction.

With the vehicle getting up speed, they all either grabbed handholds or quickly folded down seats, as the inclination took them.

"You angry because you forgot about my memplant?" asked Gant.

Thorn grimaced. "I don't know myself why I'm angry." Still showing some irritation, he sat down by the weapons console and swung the targeting visor across his face, probably to hide his expression.

"Angry or otherwise, I need you getting me up to speed concerning what's going on here," said the one called Cormac, and Eldene felt her spine crawl at the sound of his voice. She glanced round at him and took in eyes as unforgiving as lead shot, but then he smiled at her and suddenly the coldness was gone. All she could do was turn away and concentrate once again on her driving.

"Oh, I can tell you all that, Agent," said Fethan.

"Please do," said Cormac. "Beginning with why you keep on calling me 'Agent.'"

"Last I heard you was an agent—didn't think you'd retired," said Fethan.

"You know me?"

"Know of you, who don't? You're Ian Cormac—not what I'd call a *secret* agent."

"I've never been considered that," Cormac replied. "I'm a . . . facilitator, and it is sometimes useful that I'm recognized. Polity secret agents wear a different face every day and often they are Golem . . . or something else." He eyed Fethan.

"The name's Fethan," said the old cyborg. "I'm a facilitator too."

"Well, facilitate away and tell me what the hell's going on down here."

As Eldene manoeuvred the ATV around the edge of the crater and into a clear bright day, Fethan tersely detailed all that had occurred over the last few days.

"So nice to encounter old friends," muttered Cormac, when Fethan told him about John Stanton—though Eldene could hear no pleasure in his voice. Finally, some time after Eldene had stopped the ATV and powered it down, Cormac observed, "So it seems Lellan is caught. She cannot stay hidden in the cave systems because of the approach of this Ragnorak device; she cannot destroy all the Theocracy forces on the surface because that would result in a nuclear strike being used against her; she cannot lose against said forces because there would be no taking of prisoners; and in the end all she can do is drag the battle out and hope for Polity intervention here."

"But that's on its way, apparently," said Thorn. He gestured to a coms helmet lying on the floor at the rear of the ATV. "Polas earlier sent out a message of encouragement to the troops, informing them that Lellan's U-space plea for help has been picked up and relayed by an ECS dreadnought—and that same ship is now on its way here."

Cormac went very still for a moment, then asked calmly, "And the name of this dreadnought? Was a name ever given?"

"Yes, a Line Patrol ship, name of the *Occam Razor*," Thorn replied.

The euphemistic description might be tactical withdrawal, but it was called defeat in any other language, and no less than Lellan had expected. Hit and withdraw, hit and withdraw—all the way back to the mountains, where she knew she could extend the conflict almost indefinitely. To stand, out here against a force three times their number would be plain suicide. Perhaps it would have been a different matter with a few more of those war drones, or if the two she did possess had not depleted their power supplies to the point where they could just about keep up with her army's retreat, and manage an occasional counter-attack whenever Dorth's forces pushed to break the line. In the end, she desperately needed Polity intervention, because without it they would do nothing but lose.

I've destroyed us, I've completely destroyed us . . .

"Tell me again, what did he say?" asked her brother.

"He said that the *Occam Razor* is now in the hands of Separatists who are unlikely to pass on our shout for help." She remembered that cold voice speaking in her ear, then the confirmation from Fethan and the man Thorn.

"No, what exactly did he call it?" Stanton asked.

"He called it a subverted AI dreadnought, and our signal to the Polity has been updated to include that news."

"That should bring them running," said her brother.

Lellan gritted her teeth and, feigning tiredness, rubbed at her eyes to smear away the tears that were gathering there. Jarvellis had yet to contact Stanton and give him the wonderful news that the moment they had started sending the updated signal, something had begun blocking it.

"I need to wear it to prevent the gravity here killing me," explained Apis.

"Why? How would it kill you?" Eldene asked him, glad of those long talks with Fethan which had given her some understanding of "gravity" and how it was absent in space.

Mika, seated on a rolled-up sleeping bag opposite them, intervened, "His people . . . they adapted to living in space. Amongst other things, his bones would never have supported him in this gravity since, as he was then, he would have collapsed and died almost immediately."

Apis, who had been showing little inclination to sit down and continued to prowl around inside the ATV, snapped his attention towards Mika. "You say 'would' and 'was'? How different am I now?"

Mika inspected the laptop, via which she monitored the Outlinker's body through his exoskeleton. "You are improving, though I would not yet advise the removal of your suit. It is possible that you would survive it, and that the nanomycelium reconfiguring your body would be thereby stimulated to work harder, but such a move is still not recommended."

Leaning back in the driver's chair, Eldene studied the boy further. She had no idea what Mika was talking about, but it added to the mystery. This boy had previously lived on a giant space station and now had to wear the strange bulky suit to support his weight in Masada's gravity. Eldene could not conceive of anyone more unlike herself.

"Tell me about *Miranda*," she asked him suddenly.

Apis froze in mid-stride, and Eldene noted how Mika was now studying him analytically. Obviously there was a great deal more to learn here, more than she had overheard in previous conversations before the others had left the ATV—Fethan to check where the hooder had gone, and the other three to find out about this "dracoman."

Apis turned to her and replied doggedly, "What's to tell? *Miranda* was an Outlink station that was the home for millions of people, and now it is just so much floating wreckage."

Before he could turn away Eldene persisted, "But how was it destroyed?"

"A nanomycelium," said Apis, perhaps hoping her lack of knowledge might silence her.

"You have fungi here." Mika made it a statement, in her accustomed fashion. Then, with a flash of self-annoyance, "*Do* you have fungi here?"

"Orepores," Eldene replied, not quite sure of what relevance that was.

"Describe them," said Mika.

"Round things." Eldene's hands shaped something spherical in the air. "Up in the north, they feed them to the pigs."

"What you are seeing in these orepores is the fruit of a plant—the plant itself is a spread of thin fibres, some of which are too small to be seen. These fibres are called mycelia—that's the plural of mycelium."

"A fungus destroyed a place with millions of people in it?" Eldene asked, disbelievingly. Then she pointed at Apis. "And he's got one inside him?"

"It's a little more complicated than that," replied Mika, glancing towards the door of the ATV as the warning light came on beside it, then hingeing her mask back into place.

Eldene raised her mask too, and noted how Apis did not even have to—apparently devices in his clothing detected any drop in the oxygen content of the air and raised his visor when necessary.

"That was quick," said Mika, standing up and turning towards the door. Eldene had been aware that the woman was very annoyed earlier, when ordered by Cormac to stay with the ATV—so they did not later have a struggle again to drag her away from the remnants of Dragon. She wondered if they had found this dracoman they had been talking about. What she did not expect was for the door to slam back, and to hear a thud like a cleaver chopping into a cabbage.

For a moment she could not fathom what was going on. Mika suddenly bent over, something smacking into the wall above and behind her. Only when blood welled through the torn fabric of Mika's suit did it become evident that someone standing outside had put a shot through her. With a bubbling groan Mika collapsed to her knees. She turned to say something, but only blood came out of her mouth.

The Theocracy soldier who now stepped through the door seized Mika by the shoulder and hurled her outside behind him, even as he turned and fired at the Outlinker. Apis grunted as the single shot slammed him back against the wall. It was only as he began sliding down it, his eyes turning up in his head to show only the white, that Eldene thought to reach for her weapon. In a second the soldier had knocked it away, shoving the snout of his weapon up under her chin. Eldene froze, recognizing the gun—it was the very same type as the one Fethan had given her when they first left the crop lands and she knew exactly what it was capable of.

"What about this one?" asked a voice from outside.

"Leave her. She'll be dead in a minute, if she's not already," said Eldene's captor.

A second soldier, then a third, entered the ATV, and after a few minutes a fourth one closed the door behind him. The one threatening Eldene drew away his weapon as he raised his visor. It was strange, thought Eldene bizarrely, how little you could tell from someone's appearance; for she had frequently encountered plump, cheerful-looking proctors who were always ready with quips and funny anecdotes whilst they were lashing the skin off a worker's back. This man, though, with his hawkish face and twisted mouth, looked just plain evil and obviously relished the fact.

He gestured towards Apis with his weapon. "Check him out. He may still be alive."

"Should have gone for a head-shot, Speelan," said one of the newcomers.

"No, I think the good Deacon will be wanting words with these people."

"What about the other four?"

"We forget about them. I don't want to hang around here any longer." He glanced through the front screen. "Maybe that hooder will deal with them."

Eldene kept silent. To speak out, she knew from long experience, only brought unwanted attention. Transferring his gaze back inside, Speelan stared at her as if he had momentarily forgotten her presence. Almost negligently, he drew back his pistol and cracked its barrel down against her temple.

Sometimes it did not help to have the kind of mind in which blocks of logic keyed together so precisely, and life-and-death facts revealed themselves like nasty gumboils. Dragon was gone: buried under a mud slide that had raised the soil level in the pit of the crater by at least ten metres. But what the hell did that matter one way or the other, with what was coming?

"I can't and I won't believe Scar is somewhere underneath that," said Cormac, as ever revealing nothing of what he felt.

Gant disagreed. "He may be there still, but if he is you can guarantee he's not dead."

"Unlike some I could mention," said Thorn.

"I'm not dead," Gant pointed out. "How can I be? I'm a machine."

"This isn't helping," said Cormac before Thorn could formulate a reply. "Gant, why so certain he's not dead?"

Gant shrugged, turning so that the snout of his cradled APW pointed down into the slowly refilling crater. "As you know, he doesn't need to breathe oxygen. As I understand it, he is just more efficient when he is surrounded by a gaseous oxidant he can breathe in to burn his body's fuel. He can use other types of atmosphere, as we've already found out, and I know that without any atmosphere to breathe he can run on his body's fuel for days before simply going into stasis."

"And how do you know all this?" Cormac pretended interest in the answer.

"Mika. Not from her directly, but she's built up quite a database on dracomen." He nodded towards the crater. "He could be in stasis under there—or digging his way out even now."

"But do we wait to find out?" Thorn asked.

Cormac studied the two men while he considered the present situation. Maybe they should stay and wait to see if Scar would indeed dig his way out, because it seemed to Cormac that any other efforts were futile. The Theocracy would destroy the rebel army, either on the surface in straight combat, or underground—along with the rest of the population there—by kinetic missile. And it was all such a pointless drama: the squabblings of geese in a pen outside an abattoir. Cormac felt hopeless: he'd fallen so far he was not sure he could get back up again.

"Do we wait?" he asked Thorn.

"To achieve what?" asked Cormac.

Perhaps this time the bitterness came through in his voice for both Thorn and Gant looked at once confused, then not a little apprehensive.

"We should return and help Lellan Stanton," said Thorn. "She's an effective commander, and committed to the Underground cause. She deserves whatever we can give her, little as that may be."

Only half-hearing what the man had said, Cormac continued to stare down into the crater. Then something clicked. "Lellan Stanton," he said, turning back to the pair of them.

"Yes?" inquired Thorn.

"You arrived here in John Stanton's ship *Lyric II*. But how did you get through undetected?"

"The ship had chameleonware. Pretty sophist—"

"And this ship is now up in the mountains somewhere?"

"Yes . . ."

Cormac turned away from the crater and set then a rapid pace back towards the ATV. Hurrying along behind, Thorn asked, "You're thinking of hitting that Ragnorak device with it, aren't you?"

Cormac let out a brief bitter laugh, abruptly halting and turning to face the other two. "Maybe I haven't painted a clear enough picture with what I already told you, or with what I passed on to Lellan. Perhaps that's because I left out one pertinent fact." He glanced at Gant. "Your partner understands, I think, but I'm not sure he's allowing himself to understand completely."

"Skellor?" said Gant, and Cormac thought the pale grimness overtaking the Golem's expression was a superb emulation of the real thing.

"Precisely, Skellor. Skellor subverted an AI dreadnought using Jain technology, and is direct-linked to a crystal matrix AI, and surviving. I told you this, and I told Lellan this, though I'm not sure just how much of it she understood."

"Enough to know he's dangerous," said Thorn.

"Dangerous," Cormac echoed leadenly.

"Tracking him down and stopping him will become an ECS priority—something like him cannot be allowed to exist," Thorn added.

"Yes," said Cormac. "And if Earth Central knew about him, it would already have ECS tracking him down and stopping him, as you put it. You see, the fact I've missed out is that only we few on this world actually know about Skellor. We few, and whoever else we may have spoken to here."

A look of horror slowly crept into Thorn's expression as he realized what Cormac was telling him. "He's coming here . . . he won't risk letting the news get out . . ."

"He killed the *entire* crew of the *Occam Razor*," reminded Gant.

Turning to continue on his way, Cormac added, "And he's coming here in control of that ship, one capable of incinerating everything on the surface of this world, so, frankly, fuck the stupid little rebellion here and its suppression. If Lellan's transmission doesn't get through, I have to get off this world and warn the Polity. And with me off and away from here, and Skellor knowing about it, maybe he won't be so inclined to hang around killing every human being in this entire system."

For a second or two Cormac stared at the clearing, and the two tracks disappearing into the flute grasses, and wondered which particular deity was crapping on him from a great height.

"Mika!" shouted Thorn, running forwards to stoop by the bloodied form sprawled on the ground. Signalling Gant to move over to one side, Cormac pulled his thin-gun and followed Thorn out into the clearing. Glancing at Mika, he knew she had been wasted: the position of the bloodstains informed him of the entrance and exit wounds, straight through her chest on the right-hand side. Poising his gun to one side of his face, he looked down at the tracks left by the ATV. Who was responsible? That girl? Fethan? Whoever it was, he would kill them.

"Look, stop fussing. I'm all right."

Cormac registered the voice, but recognizing it just did not coincide with any kind of reality for him. He watched, dumbfounded, as Thorn helped Mika to her feet. He then stepped forward and caught her under the elbow as she appeared about to collapse.

"I'm all right. I'm all right," she insisted.

"You've been hit," protested Thorn.

Cormac tried to reassess what he was seeing: the spread of blood around one hole under Mika's right breast and a greater leakage of blood around a larger hole ripped out of the back of her jacket, the insulating layers splayed out like a thistle head: entrance *and* exit wounds. Thorn clutched Mika as she slumped drunkenly against him. Cormac used the barrel of his gun and one finger to gently part the ripped fabric on her back. There was plenty of blood there, but underneath it a nub of purplish-pink flesh like a deep-rooted tumour.

"Physician heal thyself," he murmured, releasing the fabric and stepping back, as he remembered the creature he had killed in Skellor's laboratory—the creature Mika had later studied so intensively.

She glanced round at him, a certain amount of calculation creeping into her woozy expression. "It was soldiers, Theocracy soldiers."

At Cormac's shoulder Gant said, "Survivors from that lander, probably."

"You well enough to walk?" Cormac asked her.

Mika nodded.

"Then we follow them—at least they're heading in the right direction."

"What about Fethan?" asked Gant.

"He'll catch up, I assume."

Later, as it became apparent that Mika no longer needed anyone's help, and while Thorn moved ahead with Gant, Cormac leaned close to her and said, "Doctor, you've been taking some of the Outlinker's medicine?"

"I have," Mika replied.

"And it's good, I think?" he said.

"Better than good," said Mika, tapping her finger against the contents indicator on her oxygen bottle. The indicator had gone from green through orange to deep dark red, which meant that the bottle was completely empty. Cormac wondered if, when she had earlier changed her bottle for a new one, she had done this just to keep up appearances, or if, like Scar, she operated more efficiently when breathing a suitably gaseous oxidant.

Even though Speelan delivered his report with a terseness and rigidity of control that was almost machinelike, Aberil could feel fear coming through the link. Whether that fear was of the hooder still out there, or of the expected wrath at Speelan's loss of a lander and twenty-four men, Aberil could not make up his mind. In fact he felt no wrath, just curiosity at what their two captives—one of them obviously an Outlinker—would have to say for themselves. The Proctor, Molat, who had been brought to him earlier in the day, had provided no information of tactical value and was beginning to bore him. Only the story about the siluroyne had been interesting because Aberil had known the Proctor was lying about something, but sufficient pressure had only revealed Molat's silly guilt over the sacrifice of an underling. Obviously Proctor Molat had reached the limit of his advancement within the Theocracy.

"Where is the rebel army now?" he asked generally.

"The other side of the swamp basin, First Commander," replied his logistics officer.

"So they're retreating towards the mountains, without us having to force them across the basin. It's too easy really."

"I don't think Captain Granch thought so, First Commander." The officer looked pale as he turned towards Aberil. "He has ordered the withdrawal of his remaining fighters."

"Granch, what do you think you are doing?"

The captain of *Gabriel* was quick to reply.

"My apologies, First Commander, but they must return for refuelling and arming, with the spaceport being now unavailable."

Aberil grinned across the room at Proctor Molat who, like everyone else in the command lander, was listening in.

"The one bomber we have retained is reactor-run so I do not see why it should be recalled. I am in fact adamant that it should not be."

Granch: *"First Commander, it cannot get in close enough, with those Polity machines there."*

Aberil: *"Granch, I know perfectly well that your son is aboard that plane. It will, however, remain in high orbit until required—is that understood?"*

Granch did not reply, but the logistics officer spoke up. "The bomber is returning to high orbit, sir."

Aberil turned to Molat. "You see: softness, lack of faith, nepotism. We must be harder and harsher if we are to proudly take our place in the universe before God." Then, before the Proctor could reply, Aberil turned away from him and sent over the ether, *"How far away are you now, Speelan?"*

"I have the command vehicle in sight, and will be with you within minutes, First Commander," came Speelan's abrupt response.

"Bring your prisoners directly to me here," Aberil instructed. *"And without further damage to them."*

Before Speelan could reply, another presence intruded:

"Aberil, I do hope you are not allowing your little games to distract you from your main objective."

Aberil was out of his seat in a moment. The sheer force of the Hierarch's communication almost had his head ringing, and he felt that force could not be explained just by the message being transmitted through a high channel, formerly used solely by the Septarchy Friars.

"This is not a distraction, Hierarch. I predict that by tomorrow's sunrise Lellan's forces will be perfectly positioned in the mountains for our nuclear cleansing. But I am very much concerned at why an Outlinker would want to be down here on the surface, let alone how he got here."

On a lower channel now, Loman spoke conversationally. *"Don't spend too much time finding out, if you consider it that important, use drugs, not torture."*

Aberil did not let himself object to having to forgo the pleasure of causing pain. He in fact became suddenly wary of making any response, for even on the lower channels there was something quite overwhelming about the communication from his brother.

"Your will, Hierarch."

The link closed, and Aberil swallowed and took a deep breath. In the expressions of Molat and the others, he read a hint of fear and bewilderment. They had all registered the contained power in the Hierarch, and all of them understood it not at all.

Not for the first time, Carl reached up and patted at the Polity wound dressing on the side of his face, as he stared across the swamp basin to the flute grasses on the far side. If they just opened up with their pulse-rifles they would be sure to hit some Theocracy soldiers, just as no doubt the reverse applied with the enemy and their rail-guns, but ammunition was not limitless on either side and the thick grasses had a tendency to eat up the momentum of any projectile, be it an iron slug or a pulse of ionized aluminium.

"These bastards have got thermal mesh in their body armour," said Uris, staring at the screen of a small heat detector he had managed to salvage from the tank before the vehicle got pulverized.

"Either that or you were imagining things," said Targon.

In suitable reply, a full clip of rail-gun slugs hammered into the flute grass to the right of them, with a sound like the revving of a worn diesel engine. They went face-down, flak blankets pulled over them, as the high stalks collapsed in pulpy dark green fragments. A short way off, someone started screaming, then something suddenly curtailed their noise. Another fighter broke cover and tried to dash across a channel inhabited by low plantain to seek better cover on the other side. A second rail-gun opened up, and the man just flew apart.

"Where the fuck is that coming from?" asked Carl.

Hunched up with his flak blanket over his back, Uris studied his heat detector, then abruptly gestured with his open hand. "Ten metres back from the far edge—just left of the plantain channel over there!"

"Beckle!" Carl shouted.

Beckle did not need specific instructions. He quickly set up the small mortar he had been given—as an inadequate replacement of his pulse-cannon on the tank—and fired off three rounds. Two explosions blew loam and roots into the air, but in the detritus thrown up by the third explosion Carl, as he stood up, was sure he spotted a human arm. He and Targon raised their weapons over their heads so as to clear the flute grass, and opened fire on the same area where the explosions had occurred. But then grenades started detonating to their left and the rail-gun fire became so intense that the air filled with a sleet of blasted-up mud and scraps of vegetation. Carl did not need to give any orders—his men were running again, forcing their way through thick growths of grass, stomping across already trampled spreads of moist purple leaves, staggering through muddy channels so wet that only black plantain could root there. Off to their right, others were running . . . falling . . . dying. In their own little group it was Targon who went down first. Turning to fire back behind, he looked down for his weapon and, in numb surprise, only saw his two arms ending at the elbow. He began to yell, but collapsed into the ground like a statue made of red ash, a burst of fire just eating him away.

"You bastards!"

Beckle fired the mortar and its shell slammed into a half-seen ground car on which a heavy rail-gun had been mounted. The explosion flung the vehicle out of view, and someone ran screaming to one side—his Theocracy uniform burning, then blazing white in an oxygen fire as his air bottle ruptured. The recoil of the mortar saved Beckle's life, as it sprawled him on his back below a fusillade that cut down the cover he had been fleeing towards. Carl drew his fire across, the glowing shots from his rifle acting like tracer fire as he brought it to bear on the soldier who had been shooting at Beckle, and cut him in half.

"This is not good!" bellowed Uris, dragging Beckle to his feet.

"We're outnumbered and outgunned," Beckle spat, as the three of them dived for cover in a small crater lying behind a mound of tangled roots and earth obviously hinged up from it by a recent explosion.

"Well, you know we can't win down here, so we just have to prolong it," growled Carl.

"Be nice to come close, though," said Beckle.

"Shut up, Beckle," said Uris, then grabbed Carl's shoulder and directed his comrade's attention to the other occupant of the crater. The woman sitting there was clearly an ex-pond worker, for she still had a scole attached to her body. That she was now cradling most of the contents of that body did not seem to affect the scole at all—it was still looking healthy as it drew on what remained of her blood. Keeping his head well down, Carl crawled over to her, and felt for a pulse at the side of her severely burnt neck. After a moment he shook his head and slid back to join his companions.

"Fucking things," said Beckle and, drawing his cut-down rifle, put two shots through the creature. Smoking, it pushed itself up on its legs, as if trying to retract its head, then it sagged with red oxygenated blood pouring out of it.

"It probably finished her off," observed Carl, for a moment staring beyond her with the thought that her blood had sprayed a very long way—before realizing that what he was seeing was red gallish nodules breaking out on the grass stalks, and recognizing how utterly irrelevant human drama was to the indefatigable grind of the seasonal engine. Then, peering out of the crater in the opposite direction, he ducked as a burst of fire sprayed them with fragments of the same budding growth.

"They'll put a grenade in here any moment now," warned Beckle.

"We keep running, and hold at the mountains," said Carl, relaying the orders he had just received.

"I agree with the running bit," muttered Beckle.

"Lellan?" Uris asked—he had lost his helmet earlier and did not have Carl's coms access.

"Yes," Carl replied.

"Great, she's got a plan," said Beckle as they piled over the edge of the crater and ran for the next scrap of cover.

In such horror and chaos Carl felt it necessary to believe that someone, somewhere, knew what they were doing. To think otherwise would be to give in to despair.

When consciousness eventually returned it did so with disorientating abruptness. One moment Apis felt he was waking again from the cold-coffin in the lander, then as memory caught up he assumed he was waking on the floor of the ATV. Both scenarios turned out to be incorrect as he lifted his head and looked around. He was in a lander, sure, but not the one in which he had arrived upon this planet. This particular one had its cockpit sealed off with a heavy door, some sort of fibrous matting on the floor, and cold blue lights set in the ceiling. With a grunt of effort, Apis sat up and heaved himself to a position with his back resting against the cold wall. Eldene, sitting with her arms wrapped around her shins and her chin resting on her knees, observed him silently for a moment before saying, "You haven't noticed, have you?"

Apis wondered if she was referring to the bloody dressing on her head. He reached up, with an arm that seemed wrapped in lead, and felt the back of his own head—where it had slammed against the wall of the ATV after the Theocracy soldier had . . . pushed him. He lowered his arm and stared at it, then lowered his hand to his chest and probed it with the fingers of his other hand.

"I warned them that to remove it would kill you," Eldene added.

They'd shot him, but the exoskeleton had prevented the bullet penetrating, which would not now be the case for he no longer wore it. He continued probing his chest, his stomach, his biceps, his thighs. His body felt utterly wrong to him; instead of feeling just bone and gristle under his skin he found a layer of flesh, the shapes of muscles clinging to his bones like parasitic growths—in fact, utterly unaccustomed bulk. Whenever he moved, these muscles moved with him—it did not seem quite real to him that the muscles were doing the moving, and were actually part of him.

"Why aren't you dead?" Eldene asked.

Apis considered the complicated—and to his mind incredibly dangerous—procedures involved in standing up, and rejected them for the moment.

"The mycelium working inside me—it's rebuilt me as a normal-gravity human. Mika said that the exo was taking less and less of the strain, but I wasn't sure what she meant by that."

Mika?

"Where is Mika?" he asked, not sure he wanted to hear the answer.

"Dead," said Eldene flatly. "They shot her, then just threw her outside like a sack of deaders."

Apis stared at Eldene, but somehow just could not find the energy to feel sorry. He'd lost his own people, he'd lost his mother, and Mika he had not even known for very long. He just did not have the grief to spare for her.

"Where are we now?" Apis asked, wanting to know more than just their location.

"On the way here, I saw hundreds of landing craft, and a great tent-like building erected between some of them. We're in one of those craft by the edge of the tent. We're prisoners of the Theocracy."

"What will they do with us?" he persisted.

Eldene stared at him for a long moment, then shrugged. "Probably torture us to death. There aren't any jails down here."

"They are . . . insane," began Apis. But Eldene's attention had slid over to the light beside the airlock, as it faded down from red, through orange, to yellow. Apis felt a rush of adrenalin and used it to push himself to his feet. Every movement, it seemed to him, was fraught with peril; he felt his weight as a hugely unstable load, and wondered what bones might snap in trying to support it; he felt his muscles sliding under his skin, and expected agony as they tore free from their anchor points; the clicking of his joints and the buzzing pins-and-needles in his feet terrified him, but somehow, without mishap, he stood.

The soldier who stepped through was the very same one who had burst into the ATV and shot him. Naked as he was, Apis felt incredibly vulnerable when the man negligently levelled the same weapon at his chest.

"You're standing, I see, which means that you"—he looked at Eldene—"are a liar."

Apis immediately felt affronted, was about to argue her case, but she caught his eye as she stood up too, and gave him a slight shake of her head. Only as she did that did he truly begin to understand their situation, and only then did something very adult and very callous—probably born in that moment when he had opened the airlock on twenty-three of these people, and nurtured by all that had subsequently ensued—rear its head inside him and look around. He kept his mouth closed and wondered how much he could depend on his body in this gravity; and also wondered if he would get an opportunity to use it.

Receiving no verbal reaction to his words, and perhaps expecting none, the man threw something compressed in his left hand at Apis, then stood aside to allow another guard to enter the cell. Apis caught the balled-up material, let it fall open, and saw that he had been given a set of overalls.

"Put them on," ordered the soldier.

Apis pulled on the overalls, his every measured movement carried through with the utmost care. As he finished, struggling to do up the primitive buttons down the front of the garment, he felt exhausted. When the soldier waved them both towards the door, where more guards waited with plastic ties for their wrists and hobbles for their legs, Apis felt their chances of escape fading.

Now, with the advance of the Masadan month, Calypse was being overtaken by the sun in their erratic race across mackerel skies, and had half its vast bulk sinking into misty oblivion behind the horizon as the sun set off to one side, throwing it into brown and lead silhouette. For a brief time the gas giant seemed fused to the body of the planet itself, and with its slow descent any watcher might expect the earth to tremble with this shift.

"What happened?" Fethan asked, looking intently at Thorn.

"We could as well ask what happened to you," said Cormac, studying the old cyborg's ripped clothing, and ripped skin, and noting the exposed hard white ceramals and carbon materials of his internal workings.

Thorn said, "The other two were in the ATV when it was taken by Theocracy soldiers. We are following them now."

Then, gesturing to Mika, "We've got a trace on the boy's exoskeleton."

Fethan nodded, for a moment observed the blood on Mika's clothing, shot Cormac an inquiring look, then turned his attention to Gant. "Can you move fast, Golem?" he asked.

There was too much intensity in his question for Gant to ridicule it, and he merely nodded an affirmative. Cormac glanced from Fethan to Gant, then back again.

"Trouble?" he asked.

Fethan grimaced. "We've got a hooder only two hundred metres off in that direction." He gestured beyond tall shadowed stands of flute grass, then stabbed a finger at Gant. "Me and him are gonna have to be live bait to lead it away." He turned to Thorn, Cormac and Mika. "You three have to keep going—as fast as you dare. Stay out of the flute grass as much as you can, and keep an eye up for heroynes." He stabbed a finger to the darkening sky.

"We *could* just kill it," suggested Gant, holding up his APW.

"Nah, you couldn't," said Fethan, eyeing the weapon. "That'd only piss it off."

Knowing that the gun Gant held was capable of destroying other Golem and blowing holes through steel walls, Cormac wondered if Fethan knew what he was talking about. Before he could comment on this the cyborg went on.

"That's one big fucker out there," he said. "You might manage to blow enough segments to kill it, but more likely you'd just burn it a bit, before it ripped you apart . . . Look, we gotta go."

Gant glanced at Cormac for confirmation. When Cormac nodded, Gant followed the old cyborg out into the falling twilight. Turning back to the others, Cormac said, "Let's keep moving." Then, noticing how Thorn was staring after the two rapidly departing figures he said, "They're machines, Thorn. You'd never be able to move as fast, so you'd soon get exhausted."

"Machines," Thorn repeated, then, "you know, he never told me he'd had a memplant. He lay spread in pieces on the floor of that cavern on Samarkand, and I didn't know . . . A recovery team must have come along later."

Cormac reached out and slapped his arm. "Come on."

Thorn shook himself and did as bid.

They travelled, where possible, down plantained and mossy channels, or across areas where the grass had been grazed down to its roots; and, where that was not possible, they progressed cautiously and with weapons to hand through areas of thick flute grass. All the time they were aware of the drama being enacted elsewhere by Fethan and Gant. Distantly they heard rushing sounds, as of a maglev train or a sudden burst of wind through dry foliage. At one point the reddish arc-welder flash of Gant's APW ignited the twilight, and Cormac had to wonder if the Golem had disobeyed instructions or perhaps used it just as a distraction.

"What did he mean blow enough segments to kill it?" asked Cormac as they rested briefly.

Mika was busy checking her laptop to once again locate where they should be going—roughly adapted software using the increase or decrease in signal strength from Apis's exoskeleton as its direction finder. "I only read a little about hooders, and then only out of morbid curiosity, rather than because I expected to ever encounter one," she said, hooking her screen back on her belt and turning to look at Cormac. "As I understand it they have some of the physical attributes of earthworms, with their brain not just contained in the head but spread down the length of their bodies. It would be difficult to kill a creature like that hitting it in only one place."

"What else can you tell me about them?" asked Cormac, firmly believing that once horror had been named and described, it ceased to be quite as horrifying.

"*I* can tell you a little," said Thorn.

Cormac nodded for him to continue.

Thorn went on, "Stanton told me that nothing less than an APW or missile-launcher could kill them. Apparently their shells are something like a carbon composite, and they're mainly made up of that and fibrous muscle. Both disperse the heat from lasers, and small arms just make a lot of holes. Apparently one of them once grabbed a proctor and his aerofan, which was a hundred metres up in the air."

Cormac lowered his mask and took a sip from his water bottle—his mouth now feeling a little dry. "How fast?" he pressed.

"Stanton claims they can move as fast as Terran predators. I checked that with the *Lyric II* AI. They can move even faster of course, at about a hundred kph, over this sort of terrain."

"Great," said Cormac, his previous theory about describing horror now in pieces around his feet. "Shall we keep moving?"

17

Nodding to herself the woman read on, "First into the mountains came Brother Stenophalis and high and low he searched for this enemy of the faithful, and at last found him in the Valley of Shadows and Whispers."

The picture displayed the Brother as some huge godlike incarnation astride the valley in his gleaming armour—a rail-gun of unlikely proportions clasped in his gauntlets, its ribbed power cable attaching to a lumpish power pack on his belt. Below him in the valley was something shadowy and insectile, and just looking at this made the hairs stand up on the back of the woman's neck.

She read: "Standing over the valley with the sun gleaming on his polished armour, he demanded of the monster, 'Come forth and face me!'"

Abruptly the woman realized what was giving her the creeps: the picture had taken on depth—a 3-D effect. She pressed her finger against the page and it felt cold.

"The Hooded One came forth, and Stenophalis smote it with good iron, until the valley rang and echoed with the sound of their conflict, and avalanches of rock thundered from the heights."

The Hooded One coming forth was horrible: it was a hood of chitin containing shadow and just a hint of eyes. Brother Stenophalis turned and his rail-gun spat lines of black that just dissolved into this shadow.

"But iron availed him nought against this monster, and in the end it dragged him down into the Valley of Shadows and Whispers, and his armour parted like butter under the knife of the Hooded One."

The woman stared at the scene displayed, and decided she had been right to check out this story before letting her son . . . experience it.

Hierarch Epthirieth Loman Dorth stood in his favoured viewing room in the Tower of Faith and considered what he had wrought. The Council, in their terror of him, had voted him more and ever more powers, and had thus all but destroyed their own effectiveness in office. But this was how it had always been: when Amoloran had become Hierarch, the Council had done the same thing and, over the forty years of his rule, they had their powers restored by simple delegation because, in the end, no one man could effectively control the entire Theocracy. Knowing this, Loman smiled to think of those bureaucrats who had attempted to load him with endless detail in order to expedite this natural process. Even now he could see what remained of them floating beyond the arc of the Up Mirror. What none of them seemed to realize was that, with the higher channels now available to him, now *controlled* by him, the option to take the place Behemoth had prepared for itself was now also available to him.

The Hierarch closed his eyes and felt the vast potential of the *Gift* spread through three cylinder worlds, and down to his forces on the planet surface. Poor Aberil, even with all his abilities and training he had never wondered how the likes of Brom had managed to gain such stature so rapidly on their home worlds. He had not grasped that the *Gift* was as hierarchical as the organizations it was generally employed by, like the Theocracy itself, and just as he, Loman, had clawed his way to power in the physical world, so had ascendancy in the world of the *Gift* swung over to him once his usurpation was recognized. The moment Amoloran had died, there had been that first flush of additional power as command channels opened to him—excepting those occupied by the Septarchy Friars. And now, with the Friars gone, he could truly feel the growth of his mental dominion; now he no longer had to give orders at all, as the world ordered itself to his will. Just his very expectation of something had people scrambling to provide that something, often not knowing why. However, he realized that this was only the beginning—there were even greater levels of control he could reach, there was greater ascendancy to be gained. He was coming to understand that the ultimate level—the plateau—was the entire Theocracy acting as one beast, with one mind that was his own.

Throughout the realm of the *Gift*, Loman extended his power, and the feedback to him was gratifying and sometimes disconcerting. From the surface of the planet he felt a distortion, the essence and the sense of Behemoth undissipated: something there, but something not easily definable nor grasped. From deep space he knew rather than sensed, distantly, other conglomerations of Dracocorp augs, and out there he did sense, between him and them, another distortion, something odd, twisted. Here in the tower, it amused him to feel the fear of those who served him closely. It amused him to look through their eyes and see how, to them, he had gained weight and wore small scales upon his skin, yet to himself he had changed not at all. What a strange world he had wrought, and with what senses now could he view it all—the senses of all his subjects.

"Ah, you are at the apex, Hierarch Epthirieth Loman Dorth."

The words wormed into his consciousness, almost as if forming from the random sounds of so much that he was himself hearing and hearing by proxy. With part of himself that seemed nothing to do with human senses, he felt something unfolding from quantum vacuum, oozing out like guts pressured out through a small hole in someone's torso, or perhaps like crystals growing in cooling magma—something vast, and more powerful than anything should have the God-given right to be. Even Behemoth was a pale monster indeed by comparison.

"Who? Who?"

On *Charity*, Loman looked through the eyes of technicians and saw something they had hoped very much never to see. On the *Witchfire* he felt the horror of Captain Ithos as, trapped against atmosphere, he observed missiles hammering down on him from deepest space. One after the other he felt the brief sad protest of lives snuffed out in seconds, as hugely powerful induction weapons and full-spectrum lasers scoured away small ships of every kind between the cylinder worlds, almost like a blowtorch singeing away pin feathers from three plucked birds. Briefly he heard the babbling panic of the crew in the lone bomber with its cargo of atomic weapons. Briefly he glimpsed on a screen in the *Gabriel* the trace of radioactive vapour which that craft became in high orbit over Masada, and felt the keening grief of Captain Granch.

"*I am Skellor and you see me in total, Hierarch Epthirieth Loman Dorth. Now, release your hold or I must free your hand.*"

Loman saw the sheer appalling size of the *Occam Razor*, and watched it pulverize the entire technical infrastructure of the system in mere seconds. The small ships of the fleet were burning, cargo carriers and small transports burning when not already become glowing debris. He felt the sudden groundswell of prayer from the *Gabriel*, the *Witchfire* and *Ducking Stool*, just before the missiles struck and the burning shells of these ships rolled around the planet, breaking up and contributing their substance to the growing scrapyard orbiting Masada. Then the afterglow of another titanic explosion bled across his vision, and he saw Ragnorak in harsh and brittle detail tumbling end over end down into the gaseous sea that was Calypse. Through the eyes of screaming men he saw girders and huge frameworks twisting against vast storms of colour. Then the image blinked out upon a fading wail and, alone again, he felt something reaching out from that terrible ship: something that wanted to get inside his head, something that wanted to seize from him the reins of power, absolute power.

"*You cannot have it.*"

That seemed the limp and ineffectual protest of a child caught playing with something it had been disallowed, but Loman reached out, tightened his grip, and resisted.

"*I have **work** to do.*"

Hanging on with all the sweaty grip of his mind, and the will that had allowed him to climb so high, Loman wondered at this huge emphasis on this entity's *work*.

"*This is mine! You have no right!*"

Glinting sunlight from its golden hull, and sucking away sunlight with grey Jain architecture, the *Occam Razor* slid closer, dominated the face of Calypse, and turned silver and ebony towers on its hull down towards the cylinder worlds of the Theocracy. In vacuum, the titanic flash of lased light was invisible, but it became visible as the first coherent wave slammed from the Down Mirror of *Faith*, only microseconds before that mirror disintegrated. The full horror washing through him in hot sickness, Loman leaned out and stared down into the eye of the cylinder world as the wall of fire ascended. He started screaming, as for each passing second he felt tens of thousands of his citizens incinerated; and at the last moment, when the firestorm obliterated Amoloran's Tower and the Up Mirror, he felt all contact and all power plucked from his grasp, and thought that truly cruel, before brief incandescent agony snuffed his life.

Rolling through space: *Faith* was an empty container, burnt out on the inside. The side of the big lander opened down into the tented area, in which men were now erecting dividing walls. Speelan led them round stacks of packing cases, then held up his hand to halt them by the ramp leading up into the lander itself. From the room beyond, which was obviously some sort of control centre, walked a man with a blank face and ball-bearing eyes, below flat black hair. He seemed surrounded by a kind of dead atmosphere as he descended the ramp. Perhaps that was the smell of death, Apis thought, then dismissed the idea as being far too romantic.

"My name is Aberil Dorth, Deacon and First Commander of the Theocratic forces of Masada." He gestured to the first man. "You have met my lieutenant, Speelan. And your names are?"

Apis considered keeping his mouth shut, but then wondered what point there was in that—doing so he realized would only bring about the expected violence earlier.

"I am Apis Coolant, M-tech number forty-seven of Outlink Station *Miranda*," he said, quietly pleased with his fulsome title.

Aberil Dorth stared at him for a moment, then turned to Eldene.

"I'm Eldene," she said simply.

Aberil abruptly stepped towards her, reached out and with one finger parted the stick-strip of her shirt to expose her small breasts and the dressing underneath them.

"Pond worker," he observed.

Eldene did not reply, she just closed her shirt once he removed his hand, and waited.

Aberil turned back to Apis, then pointed to something lying in a heap beside the ramp, which it took a moment for Apis to recognize as the exoskeleton he had been wearing previously.

"That suit," said the Deacon with obviously more than passing interest. "How does one remove the limiters?"

Here it comes, thought Apis: the first question he could not answer. "I don't know," he said, then seeing an opportunity to turn things away from himself, he tipped his head towards Speelan. "He killed the woman who did know."

Aberil glanced at Speelan, then abruptly reached out and closed his hand around Eldene's throat. "You are an Outlinker," he said to Apis. "You manage to stand down here which, as I understand it, is quite exceptional, but I don't want to risk killing you just yet." Eldene was now choking, fighting for breath. She tried kicking him, but he easily avoided her attempts. Apis started to move forwards, but one of the guards caught him by the hair and struck him lightly across the back of his legs with a gun barrel, so that Apis went down on one knee.

Aberil went on, "So, every time you either refuse to answer, or give me an answer that displeases me, I will do something unpleasant to your companion here. Is that understood?"

"Understood," said Apis, tears in his eyes.

Aberil gave Eldene a shake. "The correct reply from you, Outlinker, is 'Yes, your reverence.'"

"Yes, your reverence," said Apis.

Aberil released Eldene and she too slumped to her knees. Another man walked down the ramp—this one wearing a less obviously military uniform—and stood observing things from a wary distance. Aberil turned to him. "Ah, Molat, hand me your stinger."

"There's no need for this," said Apis, as the man unhooked a white baton from his belt and passed it across to Aberil.

Aberil glanced at him. "What there is need for or otherwise, I will decide. Now, my first question: how did you get here?"

"I was rescued from the station *Miranda* as it started to come apart, by a ship called the *General Patten*," Apis replied.

Aberil stared at him for a long drawn-out moment, then abruptly turned and drew the stinger across Eldene's stomach. She gasped, then clamped down on her pain, obviously determined not to scream.

"It's the truth!" Apis yelled.

"Truth," Aberil sneered, "is the *General Patten* was obliterated, and everyone aboard was killed. You arrived here with Polity spies and saboteurs." He slapped the stinger against Eldene's face and, even though determined not to, she screamed. "You came here to undermine the true faith and spread rumours and lies!" As Aberil pulled back the stinger to inflict it on Eldene once again, Apis found a strength in his legs that surprised him. He launched himself from the ground, driving himself headfirst into the commander, had the satisfaction of feeling air whoof out of him, and seeing him fold up, stagger back, then go down on one knee. Then the guards were dragging Apis away, and Aberil was standing up again, holding the stinger ready, his expression vicious.

"Oh, I tire of questions," he sneered.

Then suddenly it seemed as if the whole atmosphere inside the tent shuddered, and every one of the Theocracy soldiers jerked as if just dealt a blow. Apis watched Aberil's expression slide from viciousness to bewilderment and shock. Suddenly men were howling and dropping to the ground. Aberil bent face-forwards, his hands pressed to either side of his head. Molat was on his knees, his hands clasped as if in prayer, while Speelan was in a foetal curl with his arms over his head. Apis gaped about himself and wondered what madness had descended on them. He glanced across at Eldene, whose expression mirrored his own shock, but who reacted much faster: she stood up and, moving as fast as the hobble allowed her, went over to an open toolbox that was being used by those erecting the partitions. In a moment she had found a pair of wire-cutters to quickly release herself from her bonds, before returning to free Apis too.

"What's happening?" Apis wondered, as he discarded the severed plastic from his wrists and ankles.

"Oxygen and masks," said Eldene curtly.

Apis surveyed his surroundings. The others were all clawing at the biotech augs they wore, and the tent was filling up with a smell like seared pork. She was right: now was not the time to ask questions but to act.

Sastol grated his teeth as he watched the rebels being seemingly sucked away by the evening shadows. This squad with which they had been playing a lethal game of hide-and-seek all day was made up of only three men, formerly four, yet they had taken out seven of his own men—including Braden, who had burnt up in his own oxygen supply. Sastol wanted to go after them exclusively, but orders were orders and they must continue their slow advance beside the swamp basin, allowing the rebels to flee back and entrench themselves in their damned mountains.

"Okay, hold it here. Seems they're all pulling back now ."

Over his aug he could feel their disapproval at the order, but only Donch felt any inclination to voice it:

"It would seem like an opportunity not to be missed."

Speaking out loud, now that the rebels were quite obviously not trenching in to a new position or turning round to attack, Sastol said, "An opportunity for what?"

"Filling their backs with iron slugs, I think," said Sodar, who had moved in to crouch at his right side, dropping the heavy rail-gun—which had somehow survived the destruction of the car—on the ground before him.

"It was a direct order from Aberil Dorth. Do you want to take it up with him?" Sastol asked.

"That would not be so wise," admitted Donch, moving in close on Sastol's left. "How long do we have to hold these positions?"

"For as long as necessary—probably throughout the night." He did not look at either of his comrades, but he guessed their feelings on the matter. The previous night had been bad enough for them, what with Dominon killed by a mud snake, and that siluroyne which had charged them just before dawn, but the worst of it was the screaming during the night, the result, they had discovered, of an entire squad being taken out by a hooder. They knew about hooders— who could not know about such creatures of gruesome myth and horrifying reality?

"We'll dig in here as best we can, and wait it out," he announced.

"Seems crazy to let them get to terrain they know, and where they can easily find cover," persisted Donch.

"Do you doubt the First Commander's capabilities?" Sastol asked, staring at him directly.

"Not to his face I don't. I want to keep my extremities intact."

Sastol grinned at this and turned to Sodar. "What do *you* think—" he began, but then spoke no more, because of the sheer powerful horror of what he now knew to be happening.

"Oh my God, what is that?"

Donch's was the clearest voice of them all, over the huge rush of screaming communication that filled all channels. Sastol slapped his hand against his aug and screamed too, adding his voice to the thousands doing the same all along the Theocracy front.

"Faith . . . *it was* Faith . . . *Gone!*"

But even that was not the worst. Where once Behemoth had worked his twisted wiles, before being pushed away by the chanting and praying of the Septarchy Friars, something else loomed—and it wanted him, it wanted them all. It was reaching . . . Sastol tried to find something to hang on to, as his aug squirmed against his head and something utterly putrid overran his senses of smell and taste. Trying to mould solidity out of the indescribable, he saw himself standing with his men—and that *something* reaching out for him like a huge multibodied mud snake. But how could he fight it when there were no weapons to fire, and no physical body to fire them at? Then Donch showed him the way. Yelling angrily, the man reached up and tore away his aug, hurling it to the ground, stamping it into the ground. Sastol reached up for his own, levered his fingers behind it and pulled down. The pain, in the end, was nothing compared with the relief of blessed silence.

Seconds passed—or perhaps minutes, or hours. Sastol gazed around at his men, and those men of the neighbouring squad. Most of them were now on the ground, groaning, writhing . . . though some were ominously still. Others, who like Donch and himself had torn away their augs, were still standing and mobile.

"What the hell was that?" Sastol shuddered, unable to accept that he had *seen* one of the cylinder worlds gutted by fire, and then felt some monster trying to take control of his mind.

"Fucking Satan," Donch replied.

Sastol nodded; perhaps that was the only answer he would be getting down here. He stepped out into the open and looked around. Some of the prostrate members of the other squads were now standing again. The rattle of gunfire had him down in squat as he observed the captain of the next squad stumbling out into the open as well, with one of his men following. The second man suddenly raised his weapon and blew the captain to the ground in a bloody mess of pieces of flesh loosely connected by skin and ligament.

"What?" Sastol turned to his own men, saw Donch's horrified expression turn to one of pleading, then saw him spin away in a wheel of blood. Sodar. It was Sodar who had fired—the man standing upright with mechanical efficiency, but his face twisted as if he had suffered a stroke and the aug on the side of his head now seemingly fused to it, looking ashen grey as if burnt. Sastol observed that same ashen tint on many heads turning with the same dead eyes and wasted expressions. Without hesitation he stepped back into the clearing his squad had made earlier, snatched up his weapon and pack—and ran.

Polas read through and understood every piece of information with which his instruments presented him. Through the probe he watched *Faith* die, and the source of that death coming insystem, before the probe whited out. Then his instrumentation went insane in a way he immediately recognized as viral takeover.

"Lellan, I'm getting a viral takeover of com. Shut it down immediately!"

Whether that got through or not he had no idea, for all the equipment shut off together for a couple of seconds, before clicking back on. Then, over to his right, he saw that the holojector tank had dumped its usual program, and no longer displayed the complicated dance of the Braemar moons and other worlds and worldlets that made up the Masadan system. Instead a wasted face appeared, seemingly wearing a helmet of grey wood and blood-infused crystal.

"I will not hamper your communications," spoke a decidedly creepy voice from Dale's console. "Just as I will not hamper your inclination to kill each other. I have only one wish, and that is for you to give me Ian Cormac. Do that and I go away."

"What is this, Polas?" said Lellan from her hide in the foothills.

Polas quickly replied, "The *Occam Razor* just arrived. Are you getting the picture I'm seeing over your helmet screen?"

"I am."

"Skellor, I think."

A slow handclap issued from Dale's console—she had now pushed her chair well back from the machine, as if it might bite her—and the image of Skellor, in the tank of the holojector, grinned nastily.

"Ah, I see I have been expected—which means you know where Cormac is. Let me have him and I will let you all live."

Whilst watching Skellor speak, it took a moment for Polas to realize that an old stripfilm printer across the other side of the room was operating. Moving out from behind his console, he walked across to it and observed the printout.

"I *would* hand this Cormac over to you," Lellan told Skellor, "but even though we have been in communication, I have no idea where he is."

The message coming through the printer read:

"Sophisticated viral subversion programs all over—attempted trace of U-space transmission—closing down all links and now maintaining a watching brief—Jarv."

Knowing that the printer possessed its own small memory, Polas reached down and pulled its optic cable, before reversing the stripfilm and wiping it. Returning to his console he was uncomfortably aware of the wall-mounted security camera following his progress.

"That is a real shame," said Skellor with the sincerity of a crocodile. "That means I'll just have to kill some of your people, and keep killing them until you find Cormac for me."

"Lellan, you have to get to the caves," advised Polas. "That ship is more powerful than the arrays ever were."

"I don't think that's our main problem," Lellan replied. "We've got Theocracy soldiers attacking right now, but there's something very wrong with them." She went on to say something more, but her voice became heavily distorted, and all comlinkage then blinked out.

. . . viral subversion programs . . .

Polas turned to look at the head in the holojector as it stared out with seemingly blind eyes. There were no Theocracy soldiers here for Skellor to subvert—but there were people to kill.

"All of you, get out," he said to the personnel in the operations room.

Dale looked up at him, her expression puzzled. Perhaps it was better that way, for when white fire blasted in through the panoramic window, no one but Polas realized what was happening. And he knew it only for the half-second it took for the fire to reach him, and vaporize him along with the rest of the mountain peak.

Jarvellis lifted her hands away from the instrumentation of *Lyric II* as if it had suddenly become infectious—which, in limited electro-optical ways, it could well have been.

"Lyric . . . are you all right?" she asked, frightened that she might not believe the answer.

"No worms got through," replied *Lyric II*'s AI. "The Skellor based its attack program on information gleaned from the cylinder world it burnt out. In my terms it was pretty crude, but only crude in the way that dropping an atomic bomb on your enemy is cruder than creeping up behind him with a knife."

"Your metaphors leave something to be desired," Jarvellis replied, glancing over her own shoulder. "Remember your language."

At least the ship's AI was still hers, but things were far from all right. For the first time in a very long time Jarvellis felt frightened and indecisive. She knew that this was not wholly because of what the AI had referred to as "the Skellor"—it was because for the very first time in ages she had so much to lose.

John was out there somewhere, but to try and communicate with him would be madness—locating both him and herself for this Skellor. And then there was this ship of theirs and all it contained . . .

"Lyric, what must we do to stay safe?" she asked, more for confirmation than because she did not already know.

"Move," replied the AI. "The Skellor will have realized that was only a secondary emitter in the mountain peak, and we do not know how much information he obtained from there."

AIs were just so cold: never unable to answer any question posed. Jarvellis thought of Polas in the nursery in Pillartown One, laughing as he pushed around toy tanks for a blond-haired child. She tried to scrub the image and to concentrate on the instrumentation before her.

"We have to assume that Skellor now has full use of all the scanning instrumentation possessed by that dreadnought. In Polity terms it is an old ship, but it's still way beyond anything the Theocracy owns . . . or rather owned," she said.

"The Skellor may have more than even that," commented the AI.

"Why do you keep calling him 'the Skellor'?"

"Because it is not human, it is not AI—and because I want to," it replied.

John had deliberately programmed *Lyric II*'s AI for a certain cussedness, but sometimes Jarvellis wondered why they couldn't just have one as nice, polite and helpful as those she encountered on other ships.

"Very well," she went on, "he may even have more . . . in fact he must have, to have been able to subvert a Polity dreadnought." Jarvellis could feel herself clenching up inside. There it was again: indecision stemming from the fear of making the wrong choice—too much to lose.

"Dammit!" She slammed her hands down on the console. "We just assume a level of technology equivalent to that of the dreadnought. Now . . . this means the chameleonware field should cover us for anything, barring a real close scrutiny, but it will not cover us if we use AG."

"Agreed," said the AI.

Jarvellis stared at the screen, showing her the lake and riverine valley beyond: the looming faces of stone and tangled vegetation, which had changed from the dull beige seen upon their arrival here to dark green and red, lurid purple and light-sucking black. "So we need to use ion drive and gas thrusters to get out of this trap."

"You will then leave an ionic trail," cautioned the AI.

Jarvellis nodded. "But a diffuse one, as I'll only be using the ion engine for lift, and especially diffuse because the blast will be directed down into the river, which will soak most of it up. Would it be better to stay here?"

"On the basis of a Polity technology level, no," replied the AI.

"And if 'the Skellor' has a higher tech?"

"No again."

"Then we move," said Jarvellis.

"What about when you want to move away from the river?" the AI asked, probably annoyed about her little victory.

"There's a hundred kilometres of it before it finally winds out onto the plain. I think we'll worry about that pass when we come to it."

The AI had nothing more to add, so Jarvellis reached out, her fingers skittering across the controls with practised ease. She noted that the AI had, on its own initiative, filled the water tanks with water it had purified from the nearby source, so there was now no shortage of fuel for the tokamac running around the centre of the ship, nor for the ion function of the engines themselves, which now started up with a low thrumming. Outside she saw steam and debris blasting from underneath *Lyric II*, shells and stones splashing into the adjacent pond, and the insectile creatures diving from their rocks, perhaps confused by this sudden shower that appeared to them out of thin air. Taking a firm grip on the joystick Jarvellis gently raised and tilted it, observing on the subscreens the ship's feet retracting and folding away. Without AG, the ship handled like it was wading through glue, but she was more than capable of flying it. She considered telling its other human occupant to strap in for safety, then rejected the idea. She was confident she would not crash this ship; and the only disaster that could befall it would be discovery by Skellor, in which case *Lyric II* and all its occupants would survive only fractionally longer than the mountaintop containing Lellan's operations room.

Aberil realized it was going to burn his mind like fuse wire in a lightning strike; just as it had burnt the thousands in *Faith*, just as it had burnt his brother Loman, and just as it was burning the minds of the Theocracy army upon the planet and making each individual soldier into a dronelike extension of itself. Then something caused the "burn" to pull back from all those within the tented area.

"Outlinker . . . too crude . . ."

After these three words something, which until then had seemed as monstrously impersonal in its slaughter as a pyroclastic flow, became personal and focused. Aberil found a force of will operating more directly, on him, and he could not resist. It jerked him to his feet and pulled his hooked fingers away from their tearing at his aug. Eyes open now, he both saw and felt Speelan, Molat and the others gathering in closer as if this was necessary to bring them into the focus of the now possessing mind.

"The Outlinker boy . . . where is the Outlinker boy?"

All of them turned to survey their surroundings, bewilderment and rage roaring up in a darkness somewhere behind perception, like the oncoming wall of a tsunami. Aberil felt the others overwhelmed by the force—folding in on themselves—but for him the cold hard ideals that had so long ago crystallized his mind served as a bulwark, and he did not allow himself to go.

"I will find him for you."

Suddenly he became the full focus of that attention, and he sensed amusement spreading through the wave like red cracks.

"What a horribly neat mind you have, Aberil Dorth. It's like a Chinese puzzle: all interlocked blocks and distorted shapes."

Aberil was not sure what was meant there. All he was sure of was his recognition of *power*—terrible and godlike. He could feel it studying him, and knew that his life depended utterly on what he said next.

"There is service or death—I can see that. Give me the tools and I will serve."

Threat receded and Aberil now felt some degree of normality return. Around him stood his men: four guards, Speelan and Molat—tired and pale, but not burnt out. He could feel the strength of his linkage through to them, and the ascendance of his aug over theirs.

"These tools are yours."

The presence now mostly folded itself away, leaving only the lightest touch upon him. There were no further threats, because there was no need of them. Aberil knew the consequence of failure, but he also knew that even success would probably bring the same consequence.

"Jerrick here is a trained tracker," said Speelan, clapping his hand on the shoulder of one of the guards.

Aberil nodded and surveyed the other soldiers in the tent. Those that were not obviously dead seemed utterly brain-burned—their augs turned grey against their skulls.

"Then we'll use Jerrick," said Aberil, clapping his hands together. "Let's move!"

Aberil led the way across the large tent, pointing out supplies that should be collected, and pulling breather gear for himself from a rack by the airlock. Out in the falling night he paused and sent to Speelan:

"Where's the ATV?"

Puzzled, Speelan replied out loud, "Over to the right there, but surely we'll need to work on the ground."

Aberil turned to the rest of them. "You," he selected one of the guards, "get in that ATV and take it straight back into the flute grasses."

"For how far?" asked the man.

"You keep driving until ordered to do otherwise," snapped Aberil, reinforcing the order through the new power he derived from his aug. The man turned woodenly and headed for the ATV, climbed inside, and soon they heard the turbine winding up to speed.

"The rest of you come with me."

When they were what Aberil considered was a sufficient distance from the command tent and the landers, he sent the heavily reinforced order for them to tear off their augs, before he reached up and tore off his own.

Snarling, Skellor let run a subprogram he had paused only minutes earlier. One of the towers on the surface of the

Occam began punching lased light down at the surface of the planet, obliterating lander after lander, then Aberil's command tent, and the ATV the First Commander was clearly escaping in. Under high magnification, from orbit, a glowing line briefly cut through the wilderness as plastics and metals burnt in the intense heat, with what little oxygen there was available, before snuffing out. Then Skellor shut the program down and swore at his own stupidity.

Dragon had come down in that area, as was evident from the crater, and the Outlinker boy was also in the area—which meant it likely that Cormac was there too. Skellor felt the rage cycling inside himself. In itself the destruction and death he had just delivered did not matter, because in the end he must utterly expunge the system here of human life and burn every scrap of recording technology to dust, so that no evidence of his existence could ever leave this place. But in this case he had deprived himself of what eyes he had possessed in that area—those Theocracy soldiers in and around the landers who had not torn away their augs—and in that blast could have killed Cormac as well. Seething, he blanked the attack program he'd already downloaded to the whole subverted Theocracy army, then turned them around and set them marching back towards the landers.

"Why don't you just burn it all?"

For the first time in a while Skellor opened his human eyes and looked across the control room to Aphran—tangled in a tree of Jain architecture that had lifted her out of her seat while he had tormented her. It surprised him that she still had enough mind left to pose such a question, as she had become so fragmented it had been necessary for him to disconnect her from any form of control.

"Because I want him. He is the arrogance of the Polity and ECS, and I want him exactly where you are now. I want him to see how wrong he is, to know how foolish it was to frustrate me."

Even though she could no longer act as a submind, he had not yet wholly disconnected her from himself. He could feel her fighting not to speak, not to let what she was thinking flow into communication. And as she fought he felt her separate into two Aphrans: the one who repeated endlessly, *"I love you I love you I love you,"* and the one that now opened the mouth of the naked and ripped human body twisted between ligneous trunks, and spoke in a rusty gulping voice.

"Direct-linked to a crystal matrix AI . . . able to calculate U-space co-ordinates . . . able to control nano-technology bare-brained . . . retarded child . . . idiot savant . . ."

With crystalline scum breaking away from his lips, Skellor opened his mouth and attempted to speak too. When nothing happened he looked at himself internally and realized how much of his human body he had neglected, and with a thought he started repairs. Soon his mouth moistened and he could more easily move his tongue and lips. However, vocal speech only became possible when he started breathing again.

"Why . . . do you say that? You know what I can do to you."

"I love you I love you I love you . . ."

"It is true . . . you have the power to destroy and to build on a vast scale, yet your priority is merely to capture one ECS agent so you can say to him, 'Look at me now, aren't I clever, don't you wish you'd been nicer to me?' . . . It's pathetic."

Skellor twisted the Jain tree tighter around her, and she hissed in agony transmitted directly down her nerves.

"Please please please please . . ."

"Your need to grow is so strong, Skellor, because you are actually so small. You need to control minds so absolutely, because minds uncontrolled are free to see you as you really are."

Skellor suddenly felt fear: she remained so coherent yet he was pumping such agony into her body she must now imagine herself being skinned with white-hot scalpels. He instantly shut down on what he was doing to her and, through the mycelial structures netting the inside of her body and her brain, he gave her an intense forensic inspection. Immediately he observed that it was that other Aphran who was experiencing the pain: the animal, the primordial reptile. Somehow she had separated out the core of her intelligence, somehow . . . suddenly he also realized that there were blank areas inside her, where Jain mycelia went but where he could not sense.

"Not quite so much control as you thought," said Aphran, opening eyes dark with blood, and turning her head so she could study him.

Skellor's reaction was like a whiplash. At the same time as the Jain architecture wound itself closed, crushing and bursting Aphran's body, he concentrated heat through superconducting filaments and pumped pure oxygen through nanoscopic pipes. Broken and coming apart, Aphran suddenly flared magnesium-bright; and when Skellor adjusted for the loss of rods and cones in his eyes, and cleared the afterimages, he saw all that physically remained of her was black smoke congealing in the air. But he could not shake an echo of laughter through a structure that, in that instant, had become as alien to him as it had always been.

The explosion had flung him to the ground and mauled him through thick vegetation, before showering him with a foul mixture of heat-softened rhizomes and mud. Sitting up in that mess, as tendrils of fire flared weirdly through the night sky pursuing escaping oxygen, Molat changed his paper mask yet again, and did not have to look far to realize that he had been lucky.

One of the three soldiers who had been standing behind him had caught one of those flares even as he ran, so that from the back of his head down to his ankles his clothing had been burnt away and his skin charred black. The only part not burnt was that area of flesh underneath the scoured oxygen bottle and the ribbed pipe that snaked round to his mask. Whether or not this man was luckier than another soldier further back, who was a coiled ashen sculpture and quite obviously dead, Molat could not really judge. When the man groaned, and rolled partially to his side to look up at Molat—black skin opening red cracks which immediately began to ooze—the Proctor just wanted to get up and run away.

"That was close," the burned man said, "but God has been kind." He reached round to grope for a fresh mask from the pack attached beside his oxygen bottle. When his fingers encountered bare metal and ash, his expression turned puzzled until, in his groping around, he managed to slough away a hand-sized crust of his own skin. Then his eyes grew wide, and he started to make a horrible keening sound.

Molat closed his eyes and turned away. He wanted to vomit, but his mouth was cast in ceramic and his stomach a ball of lead. With eyes closed he heard the familiar clatter of a rail-gun nearby, the abrupt cessation of the keening, and felt something spatter against his chest. Knowing exactly what had happened, he pushed himself upright, only glancing briefly at the corpse that now lay beside him with half its head gone, and turned to Speelan who was holding the weapon with its cable fully extended from the power pack on the one surviving soldier's belt.

Handing the weapon back to the soldier, Speelan said, "Let's get moving."

Molat asked, "Get going where?"

Aberil now walked into the light cast from the still-glowing wreckage of the landers. As he looked Molat up and down, the Proctor noticed that something, perhaps a fragment of hot metal, had carved a neat coin of flesh out of Aberil's cheekbone, leaving a bloodless wound like a third eye.

"We need to find the Outlinker. Jerrick here"—Aberil gestured to the surviving soldier—"will locate his tracks and we will hunt him down."

"But why?" asked Molat.

"Because I say so," growled Aberil. Then, perhaps noting Speelan's questioning expression, he pointed a finger up into the night and added, "And because that creature up there wanted him for some reason, so he may prove useful to us. We are here now, and by God we are here now for a reason."

Molat averted his eyes from the rampant fanaticism. Personally, he would rather run off and find a hole to crawl into, but he seriously doubted Aberil would let him do that. Removing first from the front of his shirt a piece of scalp with fragments of skull still clinging inside it, he began to trudge after the other three as they moved off.

18

"In his armour of brass, Brother Pegrum came upon the valley and saw how Stenophalis had failed, but was undaunted."

The woman reckoned that, after seeing what had happened to Stenophalis, she herself would be daunted to the point of having to change her underwear. But of course Pegrum had not seen it happening, only the final result—which somewhat resembled a can of minced beef after being hit with a sledgehammer.

She continued with: "Coming astride the valley, with the sun gleaming on the polished brass of his armour, he demanded of the monster that skulked below, 'Come forth and face me!'"

Brother Pegrum looked fine and strong. The woman shook her head, and read on—she suspected there might be some degree of repetition in these stories of the variously armoured brothers.

"The Hooded One came forth, and he smote it with hard light until its scutes glowed like the sun, and below it the river boiled away."

The red beams from the Brother's heavy QC laser spat into the shadowed cowl, but only seemed to make the eyes glow brighter. Deep in that cowl the woman saw things glittering and moving, and wondered how true to life this picture might be.

"But light availed him nought, and out of a great fog of steam rose the monster to drag him down into the Valley of Shadows and Whispers."

Brother Pegrum definitely did not want to go: he was kicking and he was screaming and he was clawing at the mountainsides. The picture reminded the woman of an ancient picture she had seen, long ago, of one of the damned being dragged down into Hell.

"And his armour parted like butter under the knife of the Hooded One."
The woman paused again. "Gross," she murmured.

The flash from the screen left shadows fleeing across his vision and, even though he was some distance from the explosion itself, Stanton's ears were still ringing. From the holocam he'd dropped on top of Dorth's command tent, he was now unsurprisingly getting no response, but he had seen enough.

All communications shut down, only seconds before all those guards he had seen around the landers dropped to the ground, so he was getting nothing from Lellan, Polas or even Jarvellis on what had been going on, but then he didn't need to. Through the holocam he'd watched that bastard Dorth walking out into the grasses with five others, and then those five tearing away their Dracocorp augs only seconds before the hit. It didn't really take much figuring to work out what had happened: some sort of subversion weapon operating through aug software, communications knocked out, high-powered laser hits obviously from outside of the atmosphere . . . so the one Cormac had warned them about had arrived and started throwing his weight around. But Stanton was not going to allow that to distract him. Barring the near-miss on Brom's barge on Cheyne III, this was the nearest he had got to Aberil Dorth in decades, and he was not now going to take his eye off the ball. The only problem was that he needed to cross about five kilometres of wilderness to get on Dorth's trail.

At present the aerofan was useless—its laminar batteries so drained they had not even an erg to spare to run the LCD displays on its console—so Stanton stepped over the side rail and dropped to the ground. He tried not to allow himself to think too deeply about the kind of creatures he had been seeing in quantity during his circuitous journey here, nor to wonder what the hell was stirring them up, but there seemed something odd about the atmosphere of the wilderness—something that felt, incongruously, both alien and familiar, and threatening too. He shook his head and swore. He'd been around too long and in too many shitty situations to get the jitters like this.

Checking the direction-indicator setting of his wristcom, he was annoyed to see it had been completely scrambled by the same viral attack that had knocked out communications. No matter, the line of incinerated landers stretched from horizon to horizon and, so long as he did not go too wildly off course, he would run into that line soon enough, and once there all he needed to do was find one undamaged laminar battery. Stomping straight into flute grasses, he drew his heavy pulse-gun and a laser torch.

"I am the meanest son of a bitch in the valley," he intoned, and tried to believe it when his words seemed to stir something huge in the darkness right behind the spot where he had brought down the aerofan. He went into a squat, and peered back in that direction but, with afterimages still plaguing his vision, all he could see was flute grass and the aerofan. Then there was the rearing of a huge shadow, and something nudged the aerofan aside as it slid past . . . and just kept on sliding.

I'm dead.

He knew exactly what it was: the other monstrous predators here walked only on two or four feet, not on a hundred paddle legs. And other predators he could handle mostly, but not this one. Stanton reversed his pulse-gun up underneath his chin, as the hissing roar moved up beside him and a head like a gigantic limpet shell reared up into the darkness—the shadowed hollow of it filled with the whickering of small sharp movement. Stanton prepared himself: if it came down over him he would pull the trigger—there was simply no other option. Unbelievably the thing slid on past, its segmented body forming a wall of armour beside him that he could have reached out and touched. Then it was gone.

With care Stanton withdrew the weapon from under his chin, releasing it into his other hand. He then straightened out the crackling tension from his fingers. The heat from the laser strike, he reasoned, must have confused it—as it was in the direction of that it was now going. To his knowledge, no one had ever got so close to a hooder and survived. This, he supposed, was another example of what Jarvellis called "Stanton luck." He hoped it would hold out, since he must now follow the hooder in towards the fires.

Inside the bridge pod, Skellor checked, with his human eyes, that all that remained of his command crew was ash and smoke. In the end, he realized, only those things that were utterly of his own creation could be trusted. His eyes now opaquing, he turned his attention outward once again.

The Theocracy army would reach the landers soon enough, but meanwhile there were other matters requiring his attention. Through huge magnification he gazed down on the northern ranges of the single continent.

Hitting the rebel communications centre had been a mistake, for there they had possessed only a secondary emitter, not the actual U-space transmitter, and now his chances of tracing it had become so much less. It was somewhere there in the mountains, but had since ceased transmission, though there was still a ghost of signature for him to work with. Because of this he was able to extend the fractal calculations that fined down its location in realspace as a function of its location in underspace. But even for him this was not easy, as such maths was normally the province of runcible AIs—specifically constructed for the purpose. What he really needed was some eyes on the ground—or at least close to it. The Theocracy army was out of the question, for if he turned them back towards the mountains, the rebels, still scuttling for their caves, would probably turn to counterattack and thus hinder any search. The Theocracy soldiers were rough tools now anyway—the cerebral burn he had used leaving them as little more than automatons—and most importantly, though he could control them, they were, like Aphran, not his own creation and therefore not to be trusted. Skellor had something else in mind.

All of the shuttles inside the *Occam*, from the smallest twelve-seaters to the huge delta-wing heavy lifters, were already bound up and pierced by the growth of Jain substructure, and in some cases with the larger architecture. Luckily he did not require an actual landing on the planet—just insertion into its atmosphere—and those grabships he had returned to their holds *after* the *growth* would be adequate to that task. Through the internal vision of the Jain structure which, like an infinity of fibre optics, could provide him with views anywhere it existed in the ship, he watched the continued growth of the calloraptor-hybrid eggs in their polyhedral framework, before deciding what changes should be made. The alterations to muscle and bone structures took an infinitesimal fraction of a second for him to calculate, but for longer than that he was annoyed that practical considerations had him dispensing with a large proportion of the weight and hence the strength of those structures. Briefly he considered the installation of some form of AG, but found the idea aesthetically displeasing. As soon as he finally reached a decision on what he must do, he did it: Jain filaments darkening the albumen of the eggs as they tore and rebuilt and polished to perfection.

Beyond the Medical section, by using the old mechanisms of the ship, Skellor shifted a corridor so there was a direct connection between that area and the bay containing the grabships. As the eggs turned metallic white on completion of the processes operating inside them, they were drawn in towards the main trunk of Jain architecture passing through that section, and microscopic cilia in their billions conveyed them into the newly constructed corridor, further down which Skellor now grew another spur of architecture to convey them to the bay. Here he glued them into a three-dimensional honeycomb that expanded the grabs of three ships so that in the end it seemed they held boulders of metallic conglomerate. When the doors of the bay finally opened, and the ships blasted out into space, Skellor felt great satisfaction with his creation, and even more so as he began to program sharp little minds. In all, this particular act had taken him five and a half solstan hours—about twice the time it would take him to denude the planet's surface of human life by using the conventional weapons of this ship. But that was not something he wanted to do just yet—not while he was having such *fun*.

Through her light-intensifying binoculars, Lellan surveyed the lower slopes and still saw no more sign of the Theocracy army. There seemed no rhyme or reason to anything the enemy had been doing all night. Earlier they had kept attacking erratically: squads charging from cover in what seemed a co-ordinated attack, then that charge losing impetus once out in the open, where her own troops could use the Theocracy troops for target practice. It had been mad, horrible, and seemed to make no sense at all, yet it had produced an effect simply by attrition, because the Theocracy forces outnumbered hers by three to one. Now, though, the foe were just turning around and walking away. Lowering her binoculars, she turned her attention to the technician, who had Lellan's coms helmet lying in pieces on a nearby mollusc-crusted rock.

"Any luck?" Lellan asked. "Because I could really do with talking to my field commanders sometime soon."

The woman glanced up. "You can use it for direct radio communication right now, if you want. All the computer functions are scrambled and the only way to clear that would be a wipe followed by a direct software download from—"

"From the operations room," finished Lellan. "From Polas."

The woman ducked down and, with quick expertise, reassembled the components of the helmet, then passed it up to Lellan before turning to pack away her tools.

"Okay, who can hear me?" asked Lellan into the comlink as soon as she donned the helmet, then winced at the barrage of sound as everyone tried to reply together. "Okay, okay! I'll list each of you in your numerical order and you can reply in turn, then you can shut it unless I speak to you individually." Twelve out of fifteen field commanders answered as she said their names. Lellan nodded to herself, then went on. "I have here with me a Theocracy soldier just taken prisoner—as no doubt have some of you. I want you to listen to this, then to what I have to say after."

Turning to the prisoner on either side of whom stood Carl and Uris, she asked, "Your name?"

"Squad Leader Sastol," said the man. He looked bewildered, as if not even sure about the truth of that statement.

"Shall we pretend, Sastol, that I've had you beaten and tortured, and am now threatening to take away your air supply?" she continued. The man Sastol jerked his head up from contemplation of his feet and stared at her in confusion. Lellan went on, "What's happening down there? Your entire army was attacking us previously without any co-ordination. We've captured hundreds like you who have ripped off their augs, but those still with augs would seemingly rather die than be captured. And now your entire army has turned around."

"Something destroyed *Faith*," Sastol replied, perhaps deciding he preferred this method of *pretend* torture.

"Something destroyed *my* faith a long time ago," said Lellan. "Are you trying to tell me you've lost yours?"

Sastol stared at her directly. "Something destroyed *Faith*—the cylinder world."

Lellan absorbed that, then asked, "And the army?"

"He who destroyed *Faith* also tried to capture my mind through the *Gift*. I tore my aug away. Others did not."

Carl said, "So whose side is this Skellor on?"

"His very own, I think." Lellan paused, then said, "Did you all get that? By the numbers, give me the confirmation—or otherwise—such as you can." Seven of her commanders confirmed that they were getting the same story from their own prisoners. Two others assumed the whole thing a ruse, and did not believe that one of the cylinder worlds had been destroyed.

"As your commander I'm very interested to have your opinions. Now I will tell you how I see things." Lellan paused, obviously uncomfortable with what she must now say. "We came up from below and we attacked not because we thought we could hold the surface, but simply because we thought we could increase the ballot and create enough noise to attract the attention of the Polity—so that our cry for help would be heard and could be responded to. We had to do this because staying underground, and staying silent, would have resulted in the Theocracy destroying us down there. Are you all in agreement with that?"

The chorus of "ayes" was all she needed to continue with, "Now, we have above us an AI dreadnought, which I am told has been subverted by someone who worked for the Separatists. The Separatists on Cheyne III were supplied with arms by the Theocracy, yet, that same individual has come here and destroyed a cylinder world, and is now demanding that we . . . What is it, Pholan?"

The commander who had interrupted her gave a terse explanation, and when he had finished she went on, "Oh, not only a cylinder world, it seems—all of the Theocracy landers as well. As I was saying, this individual is now demanding that we hand over Ian Cormac. As I see it, Polas was right. The army must get under cover. You have to take your fighters back down into caves."

Lellan waited for the dying down of a storm of protest. Even in war, to be on the surface offered a kind of freedom none of them had experienced for a long time. When that protest turned to argument between various commanders, she lost her patience.

"Enough!" Argument died to muttering, then silence, and she continued, "Wake up and smell what you're shovelling. You know we cannot win a war on the surface. We have never been able to win a war on the surface. In the end we must have Polity intervention here to escape further oppression. And that we will get it is a foregone conclusion."

There came a brief flurry of further argument before they realized what she had just said. Into the silence that came after, she threw, "A subverted AI *Polity* dreadnought has destroyed a cylinder world, and has been striking at the surface. Anyone would be mad to think Earth Central Security will not come here now. What credibility they were preserving by non-intervention here is completely gone.

Separatists across humanspace will claim that dreadnought was not really subverted. ECS will come here to investigate and to offer aid—and the whole furore the Polity has been striving to avoid is now inevitable. Now they have nothing to lose by coming here, but they do have a world to gain—one that has been iconic to Separatists for a long time."

Argument continued, but Lellan was determined. "You have my orders. Obey them or not." Then she shut off her comlink.

"We retreat and hide, then?" asked Beckle, inspecting the rail-gun he had taken from Sastol.

Lellan shrugged. "If we stay up here, this Skellor could fry us from orbit any time he likes. That he has not done so yet tells me that he's in such a strong position that we're almost irrelevant to him. Either that or he likes playing games."

"You didn't answer his question," said Carl, who had sat Sastol on the ground with his hands on his head.

"No, I didn't," said Lellan.

"What are you going to do?" Carl asked.

Lellan grinned. "Well, I've been the rebel leader for long enough, and now I don't think there's much more I can do for the rebellion. I intend to head out there"—she pointed into the night—"to get hold of this Ian Cormac, and the others, and find out what the hell is happening."

"We'll be coming with you," said Beckle, closely inspecting the sight of the rail-gun.

"I didn't doubt it for a moment," she replied.

"We will also be coming," said two voices simultaneously.

The prisoner, Sastol, stared with bewilderment at the two cylinders, which he had assumed merely contained supplies. They emitted a deep humming and ignited all over with glinting lights and displays, as they rose off the ground and turned themselves upright.

The Outlinker boy, Apis, was utterly exhausted and sank to his knees on the muddy ground, but Eldene did not allow him to stay there. She grabbed his arm and began hauling him to his feet.

"We have to keep going. If they catch us, they'll kill us. And they won't do it quickly!"

He stared at her, probably too tired to know what he thought of that possibility. At first she had not understood what was the matter with him, until he'd gasped earlier, "How do you people live with this? How do you manage to spend all your lives in *gravity*?" Without his exoskeleton he was directly feeling the full effects of a force he had never before experienced.

As she finally wrestled him to his feet, he managed to formulate a response. "Do you think any of them are still alive back there, then?"

"I hope not," Eldene replied, fingering the pistol she had snatched from Speelan as they escaped. She moved in close and hooked an arm around his waist to help him along. Together they staggered on through a dark wilderness of flute grasses and churned mud; hot breezes blowing in behind them, where a hot-metal glow illuminated clouds of smoke and steam so that they appeared like a range of orange mountains—a range from behind which the upper edge of Calypse was rising as a harbinger of morning.

"Where should we head now?" Apis asked.

Eldene scanned around them and did not know what to reply. Their situation seemed hopeless: they had limited oxygen, were miles from anyone who could be considered friendly, and even heading back to their erstwhile captors was now out of the question. Where could they go? Back towards the crater, in the hope of running into their comrades, or towards the fighting in the hope of coming across some of the rebels? These were the questions she was beginning to ponder, when she heard the sound of voices from behind them.

"Keep moving," she hissed at Apis as he showed signs of sagging to the ground again. He too now heard the voices and then an order suddenly barked, followed by silence.

"Theocracy?" he whispered.

Eldene felt the skin on the back of her neck creeping—she had recognized the source of that order. She nodded to Apis as they struggled on.

It seemed the voice must have carried for some distance, for thereafter they heard nothing more until the lightening sky became distinct from the horizon of towering grasses around them. When they next heard something—the sound of someone falling over and cursing until ordered to silence again—it became evident that someone was indeed behind them, and now, in the better light, rapidly drawing closer.

"They're trailing us," whispered Eldene, at first suspecting herself of paranoia, then coming to believe her fears absolutely. How else could it be that this party, led by the one called Aberil, was still so close to them, hours after the godlike obliteration of the landers? "We have to move faster." She looked up into the Outlinker's face, and knew that it wasn't the quality of the light that now gave his yellow skin a greyish tinge, though she did wonder what was producing the appearance of worms writhing underneath that skin. He returned her gaze, his expression apologetic, before something seemed to take hold of him from the inside and shake him violently. He jerked upright and away from her—his eyes gone wide in shock and his skin turning almost orange as it suffused with blood. Then his legs folded and he went down. Eldene tried to heave him upright, but he was no longer the construct of sugar sticks and paper he had described himself as once being—but now heavy with muscle and bone.

"You go on," he gasped, his breathing raw. "I'll tell them you got killed back there." He nodded towards the now fading fire-glow.

Eldene did not like to point out that if someone was experienced enough to track them this far throughout the night, that person would surely be experienced enough to recognize that there were two of them.

"I'm staying with you," she muttered, giving herself the appearance of expertise as she pulled out and checked the magazine of the pistol before slapping it back into place. Glancing around, she saw that moving further along or backwards on this spit of rhubarb-cloaked land would afford them no better cover than at present. She gestured to the tangled flute grass beside them. "We'll go in there."

"You should go on," Apis insisted.

Eldene shoved the pistol back in the belt of her camouflage trousers, and reached down to help him to cover. Seeing her determined expression, he made no further attempt to send her away. It was obvious to Eldene, though, that he did not really want to be left alone. But then, she was staying with him for the very same reason.

The first of the Theocracy soldiers emerged into view, shortly followed by the officer, Speelan. Watching the guard inspect the path she and Apis had flattened through the purple vegetation, Eldene suppressed any hope that this group might head on past them. Their trail was too obvious, what with succulent stems and leaves crushed and oozing sap like blue paint. She also realized that, for survival's sake, she must act first. She raised the pistol and aimed it, but Apis caught her wrist.

"Wait . . . wait a moment," he said firmly.

She stared at him and saw that he no longer looked so weak and ill. Now there was something gaunt and fierce about him.

He went on, "It knows about threats to its survival, and I bet that was something that Mika did not program in. Before, it just had me operating at the lowest energy level, while it continued rebuilding me. But now it *knows*."

"What the hell are you talking about?" she hissed.

"When you shoot at them, they'll run for cover. When they go for cover, we must run on and wait for them again."

"You are up to running?"

"With the mycelium . . . I can."

Now Aberil himself and the Proctor Molat had come into view. Eldene studied Apis for a moment longer, then turned away and raised her pistol again. It was morally wrong to kill, according to tenets of the Satagents and Zelda Smythe, yet when had that ever stopped members of the Theocracy from doing so? With cold calculation Eldene chose the leading soldier, for he was obviously the tracker, and emptied one full disc of five rounds into his torso.

With a horrible grunting sound the man staggered back, the front of his jacket sprouting its insulating fibres, a haze of red exploding out behind him and hingeing down his mask as it simultaneously exploded from his mouth. His expression turned bewildered as he tried to retain balance on legs no longer under his control. Finally he collapsed beneath the rhubarb leaves.

Eldene just stared, too stunned, for a moment, to take aim at the others diving for cover. Just pressing her finger down on the electric trigger had achieved this. Shaken, she aimed at the spot where she had seen Aberil drop and scrabble towards a thicket of flute grass, and fired off another disc. To the right, someone stood and brought a weapon to bear. She fired a further disc of five rounds in that direction.

"Come on! Come on!"

She did not know how long Apis had been pulling at her arm. Slugs were now slapping with vicious force into the vegetation all around. Eldene allowed him to lead her for a moment, then freed herself when she realized she was hindering his progress. Something flicked the epaulette on her shoulder, and something else nipped her earlobe. Ahead of her she saw the back of Apis's overalls slapped, and he went over, rolled, came to his feet snarling for a moment before humanity reasserted itself and he pushed on. There was blood on his clothing for he had certainly been hit, but it must have been a ricochet—a slug with its force spent in the flute grass—and soon, sometime soon, he would replace the oxygen mask that had been torn from his face.

They came out into another open spit between the grasses, this one with black plantains spearing up through the purple rhubarb leaves, their own foliage insipid white and sprouting wormish secondary roots in the shade below. Looking around, Eldene was bewildered by surrounding light and by clouds of colour. The flute grasses here were peppered and hazed with red, yellow, white and gold, and just looking at them made her eyes hurt. Abruptly she realized that it was only the sunrise illuminating an area where the grasses were budding at last—something she had only ever before seen at a distance. Catching her breath, she glanced again at Apis.

"Your mask," she said.

Apis stared at her for a moment. Then, realizing what she was saying, he removed a new mask from a pocket in his oxygen-bottle container, tore the remains of the old one from its clip hinges in the collar extension below his chin, and clipped the new one into place.

"How?" Eldene asked.

Apis looked confused for a moment, then explained, "I'm an Outlinker—we can live in vacuum for a time, so this is no problem." He waved a hand at their surroundings, but she could see he did not believe that explanation himself. She reached towards his back and he allowed her to part the rip in his overall. She saw there only what looked like an arrow-shaped scar.

"It's the mycelium," he said.

So he *had* been hit. As Eldene stepped past him to lead the way to the next tangled stand of flute grass, dotted with white buds, she tried to focus on the realities of people trying to kill them, not the unreality of someone who should have died.

They were struggling up a slope thick with slimy vegetation, when the grasses ahead of them shuddered under a fusillade, spraying a snowstorm of buds. Eldene turned back and fired past Apis. She saw someone staggering aside, yelling, and two other figures diving for cover. Then . . . then only an electrical clicking from the pistol she was holding. What had Fethan instructed? "Double-press and hold down empties the entire magazine." She nevertheless pointed the weapon at Aberil as he slowly stood up, bloodied power pack tucked under one arm, its cable looped in front of him, and the rail-gun he had taken from the dead soldier pointed negligently at their legs. The electrical clicking continued for a moment, then ceased as some mechanism in the pistol cancelled it.

Aberil tilted his head and grinned at her. "Empty, I think, little rebel." Then he moved in close, jabbed the barrel of his weapon into Apis's stomach, keeling him over, then swept it across to knock the pistol from Eldene's hand. Clutching at bruised fingers, she held her ground and glared at him. With obvious contempt he turned his back on her. Looking past him she could see Speelan sprawled on the ground, cursing, until Proctor Molat emerged from cover and went over to help the wounded man put a dressing on his leg and also slap on an analgesic patch. Aberil turned back to face her.

"This Outlinker, I think, has knowledge which may be of use to me. You have killed one of my men and injured another." He shrugged. "I would like to have time to punish you properly, but time is not something I have . . ." Aberil paused as the sudden roar of an aerofan drowned his words. He glanced up as the machine appeared overhead and began to settle down towards them. "Then again," Aberil shouted, "it seems I *will* have time to deal with you properly."

Eldene stared at the commander then up at the descending machine. If she ran now, the other proctor would get her with the aerofan's side-mounted rail-gun, but that was perhaps better than suffering the ministrations of this lunatic. And run she was just about to do, as the aerofan dropped to hover just over their heads. Then the proctor inside it flung himself over the rail, and descended on Aberil like a flesh-and-bone hammer. Aberil dropped his rail-gun and power pack and, before Eldene could think to reach for it herself, Apis had snatched up the weapon and pointed it at Molat and Speelan, who simply had no time to reach for their own weapons. The two of them froze where they were, and could only passively observe what followed.

"Good Deacon Aberil Dorth," said John Stanton, hauling the man to his feet then driving his own forehead straight into the bridge of Aberil's nose. Eldene winced at the horrible crunching sound, then at the horrible butchering impact of each blow that followed. The Deacon tried to fight back, but he might just as well have been striking a mobile boulder, and in return he received blows from hands seemingly made of granite. Eventually, Aberil was down on his knees, groping for another mask as he spat teeth and blood. Eldene expected Stanton to finish the man, to kill him, such had been the palpable hate issuing from him. Instead he eventually pushed the Deacon onto his side with his boot, then turned to her and Apis.

"No more time for self-indulgence," he said, nodding towards the aerofan that had drifted down only a few metres away from them. "Climb in and we'll get out of here."

"What about these two?" Apis asked.

Stanton glanced at Molat and Speelan, then swung his attention back to Aberil as the man finally got his mask into place and managed to rise to his knees. "We just leave all of them here," he said. "They'll not be going far." He stabbed a thumb over his shoulder. "I have friends coming soon who'll see to that."

Choking on blood, Aberil said, "Got . . . no stomach for it . . . Stanton?"

Stanton grinned at him. "Just leaving that for someone who can do a better job."

Eldene did not understand what he meant until she, he, and Apis were high in the aerofan and heading away. When Stanton pointed out the things in the vegetation below, she knew precisely the ending of Aberil Dorth's fairy tale.

Her neck and shoulders aching with tension, Jarvellis studied with suspicion the flat expanse of rock wedged amid foothills. This was the first likely-looking landing spot she had spotted while traversing fifty kilometres of river, then five kilometres of its tributary. For a while she'd felt panic growing in her as she manoeuvred the ship between precipitous slopes or sheer walls of stone. For a time she even felt she had taken a wrong turning somewhere, somehow.

"This is the one?" she asked.

"It is," confirmed the AI. "A homing beacon has just been activated by our presence."

After a moment Jarvellis eased the control column over and boosted the ion engines to lift the ship over mounded muddy banks and rhubarbs standing three metres tall. On side screens she glimpsed vegetation steaming and slumping under the craft's ionic blast and, strangely, tricones oozing to the surface as if urged by some suicidal imperative. Coming in over the flat stone surface, she made no complaint when the AI opened out the ship's legs and feet, unbidden. She brought it down gently, but no amount of gentleness could prevent its weight crushing thousands of little hemispherical molluscs to a slurry.

"This is somewhat visible," said Lyric, flashing up on one screen a view of the trail of broiled vegetation leading from the river.

"Like I give a shit," she said, stretching her neck to ease it.

"I think that perhaps you should," said the AI. "I did not want to distract you while you were engaged in such risky flying, but now you have to know." The screen showing the vegetation now flicked over to another view that Jarvellis recognized as computer-enhanced.

"What is this?" she asked.

"The view of the sky above us, magnified, from two hours ago. You are seeing three grabships from the dreadnought."

"Shit, what kind of scan did you use?"

"Passive scan—the Skellor will not be able to trace us."

"Good . . . good. Why grabships?"

"Observe the masses of objects they are dropping," said the AI.

Jarvellis squinted at the screen. Even computer-enhanced, the picture was not very clear. She could now make out the shapes of three grabships, but would never have recognized them as such without the AI telling her. She only saw the "masses" to which the AI referred when they moved from line of sight to the ships, for they were blurred into that original image, and then only saw them for a few seconds as they glowed before breaking apart. She felt something tightening in her abdomen when she thought of John Stanton being out there somewhere, and not knowing about this. As far as she judged, to say this Skellor's intent would be hostile was an understatement, so anything that did not slam down on them from orbit—like the laser blast that had taken out Polas—was probably even worse.

"Bioweapon?" she managed, her mouth dry.

"Possibly—but a strange one. Each of the objects in the initial masses was an ovoid approximately two metres long.

This in itself is not unusual, because bioweapons dropped from orbit are usually inserted in larger packages for heat-shielded re-entry and then dispersal. However, these are not dispersing. After losing some sort of shielding after re-entry, the objects have remained in a loose cluster."

"Where is it now?"

"Directly above the mountains—and above us."

"Can you get a picture?" Jarvellis asked, puzzled.

"Oh yes. Now that they are settling lower, I do not need to use so much enhancement either," the AI replied with annoying smugness.

"Well, show it to me then."

The AI showed her, and Jarvellis could only gape at this newest insanity.

Calypse was attached to the horizon by only the smallest arc of its disc, as if reluctant to release its hold for its journey across the sky. Its swirls and bands of colour gleamed bright only for as long as it took until the sun, rising to one side of it, could throw it into silhouette. Perhaps reflection from the surface of Masada, or some luminous quality of the giant itself, cast it meanwhile in a light that gave it true depth. More than at any other time he had seen it, Cormac felt aware that this orb was truly a vast gas giant rather than some two-dimensional disc imprinted over a large proportion of sky.

"Where is it now?" Cormac asked them tiredly.

Gant did not display any tiredness, and Cormac wondered if Fethan had enough that was human remaining in him to feel any weariness. It seemed not, however, for since the cyborg had returned to requisition Gant's aid in the task of leading away the hooder, the both of them had been charging back and forth at high speed all night. This was evident from their clothing—torn from their running through the abrasive grass stalks and smeared with streaks of yellow and red juice from the crop of coloured buds the grasses had suddenly produced.

"It's moved on ahead," said Fethan. "But if that relieves you, best you know that it's not alone."

"More hooders?" asked Thorn.

"More of everything," said Fethan. "Seems the whole fauna of the planet is on the move. Must be the fighting attracting 'em, as I can't think what else it might be."

Cormac rubbed his eyes then turned to Gant. "How far do you estimate we are from those Theocracy landers?" He tried to keep bitterness out of his voice.

"Not far now," the Golem replied, looking ahead. "I can see the heat haze from here."

Cormac glanced at Fethan and noticed a hardening of the cyborg's expression. That same hardness had appeared in him when Mika reported that the signal from the exoskeleton had ceased. That event had occurred at the same time as the laser hit, so it seemed unlikely that Apis or the girl Eldene were still alive.

"We never really thought about it, but *why* did Skellor hit them?" Thorn asked.

"We're not totally sure he did," said Cormac pedantically. The massive communication over com—before it had gone dead—gave that impression, or rather what Thorn and Gant had described of it did. "But if he did, then the reason is obvious: he's knocking out all forms of space transportation prior to burning this planet down to ash."

"There you go: always the optimist," said Gant, but his effort at humour was wasted.

"You're that certain this is Skellor's aim?" asked Fethan.

"Call that scenario one," said Cormac. He glanced at Gant, and added, "The least optimistic one." He went on, "I know for certain this man will go to any lengths not to let the Polity become aware of his existence. Whatever way he sets about it, he'll want us dead." He looked now at Mika, who had been very much silent since informing them about the loss of signal. "What's *your* estimation?"

Mika winced at this assumption of her specialized knowledge. "He will not want to lose what he has acquired. The Polity would only take it away from him," she said, discomfited by her own reasoning and how it might apply to her.

"An assumption we have to work with," said Cormac. "Now, changing the subject, perhaps one of you can tell me what the fuck that is over there."

Gant spun, and aimed his APW. Thorn did likewise with his.

"Where?" they asked simultaneously.

"There!" Cormac gestured with the barrel of his thin-gun.

The half-seen bulky shape, crouching in trampled and pummelled flute grass that resembled a flash-frozen stormy sea, seemed to shrug with resignation at being spotted. Then it rose up on its hind legs.

"Scabble-dobble-log?" it wondered, unfolding its sets of forearms like some nightmare melding of the goddess Kali and a tarantula.

"Keep moving," said Fethan. "We're safe while it's talking. It's when you can't hear 'em you gotta worry."

"Who told you that?" Gant asked.

"Well . . . everyone knows that," Fethan replied, looking unsure.

Cormac observed the curving row of slightly luminous green eyes set into the white dome of the creature's head, as it watched them move on past it. When it was upright like this, those eyes were perhaps three metres above the ground. The claws terminating its multiple forearms were the size and shape of bunches of bananas, only bananas made of obsidian and sharpened to points glinting in the morning light. He had no doubt that Gant and Thorn could take this creature down with the weaponry they had, so maybe there wasn't a great deal to worry about. Then he suddenly felt very stupid, for there was something else he had forgotten about.

"Gant, Thorn, power down those APWs right now," he said. As they looked at him queryingly, he pulled Shuriken and held it ready to throw. "Something I neglected to remember is that Skellor would easily pick up the UV and radiation flash, so we might just as well be sending him an invitation to come and get us."

Reluctantly the two of them lowered their weapons and flicked certain controls on them.

"Dooble-ooble-caro-flock," the gabbleduck told them, obviously approving.

"Keep moving," said Cormac.

Soon the gabbleduck lost interest, and ducked back out of sight. As they headed on, Gant placed the two APWs in his pack, and armed himself and Thorn with two pulse-rifles instead. Almost as if something had been waiting for this, they heard huge movement in the flute grasses behind and over to one side.

"Run," ordered Fethan. "I'll try to lead it away."

"The gabbleduck?" asked Cormac as they broke into a trot.

Fethan appeared puzzled as he listened to the rushing sound. "No . . . definitely not. Hooder, I think. Something really big, anyway." He beckoned to Gant, and then he and the Golem split off to one side.

"Fuck," Thorn gasped out. "Gant's got the APWs."

"Gant'll be back . . . if they can't lead it away."

"Yeah . . . great," Thorn managed.

Saving his breath for running, Cormac did not continue this conversation. Unlike the cyborg and Gant he did not have an option. Keeping his hand tight around Shuriken, he watched his footing and just kept going. Glancing up, he saw something boiling into the air and surmised this was from the landers, and that he was getting close. When something heavy crashed past him, he turned to throw Shuriken but desisted when that something said, "Scabber-abber-abber" accusingly and accelerated away, its gait lying somewhere between that of a cheetah and a caterpillar.

"What the hell!" shouted Thorn, when something else went growling and hissing across in front of them, its hide not quite changing fast enough to match its surroundings, so for a time there were strange misplaced animal imprints in the air. Behind them, the rushing sound in the grasses was growing louder and louder—but now much less specific, for it seemed to stretch out on either side of them as well. Suddenly Fethan and Gant were with them again, as they came out onto open ground where the vegetation had been seared and flattened, and wrecked landers formed a wall of ruptured metal carcasses and scattered engine cowlings like giant cored olives. Coming to the nearest of these wrecks, Cormac stumbled to a halt, the others stopping with him.

"APW!" he shouted at Gant, but the Golem did not seem to hear.

"Bloody hell," said Gant.

Cormac glanced at Fethan, who for the first time looked utterly perplexed. Now, turning his attention back the way they had come, Cormac realized there was something very odd about this sound: a kind of slapping vibration like . . . like feet? Stepping up onto an engine cowling, he saw huge movement cutting towards them through the grasses, and shapes moving fast in the purple spaces between vegetation clumps. One of these shapes now leapt from a tangle of both new and old stalks and, trailing papery fragments and coloured buds, it thumped down into a crouch before them. This first one snarled, drawing lips back from its curving white teeth, as its fellows stormed out behind it. *Dracomen*—thousands of them.

19

"Third to the valley of the Hooded One came Brother Egris, and seeing how Stenophalis and Pegrum had failed, he was undaunted."

The Valley of Shadow and Whispers now resembled the aftermath of an explosion in an abattoir, and if seeing that mess did not put off Egris, then he must have been stupid and deserved everything he got.

"Astride the valley, he was silhouetted black against Calypse, and did not shine in his armour of iron, as he demanded of the monster below him, 'Come forth and face me!'"

The woman shook her head and drummed her fingertip against the cold page. "Bad move, Brother. You should have left it to that arsehole Nebbish."

Strangely, Egris seemed to look out of the page at her for a second, as if annoyed at her interruption, before turning his back and gazing into the coagulating darkness below him.

"The Hooded One came forth, and he smote it with thunderbolts until its scutes flamed in the air, the very ground smoked, and all that grew nearby was burned to ash."

The woman pulled her finger away from the page, because the memory fabric had suddenly warmed as Egris began using some kind of unlikely weapon it seemed idiotic to use when clad from head to foot in metal. The thing he held—something like a chrome saxophone with an image-enhancer sight—hurled lightning into the shadowed cowl, causing glassy things in there to glow like filaments.

"But thunder availed him nought, and out of dying fire the monster rose to pull him down into the Valley of Shadows and

Whispers, and his armour parted like butter under the knife of the Hooded One."

The woman paused contemplatively before adding, "And Egris spread like butter too."

Molat had no wish to have this cripple impeding him, while there was quite obviously something unpleasant moving about back there, but Aberil had kindly picked up Molat's rail-gun to replace the one he had lost to the Outlinker, before instructing Molat to help the injured man. Speelan was not exactly generous in his thanks for this assistance: every time Molat stumbled, and every time he himself stumbled, it was all put down to Molat, and Speelan regularly swore at him.

"Be silent!" Aberil slurred when this swearing became too voluble.

Speelan fell silent and bowed his head—like Molat he did not much like now looking at the Deacon's face. Whoever it was that had dropped in on them so unexpectedly, he had certainly made a mess of it.

Aberil went on, his whispering distorted by his ruined mouth, "There's something back there, and if your cursing attracts it, then I will leave you to it."

"I'm sorry," said Speelan. "I'm sorry . . . it hurts."

Molat realized the man was obviously terrified that Aberil would do what he threatened, so meant every word of his apology. A gusting hiss he heard from behind, after the earlier movement in the grasses had long ceased, immediately raised other concerns in him.

"That's a siluroyne," Molat stated.

"Yes, you would know, wouldn't you?" said Aberil, looking him up and down contemptuously. "Come on, keep moving, there might be some craft still undamaged back there."

They came out into one of the ubiquitous channels, where the ground was wetter and the plant life distinctly different. Molat wondered if it was because the soil here was wetter that no flute grass grew on it, or if the ground was wetter because no flute grass grew on it. Such was the kind of chicken-and-egg conundrum that had been the speciality of those delivering religious instruction—your answer could always be wrong, and wrong answers were always punishable.

"Damn fuck you!" said Speelan, losing his footing and painfully crunching his full weight on the leg in which the pond worker girl had put a hole.

Molat restrained the surge of rage he felt at the injustice of it all. He could not afford to get angry with either of these two, as they could have him stretched on a frame with just a word . . . if they ever got back to safety.

"Keep your mouth closed," Aberil hissed.

Molat felt his own mouth doing exactly the opposite as he continued to gaze up into the sky. Calypse seemed now the breadth of an imaginary hand above the horizon, and the sun was gnawing at the edge of reality beside it. But these were common sights to Molat, and not what drew his attention.

"What's that?" he asked faintly, unable to find any other words.

Speelan glared at him, before turning to follow his gaze. With watery eyes in his ruined face, Aberil studied the Proctor as if suspecting some trick to distract him, before looking up as well. Molat's fascinated stare could not be broken. In the sky he was witnessing something fantastical. It was titanic, this golden ship with whole cities of instrumentation blooming on its surface, and it was knotted in something grey and incongruous, like some vast opaque topaz wrapped in the mummified corpse of some cephalopod.

"It's him," muttered Aberil. "He burnt *Faith*, and now he's here."

Just then, something that felt no awe of strange objects in the sky, but rather felt some gnawing hunger in its stomach at the sight of the three individuals before it, let out a gasping hiss to get their attention.

"Oh no! . . . No!" Molat shouted, finding himself fighting against Speelan's determined grip on him. Speelan would not let go, so Molat dragged the man along with him as he tried to flee the looming siluroyne. Subliminally he was aware of Aberil taking to his heels—not even trying to use the weapon he had appropriated. Speelan did not attempt to use his weapon either, so determined was he to cling on to Molat that he dared not unhook it from his shoulder. Fighting panic, Molat finally looked away from the monster into Speelan's terrified eyes, then he drove his fingers into their sockets.

Molat was already running when he heard Speelan scream, "No, please don't!" The gnathic crunching that followed was interspersed with further wails of, "No, don't! No!" terminated by a horrible bubbling wail. *Escape* was all Molat could think of, then in horror he heard the sound of the monster pursuing him, obviously not being satisfied with its meal of just one human being.

Oh no . . . oh no . . .

Perhaps it was because his terror was even greater, or perhaps due to the injuries Aberil had suffered, but Molat soon had the Deacon in sight and was fast catching up with him.

"Wait for me!" he shouted.

Aberil glanced back, but did not slow. Behind them both Molat could hear the siluroyne's grunting snarls as it pursued. He glanced back to see it clear a tall stand of flute grass and land with heavy and sinister grace. Just that glance was enough for him to realize the creature was not even exerting itself. He felt himself like something leaden and clumsy accelerated to the limit of its capacity, whilst the siluroyne kept moving in short bursts only to keep him in sight, between slowing down to a gentle lope as it studied its prey. In its nightmare features he seemed to read amusement, but that could have been his imagination.

"Shoot it! Shoot the fucking thing!" Molat shouted to the Deacon, as he got closer to him. Aberil glanced around, gasping for breath, and obviously suffering at this punishing pace. Molat pushed himself harder and reached out for the weapon slung from a strap over Aberil's shoulder. At the last moment Aberil turned slightly, aiming the snout of his railgun downwards. A rattling crackle and Molat felt the ground drop away from him. His legs gave way and, as he went over, he caught a glimpse of shattered bone and burst-open flesh. From somewhere came a horrible keening and whimpering and, as he tried to stand but went down again, he realized it issued from himself. A shadow then drew across him.

"Please . . . no . . ." he pleaded.

But the creature had no pity—nothing in its mien or expression that was in any way *Terran* and Molat now knew he had been mistaken about its apparent amusement earlier. Caught in teeth like blue hatchets, Molat saw a torn and bloody pair of uniform trousers. The three-fingered claws, big as garden rakes on doubled forearms, closed around his torso and up-ended him. Over his shrill screams Molat heard a rail-gun opening up and emptying its magazine, but by then the siluroyne had eaten his legs and was crunching into his pelvis.

"If I ever possessed any inclination to religion, I think I'd find it now," said Gant, shading his eyes from the bright sunlight as he stared up into the sky.

"Ignore it, then," said Cormac. "We have to focus on our goal, and just that." But even he did not feel any great ease in that assertion. What Skellor had done to the appearance of the *Occam Razor* was a blatant demonstration of his power, and that he managed to hold it so easily in low orbit yet further evidence. The *Occam* was poised there like a giant overseer directing some huge chess game on the ground below, ready in a moment to sweep board, pieces, everything away. Cormac tried to focus his attention on the game, and specifically on one of those pieces whose abilities he now did not really know for sure.

All that distinguished Scar from the rest of the dracomen was his weapons harness, his loose fatigues, and the facial scar that had given him his name. Cormac remembered Mika explaining how the dracoman could easily have erased that scar, but had retained it for some reason of pride, and now perhaps for some means of identification. Standing upon the burnt-out carcass of a lander, Cormac studied the dracoman a moment longer before returning his attention to the wilderness stretching before them. Now, with the budding of the grasses, the formerly green landscape was tinged with washes of red, white, yellow and metallic gold. But these flowering grasses were now shaking with some approaching movement.

"Okay, what have we got out there?" he asked. He had a good idea—just wanted confirmation.

"Soldiers," replied Scar, before Gant could.

Gant glanced at the dracomen. "Looks like the whole Theocracy army is heading our way." He looked from side to side. "We won't be able to move fast enough to get round them."

"We go through them," said Scar abruptly.

Cormac gazed down at the thousands of dracomen gathered around the landers or in the surrounding flute grass. Every one of them was indistinguishable from Scar when he had first encountered him, and many of them seemed to have similar appetites. They had found charred corpses lying amongst the incinerated landers and had obviously decided not to let the meat go to waste. The carnivorous scene appeared hugely primitive but for other dracomen checking over, with smooth expertise, the weapons they had also found. Cormac feared Mika was allowing her fascination with these creatures to outweigh her caution as she walked amongst them, scanning and sometimes even daring to take samples from them. But then perhaps she had less fear of injury now, with the alien mechanisms operating inside her body.

"Convenient that you arrived when you did," he said to Scar.

The dracoman grunted as he surveyed his fellows, then something seemed to claw at him from the inside, and he hissed before turning to Cormac again.

"You will let me live," said the dracoman, echoing Dragon's words, and Cormac wondered if it was truly the dracoman speaking.

"Polity law." Cormac gestured to the gathered dracomen. "It was a single entity that was guilty of crimes against the Polity, but I see no such single entity here."

And so it was. Before eagerly gathering up her instruments, Mika had observed to him, *"Here's that missing fifty per cent of Dragon. Now we know what it meant about both dying and living."*

Cormac continued speaking to Scar. "But what ECS decides to do is irrelevant at present, and genocide may yet be committed." He gestured up at the *Occam Razor* before scrambling down the lander to the ground. Scar and Gant quickly followed him, and the three moved over to join Thorn and Fethan, who were listening in on radio exchanges through Thorn's partially dismantled coms helmet.

"What have you got?" Cormac asked.

"Radio only," said Thorn. "Lellan's sending her army back underground. Some of her commanders are protesting, but they're doing what they're told. It would seem Lellan sees no purpose in keeping them up on the surface. From something I heard, they probably haven't enough supplies to stay up any longer. What about you?"

It was Gant who replied. "The whole Theocracy army is heading this way, and too rapidly for us to get around it."

"The whole *subverted* Theocracy army," Cormac added.

Thorn nodded, turning his attention to the ominous shape in the sky. "Why is he doing this? Why doesn't he just incinerate this whole place?" he asked.

Gazing up too, Cormac said, "I think he wants us alive for some reason, to use or to play with, whatever. I don't see what else could possibly keep him here."

"Not so omnipotent then," said Thorn.

"No," Cormac agreed. "Still human enough to want to make his enemies suffer, and prideful enough to want to show off. Let's just hope he doesn't move beyond that stage just yet."

"Before you wax too philosophical, perhaps we should sort out what we gonna do," interjected Fethan.

Cormac glanced at the old cyborg, then turned to Scar. "Are your people ready to move?"

Scar just showed his teeth in reply.

"Then," Cormac continued, "we cut a hole through the Theocracy army, and keep going until we reach the mountains. Then you"—he glanced at Fethan—"and Thorn will take us to John Stanton's ship."

"Then what?" asked Thorn.

Almost without thinking, Cormac drew his thin-gun and checked the charge. "Let's just see if we can get that far first, shall we?"

With shaking hands Aberil changed magazines then took aim with his rail-gun. Very badly he wanted to empty this second magazine into the creature's head, but that would be more than stupid considering he only had this and one other magazine, and there were certainly other creatures lurking out here. The siluroyne no longer moved, but then with half its head ripped away that was not surprising. Molat was still moving though, which considering how little was left of the Proctor, Aberil did find surprising. Swallowing the foul taste in his mouth, Aberil walked over to Molat and watched him finally die. That didn't take long for blood was draining from him like red wine from an upended bottle.

Finally Aberil jerked himself alert, as if coming out of a trance, and suddenly was once again aware of just how bad he felt. His face seemed just a swollen ball of pain, his broken teeth aching abominably, and an overall swelling beginning to close his eyes. As if that was not enough, he felt sure some of his ribs were broken, and he was beginning to suspect that the bloody froth he'd been spitting out was not coming from the ruin of his face but from one of his lungs.

Damn you, Stanton!

He had known for far too long that he should either have left that family alone or exterminated every last one of them. Drunk on the extent of the powers granted to him as a young proctor, he had committed crimes that had led to the creation of Lellan Stanton the rebel and her brother John the mercenary killer.

Moving now with painful slowness Aberil headed back towards the landing craft, occasional fumaroles of smoke or steam rising into the sky locating them for him. Not for one moment did he consider the possibility of his own death, for he was so sure of God's purpose for him. Yes, he worked hard to preserve his own life, as he had just done with this siluroyne, for not to do so would display a punishable arrogance—but it was all part of how he was being continually moulded by the deity. Even the beating he had just received at Stanton's hands had been part of this same process. No, Aberil would not die—he had far too much yet to do.

There . . . something moving.

As far as he could remember from what he had been taught as a child, siluroynes were extremely territorial, so this definitely would not be another of them. Hearing the sound again, he tried to discount the realization that whatever was making the noise was obviously a lot bigger than the siluroyne. The sound he next heard—a whickering of rapid sharp motion—shot him through with an almost supernatural dread.

The Lord is my shepherd . . .

Much louder now—the hissing passage of a long hard body writhing through flute grass and over compacted mud. Aberil picked up his pace, wheezing now and with flecks of red spattering the inside of his mask. He'd heard that sound before: who of the higher Theocracy had not watched holocordings of rebel prisoners pinned out like bait near their mountains? But this was ridiculous surely: hooders did not venture this far out onto the plain.

As the sound grew louder, Aberil looked aside in time to see a huge segmented body hurtling past him like a speeding train. It was heading in the opposite direction, but he listened hard and could hear it curving round. He *ran*. He could get to the landing craft . . . find something there . . . there would be help. Behind . . . it was behind him. He glimpsed nightmare there, and fired a burst of slugs at it. He turned and ran on, his chest constricting so that he couldn't get his breath. He stumbled down on his knees, pain daggering into his side, his vision blurred.

As a shadow drew across him, he emptied the entire magazine at it, then groped for the spare. He realized that to preserve himself from the agony to come, he should use that precious magazine on himself, but he couldn't really believe what was happening to him. Instead he emptied the last rounds into a looming darkness, and that seemed to have no effect at all. Scrubbing at his face to clear his vision, he looked up into a circular pit of darkness that contained row upon row of mandibles glittering like surgical steel and glass, amid a constellation of red glowing eyes.

"No," he managed to protest before the hooder slammed down on him.

Tented in its chitin, his screams became both muffled and echoey—as the creature commenced, with surgical precision, to feed.

Cormac held up his hand, and Shuriken came back to its holster without reluctance—perhaps sated by its excess of killing. Once it snicked back into place he turned towards movement registered behind, as two soldiers rose out of cover and began to level their rail-guns at him. A snap shot with his thin-gun knocked one over backwards with a hole through his forehead. Gant slammed into the second, knocking him two metres through the air before the man hit the ground, following fast to stab down with one hand, then stood up and shook blood from his fingers. Horrible, utterly horrible, though Cormac was not sure if what he was killing could actually be classified as fully alive.

Mostly, though, it was not Cormac and his companions who were accomplishing the wet work. The dracomen moved at frightening speed right into the rail-gun fire where iron slugs ripped through many of them, but these creatures were of extremely rugged construction and withstood more hits than any human could possibly sustain. Cormac even saw one of them fighting on with both of its arms blown away. It had still managed to bite out the throats of three Theocracy soldiers before gunfire from elsewhere finally cut it in half.

"Keep moving!" Cormac shouted. "And keep together."

Mika proved the most wayward—she kept wanting to stay with wounded dracomen, though whether to tend to them or to see what tissue samples she might obtain, Cormac could not judge. Gant and Thorn stayed on either side of him, whilst Fethan had gone running off with the dracomen and getting himself as bloody as they. Scar had come back occasionally to check if they were still alive.

"Where the hell are your people?" Cormac asked him the next time he returned.

Showing his teeth, Scar gestured in either direction along the Theocracy lines and gave a shrug. Obviously just punching a gap through those lines had not been enough for them—now they had achieved that objective it was time for them to play. Cormac could hear plenty of gunfire, but no screams from dying soldiers—but maybe those brain-burnt individuals did not feel pain.

The whining of an electric engine sounded to the right . . .

Cormac soon had Shuriken up a couple of metres in front of him, his fingers poised over the lethal device's attack menu on its holster.

"Time to ride!" Fethan bellowed, driving in with a balloon-tyred ground car he had just stolen—the blood on the driver's seat was fresh. All but Gant, the fastest mover anyway, boarded the vehicle as Fethan turned it towards mountains now looming in the purple haze of distance below the sinking gas giant.

"Check that out," Cormac instructed Thorn, gesturing at a pedestal-mounted grenade-launcher fixed to the back of the vehicle. Thorn pushed his way past Mika who was sitting on the metal floor with her back against the side. Seeing her pull out her laptop, Cormac commented, "Hell or high water won't stop your research on Dragon or dracomen."

She glanced up at him. "There's always so much more to learn about them."

"And what more have you learnt today?" he asked.

"A lot gets revealed about a body's structure when it is torn open," she said. "Scar is asexual, but his kin out there are not."

"I wonder if that would make Scar happy or sad," he said.

"I think you miss the point. Sex has more purpose than social bonding or physical gratification."

"Well, make the point clearer to me then," said Cormac, irritated.

"The point is that we are no longer dealing with just organic constructs. We are dealing with self-determining beings who can breed—a race."

"Well, that's nice," said Cormac distractedly. Then, "Can't this thing go any faster, Fethan?"

"I'm doing my bloody best," the cyborg replied.

Crouching down to retain his balance as the machine accelerated, now jouncing all over the place, Cormac continued to Mika, "Personally, I don't see the difference between a group of organic constructs and any naturally derived race, but I will be interested to know how the Earth Central AI sees it."

"You will let me live," stated Mika, echoing both Scar and Dragon.

"Still can't *ask* even the important ones?" he asked her. "I didn't promise anything, and what I promise is irrelevant—I wouldn't be the one to pull the trigger."

Mika was about to make some bitter comeback when Thorn's sudden frantic activity distracted her. They both turned as he slammed a cartridge of grenades into the launcher and swung the device round, then up.

Just then two shadows slid over above them.

The *Occam Razor* caught the last of the setting sun, and hung half-gilded in the sky long into the evening. Observing the massive thing through her binoculars, Lellan could not help but shudder. With the riotous fighting below it, this object seemed to represent some demon presiding over one of the numerous circles of Hell described in Theocracy dogma. She lowered her binoculars to observe men looking little better than walking corpses fighting those hellish lizard creatures. The dead on both sides strewed the churned ground and flattened vegetation, and now that most rail-guns were empty, the combat was hand-to-hand, or rather hand against claw and teeth.

"If you recalled our army, who would you instruct them to fight?" asked Carl, as he turned the aerofan back towards the compound embankment.

Lellan looked round at the Theocracy soldier, Sastol, who was the only other occupant of the aerofan. "Who is the enemy now?" she asked him.

"I do not know any more," he replied. "Perhaps *they* are." Unable to point, his wrists being secured to the rail of the aerofan, he nodded towards two heroynes striding through the flute grasses some distance away to their right. As Lellan and Carl turned to observe these creatures, one of them pecked downwards and came up with something that was recognizably a struggling soldier. Tilting its head back, it tossed the man around until it had him in the right position, then swallowed him head first.

"Sweet Lord," said Sastol.

The heroyne and its companion strode on in search of further prey, whilst the struggling lump slid slowly down its long neck to its stomach. Lellan considered going after it, but what would they achieve by blowing the creature open? The Theocracy soldiers now seemed little better than automatons, and apparently did not cease fighting even when captured. From what Sastol had told her of his own experience, she surmised that the soldiers did not have much individual mind left to them, and were merely following a program, albeit a complex one. As Carl finally brought the aerofan down onto the embankment, where they found Beckle and Uris attempting to get another aerofan up and running, Lellan noticed a light flashing on the essential part of the coms helmet she had hanging on her belt. Unhooking it, she placed the speaker button in her ear and spoke into its mouthpiece.

"Yes, what is it?" she asked.

"We have located agent Ian Cormac and his companions. What are your instructions?"

"Just bring them safely to the compound, Rom," she replied, wondering if the drone's voices had become distinct from each other the moment she had named them, or if they had always been that way. In appearance they had originally been indistinguishable, but even that was no longer so—the damage each had received giving them visible individuality as well. Bringing her binoculars back up to her eyes, Lellan began searching the horizon. Shortly she located the two cylindrical shapes heading directly towards the compound, and below them, intermittently visible between still-upright stands of vegetation, came a car with an interesting collection of passengers.

Fethan and Thorn, the one with a bushy orange beard and the other with a cropped black one, were easily identifiable from a distance. Lellan had no idea who the woman was, and presumed the other, silver-haired man to be the agent Cormac. The shaven-headed trooper who had, leaping aboard at speed, just joined them in the car, she presumed to be something more than human. Lowering her binoculars she turned to lean on the rail of the aerofan and peered down the slope of the embankment. "Any luck with that thing?" she asked Beckle and Uris casually. The two men crouching by the tilted aerofan, at the bottom of the bank, had its control column in pieces between them.

Uris looked up. "Needs a new column, but we can still run it."

"Then get it in the air and head back to the compound," ordered Lellan. "See if you can find any spares there. Also get everyone prepared to move out. We don't know what these creatures are likely to do when they've finished out here."

The two men stood and with one heave dropped the aerofan back into its upright position. In disgust Beckle kicked the pieces of its control column to one side.

"You will go with them," said Lellan, stabbing a finger at Sastol. He might have surrendered himself, and circum-stances might have changed dramatically, but he was still Theocracy and she trusted him not at all. She watched as Carl unclipped the man's wrist-ties from the rail and stepped back with weapon drawn while the captive climbed to the ground.

Climbing onto the righted aerofan, Beckle sat with his legs either side of the control column base, and his arms inside the casing. Uris waited cautiously until Sastol was aboard, then climbed on behind him, his pulse-rifle covering the prisoner's back. The fans started with a slightly discordant drone, sending a spray of mud in every direction, as the machine rose and slid off over the chequerboard of ponds towards the compound. There, Lellan knew, Sastol would be wise to stick close to her two men, for the newly liberated pond workers had a penchant for removing the breathing apparatus of any Theocracy soldiers caught, then tossing them into one of the squerm ponds to see if they could survive even long enough to suffocate.

"We may find out what those creatures are all about," said Carl.

Lellan turned back to observe the approaching car, and watched in perplexity as one of the lizard creatures ran along behind it then jumped aboard without either attacking or being attacked. It seemed there were some things she still needed to know.

As the vehicle drew closer Lellan saw that more of the creatures were now emerging from the surrounding vegetation and running alongside the vehicle. Despite no signs of aggression towards the car's occupants, or of Rom and Ram considering the creatures a threat, Lellan turned to Carl. "Take us up and out a few metres."

Carl sharply did as requested, obviously glad to get out of reach.

"What's happening, Fethan?" Lellan called out when the whole strange procession had finally reached the embankment.

"Always the unexpected," the old cyborg shouted up.

As if in confirmation of that, for a second the evening grew brighter than day, then the whole plain erupted with fire and gouting explosions. With after images chasing across her retinas, Lellan saw Cormac conversing with the lizard creature in the car. The creature then turned to others of its kind gathered around the vehicle, and after a moment they melted away into the surrounding vegetation.

Then all was chaos as they fled the hellfire the *Occam Razor* laid down upon the land.

"Is this it?" asked the woman he guessed to be Lellan, removing her mask as they piled into the workers' barracks. "Is this the start of it?"

Tiredly removing his own mask, Cormac considered telling her that the start of it had been when Skellor arrived in the system, but what gain would there be in that information?

"I'd say Skellor has just realized what's been attacking the Theocracy army out there," he said.

"And what's that?" Lellan studied Scar with suspicion.

"Dracomen," said Cormac, also glancing at the dracoman. "Dragon's children, if you like." At this he saw her loosen her grip on the pulse-rifle she pretended to hold so casually. Because Dragon had destroyed the laser arrays, Cormac felt she must have some trust in that creature's intentions. He did not have time to disillusion her.

"This Skellor is attacking them? Why them specifically . . . and why now?"

Cormac thought he knew the answer to that, though he did not like it. "Because Dragon was one of those he came here to silence, and I think because I just got clear of the area, and because he likes destroying things."

"He doesn't want to kill you too, then?" Carl interjected, squatting next to an electric heater.

Cormac glanced at him. "In the same way that the Theocracy would rather capture your leader alive than kill her." He gestured at Lellan, who winced when she realized what he meant. Cormac turned to Scar. "What's happening out there now?"

The dracoman held up a claw and slowly closed it in a squeezing motion. "Many die, but we disperse and we hide."

Cormac nodded to himself—just at the last he'd spotted some burrowing into the ground. Skellor might be blitzing the area with laser strikes, but he would need to incinerate every square metre, to some depth, in order to kill every dracoman. He tried not to become too attracted to the idea of Skellor committing such genocide, and thereby obviating a future headache for the Polity. So far the dracomen had been most helpful, and had not committed any significant crime.

"They all listen to you," he said to Scar. "You are somehow linked to them." To one side, he was aware of Mika becoming more alert. "Is that why Dragon named you Cadmus?"

"They are my people," said Scar, with almost a touch of pride in his voice.

Cormac nodded. "Then you must stay here with them." He turned to Mika. "You'll continue watching them, and report?"

Mika nodded eagerly and turned to Gant. Silently he unhooked from his shoulder the pack which now contained the bulk of her instruments, and handed it across to Scar. Without any acknowledgement, the dracoman accepted the pack, its attention still firmly fixed on Cormac.

"You *will* let us live?" Scar repeated.

Cormac replied, "I'll try to save those of you that manage to survive, for now. Later, we can only hope—as the decision will rest in Polity hands . . . but I'll do all I can."

As he headed for the airtight door, Scar turned towards Mika. "She not survive with us," he said dismissively.

Mika smiled, then began unstrapping her oxygen pack, collar mask and piping. She handed these items to the soldier Uris, before following the dracoman towards the door.

"Oh, I'll survive," she said.

"What the hell?" said Lellan, stepping forward to prevent what she could only perceive as suicide.

Cormac caught her arm. "She doesn't need the oxygen we need out there." He gestured to the pack Uris held. "That thing's been empty since this morning."

"But how the hell does she . . ." Lellan fell silent as both the dracoman and Mika exited into the night.

"We, however"—he gestured to himself and Thorn—"do need oxygen. We'll need enough to get us to your brother's ship. We'll also need transport to get us there quickly."

"What—so you can escape, Polity agent?" spoke up a man who was obviously a prisoner—his wrists were bound, and he wore Theocracy uniform. There was also a dressing behind his ear where his aug should have been.

"No," said Cormac, aware that everyone nearby was much interested in his answer. "But so I can deal with our friend up there."

The prisoner snorted.

Lellan asked, "And how do you propose to do that?"

"Too many ears and eyes here," said Cormac, taking in the soldiers, ex-pond workers, and prisoners all jammed into this one airtight building. "You'll just have to trust me on that."

"I should trust you," Lellan repeated leadenly.

Cormac replied, "I am Polity, and in the end that has always been *your* only choice. Tell me, what other options have you ever had, and what options do you have now?"

Lellan fell silent for a moment, then said, "There's an oxygen refill tank in the building next door, and we have two working aerofans—enough to carry six people. We also have those two war drones that shepherded you in. When do you want to move?"

Cormac thought about that: once upon a time he'd enjoyed an utterly human pastime called "sleep," but to indulge in that now was madness as Skellor could decide at any moment that he had been playing mortal games for long enough, and that it was time to totally flash burn the planet. Without thinking about it, he took out the reel of stimulant patches Mika had given him, tore one off and, reaching inside his shirt, stuck it to his torso.

"Right now," he said.

There was almost a feeling of disappointment in having located Ian Cormac so easily, but then locating was one thing and apprehending another—as Skellor had discovered the last time he'd nearly had the man in his grasp. With a thought he shut down the lasers that had been searing the plain and focused all his instruments upon the small compound itself. The destruction had raised clouds of smoke and steam that did nothing to improve his view, and anyway the dracomen had successfully dispersed, disappearing like fog in a hurricane. But they would go with the rest of the planet, once he had Cormac up here in his bridge pod to watch the show.

Alerted by the movement of people coming out of the barracks buildings, Skellor closed in the focus of a scope so he could see each individual clearly. It annoyed him that he did not have any weapon accurate enough to target any individual from up here. Most of the *Occam*'s armament was apocalyptic—the smallest smart missiles aboard, with the appropriate range, delivered enough of a punch to take out a tank. With the right weapon he could have stripped Cormac of all his companions, before taking him; as it was, Skellor's remaining creatures on the surface would need to prove adequate to the task.

About to send his calloraptors down from the mountains, Skellor observed Cormac and some others taking off on a couple of aerofans, warded on either side by the two war drones, and heading in that same direction. All so easy, Skellor felt, and in a flush of boredom felt the urge to just wipe it all away—burn it all and move on. But then, deep in those alien structures of himself, he heard an echo of Aphran's laughter, and his vision settled clearly for a moment on Cormac turning to look up towards him. And Skellor decided to stay his hand.

The firing from orbit had been ceased for some minutes now, but Stanton was not going to head back to Jarvellis until he had drunk at least one celebratory cup of coffee laced with brandy.

"Whoever said vengeance is sweet certainly knew what they were talking about," he said, trying to put the other two at their ease.

"He killed your parents," said the boy, Apis, who claimed to be an Outlinker. "He probably killed more than them."

Setting a tin cup on the red-hot grid of his little stove, Stanton grinned to himself, then searched his utility belt for the coffee essence and a miniature bottle of brandy. The boy was groping for justification. He had obviously been as shocked by the duration of Aberil's agony as the girl had been. Though these two had reasons for vengeance themselves, they did not find it as sweet as did Stanton himself.

"Why did it take so long?" Eldene said at last, choking a little on her words. "Did it enjoy . . . torturing him?"

Stanton shook his head. "He could have shortened it all by taking off his mask and suffocating. Perhaps he didn't really think he was going to die," he said. Then, after studying his two charges for a moment, "There's no deliberate torture, really. Hooders just eat that way in order to survive. Their main diet is the grazers living in the mountains, which feed on some poisonous fungi there. The grazers' bodies are layered through with black fats that accumulate toxins. When the hooders capture them under their hoods, they need to slice their way through their prey very meticulously, to eat only what are called the creature's white fats."

"Why not kill first, though?" Apis asked.

Stanton tipped coffee essence into the rapidly heating water, then a handful of rough sugar crystals. Glancing at the boy he answered, "Apparently it's all due to the flight response. When the hooder goes after a grazer, the grazer immediately starts breaking down the black fat to provide itself with the energy to flee, and then its blood supply and muscles become toxic, too. So any serious damage to either could release poisons into the uncontaminated white fat."

"So it can't let them bleed?" Apis gaped in disbelieving horror.

"What about humans, then?" asked Eldene.

Stanton tested his coffee with his finger, then rocked back on his heels and opened his pack. For a moment the two forgot their morbid curiosity as he handed out potato bread and preserved sausage.

"Humans get treated just like the other kinds of grazers they occasionally catch," said Stanton, himself munching on a piece of sausage. "The hooder has to make the assumption that they are fungus grazers, so dissects them as meticulously, even though discovering no black fat in them. You heard the results of that." Stanton tipped some brandy into the coffee, then after taking a sip from the mug, he offered it around. He was glad when both the youngsters showed a disgust at its taste and declined more.

"That seems to be all finished now over there." He gestured over his shoulder to where the plain had earlier been boiling with fire. "We'll finish up here, then head on in. I'd stay longer, just to be sure, but"—he gestured to the remaining two oxygen bottles resting on the aero-fan's floor—"we don't have that luxury."

"Where will you go now—to the Underground?" asked Eldene.

"My ship first," Stanton replied. "That's where I keep everything that's precious to me." He looked around. "I don't think there's much more I can do here. Hopefully ECS will come soon, and perhaps it'd be better if I were not around when it does."

"What about us?" asked Eldene.

"You go underground," he said, staring at them directly, "and you wait for the Polity." He could see that they were curious to know why he should not hang about when the Polity arrived, but he did not feel inclined to give any explanations. For a minute he just sipped his way down through his cup of coffee, listening for sounds of movement in the surrounding vegetation. The laser strikes had driven away much of the local fauna, but most certainly the smell of broiled meat would bring the said fauna back, and he did not care to be around when that happened.

"Of course, you know what the irony is?" They looked at him attentively and he went on, "Eating human flesh just makes hooders, and the rest of them, sick. It's the oxygen I think—too rich for them."

"Yes, that *is* ironic," said Apis, exchanging a look with Eldene.

After packing away his bits and pieces, Stanton stood and gestured them back to the aerofan. Soon the three were settled on board, hurtling over a charred landscape below a black sky bright with a surplus of moons.

It was a bright and beautiful night to be skimming over the foothills, their two aerofans warded on either side by the battered and fire-blackened cylinders of the war drones. It was a fantastic night to be alive, and Gant wondered if he would have appreciated it any more by being so.

"There are creatures in the sky ahead of us," said Rom, its voice coming surprisingly loud to them in the roar of the wind, it being sent by directional beam.

"Probably kite-bats," Lellan said, turning towards Cormac. "Don't worry about them, they'll get out of the way."

Gant noted Cormac's quick glance, but did not have to be told to keep alert. He nodded and patted his pulse-rifle. Slung across his back was the APW he was saving for any situation warranting artillery. Focusing ahead, with his vision set to infrared, Gant made out a great flock of flying creatures circling the mountain peaks. Some of them were even roosting on peaks, turning them into a bluish melee of angled limbs and wing fabric.

"How far to the entrance?" Cormac asked Lellan.

"A couple of kilometres yet," the rebel leader replied. She pointed down with her thumb. "There are breakout caves all across here, but there's no point even trying them. Aberil was so keen we shouldn't escape that he bombed every one of them during his landing."

Gazing out into silvered night, the agent said, "You know, Skellor will be watching us right now." He gestured towards the war drones. "We're probably about the only mechanical things airborne, and with those two along . . ."

"Well," said Lellan, "unless he can also track you through stone, we'll soon frustrate him."

"He may even possess that ability," murmured Cormac.

Something was tickling the edge of Gant's memory. He knew that he could easily run a program in his head to track down that memory, but that would make him more Golem and less Gant, so he wanted to retain his imperfect recall. The flying creatures did not seem to be dispersing, in fact more were taking to the air, and now the whole flock was swirling in this direction. He could now see them much more clearly, and some of the others must already be able to see them through their night visors. There was something familiar . . .

"These kite-bats," he said, "is it the mating season or something?"

"They don't have a mating season." Lellan was leaning forwards to peer into the darkness. After a moment she pulled back on the steering column, abruptly slowing the aerofan so that Rom and Ram, and the other fan carrying Thorn, Carl and Fethan, shot ahead—then had to turn to wheel round to come back.

"Those are not kite-bats," Lellan decided.

Glancing at the agent, Gant asked him grimly, "Were there any winged calloraptors on Callorum?"

Reluctantly, it seemed to Gant, Cormac donned the night glasses Lellan had provided, and replied, "Never really looked into that. Mika would be the one to ask."

Just then, Carl brought the other aerofan alongside, and Fethan shouted across, "What are those things?"

Speaking into the comlink hooked at her neck, Lellan replied briefly, "The enemy, I think." She looked to Cormac and Gant for confirmation.

Cormac pulled up his sleeve and fingered in some complex attack programs on his lethal little weapon's holster console. Shuriken started clunking in its holster, as if eager to get out. Cormac withdrew it, and held it in the palm of his left hand. With the right hand he drew his thin-gun. He turned to Gant. "How many of them, do you estimate?"

Without even resorting to any of the counting programs that were available to him Gant said, "A couple of thousand visible. There may be more."

"Use the APW—I think the need to conceal our presence became superfluous long ago," said Cormac. Then to Lellan,

"We need to get to that cave as fast as we can. Just burn through them and keep going . . . agreed?"

Lellan had no better suggestions so she nodded, even though Gant guessed she resented the agent usurping her authority.

Cormac went on, "Does the cave have defences and, if so, what kind?"

"In the entrance we'll be using there's one pulse-cannon in the shaft leading down, and another one in the lower tunnel, then armoured doors guarding the main cavern. They just won't get through," she replied.

"Don't bet on it," said Cormac, gazing at the boiling cloud of creatures ahead. "These fuckers don't die all that easy."

Lellan stared at him for a moment then looked across to see she had Carl's attention, before making a chopping motion with her hand for them to move ahead.

"We go straight through," she informed them all. In reaction there came the cycling whine of U-chargers operating inside the war drones as they brought their energy-profligate weapons systems online. Lellan tilted her joystick forward and Carl followed suit. Both aero-fans tilted and accelerated. Moving ahead, the war drones turned in midair from floating pillars to rollers barbed with weapons. Then suddenly they were into a thunder of flapping wings, amid horrible cawings and hissings issuing from triple-jawed mouths opening all around them like satanic fuchsias. Cormac tossed Shuriken over the side, as the two drones opened up on the creatures. Swathes of violet fire left green afterimages across their night-vision glasses and visors. Gant and Thorn had also opened up with APWs, burning into this sky of moving flesh. Screaming, half-incinerated raptors dropped out of this turmoil—their wing skin seared away to leave nothing but black spiderish bone slashing at the air. Smuts of soot clouded the air like negative snow, and the flames raised a stench as of burning sesame oil. As he selectively fired into the huge flock of creatures wherever it seemed thickest, Gant saw a half-burnt raptor land on the rail and Cormac emptying the entire clip of his thin-gun into its visage to prevent it scrambling aboard. When it became evident that the creature would just not die, Gant himself turned and blasted it—and most of the rail—burning down into its fellows underneath, where Shuriken shimmered back and forth, slamming through any that tried to attack them from below.

Lellan was yelling something, but Cormac could not hear her above the racket as he removed the empty clip from his gun and replaced it with another. He leaned closer.

"I'm taking us lower!" she shouted.

Cormac nodded and hit Shuriken's recall. The device shot up from below the aerofans, where now lack of clearance from the ground gave no room for the raptors to manoeuvre, and it held station just out from Cormac's shoulder. Selecting a different attack program, he sent Shuriken off and running again. The difficulty he was finding with it was compensating for the two war drones. Shuriken's micromind possessed adequate facility to factor in the presence of "friendly fire" from armed humans or the equivalent, but since war drones of this sophistication were a recent invention, it had no set program blocks to account for them. Cormac found that the nearest he could achieve was by describing the two drones to Shuriken as human exotroops with AG packs and heavy weapons. This seemed to be working so far, though he noted some hesitation in Shuriken's flight when it came close to either of the machines. The drones, being technically more sophisticated, ignored the throwing star as they continued to incinerate flying calloraptors.

Drawing his thin-gun again, Cormac aimed single shots at the calloraptors' wing joints; these hits, when he managed them, proving more effective than any number of impacts on the creatures' heads or bodies. These calloraptors were clearly not direct kin of those that Scar had shot on Callorum—but they did possess the same miraculous ability to heal themselves as the hybrid he had encountered in Skellor's laboratory. Nevertheless, even ability to heal did not negate the effects of gravity once a wing-joint shattered and the wing collapsed. The ones he thus crippled soon ended up far behind and out of the chase.

"We're coming up on it now!" Lellan yelled. She was flying one-handed, holding a pulse-rifle in her right hand, its light stock resting in the crook of her arm.

"Call the drones in behind us!" Cormac shouted back, then found himself knocked to his knees as a raptor, its wings burned down to the bone, crashed down on top of him. Like a bird the creature had no arms, so it grabbed at him with its powerful foot claws and tried to close its two remaining jaws on his shoulder. Even in such an extremity, Cormac realized the creature was not actually trying to kill, but merely immobilize him. The aerofan lurched aside as Lellan was nearly knocked over during the ensuing struggle. Cormac caught a glimpse of a rockface speeding past him to the left, then one of the drones dropping back overhead. With his hand gripping his attacker's throat he fired repeatedly into its skull, hoping the raptor's brain would not heal as quickly as the rest of it. Just then Gant grabbed the creature from behind and wrenched it upright, tearing away one wing and snapping its double spine. The broken bone in its back quickly realigning, it turned to attack Gant instead.

A sudden impact slid Cormac along the floor of the aerofan, now tilting at thirty degrees. He caught what remained of the rail on that side, his legs lunging out into empty space over rock speeding by. Then they were dropping down into a shaft, screaming raptors all around them still. Behind them flashed the arc-welder stuttering of a pulse-cannon, and they spun out of the main shaft into another tunnel. Struggling to climb back on board, Cormac spotted Gant and the calloraptor tearing at each other with hideous ferocity as they sailed past him. He glanced back to see a war drone, clad in a skin of attacking raptors, hit the cavern floor and bounce end over end. While avoiding this, the other aerofan clipped stone and flipped over, three bodies disappearing amid the mass of wings and nightmare mouths just as Gant had.

"Don't slow down!" Cormac bellowed, when he realized Lellan had started to do so. She gestured forward, just as pulse-rifles filled the cavern with a blizzard of blue stars.

20

"Now we're getting to it," said the woman as she observed Brother Nebbish with his robe of sackcloth, his expression of pious disapproval, the slight aura around his head, and a book clutched in his right hand.

"At last into the valley came Brother Nebbish, and when he saw how Stenophalis, Pegrum and Egris had failed, he was undaunted."

Nebbish was staring bug-eyed at the mess strewn across the valley floor as he walked into the place. The remains of the other three were huge in comparison to him, and he did not stand astride the valley.

"Warded by his faith and armed with the Word of God, Brother Nebbish demanded of the Hooded One, 'Come forth and face me!'"

The woman choked on her laughter when in the picture the good Brother dropped his book, hauled his robes up over his knobbly knees, and took off down the valley like an Olympic sprinter.

"Standing always in the light of God, Brother Nebbish smote the monster with the iron of God's law, and the monster was bowed."

Nebbish had fallen flat on his face at this point, as the shadowy creature rose up to follow him. His face thick with ash, Nebbish looked back at it as he scrambled to his feet, and with his mouth hanging open in what had to be a perpetual scream, he sprinted on.

"Standing always in the light of God, Brother Nebbish smote the monster with the radiance of God's justice, and the monster was blinded."

Nebbish could certainly shift, but he just didn't have quite so many legs as the thing that was coming after him.

"Standing always in the light of God, Brother Nebbish finally smote the monster with the thunder of God's truth, and the monster was cast down."

The woman had never before seen a realistic depiction of a man being peeled like a potato. She was also intrigued to watch the movement of muscle and sinew, as the skinless Brother Nebbish ran screaming on a conveyor belt of chitin, towards the deep shadow containing a glitter of horrid eyes.

"And what moral does this story have?" she wondered.

"Hooders have more fun?" the book suggested.

She dropped the book as if it had tried to bite her.

Stanton eased the aerofan down on a rocky outcrop and the machine made a crunching sound as it crushed the countless molluscs colonizing the surface. As the machine's fans wound down to stillness, he held out his hand to Apis, who handed over the binoculars he had been gazing through.

"Primitive, but effective enough in this light," the boy commented.

Stanton thought at first he was referring to the great mass of creatures ahead, then realized Apis meant the binoculars—being an Outlinker he had probably only come across such technology in a museum. Stanton then found himself amused, realizing the boy had only spoken thus to highlight the fact, to the girl, that he came from the *superior* Polity.

"You do tend to find that with some technologies," said Stanton, bringing the lenses up to his eyes. "They reach the limit of their development. I wouldn't call these a satisfactory limit though. I could do with autotracking lenses, shake compensators, and image enhancement." He paused to study the view ahead, continuing, "Then again, I doubt those would tell me anything different." He lowered the binoculars. "I haven't the faintest idea what those creatures are, but even in half-light they look like killers to me. We'll have to go round them to try for the ship."

*

Thorn kept his head well down and tried not to think beyond surviving the next few minutes. The pulse-cannon was only a few metres ahead of him. It was firing away at full power, its shots passing only a metre above his head, yet still the creatures were somehow getting past it—to fly straight into the fusillade coming up from the rebel soldiers who he saw were now retreating towards the armoured doors. To his left his aerofan lay on its side draped in pieces of smoking calloraptor remnants—the same unpleasant fallout that was presently snowing down on himself. The soldier Carl was tangled in the wreckage of the crashed fan. He was wasted, as not even these creatures could have survived what had happened to him. Further back, the war drones were down and out of it, their energy sources drained beyond any possibility of self-recharge. Somehow knowing this, the calloraptors had quickly lost interest in them and were going after more mobile prey.

The old cyborg, Fethan, had been flung much further along the cavern. By running like a madman, he had made it to the rebel line—only losing the skin off his back to one tenacious creature that would not let go until blasted to fragments. Thorn considered fleeing too, but the fractured bone sticking out of his shin told him he would not be running anywhere; just as the piece of fan blade imbedded in his forearm told him he would not be playing the violin for a while. That he had managed to retain his APW he considered a miracle, and he wondered for how many minutes it would extend his life, should he finally make some move.

Just back from the wreckage of the aerofan was a door he had seen one of the creatures tear open, perhaps hoping this would provide another route into the rebel stronghold. When the creature emerged from it shortly after, Thorn guessed some sort of maintenance room lay beyond the door. Perhaps a place for tools, even spares for the pulse-cannons. Maybe if he could just . . .

Suddenly the nearest pulse-cannon ceased firing, and immediately the creatures were swarming past it overhead.

He turned back to see them landing by the armoured door, and tearing at it in mindless anger. Others turned their attention to Lellan's abandoned aerofan, ripping the grounded machine to pieces. But his simple turning motion betrayed him, and three of them dropped from the flock to come hissing towards him like gulls after a discarded fish. With his left hand he swung round his APW, and managed to incinerate two of them before the third was upon him. He smashed away with his weapon and tried to bring the barrel to bear. But the creature had closed its claws into his clothing and the flesh of his stomach, its wings wide open to steady it as its pink star of a mouth stabbed towards his face. Flinching back, he saw silver hands close round each shoulder of the creature's wings. With a new screaming, it tore apart before him, its double chest parting down its central channel. Then a figure stepped through, grabbed Thorn by his collar, and dragged him at speed to the maintenance room. There Thorn pulled himself up on one leg, and stared across at what was still recognizably Gant, as the Golem drop-kicked a pursuing calloraptor back amongst its fellows, then fired a shot that sent the lot of them tumbling backwards.

Through gritted teeth Thorn said, "Seems we've been in caves like this before, old man."

Gant glanced at him. "Tell me you've got a mem-plant," he said.

"'Fraid not," Thorn replied.

"Best you survive then." The Golem then hauled closed the steel door, and braced his back against it.

In one bay Skellor found a shuttle that was not so interpenetrated with Jain substructures as to be almost unrecoverable. Those stems and branches that had penetrated its hull, he quickly withdrew, initiating the necessary repairs on their way out. Whilst transporting its egg from Medical through the strange organic spaces of the ship, he accelerated the growth of this one chosen from a new batch of calloraptors. Upon getting it to the bay, he paused only to retard its wing growth and then make swift surgical alterations so that when he stripped the egg case away the raptor tumbled out possessing only long bony arms ending in optic interface plugs. Skellor then wrapped the new creature in a Jain pseudopod, inserted it into the pilot's chair of the shuttle, tore away the manual controls, and connected it directly into the craft's main systems. Now he was ready: he had his way of bringing Cormac to the *Occam*. Skellor then opened the bay doors and ejected the craft and its raptor pilot into space—another of his experimental creatures wrenched painfully into the world.

Looking through the eyes of his other creatures on the surface, Skellor now felt a grinding boredom at the inevitability of it all. He had destroyed every spacecraft evident on the surface of the planet, and though there might be something hidden in the caverns, it could not get off the ground without detection. So really Cormac, as much as his two companions trapped in that store room, had nowhere to run. The agent might choose to take his own life rather than be captured, but Skellor's anxiety about that was leavened, for he knew he could rebuild and revive anyone who had been dead for up to ten hours. Skellor's greatest fear was that Cormac might select a form of suicide that could utterly destroy his brain—as Captain Tomalon had done—for not even Skellor could recreate something for which he possessed no pattern.

Though the remaining pulse-cannon was still destroying his creatures in great numbers, he knew it could kill no more than an eighth of their number before they finally broke through. Of the remaining raptors maybe half would be killed inside the cavern itself before the human population was slaughtered and Cormac finally taken. Their losses didn't matter very much, because Skellor did not intend to retrieve his raptors. Once Cormac was safely aboard the shuttle that was even now going into descent, Skellor could break this planet like he had broken the moonlet from which he had obtained materials for growth.

Cormac glanced at the empty Shuriken holster on his wrist and swore. It seemed to him that he suffered nothing but loss all the way down the line, and he was damned if he was going to lose any more. Gazing around the huge cavern in which he stood, anger and suppressed grief prevented him from feeling impressed. All he saw was another trap—and that was not where he wanted to be. Lellan was over conferring with her men, setting up heavy weapons for the moment the raptors broke through the door—as they most certainly would, any time now. She had said she would be back soon, but minutes dragged slow and leaden. Did she not realize how unimportant all the little battles down here really were? Abruptly, Cormac came to a decision. After a conversation held with Lellan, before they had come here to the mountains, he had learned that he needed exit cavern seventeen, which lay to the right of something called the watergate. He gazed along the river's length winding past the pillartowns and the ponds, the crop fields and storage bunkers. It had to be there: one of those tunnel entrances beside where the river entered the huge cavern. There must be the watergate.

Cormac walked away past a big antique rail-gun now being bolted to the stone floor, past soldiers setting up a barricade—something pretty futile considering their attackers could fly. He headed on down an alley leading between two large warehouses, to an open space where various military vehicles had been abandoned. As he walked along, he found it a relief to be breathing again without a mask over his face. Reaching the empty vehicles, he climbed into something that resembled the bastard offspring of a jeep and a golfer's cart, engaged the simple electric drive, and headed away. Someone shouted after him, but he ignored that. He would have readily shot anyone who attempted to stop him.

Now on the move again, he did have a little time to spare for his surroundings. Just as Blegg had informed him: the Underworld was bigger than the surface colonization, and from what he could see was well organized. Whether it was better in this respect than what he had briefly seen above he could not judge, as all he had seen up there was ruined by war, and the one city he had only glimpsed. Studying the fields and ponds down here he saw that the inhabitants had taken the same agricultural route as the Theocracy, and as so many other planetary populations: the usual cereal and vegetable crops, but also protein harvested from species of fast-growing crustaceans and chilopods that were not the product of natural evolution, but genetically spliced for this very purpose hundreds of years in the past. He wondered how the Theocracy, farming the same unnatural creatures, could square that with their rigid beliefs, but then recalled how religions had a long history of "squaring things" so their senior echelons could live comfortably whilst the lower ones did the labour and suffering.

The stone track he drove along sat well above the ponds and fields stepping down in tiers towards the central river. He noticed the marks of cutting tools on stone and realized that every field and every pond had been excised out of rock. Looking round at the immensity of the cavern, with its gridded ceiling and pillar-towns, he wondered just how much had been excavated and how much was natural. But, then, over a couple of centuries it would have been possible to shift a lot of stone.

Eventually the track curved directly past the plascrete banks of the river, near where a couple of waterwheels, maybe fifty metres in diameter, were constantly churned round by the current. Cormac wondered if the river itself was the only source of energy here—generating the power to supply heating and lighting, while the plants growing under those lights provided the oxygen. Or if there was somewhere a hidden fusion plant or geothermal energy tap? He reckoned there must be something like those, for this place was not just some agrarian idyll. There had to be industries here for the building of the pillartowns and the manufacture of tools and weapons. This underground world was definitely not low-tech.

Beyond the waterwheels, lock gates reached halfway up the height of the cave mouth from which the river issued. Hinged on either side to the walls of the cavern, these were driven by huge hydraulic rams, and were presently open. Cormac could not discern the purpose of these gates until he drew closer and saw that, just back from the cave mouth, another tunnel led off to one side, opening just above the surface of the water. Closing the lock gates would force the water level to rise and be diverted into this alternative tunnel. Perhaps this was to provide further hydro-electric energy from a hidden generator, or maybe just a flood-prevention measure.

Behind the waterwheels, but before the lock, a level bridge stretched across the river. Cormac observed that tunnels had been bored into the wall on either side of the river's entrance. Lellan had told him earlier that exit seventeen lay to the right of the watergate, and this was soon confirmed for him when he saw the large 17 etched into the rock above one tunnel right ahead of him. Soon he plunged into it, lights coming on automatically above him. The tunnel drifted left in a slow arc and eventually emerged into the natural cave cut by the river. For a while he motored along on a narrow track beside the thundering white water, then his route cut away from the river bank and began to rise. When he began to find himself gasping for breath, he had to flip his breather mask up, realizing that it wasn't the airlocks that retained the oxygen in the larger cavern. He guessed that it must be continually topped up, which confirmed his suspicion about there being other sources of energy, since greenery would not be able to do the job alone.

A few minutes after donning his mask, he came to an open area where a couple of vehicles were parked in front of a circular armoured door, with a smaller door set into it. Three soldiers stepped out of their vehicles, as he halted his own and got out. One, who was evidently an officer, approached him.

"We are to offer you all assistance," she said, her fingers resting against her coms helmet, while she listened to instructions delivered through the device.

Cormac studied her and then the two big men with her. He was frankly tired of seeing people around him die. "Just confirm for me how to get to *Lyric II* once I reach the surface."

"We'll take you there," the woman insisted, taking her fingers away from her helmet at last.

"No, just give me the directions," he repeated.

The woman gestured behind her. "There's only one route down the hill, which takes you directly to the river. You follow that downstream to the Cistern, and the ship rests on the largest beach. You won't see it though."

"I know all about the chameleonware," Cormac replied, heading for the smaller door. Then he paused and turned back. "Tell Lellan . . ." He paused, momentarily unable to go on. If he failed in his attempt, this whole planet would be denuded of human life. If he succeeded, however . . . he succeeded.

"Tell her the Polity *will* come."

The woman smiled at this, and he did not add that they might well be coming to inspect an ashpit over a charnel house.

The calloraptors' racket outside ceased once the pulse-cannon started up again. Gant had dragged over a heavy pedestal-mounted grinding machine, and jammed it against the warped and mutilated door of the workshop, before turning back to Thorn.

"We'll need to do something about that." The Golem pointed at Thorn's shattered leg.

"No, really?" said Thorn, groping in the bag of medical supplies he had earlier retrieved from the ATV. Finding what he wanted he slapped three drug patches on his knee, and a further one on his biceps. Gant moved off to scour the workshop and small storage room attached. Shortly he returned with rolls of insulating tape, a plascrete sprayer, and varying lengths of alloy tube that was probably used for water pipe.

"I can see what you're thinking, and I don't think I like it," murmured Thorn. Before the analgesic patch on his biceps had fully done its work, he wrenched out the aerofan fragment imbedded in his arm. That there was no instant gush of blood to denote a severed artery almost surprised him, as that was the way his luck had been going. He then caught the roll of insulating tape Gant tossed him, and wound some of it tightly around the wound. Meanwhile, Gant was studying his leg.

"Here, take this," the Golem said at last, holding out the plascrete sprayer.

"So you're qualified in field surgery?" said Thorn, groping for humour.

"Who took that bullet out of your arse on Thraxum?" Gant muttered.

"I was trying to forget about that." Thorn looked away while Gant taped lengths of the alloy tube to his boot, and bound them close to the protruding fracture.

"I'll pull it straight," said Gant. "When I give the word, I want you to start spraying the plascrete."

Thorn nodded, then yelled out in agony. He watched in morbid horror the splintered bone drawn back into his flesh as Gant pulled the leg straight. When the limb seemed about the correct length, Gant gave the order and Thorn began to spray. He yelled again as the reacting epoxies burned the open wound. As soon as his lower leg was encased in its makeshift cast, Gant hauled him to his feet.

"At least you can walk a little now," said Gant.

"I'll not be winning any races," growled Thorn.

Gant turned to look towards the entrance. "You know, if that pulse-gun stops again, that door won't hold them out much longer," he said.

Thorn shrugged. "Do we need *longer* to formulate an escape plan?" he asked.

"You know, you get even more sarcastic as you get older," said Gant.

"At least I have that option," said Thorn. Then noticing Gant's odd glance, he added, "To get older, I mean."

Gant stared at him. "It bothers you that much, about me?" he asked.

"I grieved for your death, and now I feel cheated," said Thorn.

"You may not have been cheated, as whether or not I am really Gant is a moot point. I never intended for you not to know, but I had the memplant put in thirty years before I even met you—when I was a kid back on Earth. It just never seemed important enough to mention."

"That you were immortal?" asked Thorn.

"Is it immortality? I don't know. I *do* know that many other Sparkind have memplants, so why don't you?"

Thorn shrugged. "Just never got round to it."

The firing of the pulse-cannon ceased again, followed by the roar of calloraptors storming up the tunnel outside.

Gant headed towards the door. "Do me a favour," he said. "If we ever get out of this, get yourself mem-planted, will you?"

"Can you still get drunk?" Thorn asked as Gant stepped over to the door, and braced himself against the grinding machine.

"I have that option," Gant replied, his expression puzzled.

"Then I will get it done, and we'll celebrate in *Elysium*."

Gant did not get much chance to reply to that as the first calloraptor hit the door and managed to wriggle its head around the warped metal.

Eldene woke with a start. She had fallen asleep despite the cold, her back propped against the rail and her head resting on the Outlinker's shoulder. He seemed to put out plenty of warmth, though, and when she realized he had his arm around her she felt a surge of some feeling she did not really want to identify. She realized that Stanton—a bulky silhouette against the stars and one tumbling moon of the predawn sky—must have spoken and that was what had woken her.

"About ten minutes," Stanton continued, and from that Eldene surmised they would arrive on solid ground soon. Apis did not remove his protective arm from her. Glancing at him in the half-light, she saw no sign of embarrassment at such new-found intimacy.

"Ten minutes until we land?" Unsteadily she stood, the rail seat flipping back up behind her, and looked out over the lightening mountains. Behind them, Calypse was a brown dome blistering up from the horizon, which was barely distinct from the sky above it. Below was a river valley, deep in shadow, but she could still distinguish the mercurial glitter of water.

"Yeah, ten minutes," Stanton confirmed. "Do either of you know how to fly one of these things?" He tapped a hand against the steering column.

Standing up also, Apis said, "The controls seem simple enough. I don't see any difficulty."

Stanton said, "Well, if, as you said, you brought in a lander without ion engines, I should think you able enough."

"Why do you ask?" Eldene inquired.

"Because, when I head for my ship, you can take this aerofan to the nearest Underworld entrance." He looked at Eldene. "You remember where it is?"

Eldene nodded, feeling an immediate sinking sensation. With one incident so rapidly following another, she'd had no time for thoughts of the future. It had often in fact seemed laughable that she might even have a future. Now she just didn't know . . . she just didn't know.

Ahead, a wide lake caught between sheer rock faces became visible, but from this angle it took Eldene a moment to recognize it as the one they called the Cistern—the landing spot of *Lyric II*. The ship, of course, was invisible somewhere on the further shore. In a moment Stanton brought the aerofan down low, its down-blast disturbing insectile shapes from their roosts on half-submerged rocks in the lake, and causing the flute grasses behind the shore to roll like sea waves. Stanton eventually landed them on a narrow beach Eldene recognized. As the fan motors wound down, Stanton opened the rail gate and stepped down onto sand and shells. Eldene noticed the insect things crawling back up onto their rocky perches.

"I'll be back in a moment," he said, "then you can head off." He turned away and started walking up the beach.

"As he walks towards it, he'll disappear," she informed Apis.

"Yes, chameleonware, I know about that," the Out-linker replied.

Eldene felt a flash of anger at his conceit, but still she was glad to be with him. "They used it on *Miranda* then, did they?" she asked.

"No, no, they didn't," Apis replied.

"How do you know about it then?"

"I was taught . . . educated . . ."

"Gosh, you are *so* clever," said Eldene, and had the satisfaction of seeing him flush with embarrassment.

Something was wrong. As Stanton kept on walking, he remained perfectly visible in the breaking dawn. By now he should have disappeared into the magical field projected from the ship. There was a clattering of falling stone, and Stanton turned to a rockfall on his left, his heavy pulse-gun drawn and aimed in one smooth motion. In a motion that was even smoother, a figure rose from behind a nearby boulder, took a few fast and silent steps, and pressed the snout of a smaller gun into the back of Stanton's head. Eldene had no time to yell a warning, but now grabbed up the rail-gun abandoned on the floor of the aerofan, and stepped out with it aimed at the newcomer.

"Girl, you better put that down before you hurt someone," said a voice behind her.

Eldene swung round to see Fethan, and felt a surge of joy—then dismay when she saw what had happened to him. Confused, she lowered the weapon and looked back at the drama ahead. It was the agent, Ian Cormac, who had captured their rescuer, and now Eldene was not sure where her loyalties lay. She watched silently as Stanton was disarmed and herded back towards the aerofan. Standing beside her, Apis gently took the rail-gun from her.

"Well, John, seems we've been here before," said Cormac. He glanced to Fethan. "I wondered who that was creeping through the grasses."

"Lellan sent me after you," Fethan replied. "She thought you might need some help."

"What I need is a ship," said Cormac, returning his attention to Stanton. "I can see where it landed but, 'ware shields or not, it certainly isn't there now."

Stanton, with his hands clasped on top of his head, remained stubbornly silent. Eldene noted the complete lack of warmth in Cormac's expression, and feared he was about to pull the trigger. Then abruptly the agent stepped back, holstering his own weapon, then moved around Stanton to face him. Weighing the prisoner's heavy gun in his hand for a moment, he abruptly tossed it to him. Stanton's hand snapped down, caught it and aimed it in one movement. Now Eldene thought it was Cormac's turn to die.

"It's like this, John. You shoot me and everyone dies. If I get up there in a ship, meaning your ship, everyone still has a chance to live. Of course, you can get to that ship yourself, and escape, but I don't think you'll do that."

Stanton abruptly concealed the gun. "Jarv will have taken it to a prearranged spot. We can be there in an hour or so."

Cormac gestured towards the menacing shape of the *Occam Razor* poised in the morning sky like a diseased eye. "Well, let's go before we get seen. Now is *not* the time for that to happen." He turned to Fethan. "Get these two down into the caverns. Calloraptors or not, that'll still be the safest place for a while." He reached out and squeezed Apis's shoulder. "Mika will probably find you, and I think she's going to be pleased about that—we all thought you and Eldene had died."

Eldene wondered if that was the most human emotion the man could ever show. She herself was glad of Fethan's arm across her shoulders, and Apis close at her side, as they watched Cormac and Stanton take the aerofan up into the air, then back along the course of the river. She shivered. It was cold, very cold that morning.

The workshop door was no longer recognizable as such, and Gant threw the grinding machine into the mass of calloraptors that were jammed together in their eagerness to get through. Using their APWs at the lowest setting, Gant and Thorn fired into the winged mass until the creatures did break through, then strategically brought down the ones that would impede the rest. But they still had to keep moving back, and in the little workshop there wasn't room to retreat.

"I'm not dying here in a fucking cupboard!" Thorn yelled.

"Can you make it to the main cavern door up there?" Gant slammed a raptor to the ground with the butt of his weapon, then burnt its head off when it began to rise again.

"I can make it—so long as that pulse-cannon doesn't start up again!"

"Now then!"

Both of them upped the setting on their APWs, and the air thumped with the detonations. Violet fire tore through a wall of alien bodies, and black smoke exploded in every direction. Firing repeatedly they advanced, breaking into the main tunnel, swarming with the calloraptors. Thorn now realized that the pulse-cannon would not start up again, because the creatures had somehow torn it from the wall and smashed it. Firing into the cavern to try and clear a path, Thorn began his painful advance, Gant staying right beside him. They made twenty paces.

"Oh fuck," Thorn managed as his weapon died on him and its displays went out. Still heaving himself along, he jammed the weapon's barrel into the mouth of his nearest attacker, then drove his fist into the throat of another as it dropped towards him. It felt like thumping a tree.

"Here!"

Gant threw his own APW across to Thorn, and unshouldered his pulse-rifle. Thorn caught it and fired upwards, clearing the air above them. They now moved back-to-back, only Thorn's shooting being really effective. Gant emptied his rifle and had to resort to his Golem strength—tearing the assailants apart as they came in. Soon they ended up with their backs to the wall.

"Double fuck," muttered Thorn, as the second APW also spat its last and faded out.

Then they heard something like an inhalation, as the calloraptors drew back from them and ceased their onslaught.

"You do know that fucker Skellor is watching us through them," said Gant.

After the chaos that had preceded, the sudden silence almost made Thorn's ears ring. Then he noticed a strange whuckering sound as of an imbalanced aerofan. As the calloraptors suddenly stormed forwards as one, Thorn knew he was about to die. But something flashed across in front, and with a triple thud and sprays of pink liquid, the three leading calloraptors fell out of the air in pieces. Further flashes were followed by more creatures disintegrating. Their attack stuttered to a halt and they drew back. Shuriken dropped into view in front of Gant and Thorn, flexing its chainglass blades to slice away pieces of raptor flesh.

The two of them just stared at each other, then along the tunnel to where the raptors had now broken into the main cavern. That was why they were no longer under direct attack, but these few seconds Shuriken had given them might prove the difference between life and death. They watched in silence as the creatures just flew on past them now, simply ignoring them. They watched as partially burnt raptors approached from further back in the tunnel, following their flying brethren—the whole crowd cramming towards the chaos of gunfire by the cavern door. Still without saying anything, they simultaneously moved over to crouch behind the wrecked aerofan lying nearby, though the creatures continued to ignore them. Shuriken hovered over them for a second or two longer, until Thorn held out his hand. The killing device hesitated for a moment, flexing its blades in and out in agitation, then abruptly closed them up and dropped into his palm.

"I'll return it to Cormac when I see him next," he explained.

"Yeah, you do that," muttered Gant.

Jarvellis felt a sudden surge of gladness immediately tempered by fear when she saw who accompanied John Stanton on the aerofan. She watched carefully as the machine came in to land on the patch of wilted rhubarbs beside the river.

As the two stepped out from it, neither had their weapons drawn, but that meant little since perhaps John was wearing an explosive collar and the agent's finger was on some remote trigger. No matter how much John had come to terms with the Polity, after the previous crimes he had committed, it would never accept him.

"Lyric, use the laser to target that man with John," she instructed.

On one of the subscreens she watched as a close-up picture of Cormac was overlaid by a grid; the square covering the man's head blanked out as the picture froze for a moment, then the picture started to shift again, as the grid faded to leave a single targeting frame centred on the agent's forehead. Of course, if John was wearing an explosive collar, it was likely Cormac carried a dead man's switch for it, so Jarvellis restrained herself from killing the agent right then. Also John was unlikely to have led his captor here . . . Dammit! Jarvellis thumbed the control for the external speakers.

"John . . . is everything all right?" she asked.

The two men paused. John seemed to gaze straight at her, though there was no way he could yet see *Lyric II*. He grinned and reached up to pull down the uniform shirt collar he wore, to expose his neck. Sometimes she just hated the way he seemed to get inside her head.

"What's happened, John? Why is he here?"

Moving again, Stanton replied, "He wants to save the world, and to do that he needs our ship."

As the two of them entered the 'ware field Jarvellis hesitated to operate the airlock control. What the hell could this ship achieve against a Polity dreadnought, and was she really prepared to risk so much?

"Jarv, the door," said Stanton.

Swearing again, she thumbed the control, then stood up and headed back into the cargo area. Clumping aboard, the two men seemed to fill the small space.

Jarvellis glanced down. "Careful!"

Cormac lifted his foot off the interactive storybook he had just stepped on. He stared at it in some puzzlement, then at the other toys scattered across the floor. A small blond-haired boy charged out from wherever he had been playing, a toy dark-otter clutched in one hand. He hesitated for a moment, then with a delighted yell rushed over to Stanton, who picked him up.

"Ian Cormac, meet Cormac Stanton," said John Stanton, trying to hide his embarrassment. Jarvellis noted this, just as she noted the agent's expression turn from something cold and hard to something merely tired. She guessed that was to do with the ship, and what he wanted of it, and there being an innocent child aboard.

In Thorn's estimation a couple of thousand of the creatures had now swarmed into the main cavern. Judging by the receding roar of gunfire, the rebel fighters were being driven back. Beside him Gant stood up and offered him a hand, and Thorn rose up onto one foot, supporting himself against the Golem's unyielding strength.

"Well, frankly, I'm surprised to be alive," he said. "I gather, from something Cormac said earlier, that you've met these bastards before."

Gant shrugged. "A couple of kinds, yes. The normal predators on Callorum weren't too much of a problem, but then there was something Skellor created—and neither type had wings."

They moved out from behind the aerofan, Thorn glancing at what remained of the soldier Carl before he turned his attention to the other debris on the tunnel floor. Those creatures, it appeared, had to be scorched almost down to the bone, or completely blown into pieces, before they would actually die. The remains of such carnage lay everywhere in drifts upon the stone. Underfoot something white and glassy crunched and fragmented. He noticed one creature burnt down to bone yet still moving, some pinkish substance oozing out between its bones. It fixed him with gleaming dots of eyes set deep in dark pits, and even tried to open its mouth to hiss. This small action used up the last of its strength for then it shuddered, and the pinkish substance began turning the same white as the frangible layer on the floor.

"What the hell?" muttered Thorn.

"Jain tech," explained Gant.

"Nasty," said Thorn. "Now what do we do?"

Gant studied him. "How much oxygen do you have left?"

Thorn glanced at his bottle's readout. "About two hours—so there's only one direction for me to go." He pointed towards where the calloraptors had gone.

Gant abruptly turned and headed back to the aerofan, stooping over the body of Carl. First discarding a pulse-rifle which was bent and broken, he next came up with the man's breather pack and removed its oxygen bottle from the blood-soaked bag. Returning with this item he said, "Another hour from this, though not enough to get you anywhere far. But I don't think that matters now." He looked back the way they had originally come in.

"More of them?" Thorn was looking around for something to use as a weapon.

"No, dracomen," said Gant.

"How can they be here?" Thorn asked, puzzled.

"Oh, they can. I worked with Scar for quite some time, and he can run faster than the top speed on one of those things." Gant gestured to the aerofan.

"So what do they want here?"

"To kill calloraptors, I expect," said Gant. "It's something Scar took great pleasure in."

Thorn considered that. "I think we should move over to the side of the tunnel," he suggested.

In the seat beside Jarvellis, Cormac clipped his harness into place and watched her expert manipulation of *Lyric II*'s controls. The ship responded with a deep thrumming, like a musical instrument being played by an expert hand. He watched her take hold of the joystick as the screen revealed the debris being blown about outside. *Lyric II* lifted and tilted, its legs and feet quickly retracting before the toes could stub themselves on surrounding rock.

Bringing the ship over wilted vegetation towards the river, Jarvellis glanced up as Stanton returned to the cockpit. "All done?" she asked, and Stanton nodded.

At least in cold-sleep the boy would feel no pain should their ship be destroyed, thought Cormac. But then he doubted that any of them would feel very much—it would be so very quick. The unexpected presence of the child left him feeling hollow inside, though no less resolute. In the end duty had to come first.

"How long?" he asked.

"Lyric?" Jarvellis prompted.

The AI replied, "We should achieve escape velocity in one half of an orbit—that's two hours nominally. One hour after that we will be able to submerge in under-space."

Cormac nodded to himself as the screen now showed them coming up out of the river valley and achieving enough height so that Jarvellis did not have to navigate the ship along the watercourse. Higher still, and the ion engines were now cycling up to a steady roar. Though the screen continued to show the forward view as they accelerated, he guessed that the ship was now beginning to tilt into their vector so that the engines could blast out directly behind. Air turbulence began to give the craft the occasional tentative shake as it accelerated. It maintained that more due to brute force than to aerodynamics—like most ships of the time, *Lyric II* was built to land and take off by using antigravity.

Cormac recalled a conversation he'd had with Jarvellis: "The 'ware effect doesn't hide AG, it merely blurs it over a number of kilometres," she had told him. "That was good enough for Theocracy detectors, but not to get us by a Polity dreadnought."

"What about the fusion engines on this?" he'd then asked her.

"Taking us straight up, the blast would flare visibly outside the range of the 'ware effect. Skellor would detect us that way too."

"I guessed so," said Cormac. "Can we slingshot around the planet on ion boosters? We'd leave a trail, but that's something we'll have to risk."

In response Jarvellis had opined that the trail would be one of wreckage—*Lyric II* not being built to withstand such forces. However, they had little choice.

"Approaching Mach one," she announced now. "Let's hope Skellor's got no one listening down there, because the 'ware only covers us for long-distance checking of air disturbance. They'd still hear the sonic boom."

"Let's hope that, indeed," said Cormac—and didn't really like to think beyond. It seemed to him that the processing power and technology Skellor had under his control meant the man was only limited by his own imagination. Probably Skellor was watching through the eyes of his calloraptors, but would it occur to him to listen also? No doubt, from where he hung geostationary, he could see in great detail much of what occurred on the planet, but what was his focus? He had certainly missed the journey Stanton and Cormac had made on that aerofan, probably because his attention was directed entirely towards his creatures' attack on the cavern. Had it occurred to him to set up listening posts? Did he have anything watching on the other side of the planet? Much depended on the detail: it wasn't good enough to have the power of a god without a god's universal vision.

A subscreen gave them a receding view of the *Occam Razor*, while another screen presented a view across the top of *Lyric II* whereby Cormac could see that they were now flying perpendicular to the ground so that the ion engines could operate most effectively. The ship had started to vibrate, and from somewhere there came a whistling scream, like a bombshell coming down but never hitting. Every now and again the craft gave a shudder as if something structural was about to break.

"Let's drop the Mach readings: we just passed five thousand kph," said Jarvellis.

The ground was now far enough below them for many small details to be lost, not that there was much diverse detail over this wilderness. The open plains receded underneath them, changing from greenish blue pocked by great splashes of red to a sudden band of grey stone, then cerulean ocean. Jarvellis adjusted a sub-screen to show the continent receding behind them like a thick blanket of mould skimmed back off the oceanic surface. The ship was now howling and shuddering constantly, and by the way she was white-knuckling the joystick Cormac suspected that Jarvellis did not consider this at all a good sign.

"Do you have stress readouts for this craft's superstructure?" asked Cormac.

"Yes, I do," admitted Jarvellis. "But I'm not looking at them."

Soon they were puncturing cloud as they flew on into night. Looking at the screen with a view all across *Lyric II*, he observed ice building up and flaking away in glittering contrails.

"Are we leaving a vapour trail?" he asked her.

"No, the exhaust is too hot. Our only problem right now is the ionic trail and, as you said, we just have to hope he doesn't spot that."

"Other problems?" Cormac persisted.

"Proximity lasers online," the AI chose that moment to announce.

"That problem," Jarvellis replied. "Your Dragon creature did a fine job of destroying the laser arrays. Shame it left the debris up here as well. I've set our course to avoid the worst of it, otherwise I'll dodge the larger fragments whilst Lyric here vaporizes the smaller ones."

"But surely you'll be able to do all that inside the 'ware field?" Cormac pointed out.

Stanton interjected, "Sure they'll get vaporized inside the 'ware field, but that vapour won't stay inside the field for long. You were worried about a moisture vapour trail lower down. Now you can worry about a metallic vapour trail up here."

Cloud banks lay below them like a mountain range of crystal sulphur and snow, with jade ocean glimpsed far below through deep crevasses. Above this they hurtled further into space that could never get completely dark because of the Braemar moons suspended like lanterns, and behind them, the shining glass sculpture of the distant nebula. Cormac registered U-chargers powering up then on a subscreen and observed vapour explosions as the ship's lasers obliterated obstacles that were too small to be visible but large enough to punch holes through the hull. Operating the steering thrusters, Jarvellis took the ship swaying to one side to pass a lump of wreckage resembling half a piano made of polished aluminium. For a short while the lasers continued operating at full capacity, though not well enough, for they could hear the sharp bullet-cracks of impacts.

"Lyric, damage?" Jarvellis spat, when these impacts finally ceased.

"Four micropunctures, now sealed. One large hole in the hydraulic cylinder for landing foot two. I've shut off the hydraulic fluid supply to it, but cannot repair. We need to space dock for that," the AI explained.

"Be glad of the chance," Jarvellis muttered, glancing at Cormac.

He was observing the display that noted their speed in kilometres per hour. Now pushing twenty-five thousand, he saw that they had achieved escape velocity, and that now the arc of the horizon was dropping below them.

Stanton confirmed this for them by asking, "What now, Agent? What do we do now?"

"Depending on the circumstances, it would take about an hour for the underspace disturbance created by a ship this size to disperse." He turned to Jarvellis. "Get the *Occam* up on the main screen, will you."

Jarvellis did as requested, and soon the Polity dreadnought filled the main screen, looming utterly clear now in the clarity of vacuum. For a second Cormac allowed himself misgivings: Skellor had so obviously moved far beyond anything Cormac himself could easily judge or understand, let alone manipulate.

"One hour at the present velocity will take us far enough out of the well for you to use U-space engines. You don't need greater velocity?" he asked.

"No. We have modern engines on this *Lyric*," Jarvellis replied tartly.

"Okay . . . if you use your fusion engine—"

"Fusion mode," Jarvellis interrupted. "The engines are dual-function: ionic and fusion."

"Whatever," said Cormac, irritated. "If you use fusion mode, how quickly will you be able to go under?"

"Ten minutes, maybe less. Lyric?"

The AI replied, "Seven minutes and thirty seconds . . . mark."

"Use fusion," said Cormac, "for the last few seconds—and in those last few seconds I want you to send a message for me as well."

"Just say it, and Lyric will record it," Jarvellis told him.

Cormac cleared his throat and addressed the image on the screen. "Skellor, it seems you missed me again, but I guess mistakes are to be expected from an intelligence stretched so far beyond its capacity. Now I want to make you an offer: come and work with the Polity on studying the technology you now control. All previous misdemeanours can be forgotten, since you know that Polity AIs do not countenance vengeance, and in exchange for what you now possess, you could have almost anything you ask for." Cormac glanced round at Stanton, who seemed set to explode. He continued, "I do understand that you will not want to compromise your safety. When I arrive, I'll send a message to that effect into the Polity, and you can thenceforth communicate with ECS yourself and make the right arrangements. Please give this offer serious consideration. Message ends."

"Are you out of your fucking mind?" Stanton growled.

"Trust me," said Cormac, then smiled at the rustling of material that told him Stanton had just drawn his weapon. He went on, "What did I just say to him?"

"You offered him anything he wants," said Stanton.

"I also said 'When I arrive, I'll send a message to the Polity,' so what do you think he'll work out from that?"

Stanton thought for a moment then said, "He'll know you're not going right into Polity space."

"Precisely, so he'll think he still has a chance of silencing me," said Cormac. "And when he moves to pick up our trail, and tries to follow us through U-space, he'll see that this is true."

"You haven't told me our destination yet," said Jarvellis. Cormac now told her.

So engrossed had Skellor been in the underground battle that he felt a surge of panic as in a microsecond he became aware of fusion spillover from a 'ware field. Immediately he put the relevant laser battery online, whilst experiencing huge loathing and contempt for himself. With all his available sensors he had watched out for Polity technology, and so just not expected anything else. That was his own damned chameleonware on some small ship, and it had nearly got the vessel past him. Targeting the calculated centre of the 'ware effect, he immediately became suspicious: why was he seeing fusion spillover now? It seemed almost as if the pilot of that ship wanted to be seen. Then Cormac's message arrived and Skellor screamed with rage at his own stupidity, and fired his lasers, only to see their blast igniting vapour over a fading U-space signature.

Skellor immediately engaged the *Occam*'s fusion engines to take him out of low orbit. As he did this, he imposed self-control and re-examined the content of the man's message.

"*When I arrive I'll send a message to the Polity*" was a provocative phrase. Skellor felt it was a ploy to get him to follow the ship to some dangerous destination on the Line. Yet there could be no trap laid there, because no one outside of this system knew anything about him. Hammering up towards the rapidly fading signature, Skellor probed and was further bewildered when he discovered what the little ship's destination was.

What did this Agent Cormac think he could achieve by leading Skellor there?

It took Skellor a huge adjustment of perspective to understand what was happening: if he did not pursue, then Cormac would get to the Polity and Skellor's secret would be out. If he did pursue, the chase would take him two solstan months, and in that time the Polity would be sure to have gone to Masada to find out what had happened to its people—and to this very ship—and again the secret would be out. Obliquely, Skellor realized what he was truly being offered. Cormac was sacrificing himself for this remote world. The agent realized Skellor would never follow the trispherical ship anywhere under Polity control, as that would be suicide for him, thus Cormac would not now be heading into Polity space. The circumstances were such that Skellor had a choice: he could stay here and incinerate this world, or he could follow the ship and capture Ian Cormac. Without a second thought Skellor dropped the *Occam Razor* into underspace.

"Pull back! Pull back into Pillartown One!"

The man with the still-working coms helmet who was loudly relaying Lellan's orders let his gaze stray from the air above him for too long. Two calloraptors hit him simultaneously and dragged him screaming up into the middle of their flock, where his screams were soon curtailed as they ripped him apart.

With the taste of bile in his mouth and with his hands shaking, Apis quickly changed the energy canister of his pulse-rifle. It was an automatic action—which he had done six times already. Long before he, Eldene and Fethan had arrived, the battle had become a diffuse and chaotic thing, for the calloraptors, once through the cavern door, had room to take to the air and attack at will from overhead.

"Where is Pillartown One?" he asked Eldene, as she fired several short bursts overhead. She pointed to a building beyond the hovering raptors, then led the way.

Watching his footing on the rocky terrain—for he still feared falling over more than physical attack—he followed Eldene as she continued firing short bursts upwards. He saw she was certainly a better shot than himself when one burst she fired separated a raptor's wing, and the creature came thwacking like a broken sail to the cavern floor. Before it even hit the ground, three dracomen were upon it and tearing it apart. Apis noticed that one of them wore a weapons harness, and he wondered if that might be Scar. Difficult to tell, for they were all so similar. It had taken some time, and much reassurance from Lellan, for the rebel forces to realize they were friendly. However, though they made ferocious allies, they could not fly.

"We have to move faster!" Eldene yelled.

Glancing aside, Apis saw the rebel forces in full retreat. He ran to keep up with Eldene, ducking a claw that passed dangerously close to his head, then ducking the dracoman that leapt straight up in front of him. The thump from above told him that it had seized its prey, and he glanced back to see dracoman and calloraptor hit the ground in a flailing bundle.

"Keep moving!" shouted Fethan, sprinting past. Apis broke into a run again, till soon he was back abreast of Fethan and Eldene.

To either side of them, commingled rebel forces and dracomen were retreating under the onslaught from above. The running seemed to go on interminably, with the pillartown seemingly always distant from them. Then, as if he was coming out of some nightmare, Apis found himself in its shadow, and saw rebels and dracomen ducking through the shattered doors ahead of him. Driven wild by the prospect of their prey escaping, the raptors descended in vicious onslaught.

"Watch out!" Fethan yelled.

Apis ducked, and the creature went straight over him, and knocked Eldene to the ground. Apis leapt forward, and slammed himself into the raptor just as it was trying to drag Eldene upwards. He brought it down and, pinning it underneath himself, he emptied his rifle into the monster's chest. Fire flared underneath him, and claws closed on his leg. He felt himself being jerked up, but with his head towards the ground, and with horror saw the one he had just eviscerated with fire flapping to its feet, with fibrous pink chyme welling up in the burn holes on its midsection, then going for Eldene a second time. Hauling himself up, Apis swung his weapon with all the force he could muster, smashing one of his own assailant's wing joints, and both he and it crashed to the ground. His rifle gone now, he was defenceless as the raptor loomed over him, its triple mouth opening to tear off his face.

"Fuck you!"

His fist smacked hard into its double-keeled chest, and it coughed. He thought of *Miranda*, and hit it again in exactly the same place. As something gave under his fist, he assumed it was his own bones breaking. Amazingly the raptor continued coughing. He struck it again, now thinking of all those who had died on the *General Patten*. Then for his mother, he followed that blow with one up and under the monster's ugly head, then another . . . then another. It suddenly seemed to go soft on him. He felt its neck snap, saw its flesh tearing—that pinkish chyme welling up to make repairs.

"And double fuck you!" he yelled, remembering one of Gant's favoured curses. His next blow tore the creature's head from its body.

Apis did not allow himself time to feel appalled at what he had just done, he turned and immediately went for the one attacking Eldene. By then the dracomen had realized where the rebels were heading and had closed in. During the confused and vicious fight that followed, all the rebels were soon undercover, and dracomen manned the doors, joyfully countering any intruding raptors.

"Skellor programmed 'em to attack and kill, but not much beyond that," observed Fethan. "They're at a disadvantage when they land." He then turned to inspect Apis thoughtfully. "Take it you finally got over your fear of falling."

Apis fought to recover his breath, still not quite believing what he was now capable of doing, even though he had worked it all out. That was the Jain nano-mycelium working inside him—likely the very same stuff that effected such rapid repairs to those raptor creatures. Even though the same tech worked inside, he had beaten the creature simply because its strength was related to its density, so the raptor could not be as strong as himself since it needed to be light enough to fly. After a moment Apis stood upright and noticed Eldene was watching him with something approaching awe. He turned back to Fethan. "If they keep having to land in order to attack, the dracomen will eventually get them all," he suggested.

"Only thing to stop them fighting themselves to death would be a bit of Skellor's reprogramming," said Fethan with satisfaction.

"There's nothing to stop him doing that remotely," Apis stated.

"I doubt he can do it from underspace," replied Fethan with a grin.

"He's gone? Skellor's gone?"

"That's the word, boy. That's the word," Fethan replied.

Apis could only believe it as he watched raptor after raptor land outside and enter the building, only to be torn apart by the waiting dracomen, and as what had been a desperate fight in the open devolved into a slaughter—an extermination.

Lyric II spun out of underspace, exciting a photonic trail, before its fusion engines ignited to decelerate it down into the system. Being identified as one of the numerous large cargo ships that usually arrived at and departed from the sprawling structures coming into view, its AI was soon queried by a local AI, its presence noted and directions given, then it was all but forgotten. Aboard the ship, Cormac sipped hot coffee and tried to shake off the last dregs of cold-sleep that seemed to clog his head with wet tissue-paper. So much would depend on what happened in the next few minutes that, in his present debilitated state, he was finding it difficult to accept it all as real. Eyeing Stanton and Jarvellis, he saw that they were having no such problems accepting reality: she appeared white and ill, while her partner wore an expression of grim determination.

"He may not be prepared to take any more risks with us." Stanton at last voiced what they were all thinking. "If he fires on us as soon as he surfaces, that's it—all over."

"But he won't," said Cormac with a confidence he did not feel. "He'll want to gloat, if only for a few minutes, and while he does that we'll be sending *our* message on ahead. I would even bet he'll open communications with us in the hope of getting some response out of me."

"And *our* response to that?" said Jarvellis.

"I will talk to him," said Cormac. "Every second we gain . . ."

"In that respect," said the captain of *Lyric II*, "it's time to start counting."

The *Occam Razor* slid out of underspace a thousand kilometres behind them, so that it seemed a tangled, dead thing, wrapped around something glorious and precious, was folding out of blackness there. Observing the great ship, Cormac was struck this once by how strangely beautiful it was. Perhaps this was because it would be the last time he ever saw it.

Through the myriad senses at his disposal, Skellor observed *Lyric II* like a fleck of matter against the sprawling backdrop. He studied the cylinder worlds like displaced towers, and the fragile chains of habitats, the huge manufactories and refineries, and the swarms of ships. Here was another place open to subversion, to takeover—throughout it he could feel the presence of Dracocorp augs, in loosely aligned communities each held together by the creeping dominion of one of their members. His arrival at Masada, and what he had found there developing under the Hierarch, had made him understand the subtle route Dragon had used to dominate humans—a route Skellor had very unsubtly ripped wide apart. But that was all something he must return to later, for here he was much too close to the Polity, and already could feel the U-space probing of a runcible AI. No, the one ship ahead of him he would take, and that would be all and enough. He opened the bay from which he had earlier ejected the raptor-piloted lander, and accelerated down onto *Lyric II*. As he descended, he spread himself out through Jain structure, substructure, architecture in a kind of rapturous stretching as of some creature extending great wings and claws.

This is it, Agent. I have you now.

Horrible laughter then echoed within him—and it wasn't his own.

You are dead, he told the source of that laughter.

You made me, replied the ephemeral voice of Aphran. He tried to find it, encompass it, smear it out of existence, but he was chasing mere shadows through the vastness of himself.

You haven't seen it yet, have you?

I haven't seen what? he asked, hoping this time that when she spoke again he would be able to nail down exactly where she lurked.

The light, Skellor. The light.

Standing in the sharp blue shadows of his favourite cyanid, Dreyden drew hard on his cigarette, its glowing tip reflecting off his chromed aug, then blew out a cloud of smoke over the exposed yellow convolutions inside one of the plant's opened pods. The convolutions all immediately zipped themselves up like a swarm of worms passing over the surface of this alien flower, then after a time unclenched again.

It was only here that Dreyden truly felt he could relax. Or perhaps he was kidding himself that relaxation was even possible for him: he had been described as being "taut as monofilament" from his childhood—full of crazy hopes and numbing fears which he felt were the driving forces of his success. He knew that sometimes his fears strayed into the irrational, and it was good that he did know this, for Lons and Alvor would never tell him: Lons because Dreyden's sanity or otherwise was not a matter of interest to him; and Alvor because he was always looking for an angle, for a way to manipulate his boss, to scrabble another couple of rungs up the ladder.

Across the ground before him a flattened worm of jelly oozed with slow ripplings that caught the lights from his apartment. To his right he saw that a plasoderm's grey seedcase had hinged itself completely open, and that the object crawling before him was the last of its slime-mould spore carriers to be released. He threw his cigarette butt into the empty seedcase where it hissed out in the damp interior. The accuracy of his shot gave him a second's satisfaction before his whole world collapsed on him.

There was no alarm mode in his aug, as he considered that for anything *that* urgent he wanted no delay. His connection, which had been a low buzz of activity in a place impossible to point to, suddenly slammed back with such force that he staggered against the lethal edges of the cyanid leaves.

"Battle stats and alarm to all areas lock down and seal gate connection break . . ."

Alvor was rattling off instructions so closely auged in that he became part machine himself for that brief moment. Lons had already moved beyond the verbal and was dealing in logic blocks and prestored sub-programs. Below Dreyden's hands, virtual consoles flicked into existence, and all around him flat and holojected displays folded out of the air. There he observed huge transfers of information as the bulwarks of his empire were automatically dropped into safe storage. However, his attention was immediately riveted on one small screen. A touch at the non-existent console expanded the screen to reveal the huge Polity dreadnought bearing down upon *Elysium*.

"Lyric II pursued. Message coming in from John Stanton."

Dreyden had not needed Alvor to tell him this. He was on top of things now.

"Dreyden, you've got to cover me. He is seriously pissed about those drones," said the holojected image of John Stanton.

Dreyden felt his insides clenching in a brass fist as he studied the man—Stanton seemed scared, and that was a first.

"What about the drones?" he asked.

"Signal code broken. Signal code broken."

Dreyden pressed his hands together to stop them shaking, as Stanton flickered out of existence and was instantly replaced.

"Donnegal Dreyden," spoke a hated image. "This is Ian Cormac of Earth Central Security. You have thirty seconds to transmit all your control codes to this Polity dreadnought. If you fail to comply I will be forced to fire upon you."

Something was wrong with all this, but Dreyden could see no way to discover what, nor had he been allowed time.

"You *know* what my reply has to be," he said, not believing he was speaking these words, nor knowing what else to say. "I did warn you last time you were here."

"Do you really think your pathetic mirrors will manage to cut through the armour on this Polity dreadnought before it destroys them?" And now Cormac's expression turned furious. "Do you really think that ECS can countenance you supplying terrorists with high-tech Polity war drones?"

"But I—"

The link cut off and Dreyden was left staring at darkness. *"He can't be that stupid."*

Dreyden was in complete agreement with Alvor's assessment: Agent Cormac of ECS had to know the mirrors were capable of raising in seconds the temperature of *anything* to that of a sun's surface. The agent must want to die aboard that great ship, and Dreyden did not have the option to persuade him otherwise. Already he was sending the signals that would give him total command of each mirror. Before him a depiction of *Elysium* sprang into existence, and each mirror gained a shimmering halo as it came under his control. His hands moving across and through the consoles, he spidered the air with bright lines as he plotted trajectories and sent further commands. In that moment he moved into the language of machine code, and felt himself connecting more deeply into his own realm. He knew that, like those images of consoles and screens around him, the feeling itself was illusion, but he *felt* the glide of massive hydraulics, the acid fire of thruster motors, and the huge shifting of mirrors at his command. Subliminally he noted a grabship caught in momentary focus, turning mercury-bright then transforming into a ball of light expanding and dispersing. Then plotted trajectories intersected on what was even now becoming visible through the glass dome above.

The *Occam Razor* gleamed then glared in sunlight—a strange gem flashing into existence over *Elysium*. To one side Dreyden saw the hologram of someone appear and turn puzzled bloodshot eyes towards him. It was recognizably human but horribly tangled, and melded with both the organic and the mechanical.

"*Subversion access! Subversion access!*"

He didn't need to be told, as he was already fighting to prevent it killing the tracking programs in the mirror-guidance systems. The figure was screaming now as the heat delved down to it inside the dreadnought, white light all around it and holographic smoke filling the imaging area. Equally, the *Occam Razor* was howling across the sky with fire flaring across its surface and Jain structure ablating away into space. Then it rolled, bringing to bear another surface as yet untouched by sunfire. Dreyden felt a huge surge of energy through solar collectors and, with a thought, folded out a screen to view one section of *Elysium* itself. He saw an expanding mass of wreckage: burnt and burning habitats, domed forests falling out into blackness, human bodies . . . and a line of fire tracking across, searing and smashing and killing.

"You bastard!" he shouted, not entirely sure whom he was cursing.

The fire died as the weapons exposed on this new face of the *Occam Razor* collapsed into the boiling plain of its hull. To one side the image of the man-thing flickered out, and the ship seemed suddenly to alter its shape. For a second everything blacked out as a safety system cut into the visual feedback, then it cleared on the red eye of an explosion, and spreading sheets of molten metal and incandescent gas.

EPILOGUE

The sun had overtaken Calypse and, preceding the gas giant behind the horizon, had thrown it into partial silhouette—its whorls and bands of colours turning the hue of ancient cathedral paint. Out over the more vivid colours of the flowering flute grasses, Ram and Rom reflected nothing but this colour from their polished cases as they slid silently through the air. Seated on a cold mollusc-studded rock with Eldene pressing close to his side, Apis wondered if he would ever become inured to the fantastic sunrises and sunsets here—and hoped not. He then transferred his gaze to the approaching vehicle that the two war drones guarded.

"I wonder if she found her hatchery," Eldene said.

"I doubt she had the time."

They both watched the ATV come out of the grasses and into a lane of black plantains, against which the multicoloured pollens splashed all over its surface showed up clear like a strange camouflage.

"Here come the others," said Eldene, pulling closer so that he would put his arm around her. Obliging her he glanced aside at the encampment from which Lellan and Fethan approached. Lellan had long been essentially the dictator here, but then Fethan had pointed out that when ECS came to *help* them, and once it established a runcible on one of the Braemar moons, there would be another dictator and it would be made of silicon. She had not seemed particularly averse to the prospect.

The ATV drew to a halt on an area of crushed-down rhubarb that abutted the river winding out from the foothills. First out of its door was Gant, carrying Mika's huge sample case. Next came Thorn—very nimble on his feet since one of Mika's "little doctors" had established itself inside him, but then Apis knew exactly how *that* felt. Thorn, like himself and Mika, no longer wore a mask. Sometime soon Apis hoped Eldene would follow the same route, for if they were to become true Masadans they must learn to *live* on the surface, not merely exist.

"Let's get down there," said Apis, removing his arm from Eldene's waist.

"Oh, all right," she pouted, mock angry.

They clambered from the rock and side-by-side walked down the scree slope towards the vehicle, as next emerged Mika and Scar. Lellan and Fethan joined them and the four approached it together.

"Did you find the site?" Fethan asked.

"Yes, fragments of shell from where they burrowed their way out of the ground," said Mika. "I'll need excavators to dig down deep enough. The whole thing will have to wait until ECS gets here."

Apis noted her distraction as she stared upriver to a shuttle that rested half in the water. This craft bore some resemblance to a huge U-shaped section of grey pipe, but with thruster motors and guidance fins attached.

"I don't think I've seen one like that before," she remarked.

For enlightenment, Lellan and Fethan looked to Apis, who said, "It's a good century out of date." When Mika just stared at him, he explained further, "We studied landing craft on *Miranda*. It was one of our more academic subjects." He shrugged, very aware that much had since ceased to be academic to him.

Turning to Lellan and Fethan, Mika stated, "You have been inside it."

"Door's open," said Fethan. "We had a look then decided to leave it until you got here. No telling what it might do."

Mika's expression showed both curiosity and irritation. "What might do what?" she asked, wincing at the clumsiness of her question.

Fethan gestured towards the grounded craft, and the group of them began walking in that direction.

"What more do you think ECS will find . . . when they get here?" Lellan asked, studying Scar as she brought the conversation back to Mika's recent jaunt into the wilderness.

Mika shrugged. "I'll probably only get confirmation. Dragon converted most of its own mass into eggs hidden underground, out of which eventually hatched the dracomen. It's the same method employed by Skellor for his raptor creatures."

"Very similar technology," Lellan observed.

"Very," Mika agreed, "though the raptors were not intended to breed."

"Pardon?" said Lellan.

Mika glanced at Scar. "Oh yes, the dracoman population here is set to rise—and I think that maybe that will be a good thing."

"Your idea of a good thing might differ from everyone else's," muttered Thorn.

Shortly they reached the craft and, staring at the open door with its extended ramp, Apis could not repress a shudder. He too had seen the Polity and Jain technology melded to the mutilated calloraptor. So he and Eldene held back with the others as Mika followed Thorn and Gant inside. Apis listened to the creature within's painful hissing, and its truncated struggle in attempting to pursue its programmed instinct to attack. Shortly, the interior of the craft was filled with the viridian arc-welder flashes of Gant's and Thorn's APWs, a sound like the exhalation of a giant snake, then stillness. Exiting the craft, Gant and Thorn wore grim expressions, and even Mika's perpetual curiosity seemed tempered.

Nodding half to herself, Mika said, "Dracomen . . . any of them really. I think we're going to need all the allies we can find." She gestured back into the craft. "It's out of its box now and I don't think there's anyone who can put it back."

Apis knew she didn't mean the creature itself, but the technology it represented.

A woman danced in space, surrounded by diaphanous white material. Close focus now revealed that she had floated out from the shade of a shattered habitat, and the last vital fluids were boiling from her body. The silver-haired man shut off close focus before the child on his knee decided to ask him a question about the revealed image. Observing at a distance the broken bodies desiccated by vacuum into rolling woody statues, the mass of shattered biodomes, and the habitats melted into grotesque baroque shapes, his expression turned utterly cold.

The boy reached one pudgy hand towards the screen. "Dead?" he asked, his eyes wide.

"Oh yes," said the man. "Certainly that." He paused for a moment, then in a bitter voice explained, "You see, this is what is called a Cadmean victory."

Pulling his hand back, the boy put his finger in his mouth as he stared at the screen. After a moment his attention wandered to those toys of his scattered on the floor.

Abruptly he swung back to the man. "Story now?"

When this elicited no response, the boy began to fidget. Eventually the man reached across and picked up the storybook from the chair beside him. Opening it, he observed a heroyne, caught in the damaged memory fabric of the page, in a cycle of perpetually swallowing the same priestly individual. He closed the book and returned his attention to the main screen.

With his gaze fixed, and his eyes hard as nail-heads the man began, "Once upon a time . . . on a planet far far away . . . there lived a Dragon . . ."

Neal Asher is a science fiction writer whose work has been nominated for both the Philip K. Dick and the British Fantasy Society awards. He has published more than twenty books, many set within his Polity universe, including *Gridlinked*, *The Skinner*, and *Dark Intelligence*. He divides his time between Essex and a home in Crete.

THE ADVENTURES OF
IAN CORMAC CONTINUE . . .

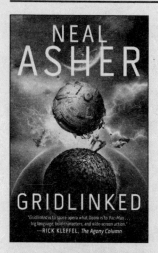
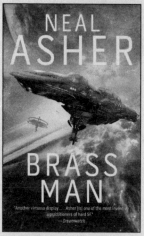

THE ADVENTURES OF
IAN CORMAC CONTINUE . . .

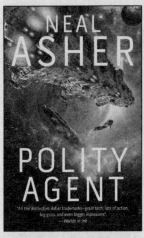

POLITY AGENT
The Fourth Agent
Cormac Novel
978-1-59780-981-0
Mass Market / $7.99

"A terrific read with all the distinctive Asher trademarks—great tech, lots of action, big guns and even bigger explosions."
—*Worlds in Ink*

LINE WAR
The Fifth Agent
Cormac Novel
978-1-59780-982-9
Mass Market / $7.99

"A highly engaging, smart, and fulfilling close to the Ian Cormac series . . . strongly recommended."
—*Fantasy Book Critic*

AVAILABLE FROM NIGHT SHADE BOOKS
WWW.NIGHTSHADEBOOKS.COM

MORE NOVELS OF THE POLITY

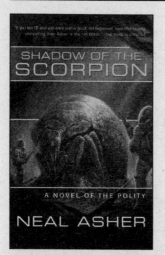

TRANSFORMATION: A POLITY TRILOGY

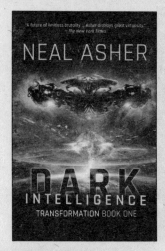

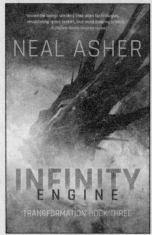

DARK INTELLIGENCE
978-1-59780-844-6
Trade Paperback / $15.99

WAR FACTORY
978-1-59780-882-8
Trade Paperback / $15.99

INFINITY ENGINE
978-1-59780-910-8
Trade Paperback / $15.99

AVAILABLE FROM NIGHT SHADE BOOKS
WWW.NIGHTSHADEBOOKS.COM

THE OWNER TRILOGY

THE DEPARTURE
978-1-59780-447-9
Trade Paperback / $15.99

ZERO POINT
978-1-59780-470-7
Trade Paperback / $15.99

JUPITER WAR
978-1-59780-493-6
Trade Paperback / $15.99

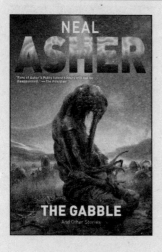

NEW FROM NEAL ASHER
AND NIGHT SHADE BOOKS

**THE SOLDIER
RISE OF THE JAIN
BOOK ONE**
978-1-59780-943-6
Hardcover / $26.99
(available now)
Trade paperback / $15.99
(coming November 2018)

"With mind-blowing complexity, characters, and combat, Asher's work continues to combine the best of advanced cybertech and military SF."

—*Publishers Weekly*,
starred review

In a far corner of space, on the very borders between humanity's Polity worlds and the kingdom of the vicious crab-like prador, is an immediate threat to all sentient life: an accretion disc, a solar system designed by the long-dead Jain race and swarming with living technology powerful enough to destroy entire civilizations . . .

In *The Soldier*, British science fiction writer Neal Asher kicks off another Polity-based trilogy in signature fashion, concocting a mind-melting plot filled with far-future technology, lethal weaponry, and bizarre alien creations.

Marco's ship surfaced from the faster-than-light continuum of underspace into realspace, and was quickly back within Einstein's laws. His vessel came to an abrupt stop in the permitted zone lying five light-minutes out from Musket Shot—a dark planetoid whose mass was over 50 per cent lead. Had Marco surfaced his ship just a few thousand miles outside this spot it would have lasted a little over four microseconds, so he had once been told by the Artificial Intelligence Pragus. This was how long it would take the three-foot-wide particle beam to reach the ship from the weapons system watching that area of space. Of course, Pragus could have been lenient and delivered a warning, but any traders who came here never missed that spot. Apparently two other ships had arrived in the proscribed zone. One had been owned by a tourist who had ignored all the warnings delivered to anyone who programmed these coordinates. The other had been a ship controlled by separatists out of the Polity in search of new terror weapons. Both were now cool, expanding clouds of dust.

Or so Pragus said.

"So, what do you have for me, Captain Marco?"

The voice issuing from his console made Marco jerk, then he grimaced, annoyed at his own reaction. He'd made the deal, it was a good one, and certainly not one he could renege on, considering who he'd made it with. He shrugged his shoulders, like he did before going into a fight, and opened full com. The image of a chromed face appeared in the screen laminate before him, and Marco forced a smile.

"Something interesting today," he replied gruffly.

"I never thought otherwise," said the AI Pragus.

Interesting was what Pragus needed, what all the AIs out here on the defence sphere needed. Marco had learned the story from another trader who used to do this run before him. Here the AIs, each stationed on a weapons platform, were guarding the Polity from one of the most dangerous threats it had ever faced. Automatic systems would never have been sufficient, for the format of this threat could change at any time. But the problem with employing high-functioning AIs as watchdogs was their boredom. Three AIs had to be pulled out of the sphere in the first years, having turned inward to lose themselves in the realms of their own minds. That was before Orlandine—the overseer of the sphere project—decided on a new approach. She allowed contact with the Polity AI net, and she permitted traders to bring items of interest to sell. AI toys.

"You can come in to dock," Pragus added.

"Thank you kindly," said Marco. Then, trying to find his usual humour, added, "Finger off the trigger, mind."

"I don't have fingers," said the AI, and the chrome face disappeared from the screen laminate.

Marco reached down to his touch-console, prodded the icon for the docking program that had just arrived and simply slid it across to the icon representing his ship's mind. This was the frozen ganglion of a prador second-child—voiceless, remote, just a complex organic computer and nothing like the living thing it had once been. It began to take his ship in, then Marco used the console to pull up another view in the screen laminate to his left.

From this angle the accretion disc, around which the defensive weapons platforms were positioned, looked like a blind, open white eye. It seemed like any other such stellar object in the universe—just a steadily swirling mass of gases and the remnants of older stars which would eventually form a new solar system. His ship's sensors could detect scattered planetesimals within it, the misty bulks of forming planets and the larger mass of the dead star at the heart of the disc. Occasionally that star would light, traceries of fusion fire fleeing around its surface like the smouldering edges of fuse paper. One day, maybe tomorrow or maybe a thousand years hence, the sun would ignite fully. The resulting blast would blow a large portion of the accretion disc out into interstellar space. Marco knew this was the event to be feared, since it was the job of weapons platform AIs like Pragus to ensure that the virulent pseudo-life within that disc did not escape.

Marco shivered, wondering how the subplot in which he had been ensnared related to that. Certainly, the creature who had employed him was a conniving bastard . . . No. He shook his head. He could not allow his mind to stray beyond his immediate goal. He banished the image and, as his ship turned, watched Pragus's permanent home come into view.

The weapons platform was a slab ten miles long, five wide and a mile thick. The designer, the haiman Orlandine, had based much of its design on the construction blocks of a Dyson sphere—a project of which she was rumoured to have been an original overseer. After his first run here, Marco had tried to find information about this woman from the AI net, but there was little available. It seemed that a lot was restricted about this haiman, a woman who exemplified the closest possible melding of AI and human.

The platform's only similarity to a Dyson sphere construction block was its basic shape. The numerous protrusions of weapons and shielded communication devices gave it the appearance of a high-tech city transported into space. But the skyscrapers were railguns, particle cannons, launch tubes for a cornucopia of missiles, as well as the attack pods of the distributed weapons system that the platform controlled. And all were needed because of Jain tech. The accretion disc was swarming with a wild form of technology, created by a race named the Jain. These creatures had shuffled off the universe's mortal coil five million years ago but left this poisoned chalice for all ensuing civilized races. The technology granted immeasurable power but, in the process, turned on its recipients and destroyed them. Quite simply, it was a technology made to destroy civilizations.

Marco's ship drew closer to the platform on a slightly dirty-burning fusion drive—a fault that developed over a month back that he'd never found the time to fix. Its mind signalled on the console that it had applied for final docking permission, and Marco saw it accepted. He looked up to see a pair of space doors opening in the side of the platform. Having used these before, he knew they were more than large enough to allow his ship inside. But, at this distance, they looked like an opening in the side of a million-apartment arcology.

His ship drew closer and closer, the platform looming gigantic before it. Finally, it slid into the cathedral space of what the AI probably considered to be a small supply hold. Marco used the console to bring up a series of external views. The ship moved along a docking channel and drew to a halt, remora pad fingers folding out from the edges of the channel to steady it, their suction touch creating a gentle shudder he felt through his feet. He operated the door control of his vessel then stomped back through his cabin area, into his ship's own hold. He paused by the single grav-sled there, then stooped and turned on its gesture control. The sled rose, hovering above the floor and moving closer to him at the flick of a finger, as he turned to face a section of his ship's hull folding down into a ramp. An equalization of pressure, a whooshing hiss, had his ears popping but would cause him no harm.

By the time the ramp was down, pressure was back up again. Marco clumped down onto it in his heavy space boots, the sled following him like a faithful dog. He gazed about the hold, at the acres of empty grated flooring, the handler drays stuck in niches like iron and bone plastic beetles. Spider-claw bots hung from the ceiling like vicious chandeliers, and to one side the castellated edges of the space doors closed behind his ship. The sun-pool ripple of a shimmershield was already in place to hold the atmosphere in. As soon as he reached the floor gratings a cylinder door revolved in the wall ahead. Marco grimaced at what stepped out of the transport tube behind.

The heavy grappler—a robot that looked like a giant, overly muscular human fashioned of grey faceted metal—made its way towards him. It finally halted a few yards away, red-orange fire from its hot insides glaring out of its empty eye sockets and open mouth. But Pragus had used this grappler as an avatar before, so Marco knew he should not allow the sight of it to worry him; he should not let himself think that the AI knew something. He had to try to act naturally. He was just here doing his usual job . . .

"Still as trusting as ever, I see," Marco said.

He could feel one eyelid flickering, and felt a hot flush of panic because he knew the AI would see this and know something was bothering him. He quickly stepped out onto the dock, boots clanking on the gratings. At his gesture, the sled eased past him, then lowered itself to the floor. Sitting on top of it was a large airtight plastic box. The grappler swung towards this as if inspecting it, but Marco knew that Pragus was already scanning the contents even as it sent the grappler robot over. In fact, the AI had certainly scanned his ship and its cargo for dangerous items before it docked, like fissionables, super-dense explosives or an anti-matter flask. The more meticulous scan now would reveal something organic. Hopefully this would start no alarm bells ringing because the contents, as far as Marco was aware, were not a bio-weapon. Anyway, it was not as if such a weapon would have much effect here, where the only organic life present was Marco himself, as far as he knew.

"What is this?" Pragus asked, its voice issuing as a deep throaty rustle from the grappler.

"Straight out of the Kingdom," said Marco, sure he was smiling too brightly. "You know how these things go. One prador managed to kill a rival and seize his assets. One of those assets was a war museum and the new owner has been selling off the artefacts."

It was the kind of behaviour usual for the race of xeno-phobic aliens that had once come close to destroying the human Polity.

"That is still not a sufficient explanation."

"I can open it for you to take a look," said Marco. "But we both know that is not necessary."

When the box had been handed over to him, Marco had been given full permission to scan its contents, though he was not allowed to open it or interfere with them. He knew that Pragus would now be seeing a desiccated corpse, like a wasp, six feet long. But it wasn't quite a single distinct creature. Around its head, like a tubular collar, clung part of another creature like itself. Initial analysis with the limited equipment Marco had available showed this was likely to be the remains of a birth canal. Meanwhile it seemed that the main creature had died while giving birth too. A smaller version of itself was just starting to protrude from its birth canal. It was all very odd.

"Alien," said Pragus from the grappler.

"Oh certainly that," said Marco. "You want the museum data on it?"

"Yes."

Marco reached down and took a small square of diamond slate from his belt pouch and held it up. The grappler turned towards him, reached out with one thick-fingered hand and took the item between finger and thumb. Marco resisted for a moment, suddenly unsure he should carry this through. He realized that on some level he wanted to be found out, and he fought it down, releasing the piece of slate. The grappler inserted the square into its mouth like a tasty treat. Marco saw it hanging in the glowing opening while black tendrils of manipulator fibres snared and drew it in. Doubtless it would next be pressed to a reader interface inside the grappler's fiery skull.

It would not be long now before Marco knew whether or not he had succeeded. Minutes, only. The AI would put its defences in place, then translate the prador code before reading it. Of course, it had taken Marco a lot longer to translate the thing and read it himself—in fact, most of his journey here.

He had found out how, before the alien prador encountered the Polity, they had come upon another alien species whose realm had extended to merely four solar systems. The prador had attacked at once, of course, but realized they had snipped off more than they could masticate. What had initially been planned as the quick annihilation of competitors turned into an interminable war against a hive species whose organic form approached AI levels of intelligence. These creatures quickly developed seriously nasty weaponry in response to the attack. The war had dragged on for decades but, in the end, the massive resources of the Prador Kingdom told against the hive creatures. It was during this conflict that the prador developed their kamikazes and, with these, steadily destroyed the hive creatures' worlds. It seemed the original owner of the museum had been involved in that genocide, and here, in this box, lay the remains of one of the aliens the prador had exterminated.

"What is your price?" Pragus finally asked.

"You've been doing some useful work with that gravity press of yours?" Marco enquired archly, his acquisitive interest rising up to dispel doubts.

"I have," Pragus replied.

Marco pondered that for a second. "Don't ask for too much," the creature had told him, "and don't ask for too little."

"I want a full ton of diamond slate."

"Expensive and—"

"And I want a hundred of those data-gems you made last time."

This was a fortune. It was enough to buy Marco a life of luxury for many, many years. He had also calculated that it was about all Pragus would have been able to make with the gravity press since the last trader visit, when it wasn't using the press to make high-density railgun slugs. But was the dead thing inside that box worth so much? Of course it was. Material things like diamond slate and data-gems the AI could manufacture endlessly, filling the weapons-platform storage with such stuff. But the alien corpse would contain a wealth of what AIs valued highest of all: information. It was also so much more to weapons-platform AIs like Pragus: the prospect of months of release from the boredom of watching the accretion disc.

"You have a deal," the AI replied.

Marco had no doubt that Pragus was already having handler drays load the requested items onto themselves. He felt a species of disappointment. Weren't Polity AIs supposed to be the pinnacle of intelligence? Surely Pragus should be able to see to the core of what was happening here . . . surely the AI would have some idea . . .

The grappler stooped and carefully picked up the box, then it froze, the fire abruptly dimming in its skull. Marco had seen this before. It meant that Pragus had suddenly focused its full attention elsewhere. Had he been found out?

After a moment the fire intensified again, and the grappler turned towards the door of the transport tube.

"Something is happening," it said.

"What?" Marco asked, his mind already turning to the prospect of getting away from here as fast as he could.

"Increased activity in the accretion disc." The grappler then gave a very human shrug. "It happens."

Marco simply acknowledged that with a nod, hoping it would not delay his payment or his departure. This, he decided, would be his last run here. He wanted no more involvement with giant weapons platforms, Jain technology or Orlandine. He also, very definitely, wanted no more involvement with an alien called Dragon—a creature whose form was a giant sphere fifty miles across. A creature who, some months ago, with some not so subtle threats and the promise of great wealth, had compelled Marco to make this strange delivery here.